Igor H. Stone was originally a television director. He makes TV documentaries and other programs for television.

Igor is currently living in Budapest, and *Dark Ages Reloaded* is the first part of his Dark Ages trilogy.

I wouldn't have thought that a conversation whilst having a coffee would inspire me to write novels. Yet my friend, Mihály Vadas, persuaded me to start writing. So, I have to say, subsequently, that he was right. Without the help of my wife, this book could not have been born. My family's patience and encouragement gave me a lot of power/strength to write the novel.

Igor H. Stone

DARK AGES RELOADED

AUSTIN MACAULEY PUBLISHERS™

LONDON • CAMBRIDGE • NEW YORK • SHARJAH

A CIP catalogue record for this title is available from the British Library.

ISBN 9781528976282 (Paperback)
ISBN 9781528976299 (Hardback)
ISBN 9781528976312 (ePub e-book)

www.austinmacauley.com

First Published (2020)
Austin Macauley Publishers Ltd
25 Canada Square
Canary Wharf
London
E14 5LQ

A thank you to my friend, Mihály Vadas, for the encouragement, to my wife for the many nights awake, to my daughter for pictures.

A special thanks to Elza Kádár for the editorial work. Furthermore, I am grateful to Walter Scott, Jules Verne and Alexandre Dumas for the inspiration.

Prologue

The Spanish Queen, Esmeralda, looked contentedly at her reflection in the huge mirror that stood in the corner of the room, showing her whole figure. Her raven black hair framed her slightly round face. Her black eyes and dark eyebrows stood in subtle contrast to her immaculate white skin. Her thin, translucent nightgown showed her slender body, rounded hips and shapely breasts. Her dark brown nipples showed through the light fabric.

The mirror had been brought from the Kingdom of Italy, from Murano, where they made mirrors that did not distort her figure at all. Esmeralda began combing her hair. She liked to do this herself; not because her servants were clumsy, but because she simply enjoyed combing it. When she was done, she took a step back and looked at herself once again in the mirror.

Then she approached the table in the centre of the room and poured herself a shot of liquor. She usually drank wine, but she needed something stronger now.

The drink worked immediately, and she quickly had to gulp down a glass of water as she began to hiccup and felt the alcohol spreading through her body. She sat down on a comfortable chair, closed her eyes, and let the spirit do its work, to relax her from head to toe.

There was a soft knock at the door. Esmeralda opened her eyes, took a deep breath and said,

"Come in!"

The door opened, and Bishop Oscar Martinez entered. His squat-figure seemed even smaller as he approached her bent at the waist. He spoke with his head turned slightly sideways and was simultaneously excited by Esmeralda's scanty clothing.

"My lady, I've made arrangements, he's outside the door."

"Stop this stupid, grovelling behaviour! Nice work by the way. Send him in at once!"

"Yes, my lady." Martinez backed out of the room, stealing a furtive glance at the queen's breasts as he did.

Soon a man appeared in the doorway. Esmeralda walked over to the wide bed and sat down.

"Come closer, let me have a look at you!"

Pablo Lopez did not dare to speak; he obeyed her silently. He stopped a few metres in front of the queen.

"Closer!"

She had a good look at the man before her. She had never seen a peasant up close before. They all looked the same through her carriage window. Lopez was tall and profoundly muscular; and the long days of toil had wrinkled and tanned his skin, though he was well under 50. She could smell the strong scent of perfume wafting from him. Her servants had been generous with the expensive cologne. But Esmeralda's stomach still turned as a whiff of stable smell crept up her nostrils. She knew this was impossible, and that it was her high-born nobility playing tricks on her mind, as no one would allow a person visiting her chambers to arrive there smelly.

She liked his eyes; she loved wild, sharp-eyed men. There was something atavistic in them—an unbridled power that always awoke her dormant passions.

"Is it true that you have 15 children?"

"Yes, my lady," Lopez replied with his head bowed, as he had seen even from the doorway that the Queen was practically naked. He was embarrassed, and he could not imagine what the first lady of the country could want from him.

"How many times have you lain with your wife?"

The man could not believe his ears. She asked the question so lightly, as if inquiring about the weather. He wanted to hide beneath his shame, but the beautiful terrifying woman who sat before him was expecting an answer.

"Almost every day, my lady," he replied. He still could not comprehend that all this was happening to him.

"Undress!" the Queen commanded sternly, and then in a single motion, she slipped out of her nightdress where she sat. Lopez fumbled with his clothes. When he was done, he stared ashamedly down at his firm member. The Queen began to slowly stroke his manhood and then grabbed it and pulled it gently up and down. The repetitive motions achieved the desired results, as Lopez became so stiff, he thought he was going to explode. Then the Queen pulled him onto her, and he slowly came under her influence; his mind consumed by desire. Moments later, they began making love.

Esmeralda felt a strong pain. As she did not want the man, her dry chalice ached from his entry. She could have handled this, but Lopez's glassy eyes and far-away lusty stare were too much for her. She pushed him away with both hands while drawing her legs to her and pulling away from him. Then she turned around onto all fours and pushed her shapely behind towards him. She thought this would make it easier, but the situation did not get much better. It's true that she was free from his lusting stare, but only animals mounted their mates from behind like this. She felt the position to be very demeaning. Meanwhile Lopez was completely immersed in making love, and he thrust forward powerfully grabbing one of the Queen's breasts with his left hand and slapping her snow-white behind with his right. The Queen endured this through clenched teeth, but after a while, though she could not admit this to herself, she began to enjoy it.

Soon, amidst loud moans, the man reached his climax.

"Alright, that's enough! Now get out!" she shouted. Lopez hurriedly put on his clothes and then quickly left the Queen's chambers. Two soldiers were waiting for him by the door, and they escorted him through the castle district and then left him there.

He was well into the suburbs, but he could still not rid himself of the effects of his experience. What would Diego, his best friend, say when he told him what had happened. He wouldn't believe him. As he recalled the Queen's beautiful body, his manhood began to harden again—those swaying breasts, and her thighs opening shamelessly. When he got home, he would ravage his wife, he decided. He was almost there when two silhouettes appeared in the moonlit night. As he approached them, he feared they were bandits, but they were soldiers. *They must be on the evening patrol,* he thought.

When he passed them, he suddenly felt a sharp pain, clutched his stomach and collapsed. Lying there on the cold stone, he stared at the blood flowing between his fingers. He knew that he would die soon, but he was not afraid. He did not feel pain. He prayed to God. Only one urgent, unpleasant question haunted him, "Why?"

Chapter One

Councillor Alain Perrier sat confidently on his horse. The premier leader of the French kingdom—after the king, of course—had to travel a lot, and so had had time to get to know horses. He did not like carriages; they were too conspicuous and often got stuck on muddy roads.

That day, he made a loop of the inner territories surrounding the Paris Castle.

The area was under strict supervision because the castle was the king's residence, so it had at all times to be surrounded and under-control. The district surrounded by high walls was constantly guarded. Only five, heavily monitored gates allowed access inside. And, after sunset, one needed a very good reason indeed to enter. The roads of the inner district had been paved for a year now. The new surface afforded the city with new peculiar sounds. The pitter-patter of women's shoes, the heavy footfalls of men, the metallic ringing of horses' hooves, the humming of carriages and carts…all created a unique atmosphere. These soft noises were completed by the hullabaloo of the populace, the ringing of smithies' hammers and the performances of comedians.

Residence in the district was dependent on the councillor's permission, as was doing business or simply existing therein. Residents had to report everything they saw to the king's chief confidant. Furthermore, taxes were far higher here than in the outskirts of the city. Despite all the unpleasantness, it was still lucrative to live in the inner city, as the throngs of people meant business was thriving.

Perrier was over 50, but did not look like it. His movements remained dynamic, his posture taught, and only his greying hair and beard belied his age. He was a handsome man with noble features and cold penetrating eyes. Everyone in the kingdom was afraid of these eyes, and people had good cause to feel this way, as there were many rumours about missing citizens, peasants, soldiers and noble-men.

The Councillor rode at the centre of a small group; on his right, his aid, Vincent Farall. To the front and behind them were two black and red-armoured liquidators—armed to the teeth.

"You know, Vincent," Perrier said turning to his aid, "if something is really important to you, you have to do it yourself. Why do you think that is?" The boy thought about this and then ran his fingers through his thick black hair. Women's eyes followed the muscular, gentle-featured boy. He had sad eyes, which did not suit his 20-year-old face.

"Because no one can be trusted?" Farall asked back.

"Because your cause is never as important to anyone as it is to you. They will complete the task assigned to them, but that is all. If they complete it, good; if not, that's good too."

"Who would dare take your orders so lightly, my lord?" the aid said in disbelief.

"I'm not saying they take them lightly; no one would do that, but they would not go to any lengths as I would. You know, I hate excuses."

"Councillor, I went there, but he wasn't there. I cut his throat, but he did not die…"

"I don't do excuses, I complete tasks. Since I cannot be everywhere at once, I am forced to entrust others to act in my name, but I do not value these people very highly. This is another reason I change my staff so often," Perrier said watching his aid's reaction.

"You mean that's why you kill them?" Farall asked, raising his eyebrows, and then quickly realised that he may have spoken too bluntly.

"I value useful people greatly; the others do not matter." Perrier did not seem like he had taken the comment to heart. "Those that have disappeared are good for keeping the ones who remain in fear."

There had been many such conversations between them over the past years. At these times, the Councillor was teaching and testing all at once. They both enjoyed this intellectual game thoroughly.

On the largest street of Paris, simply called Main Street, the immense proportions stunned visitors, especially those used to countryside shacks. The buildings came up on one another and were often three-storeys tall. Their brightly painted window frames stood in stark contrast with their whitewashed walls. The road was so wide that two carriages could pass each other with room for many pedestrians to spare.

Farall watched the people jumping around in the street. When a carriage or cart approached, they quickly moved to the side; and as soon as the road was clear, they returned to the centre. In the larger cities of the known world, the custom of residents throwing the contents of their bedpans out the window of multi-storey buildings had become common place. Unlucky pedestrians usually responded to a collar full of excrement with vehement swearing, but the situations often devolved into serious fights. This custom of emptying bedpans was also an infinite well of humour for the residents. The aid knew that those in the centre of the road were not Parisians, because locals walked on the side and did not fear being spilled on, as no one threw anything out their windows in the inner district. Farall stole a glance at the Councillor. He remembered how his superior had put an end to the custom. A few years ago, they had been planning on entering the Four Heroes Tavern when the Councillor caught a large dose of bedpan juice on his neck. His eyes flashed, but he did not shout. He went inside and asked for a basin and washed. He sent a liquidator to the castle for new clothes. Then he took the tavern owner woman, who was the perpetrator, to the castle. The woman begged for forgiveness, but Perrier said nothing. He ordered hangmen to cut off both her arms, and then doctors to dress the stumps. When

13

the poor woman recovered, he had her returned to the tavern by two liquidators. A sign was hung about her neck saying, "I poured filth on Councillor Perrier." Farall would have understood if he had punished her then and there, but he could not comprehend this premeditated cruelty. That day, the Councillor asked him:

"Do you know why I did it?"

"Because you want to teach people not to empty their bedpans out the window?" Farall asked meekly.

"Teach? No, only smart people can be taught, those who understand words, like you. I teach you. But the people only understand fire and iron, they have to be tamed. Do you know what they do at the docks if the rats become too numerous?"

"No," he replied.

"They catch one and burn its eyes out with hot steel. The screams of the tortured rodent scares away the others. I needed the tavern keeper's mouth, not her hands. She will be my blinded rat."

The aid could not forgive the councillor for what he had done to the woman, even if Paris' streets were free from excrement since then.

Their procession would have usually moved faster on a weekday, but a day before the Knights Tournament for the Kingdoms of the Known World, the city was packed. Rich knights stayed in the taverns of the inner city with their entourages; poorer ones only came in during the day. Those clever enough managed to stay inside for the night too, because, in exchange for two gold pieces, the locals would become anybody's relatives, offering a cheap alternative to the overpriced taverns.

The Councillor took a deep breath of city air, smelling horse manure and food. He could see that the locals pulled aside fearfully as he passed through with his procession. The grey uniform of his profession had the desired effect. But the outsiders were a little less enthusiastic in the movements.

"I want you to call me by my first name from now on!" He looked into the boy's eyes. "Do you know why?"

"Because you like me, my lord?" Farall could not think of a better response in the moment, though he knew the Councillor expected a better answer from him.

"Do I seem like a sensitive idiot to you?" Perrier growled, and even his horse twitched as he spoke.

"Of course not. Then it's because you trust me."

"If I did not trust you, then you wouldn't be my aid, nor would you be alive anymore," Perrier said visibly disappointed. He clearly expected more from his protégée, but he did not mention his discontent. He continued a little impatiently, "The reason is power. There are not many who can call the Councillor by his first name, and those who can have increased power, they are feared and obeyed immediately, and they are not doubted and can act freely. And why would I want you to have greater power?"

"So that I can complete your commands more efficiently, Alain," the aid replied. The Councillor gave a half-smile.

"Smart boy," was all he said.

Perrier personally visited the larger taverns and brothels along the main road, because he wanted first-hand information. He did not want to have any scandals during the event. The French court could simply not afford to allow relations to deteriorate further between the kings in the current tense climate. Therefore, he wanted to know about everything—who were coming, what they talked about, who'd brawled, who spoke ill of the king, and who the likely contestants of tomorrow's games were. He couldn't question all his informants in a single afternoon, so he only went to the more popular places. He visited Fat Jean's Tavern; the White Horse last.

The Councillor waved, and the procession stopped. As he dismounted his horse, he called to the leader of the liquidators.

"Commander Azor! You, my aid and I will enter—three men stay outside. No need to stable the horses; we won't be long."

"Councillor! It is dangerous with only three of us."

"I've noted your warning and choose to ignore it," Perrier answered icily. When he used this tone, no one dared oppose him. Azor swallowed and then nodded.

When they entered, the din of drunkards, the laughing of prostitutes, the smell of food, smoke and sweat greeted them. Those inside did not notice them enter, which allowed the Councillor to look around unhindered.

The ground floor of the tavern consisted of an open hall where people could eat and drink. It was a large room, with 15 or 20 round wooden tables surrounded by chairs. No space was left unused. The patrons were knights competing in the next day's games, pleasure girls looking for a lucrative customer and rich peasants and craftsmen. There were many foreigners, but luckily everyone was speaking a common language now, so there was no cause for silence. Perrier walked between the tables, towards the back where the innkeeper had probably gone into the kitchen to check on the cooks. He was in the middle of the room when he tripped on a sword that was hung over the back of a chair. The owner of the sword, a Spanish knight, yelled at him drunkenly,

"Are you blind, you idiot?"

"Calm yourself! Can't you see the grey cape? This is the councillor! I think you had better choose your words carefully if you wish to live," Azor said setting the stranger straight. The Councillor waved his hand indicating disinterest, and that they should move on, but the Spanish knight could not leave it be.

"Go to hell!" he growled drunkenly and then jumped up pulling his sword from its scabbard.

After that, everything happened quickly. Perrier pushed the Spaniard away with his left hand; and at the same time, he drew his dagger at lightning speed with his right and lunged. He felt that he had not caused serious damage in his opponent who wore a chest plate, but it had stopped him. He also knew that Azor the liquidator stood behind him; so after the lunge, he stepped aside to allow his man to attack more effectively. One cut was all the Commander needed, and the knight collapsed with a slit throat. Meanwhile, the Spaniard's two friends sprang to their feet and began backing up—their swords drawn. Fear had sobered them up instantly. People scattered, making room for the combatants. Farall attacked the man on the right with his sword while Azor had a tight grip on the knight to the left. This was not the first time Perrier had experienced his thoughts speeding up during a fight. He had time to think through his next move despite the fast-paced action. Now he decided to help Farall; clearly the aid was far more valuable than the liquidator. Farall's opponent was immersed in battle, so the Councillor could easily reach under Farall's arm and stab him. Farall had a much easier task of it now, and he quickly found the lethal blow. The Commander had no trouble with the remaining man.

At the sound of the skirmish, the other liquidators barged into the tavern.

"Commander Azor! Go back to the castle and send a few soldiers to get rid of these scum. A big hole somewhere in the outskirts should suffice." The Councillor showed no signs of just having done battle. He gave his orders with absolute calm, as if he were organising a royal feast.

"And you," he turned to the other liquidators, "take the corpses out back till they collect them. I don't want to hear another word about my safety! When you're done, wait outside; my aid and I will question the innkeeper."

Finally, Fat Jean appeared out of the kitchen, kneading his knuckles and swaying as he waited for what was to come next. He was short, and beads of sweat formed on his bald head.

"Innkeeper! Let us go to a quiet place, I want a word with you!" the Councillor said.

The patrons resumed their places as if nothing had happened. After all, it was much better to have seen nothing than to interfere in the Councillor's business. The people began to murmur. The last few minutes would provide fuel for several days of conversation.

Fat Jean led them to one of the guest rooms upstairs. It could not be called cosy. There was no window, and just a few candles illuminated it. The furnishings consisted of a bed, a closet, four chairs and a table. As they went, Jean whined incessantly.

"I didn't know who they were, my lord. They must've come in through one of the five gates. I'm sure your soldiers checked them out. They were quiet until now. How could I have known what sort they were?"

"If you speak another word without being spoken to, I'll cut off your hands," Perrier said growing bored of his antics. "If you have anything edible, bring it." He hadn't eaten all day, and his stomach was rebelling against the hunger.

Jean sprang up, ran out and soon reappeared with a large tray of ham, cheese and bread.

"You eat first!" Perrier looked sharply at Fat Jean.

"My lord, you wouldn't think that I would try…"

"Shut up! Don't talk! Just eat!" While Jean cut some ham, the Councillor sat down and glanced at Farall.

"Nice work, Vincent!"

"Thank you," the aid replied, though he knew that Azor and the Councillor had done the lion's share of the fight.

Perrier began to eat and thought about his training. They had first been taught the Councillor's first lesson, which stated: everyone has a weakness. Interestingly, in his experience, most people had not one but many weaknesses. And this halfwit Jean had a plethora, and nothing else besides.

"Whose lodging with you?" he suddenly began the interrogation. At these times, Farall never interjected; he just sat and listened. Sometimes, Perrier would send him to interrogate people, but if they went together, then the Councillor always asked the questions.

"Ten or so men and five women," the fat man said. One of the boys has noted down their names. I did as you asked, which is why I hired a boy who could write.

"Good, I'll have a look on the way out. And how many new 'relatives' have you?"

"Errr... Well, two. But I had that written in the book too."

"All accommodation in the city is full. This room is empty. Why?"

"Well, the thing is, sometimes girls come in here with their Johns," Fat Jean muttered, and thinking about the girls, he inadvertently licked his lips.

"And you don't pay tax after them, you weasel! I think I will cut your hands off!" Perrier said wagging his head. He wasn't actually angry, just bored of the situation.

"Well, errrr, I don't really get money for it; they pay me in kind."

"Look, innkeeper! Who should I tell this to? The archbishop who might torture you or your wife?"

"My lord, I'll do anything."

"We'll see if you're lying or not."

This halfwit responds to quick questions with wither the truth or lies so stupid, they're impossible to notice. the Councillor thought.

"And what are people saying, who will win the games?"

"Well, in truth they think the French champion is most likely."

"Fat bastard, tell me the truth!"

"Yes, my lord, forgive me! The English knight, Sir Thomas Parker."

"And in fencing?" the Councillor asked languidly, while his thoughts drifted to his next task for the day. He wanted to check the locations for the games tomorrow. The number of participants required seeding rounds, and these would not be held in the castle gardens, so they were not of interest. The finals were important. Which king would sit where, when they would enter, how their security could be insured, organising the dinner and so on. The tasks were infinite, and the time till the games was drawing short.

"Well, there are several likely ones. Most are betting on the German knight, Hans von Basel," the sweating inn-keeper replies.

There was a knock at the door. All three looked at the makeshift door.

"Inside!" Perrier commanded. Who would dare disturb them during an interrogation? He hadn't positioned the liquidators by the door, just so they could let anyone in—he fumed to himself.

"Forgive me, Councillor," the young man who entered began. Perrier could see from his clothes that he was a Royal messenger. "My lord, you must come at once; the king has assembled a special council."

"Alright, I'll join the council shortly, you may go now!" the Councillor said with disinterest.

"But they told me that you should come immediately." The soldier's beading brow revealed that he would rather be anywhere else in the world than here before the king's most-terrifying servant.

"Who told you?" The questions seemed to rent the air.

"Archbishop Cain Leroy, my lord," the messenger's voice was shaking.

"And I am the councillor; I won't jump about for a mere priest!"

The messenger left hurriedly, and the Councillor calmly finished his meal and then headed for the street. He knew that he couldn't make King Auguste Lefebre IV wait for long, however much of dunce he was.

The King sat on his throne. Perhaps no other king before him had been able to sit atop the all-powerful throne with such a lack of dignity. He kept his left foot up on the noble chair and dangled his right in the air.

The King was not long-gone 30 years of age, but looked closer to 20, which filled him with significant satisfaction. He was considered a handsome man, though his features lacked a harness and power, which translated into his personality also.

The throne room was adorned on one side by huge windows, through which the April-sunlight streamed unhindered. On the opposite wall, previous rulers looked down from their portraits. The magnitude of the hall seemed to compress those who were in it. Opposite the King, a long table was set around which were seated the honorary members of the King's council. The chair to the left of the King stood open; this was the councillor's place. Beside him sat the stocky archbishop, Cain Leroy. At the end of the row to the left sat the fidgety, nervous figure of the treasurer Leopold Dubois. To the right of the King sprawled the Marquis Philippe Bertrand. He represented the nobility; more precisely, the noble men who were loyal to King Lefebre. The other half of the nobility kept their distance from the King's court; they did not openly oppose the ruler, but their loyalty was highly suspect. Next in line was a silent, gaunt, scar-faced, uniformed man: Head liquidator Luc Moreau. He was followed by another straight-backed man in uniform—young for his rank at 38—this was the commander of the army, Marcell Durant. At the end of the row sat a humble old man, Raimund Petit, representing the guilds of the tradesmen. The members of the council looked down on him for his lowly origins, but the taxes paid by the guilds formed a significant portion of the treasure, forcing the noble men to tolerate their presence.

"When the Councillor arrives, I will have to listen to King Mortimer's rude rants all over again," the King moaned.

"Your Highness, that is truly terrible," Leroy simpered, "I sent out a messenger long ago to bring Perrier here immediately. I don't know who he thinks he is. He simply cannot do this."

At that moment, the Councillor arrived. True to his character, he moved silently, seeming to glide above the flagstones. He swept along the room and then sat down on a chair. Though he had heard the last few sentences, he said nothing, only once he had made himself comfortable.

"Your Highness! Gentlemen! I apologise for my tardiness, but news of this impromptu meeting reached me late. I can see that some would like to use this to besmirch my name before the council."

"I didn't mean it like that," the Archbishop said going crimson.

"There is no other way to mean it, Father," the Councillor looked directly into the eyes of the man beside him. Not many people could hold his stare, and Leroy lowered his eyes.

"Where have you been, Councillor?" the King asked.

"Your Highness, the seeding rounds begin tomorrow. I had to ensure the transport of our guests, the condition of the locations, and, most importantly, Your Highness' safety."

"Alright," said the King softening. "I'll tell you briefly why I have called this council. The English King, Arnold Mortimer, has offended me and the French kingdom," he said while drawing his other leg onto the throne. Sitting there, he looked like an ill-mannered teenager.

"What happened, my lord?" the Councillor inquired.

"When the English party arrived, their king said to the noblemen that I'd sent to greet them: 'The King of England is greeted by peasants in this rat hole. I take offence; I should be greeted by none other than the king'."

"That is indeed uncouth behaviour," Perrier nodded, though he did not seem too distraught by the news.

"Uncouth?" Marquis Philippe Bertrand exclaimed. "I about died from shame," he said with dramatically flare and gesticulation.

The Councillor could not resist a mocking sneer.

"I do not believe your shame is of importance here. The French King has been wronged!" Commander Marcell Durand interrupted him.

"Gentlemen!" Perrier looked around wagging his head, all the while looking at the council as if they were a congregation of children. "We are not going to war over a silly line. I will solve the problem diplomatically."

"Diplomacy!" the Marquis waved it off. "Not worth a thing!"

"Dear Bertrand," the Councillor replied coolly, "When I say diplomacy, it means the fate of countries, war and peace, life and death, depend on it. Everything depends on how we relate to the occurrences around us. We cannot act without thinking."

"So, what do you suggest?" the King inquired. He was clearly ready to suspend the meeting. He was not capable of concentrating on something for long, and state affairs had never interested him much.

19

"Relations with the English are very tense at the moment, so we have to proceed carefully," the Councillor continued his lecture.

"Now that he is in Paris, we could kill Mortimer. It is a unique opportunity," Head liquidator Luc Moreau interrupted.

"Yes, we could easily do so; in fact we could even blame the assassination on someone else, but who would believe us?" Perrier replied patiently. He considered the head liquidator a simple, straightforward man and held no grudge against him.

"I am the king of more than five million people. Why would I be afraid of anyone?" Lefebre asked haughtily.

"Your Highness, this is true, but if you remember, England is six million and could easily form an alliance with the seven million strong Germany or the Spaniards or the Russians who may number as many as ten million, and then we'd really be in trouble."

"Are you saying we would lose in a war against England?" Lefebre sprang up from his throne and ran to the window.

"No, my lord, but we cannot wage war against the whole known world. And if the king of a large country falls victim to assassination, here, in Paris, then they will unite against us," the Councillor finished.

The King turned from the window and faced the council, dismissing the matter with a nervous wave,

"Alright, do as you see fit. And now, leave me alone! Councillor, you stay here a while longer."

When the others had left, the King stepped close to Perrier and whispered:

"Sir, I need you to take care of something again today!"

"Naturally, my lord, you can count on me," the Councillor whispered back. "What would you have done, my lord?" He acted as if he did not know what this was about, as if this were the first time. The King was asking for a discrete favour.

"Oh, just the usual. Look, make it one redhead, with a nice, full-figure. And be very discreet!"

"Of course, my lord, as always." A sly smile crept into the corner of Perrier's mouth.

Exiting the throne room, the Councillor remembered the first lesson of his training for the second time that day: everyone has a weakness. How true. It just has to be found.

Chapter Two

Arnold Mortimer sat suddenly down in the chair by the huge table that was the centrepiece to his room. The movement was at once quick and stilted; he wore mostly heavy armour, which made him move in this way. He started his movements quickly, because his heavily weighted limbs had to be brought into momentum, and then he had to slow it down so as not to drag him too far. Heavy armour hinders a fighter's speed, one must learn to coexist with the metal skin— he was fond of saying. He wasn't wearing armour at the moment, but it was like a sailor's unsteady gait on dry land. Old habits could not be shrugged off so quickly. The English King was bothered by his ceremonial garb; he felt much better in knights clothing.

"I hate these frilly things," Mortimer poked at his clothes. "I have to suffer this for two more days, but as soon as I'm headed home, I'll tear them off, I swear it."

When he had sufficiently angered, he turned to the man standing before him.

"Let's go over it one more time: what do we know about the Councillor?" In the known world, it was not customary to speak of councillors behind their backs, not even in royal circles. But they had gone over what they knew again and again, in the hope of coming across something important; they may have missed, that might shed light on the doubts they had about the councillor.

"First, Your Highness, let's look at the fact that we know to be true," Sir Lemmy Black replied, who was known around the world as the strategist, because he never lost a war, even though he had been at war all his life. He wore tight-fitting leather clothes that showed his thin, muscular frame. His slightly bony, yet gentle and proportional face, was framed by a straight-cut black hair and beard. Some would call him handsome, but his roving, searching eyes made people feel uneasy. He held the rank of warlord to the English crown, but his real power came from his close relationship with the King of England himself.

"The councillors appeared a few decades after the collapse of the old age," Black went on.

"Are you sure this old age existed, and it's not just something they made up?"

Mortimer inquires. While he waited, his clothes seemed scratchy, or maybe he was just imagining it. Everyone knew about the old times, but they could only progress through important matters if they questioned everything other people took for granted. The King lived by this philosophy.

"I don't think so, my lord. Though all the ancient books have turned to dust, the royal scribes have copied all volumes over and over again, so we still have volumes from those times, and all sources seem to indicate that it existed. I think there was an old age, when many people lived in gigantic cities. What's more, strange artefacts and ruins have been found in every kingdom; there are too many signs indicating that it is true."

Black stood before the king with the same posture as he had at the beginning of their conversation. He displayed no emotion on his face. For the most part, he did not express himself erratically.

"Alright, so the councillors appeared. Go on!" Mortimer said raising his voice. He was always impatient, and the upcoming games and protocol were making him increasingly insufferable. Sir Lemmy was visibly unfazed by the King's state of mind.

"They made order from chaos, and united the warring hoards into a kingdom. They formed laws, the common tongue, introduced current religion, stopped plagues, helped peasants farm, leading to greater yields, and every king was assigned a councillor," Black listed the commonly known facts.

"How could they do all this when there were so few of them?" the King interrupted.

"They were in possession of a higher knowledge, as they are now. To this day, they supervise agricultural work, make medicine, direct the church and advise the kings," as black answered, his lip curled, which was a large gesture by him. Even Mortimer noticed the unusual expression.

"Something not to your liking, my friend?" the King chided.

"Of course, I don't like it, my lord," Black said scratching his chin.

"You should be in control, and of course my advice is more valuable to you than the false wisdom of some councillor."

"This is true, but we cannot openly oppose old councillor Ed Wilder, not yet…" Mortimer smiled.

"This is true, my lord, we must be careful, though Wilder is certainly aware that he is not in control of the Kingdom of England."

"Let's go on!" Mortimer ordered. Meanwhile he adjusted his shirt collar vehemently to the detriment of two lost buttons.

"We know that the councillors wear a ring that has poison in it," Black went on, "which is how they protect themselves from interrogations. Do you remember, my lord, when we wanted to capture the Estonian councillor?"

"Don't you dare mention that!" Mortimer barked. They had organised everything. A small team of English soldiers in disguise kidnapped the Estonian councillor, while Mortimer was at dinner with King Badolfin. He had even helped in the search effort, so as not to be suspected. The mission was a success, and yet it bore no fruit. They wanted to interrogate the councillor, but even though he was held down, he managed to activate the ring with one hand and died instantly.

"When a kingdom wants a councillor, they must place white flags on the castle tower," Black said glossing over the uncomfortable topic. "They have no obligation to request a councillor, but if a country does not request their help, they mysteriously seem to have plague. Their crops fail or some other calamity befalls them. This is no coincidence; they organise it somehow. They exploit their superior knowledge and force the country to request their aid."

"You may be right, damn them!" Mortimer fumed, and then jumped up and went to the window. Outside, in the courtyard, the preparations for tomorrow's games were in full force. Workers were assembling the stands; weapons masters brought swords, helmets and shields.

"We don't even know where councillors come from," Black said, who was stuck in his usual rigid stance. "They say their kingdom lies past the Russian kingdom in the frozen planes. Of all the expeditions that have gone there, none have returned. The councillors explain this by saying the cold killed them, but I don't believe that. They call their country Atlantis, after a mysterious city from folklore, and no-one from the known world has ever been there."

"It does sound unbelievable, but we can only go on what the councillor told us," observed Mortimer, as he turned away from the window and sat down again.

"Everything in this world happens for a reason, my lord," Black replied, "there are no coincidences. I cannot see the reason for the councillor's actions, and that worries me greatly. Why would they help if it does not benefit them or their country? In two thousand years, they have never tried to conquer any of the kingdoms. They asked for nothing in return for their services—of course they are wealthy men, but they are not motivated by wealth, so what is it? If they possess such great knowledge, why do they have to keep Atlantis a secret? What do they want from us? The greatest mystery is that they have been here for two thousand years, but nothing has changed."

"What do you mean?" For a moment, Mortimer even forgot about his robes.

"We know how people used to live, cramped in gigantic cities. The old books even tell us that there were even earlier times when life was completely different; several completely different worlds changed places constantly."

"And?" Mortimer still didn't understand where the warlord was going with this.

"Our time has been unchanged for two thousand years now. Before our age, there was never such a long period of things staying the same. As if we were being held back."

"Who? The councillors?" The King was beginning to glean the meaning.

"Well, do they not control our world?" Black asked back.

"I will not rest until I get answers to these mysteries."

"So be it!" the English King said finally and then finished off what was left of his collar with a determined wrench of his hand.

Didier Ponga looked pleased as he entered the huge tent reserved for the fighters. The long tables were lined with equally long benches. He sat down on the edge of a bench and ate some of the free food. He had wanted to compete in the games his whole life. It had not been an easy road, but it had been worth it. He could still barely believe that he could be here, at the Knights Tournament for the Kingdoms of the Known World. In order for someone to participate, he had to be knight, which meant that they had to have a full set of armour, weapons, a second and the ten-gold entry fee, which was considered a considerable fortune. He felt like the world was his—he had just turned 24, and his best years were yet to come. His smoothly shaved face impressed the women, and soon he would be champion and his dream—fortune and fame—awaited him just two days ahead.

A lot of knights had entered the tournament. Five large tents had been erected to greet the participants, and all of them were beginning to fill up. Ponga looked around. The knights formed small groups; the rich noblemen wearing expensive armour did not mix with the poor ones. Any free man with the right weapons could become a knight in a kingdom, but noblemen were born that way. Simple knights could never dream of entering the tournament. The costs were too high, a battle horse, stable fees, armour—for the horse too—a practice pillow, keeping a second.

The weapons-master for one of organisers entered the room holding a scroll, which he self-importantly unwound and began to read.

"Attention! The tournament will proceed as follows!"

"Look, weapons-master!" a knight wearing blood red armour interrupted him. The armour he wore was worth a small village at least. "Why did we have to leave our weapon-bearers outside?" he asked.

"My lord, we can barely fit in the tent as it is. This once, you will have to pour your own wine."

"Insolence!" the nobleman shouted taking offence, but everyone in the tent was laughing so loudly that he thought it better to stay silent.

"So, the tournament will proceed as follows."

"Hey Geezer, we know all this! Get to the point," shouted someone from the crowd. Everyone nodded in approval, and there was a sudden commotion.

"Silence, dammit!" shouted the knight's weapons-master, "anyone calling out will be barred! Anyway, I'm not reading you this out of the goodness of my heat." He looked around and was pleased to see that everyone had fallen silent. No one wanted to drop out before the fights had even begun. The old weapons-master looked at the scroll again, cleared his throat and went on.

"One sword combat, no shirts, half-sharpened blades, next mounted combat, blunt-tipped spears. Both events will have 500 participants each. The seeding will take place today, on the first day. Only 16 knights will remain for tomorrow. They will fight before the kings. The rules will be read before every contest, and if anyone breaks them, they will be barred. If there are any fights in the tents over the next two days, those involved will be barred. That is all."

As the weapons-master left, the noise in the tent increased. The knights taunted one another, they all wanted to appear bolder and more confident than the others. Ponga did not take part in the verbal battles; he watched the bragging warriors, who were behaving just like the cockerels in his father's yard. He had seen the stupid beasts puff themselves up and spread their wings a thousand time, emitting loud noises as they strutted, convinced that they were the best in the world.

Ponga had known, even as a child, that he was not like the others. He was different in one important respect—and that was his speed. He was not simply faster than the others but devilishly fast. At an early age, he figured out how to use his special skills. He did not become a performer but rather duelled for money. Only one fight per village, and then, before news of his skills could outrun him, he moved on, as no one else would challenge his lightning speed after they'd seen it. He had left his home when he was 16. Sweating in his father's smith shop was not enough for him. When he escaped, he took a good sword, his father's savings, which was not much but enough for a start. It took him eight long years to collect the money for a set of knight's armour. Even so, he could only enter the fencing tournament, as he could not afford armour for his horse.

It was almost noon when his name was called, "Didier Ponga, to combat!" He'd been afraid he's stuck there all day. He stood up quickly, and a servant led him to the battlefield. It was about a hundred pace till they reached the spot. There were several arenas, close to one another. The fights took place in a ten-metre wide enclosure. Before he was allowed in the circle, he had to strip his shirt off, and then he was given a sword and a shield. Both sides of the sword were only half-shard, but it could still cause serious injury to the half-naked combatants. As he entered the ring, his opponent, an almost two-metre tall giant was already there. The weapons-master in charge read the rules:

"Anyone leaving the ring will lose. Whoever draws first blood, wins. No other rules. The fight begins on my whistle."

Outside the ring, simple folk thronged around them. They made bets or just stared or shouted encouragement at the knights. They moved around in their excitement stirring about a huge dust cloud that dulled the bright spring sun.

Ponga could hear people shouting, but he was focussed on his opponent. The shrill whistle reached his ear, and the fight was finally under way. The giant, certain of his advantage, advanced with a smile on his face. The crowd was wild.

"The big one will win, five more silver on the giant!" someone shouted.

"The little one had no chance!" a fat woman shrilled. As the giant moved towards him, Ponga began circling the edge of the ring.

The both held their shields before them. The moment the giant reached within an arm's length, he swung his sword downwards. The giant had expected his opponent to put all his effort into holding the shield, so he put all his weight behind his blow. But, at the last second, Ponga turned to the side at superhuman speed, and his opponent didn't even have a chance to slow down. His sword, the dust and his body followed its momentum onto the ground. The audience laughed loudly and shouted mockingly.

"What you doing? Can't you stay upright?" asked a pockmarked viewer.

"Stop hiding, coward!" the giant shouted, and jumping up from the ground, he attacked again. His charge was inspired, and it was clear to see that anything that got in the way of this tower of meat would be demolished. Ponga waited for the knight to draw near and then moved out to the left, and gathering all his strength, he struck his opponents back as he passed by. The cut drew a deep line from the giant's left shoulder to his right hip bone. The giant screamed, a shower of blood painting the sand red. The sight of the blood drove the audience into a frenzy as they cheered the champion, and no one felt sorry for the loser.

"Knight Ponga, winner!" the weapons-master announced the results.

Strange, Ponga thought, *everyone here is so happy, as if they'd won the fight themselves.*

As he pushed his way through the cheering crown, his eyes rested on a hooded-figure, a member of the beggars' guild. He didn't know why the priest's face had caught his eye in this throng; perhaps it was the all-seeing, piercing-grey eyes that had captured him. They drew closer to each other. Perhaps it was just the crowd bringing them closer, but maybe the priest was making his way through the crowd—he could not tell. When they were face-to-face, the priest leaned in to him and whispered in his ear.

"It's disgusting how a little man always avoiding risk enjoys basking in the lime light of his success."

By the time he could answer, the priest was nowhere to be seen, but his words rung in Ponga's ears all day.

That night at Fat Jean's Inn, Didier Ponga was drinking his second glass of wine. He had fought a total of five battles that day and had won all of them. He was now one of the 16 knights who would fight before the kings tomorrow. Of course, he knew that the main attraction would be the jousting, but no matter, he could participate in that number another time. Of the participants from poor backgrounds only he remained, because the sons of rich families had all received the best training. Brute force in a fight was not enough. Technique and experience were more important.

The inn was full. The innkeeper was running between the kitchen and his customers, loudly berating the staff as he did so. The evening atmosphere was the usual—cacophony, drunks, pleasure-girls and the smell of food. All the tables were crowded, only Ponga sat alone. He wanted to drink alone, and Jean could not refuse his request, and there was no one in the inn stupid enough to pick a fight with an undefeated knight. Recently he had thought a lot about his abandoned family. For the first few years, he had sometimes thought about his parents, his brothers and sisters or the neighbour's daughter, Blonde Ann. Today, the memories seemed to flood his mind. He thought his heart was touch enough that he could not be surprised, and that his memories would let him be for the rest of his life. What would his father say if he could see him now? Would he be proud, or would he never forgive him for what he had done?

He would never know, because he would never go back, that was certain. What would he tell them after he had robbed them and left them without as much as a farewell? But, from another perspective, if he had not escaped then, he would not be here to celebrate his victories. Yet, he could not be entirely happy, he felt sorry for himself, or perhaps for those he had left behind, who knows? He was jolted from his reveries by a figure suddenly appearing before him.

"Is the taste of victory so bitter to you?" the man asked.

Ponga looked up and stared in disbelief at the same hooded priest who had whispered to him after the first fight.

"Our meeting again can be no coincidence, you must have followed me. What do you want from me?" Ponga asked ignoring the priest's question.

"True and also false. I did not follow you, but there are no coincidences in life. God has ordained our paths to cross. But now, I reckon, you do not want to deal with questions of faith. May I sit down, provided that you buy me a cup of wine?"

Without waiting for an answer, he sat down. Ponga noticed how lithe and youthful his movements were, though he seemed to be an old man. His eyes stood out from his thin, stubbly face; they were a mixture of green, yellow and grey swirls.

"Sure, I'll buy you one. Why do you want to sit with me?" Ponga inquired, as he drained his cup and turned towards the bar.

"Jean! Fetch us carafe of the good wine and another cup," he shouted to the innkeeper.

"Right away, sir!" came the answer from the direction of the kitchen.

"Why here?" asked the priest. "Can you see any other free spaces?"

"And what makes you think my victory is bitter?"

Meanwhile, Fat Jean arrived with the carafe and the cup, placed them on the table and rushed off. Ponga poured for both of them and then looked at the priest.

"Why bitter? Because of the empty seats beside you."

"I don't get it," Ponga said confusedly.

"Those who celebrate merrily do not sit alone in a crowded inn," the priest smiled.

They did not speak for a while, and the hubbub of the inn filled in the silence between them. Ponga had a feeling as if they had known each other for eternity. The priest unexpectedly looked Ponga in the eye and said:

"I know that you will think what I'm about to say is stupid. Your incredible speed may cost you your life tomorrow. If you feel the danger, run, and I will help you."

Without waiting for an answer, the priest stood up, and within moments had disappeared through the throngs of people. Ponga wagged his head. *"I won't let a slit-eyed old man ruin the best day of my life,"* he thought. *"I'm going to have a good time anyway!"* He determined, and yet an unpleasant feeling overcame him, a feeling he could not shake all night.

Chapter Three

The clock struck midnight in the Royal Paris Castle. They say it is the witching hour. Cloaked figures often dart across the halls at these hours. The light of the torches paint their silhouettes onto the walls. The king's guards, the liquidators and the soldiers defending the castle were terrified of these late-night ghosts. Not because they were afraid of ghosts—how simple life would be if other worldly creatures lurked in the night—but they were afraid of flesh and blood people creeping around.

If they do not catch them, they are not fulfilling their duty—because what if a stranger is lurking in the castle, might they be an assassin? In that case, they would answer for their negligence with their heads. Or, if they stopped them, and it turned out to be a marquis, or even the King sneaking out for a late-night date. Then they would be in even bigger trouble than if they had not guarded the castle in the first place. This night was unusually busy. Councillors flooded the halls and walked past the soldiers as if they weren't even there; for them, the saluting men were nothing more than the statues that lined the halls. The guards were surprised, because most of them were too young to remember the night some ten years ago when the councillors had walked the castle in the same way. That had been during the Paris Knights Tournament as well. At least they did not have to stop and check them, because the grey robes of their profession identified them.

The councillors' meeting was always led by the Atlantis communicator. This role had been filled for the past five years by Pedro Garcia, the Councillor to the Kingdom of Spain, who now sat on a pedestal at the far end of the meeting hall. He maintained direct contact with Atlantis and passed on the orders received from home, which all councillors were obliged to obey. He drummed his thin, bony fingers of the table. His long-face, aristocratic moustache and shortcut beard, and deep-set steel blue eyes all radiated authority. Though he was only in his 40s, he was distinctly grey.

Before him, the lines of chairs were almost all taken. The councillors arrived and took their places in silence; no one said a word. Garcia knew that he would have to break this silence, but only once everyone had arrived, and he was given the signal that the room was safe, and no one could hear them.

The communicator looked around the room. *A perfect setting for a secret meeting,* he thought. The high walls of grey stone blocks rose and seemed to almost swallow the flickering light of the torches. The darkness made the room ominous and imposing. The first rows consisted of the councillors for the major kingdoms, behind them the others who served the lesser kingdoms and were far greater in number. *As if we weren't equal, as if we weren't working for the same goal*, he fumed quietly. Then he received the signal, and the meeting could commence. He stood up. All eyes were upon him, and he began:

"My lords, we haven't much time, let's use it well. We are only able to meet once a year at the Knight's Tournament. We have no chance of discussing all matters, so we will focus on the most pressing issue, the tension between the English and French thrones." As he looked around, he saw someone in the back raise their hand. He nodded at them.

"Unfortunately, there are more and more mutation," Nicklas Bjorn said, the Councillor to the Norwegian throne, and this is affecting all the kingdoms now.

The communicator never liked this jumped-up Bjorn, but he answered patiently.

"You are right, Nicklas, but we have no time to deal with this now," Garcia said silencing Bjorn. "We will continue to follow order from the Atlantis Council on the matter that is we must liquidate all mutants, even if they have positive traits, because they upset the balance of society. We cannot allow them to breed. And now let's get onto the French-English situation."

Garcia sat down and brushed his long hair back with his hand. He was certain that they would have a tiring night, so he quickly continued.

"I'd like to call on the councillors of the countries in question. First, Councillor Alain Perrier."

He stood up nice and slow and looked around. He visibly enjoyed situations like these when he was the centre of attention.

Meanwhile Garcia had time to think about the matter Councillor Bjorn had raised—it was indeed a grave problem. It was a fact that there were more and more mutants, he analysed the situation internally, though the situation had not escalated to a level where they should be seriously concerned. The problem was not with the visible mutations; those were easy to filter and could easily be weeded out with the help of the church. Those who were different, in opposition to God, 'aberrations' were handed over by their community willingly. Public burnings were very popular in all the kingdoms. The problem is with the ones where you couldn't see the change; these people kept their differences secret, though there weren't many such cases nowadays, but their number were increasing.

"So," Perrier began, "the Kingdom of France will not start a war, I'll make sure of it." He held a dramatic pause after his announcement and looked for people's reactions. The councillors seemed a little reassured by what he had said.

"The King is under my control," he went on "and it is not in the noblemen's interest to wage war; the costs are too high. A war would eradicate the relative comfort that exists in the country for years. Commander Marcell Durand…"

"By the way, are the French ready for war?" Philipe Derm, the Belgian Councillor interrupted. He jumped up as he asked this. His tall, gaunt-figure towered above the seated councillors. Perrier looked at him in an equally offensive and deprecating way. He stared at the Belgian until his assailant lowered his eyes and became like a guilty puppy.

"Sit down, my young friend!" Perrier said after a long while, in a cold, piercing voice that had no hint of friendship in it. "I seem to recall that I was given the right to speak."

Derm sat down and knew from Perrier's first words that he had made a mistake. He had not been to a meeting before, and he'd wanted to make an impression. He'd heard of Perrier before, but had not believed that he would be such a formidable opponent face-to-face. But from that moment he knew that the French Councillor would crush him if he got the chance.

"So, if you don't mind, kind sir...?" He looked at the increasingly embarrassed Derm.

"Philipe Derm," the Belgian Councillor whispered.

"Interesting, you are much more quiet now than when you interrupted me, dear Philipe," Perrier smiled.

"So, dear Philipe, my dear friends! The French kingdom is obviously prepared for the eventuality of war. Commander Marcel Durand is an excellent leader, and we will not be caught unawares. In any case, the question is not whether we are prepared for war, but what situation is advantageous to us."

"Thank you, Alain," Garcia said interrupting the French Councillor, because he knew that if he didn't, they would have to listen to his explanation for a long time yet.

Perrier took a little offence; he would have liked to have kept going. He shrugged noncommittally and sat down.

Garcia waited for the whispers to die down and then spoke:

"And now let us listen the councillor to the English throne, Ed Wilder."

The old man got up very slowly. He was one of the oldest councillors, well over 60. He sat in one of the middle rows, though his age and rank would have placed him in the first. Perrier and several councillors in the front had to turn around to see him.

"Well," Wilder began kneading his knuckles as he spoke. His eyes fixed before him, "the situation raises much concern."

"The English are preparing for war?" Garcia said, trying to get to the point, staring at Wilder with furrowed eyebrows.

"It would not surprise me, as Mortimer the knight king has been at war his whole life. He's battled the Irish, the Scots, the Danes, the Norwegians and the Swedish, and he's always won. True, the French kingdom has a far larger army than any adversary Mortimer has faced. It would not make sense to attack an equally large and strong kingdom."

"So, there will be no war?" Garcia did not take his eyes from the aged councillor for a second, and his question belied impatience.

"I don't know," Wilder replied. As he spoke, he continued to stare ahead of him. He didn't want to meet anyone's eyes, especially not Garcia's.

"The problem is Sir Lemmy Black, the strategist. The king relies on him for all decisions, not just military. Black's moves cannot be predicted. He's not only won every battle on the field, but in the King's court too. The church, the council and the noblemen have no rights in England—the king is all powerful. Whatever Lemmy wants to happen, will."

"How could they oppose the authority of the council?" Garcia asked in disbelief; though spies had informed him of the situation in England, he had not seen the situation to be as dire as this. Till now.

"I feel like he can predict my every move," Wilder almost whined. "Not long ago he captured one of my men, killed him probably. I haven't seen him since, but he pretended not to know anything about it. He does not openly oppose me, but he is a constant threat. I think my life is in danger too. Not that an old man's life is worth very much, even if he is councillor, but I worry for the known world."

"Thank you, Ed," Garcia took over. "Who has anything to add?"

Perrier's hand shot up halfway through the question. Garcia sighed and turned to Perrier:

"You have the right to speak, Alain."

"Thank you," Perrier said standing dramatically. "I think our friend Ed Wilder here sees the situation too darkly, perhaps his age has something to do with that…Excuse me, Ed," he said with a condescending look at Wilder, then he went on: "One person cannot have that much influence on the known world and cannot challenge the council alone. We've had wars before; in fact, many councillors have had to use their rings, but nowadays our situation can be called stable. Please, Pedro, allow me to meet Black; I would like to assess my enemy myself."

"So be it, as you wish, Alain," Garcia said. He felt in his bones that Wilder was right, and that the situation was far worse than they had believed.

Vincent Farall was waiting for Perrier in the councillor's chambers. He sat opposite his superior's favourite place on a simple chair. He would never have made the mistake of taking the councillor's seat.

The room did not resemble real chambers—simple, thick, undecorated wooden furniture, a wooden bed with a mattress, a round table (that could have been in Fat Jean's Inn) and a few chairs for those rare visitors—there was no mark of extravagance. The only peculiarity was a large chest of drawers. The oaken piece was heavy enough to challenge the strength of six men. There were no paintings on the walls—though there was nowhere to hang them either, because the walls were covered with thin book shelves.

Farall had been serving by Perrier for 15 years, but he still did not know his way around the councillor. The councillor was known in the court, and in fact in the whole kingdom as a powerful, ruthless man who loved no one. Farall was the only one who saw him in a different light.

He often remembered—in fact it had become a permanent fixture in his life—the day they had first met. He had been ten years old then and had been living in a monastery for four. His parents had sold him to the priests, no doubt for a tidy sum. When they bid farewell, his mother told him that she loved him very much, but that she could not raise him or his siblings, so he would go to the monastery because the gold they received would be enough for years, and that he should not worry, he would be well taken care of. His father said nothing, nor did he look at him. He could never forgive his parents for selling him like cattle, that he meant nothing more to them than another source of income in the family books. He hated the priests because they humiliated him on a daily basis, but at least he could learn, and he never went hungry. On the day they met, the town where the monastery was on the northern side of the kingdom was attacked. Later he learned that they were northern pirates, looting undefended weak settlements. The attackers took everything they could carry: food, drink, women and children. What they left behind they burned, and the people they couldn't take with them, they killed. Only those who managed to hide survived, nor did they spare the monastery. The priests were hanged, and the students kidnapped, and those deemed useless were slaughtered. He had climbed into the lavatory with only his head barely poking above the rancid water. He knew they would not find him there, and even if they burned down the monastery, he would survive. He was right, and he survived. Even after so many years, the terrible murders and the rancid smell of vile excrement were sharp in his mind.

That day, a small group of riders arrived from the king's court. Their leader called the survivors into the town square and promised to help with whatever he could. He gave them gold and told them that he would send food and workmen who would help rebuild the town. When he finished talking, he noticed Farall and approached him.

"Well, why are you so soiled?" he asked with a hint of pity in his eyes.

"Because I hid in the lavatory, Councillor Perrier," he replied politely.

"How do you know who I am?" the stranger asked in surprise.

"You wear a grey uniform, sir, and your badge holds the motto of the councillors: 'Kingdom or Death!', and there is only one councillor in the Kingdom, and he is called Perrier," he'd replied.

"You can read?" Perrier asked in disbelief.

"If I couldn't, how would I know what's on your badge, sir?"

"You may have heard it. Now my men will clean and feed you, and then I want to talk to you!" Without waiting for a reply, he turned and left.

That night he was alone in a desolate room. He got clean clothes, a hearty dinner, and then he was locked in. The vicious pirate attack combined with the hard years in the monastery weighed upon his decade old soul, and he could not bear the dark unfriendly place any longer, and he burst into tears. That was when the Councillor entered. He approached Farall, squatted down next to him and said,

"You had better learn, my son, that you never show weakness, because they will crush you immediately. Don't cry, I will take you with me, and when you grow up, you will be my aid."

"But, my lord," he sobbed, "you already have an aid."

"A minor problem, I'll take care of it," Perrier replied, and then did something he had never done since—he hugged Farall. It was only a hug, and yet it meant so much to him. There in the empty room, waiting for the councillor, he relived that moment that changed his life forever.

The door opened, and steel-heeled scraped the floor. Perrier entered momentously and sat down in his favourite chair.

"Why have you been sitting on that thing? My place was here too," he scoffed.

"You know I would never sit in your chair. That would be like trying to take over your position," Farall answered and ran his hand through his thick hair.

"Eat a little!" Perrier encouraged him and poked at the fruit bowl on the table.

They sat down opposite one another and pecked at the dried fruit. Farall broke the silence.

"What happened at the meeting?"

"Everything went exactly as I wanted it to. I convinced the councillors once more that I am a bilious wart. Do you know why that's important, Vincent?"

"That the council see you as arrogant? I have no idea." He shook his head and then looked at the Councillor questioningly. Perrier wagged his head—he had secretly hoped that Farall would know the answer—then glancing at him sternly, he replied,

"Look! The councillors like to categorise people. That makes it easier to predict people's moves. If they think I am different from what I am, then they will make wrongful assumptions about my future actions. Transparency is a mistake we cannot afford to make."

"I thought the councillors all served, Atlantis," Farall said nonplussed.

"Of course, but we all do so with our own tools. I don't think every councillor is up to the task they have been given, and I'm not just thinking of old Ed Wilder. And I will not expose myself to their incompetence."

"Did you achieve what you wanted to?" Farall inquired, though he did not quite understand what Perrier had expected from the secret, late-night meeting. The Councillor replied contentedly:

"Yes, I received permission from Garcia to meet Sir Lemmy Black, the strategist."

"What do you expect from that meeting?"

"Nothing special. He certainly won't tell me any military secrets."

"So why do you want it so badly."

Perrier smiled; he leaned back in his chair and only answered after a dramatic pause,

"I'm terribly curious about Sir Lemmy."

Chapter Four

"Get up, Mr Knight! Get up, Mr Knight!" Ponga felt like his brain was being drummed on, and on top of that, someone was shouting at him.

"Get up, Mr Knight! Get up, Mr Knight!"

"Alright, alright, just stop shouting!" He yelled at the door. "What time is it?"

"Almost 7:00, your weapons-master is waiting for you downstairs," came the answer through the door.

"Dammit!" Ponga shouted and sprang up. At that moment, a sharp pain pierced his head. He had to sit back down. *Dammit*, he thought, *how will I get to the city for the tournament in this state?*

"I'll be right down, just getting dressed," he shouted at the door.

"Hurry up! I'll wait here. I won't go down without you, or your weapons-master will kick me in the ass again," answered the servant.

"If you shout again, I'll be the one to kick your ass!"

Ponga threatened and began preparing himself. It was not easy, he could barely get his trousers on. When he bent over for his boots, he was certain he wouldn't straighten up again. He didn't even put his shirt, belt or weapons on; he just held them under his arm and left. He was very dizzy and had to hold onto the servant down the stairs. When they reached the ground floor, the weapons-master was impatiently waiting for him.

"Damn you! If we don't get there quickly, you'll be out of the tournament. The knights will be introduced to the kings soon. Hurry!" He blurted in one breath.

Only scattered memories of the trip remained to Ponga. He battled with nausea all the while trying to comprehend his situation. He hadn't drunk much the night before, he'd known today was his big day, so he stopped after a few cups of wine. And anyway, he held his drink well. He'd awoken at 5:00 a.m. every morning since he was a child. What's more he had left instruction to be awoken the night before, just to make sure. So how could all this have happened? As they ran towards the arena, the figures moving before him were blurry, and he kept bumping into them.

"Look where you're going, Sir Knight!" his escort chided. "How could you get so drunk when you knew you'd be fighting today? I won't be betting on you that's for sure," huffed the weapons-master as he helped the knight along.

They arrived and Ponga hurriedly put on his shirt and strapped on his weapons. They had arrived just in time; the knights were just exiting the tent for the ceremonial introduction. He joined the line. The court's weapons-master in charge of fencing—if he remembered correctly, was called Luc Remi—shouted at him.

"You're just in time, but in the state you're in, you should have stayed at the inn."

The others laughed and chided him.

"I hope I get you for my fight!"

"My auntie would have a better chance than you!"

"Can you tell the difference between your sword and your prick?"

As they went, fear swept over him. "What if I can't fight?" he asked himself, but for the moment, he focussed on walking straight. He knew he would have to bow at the introductions. It would be embarrassing if he just stood there swaying. The kings may even think he was mocking them.

Meanwhile, they arrived in front of the kings' watch stands. He had never seen such a monumental construction. The kings of the greater kingdoms, their families and closest courtiers sat on the lower level. All the balconies were adorned with richly sown curtains separating them. In the middle, the host, the French King and his entourage, to the right Mortimer the English King and his group. On the ground level, there were also the German, Russian, Spanish and Italian royal families. On the upper levels sat the kings of the more minor countries. There were four levels in total, staggered horizontally to avoid the kings being above one another. Opposite the construction sat the common folks on a huge hill designed so as not to be too steep to sit on. The contestants lined-up in front of the French King.

The ceremonial introductions began. The day before the master of ceremonies had questioned each knight so that he could say something interesting before the kings, making it easier for the king to decide who he was pulling for. First to be introduced were the mounted knights, who were far more important in the eyes of the nobility.

"Sir Thomas Parker," the master of ceremonies began, "descendant of the noble Yorkshire line of Parker and heir to their estate. Champion of four tournaments. Sir Thomas has never lost a fight."

Parker stepped forward and bowed elegantly.

I still have some time, Ponga thought. And he tried to calm himself by looking around.

Of course, he could not turn his head in front of the kings, the greatest rulers of the known world were right before him. There sat the young, pubescent-face French ruler Auguste Lefebre IV, beside him Queen Josephine who looked very sad indeed. *She's not even that pretty,* he observed. Next to the King sat many lavishly dressed lords whom he did not know. Then he stole a glance at the

English King. He was not called the Knight King without reason—if he took his cloak off, he could've joined the knights below. *Every king should look this way*, Ponga opined, *muscular body, open demeanour, noble visage.*

He could stare no longer, because the participants of the number more popular among the common folk, the fencers were being introduced. Ponga was the only commoners in this group. There were many poor knights here, but the thorough training the nobility received gave them a big advantage.

"Sir Hans von Basel, who is without match in the German kingdom. He is here today to defeat all the knights of the known world," the commendation of the day's heroes continued.

"Sir Pablo Don Perez, pride of Andalusia, the undefeated knight of the Spanish kingdom. Before the fight, the knight said that he had personally promised the Spanish King Carlos V that he would not return from Paris empty-handed."

Perez moved forward with a light, bouncing gait, and then, in the Spanish custom, he gave such an elegant courtesy that the noble women in the stands all sighed as one. Most of them could surely imagine the knight in their beds, of course only in secret and only for one night.

"Oleg Borosilov, whose noble father Mihail Borosilov has won this tournament once before." The boy was here to prove that he was worth as much as his father. The Russian knight approached the king with a military march, quickly bent to one knee and bowed his head so vigorously that the audience thought he would hit his nose on his chest plate.

"Sir Didier Ponga," the master of ceremonies scowled a little before he went on, "here today to gain a reputation."

One step forward, bow, straighten, back away, Ponga encouraged himself and then set off. Considering the circumstances, it went quite well. *Well, at least I didn't mess that up, even though I still feel sick*, he thought.

The fencing always came first in the tournaments; then during a short break, the arena was prepared for the jousting.

"Only a few minutes left," he shuddered. He felt like his condition had not improved much since he woke up.

The crowd murmured, and the royalty awaited the action with elegant indifference. The matches were drawn. Ponga was first against the Spanish knight, Pablo Don Perez. The noble knight looked at him with proud disdain. They both stripped half-naked and received a shield and a half-sharp sword. These swords could cause a nasty wound, and it was not hard to assess a successful hit, because someone hit by such a blade would not escape unscathed. A long time ago, a few hundred years ago, they had used real, razor-sharp swords, but due to the many deaths, the councillors had changed it to safer, half-sharp weapons. Of course, the deaths of common folks did not matter, but the lives of the aristocratic youth were too valuable.

"And now the final matches for the Knights Tournament of the Known World will begin," shouted the master of ceremonies. "I call the first two knights to come forward and decide who will continue in the tournament."

They entered the circular arena, and the combat began. Ponga found moving sideways to be a chore, yet he could not charge forwards, especially not in his state. He could barely hold the heavy shield in his left hand, and the sword in his right felt like it weighed a ton. Perez was a proportionately muscular, young man, giving the impression of a well-trained fighter; his movements belied the teachings of a weapons-master, the way he held the sword, the way he circled, all the while exposing the bare minimum of undefended area. Ponga waited; though he was not sure what he was hoping for, he still felt terrible. The Spanish knight decided to attack. He started straight forwards. Ponga could see what was coming and prepared for a quick change of direction. After two steps, Perez struck, and though Ponga stepped to the side, he was not fast enough: the sword struck his shield with such force that the shield hit him in the nose. With great difficulty, he straightened up blood dripping from his chin and pulling a thick red line down his thin, muscular body. Though he was bleeding heavily, the fight could go on; the injury had not been inflicted by a sword. In cases like this, the injured party could decide. Ponga signalled to the weapons-master that he was ready to go on. Don Perez leapt at him a second time, but this time Ponga held onto the shield more tightly. After the attack, the Spaniard did not retreat but sent his knee flying hard into Ponga's left ribs. Ponga was not used to experiencing pain during a fight, he had been in countless battles, and yet his opponents had never been able to touch him. His advantage in speed had made him believe that he was invincible. The sudden attack felt like an explosion in his side, tears filled his eyes, but something else also happened. The fear and rage caused by the pain cleared his mind. In an instant, he felt like his old self again. He pushed the Spaniard away and awaited next attack. Don Perez felt his victory to be near and attacked a third time. Ponga could see that his opponent had thrown caution to the wind as he ran towards him. *Now we will see if I've regained my speed. If not, it's all over anyway*, he thought. He took a deep breath and waited for the last moment, and then, fast as lightning, he stepped aside. When the Spaniard flew past him, Ponga stuck his sword into his opponent's side. Don Perez fell to his knees and let out a howl. His eyes flamed with rage and incomprehension. He threw his weapons to the ground and clapped his hands to his bleeding side, shouting,

"I'll kill you next time, you vermin!"

"What next time?" Ponga asked. "I won, you can go home now!"

"The winner is Sir Didier Ponga, entering the round of eight!" the master of ceremonies announced.

The fights had been going for an hour and a half when a French royal messenger arrived in the English balcony. He bowed and whispered something in Sir Lemmy Black's ear before he left.

"You must have received a very important message if they dared disturb the English royal balcony," noted Mortimer turning to Black.

"Yes, Your Honour," Black nodded.

"You want me to beg you, or will you tell me? I'm dying to know," the King grumbled.

"Councillor Perrier would like to speak with me in the break before the jousting in my chambers," Sir Lemmy replied. He displayed no emotion on his face. His coolness disturbed even Mortimer sometimes. Though it did not take much to annoy the King.

"And?" Mortimer said raising his voice. Those seated around them looked up as they heard the King raise his voice, then quickly looked away pretending as if nothing had happened.

"Of course, I will go, provided you do not have orders to the contrary, my lord," Black replied.

"Well, my dear knight, you go so willingly into the lion's mouth," Mortimer laughed.

"Yes, my lord, I want to see what's in his belly,"
Black replied.

"I can't believe it," said the King wide-eyed, "it was almost as if you smiled. I'll call the chroniclers to write it down."

"I don't think such an act is so important, my lord," Black retorted.

"Watch your skin, I'm going to need you in the future. And after the meeting, tell me everything, word for word," Mortimer said finally.

Ponga felt great. His injuries were not severe, and there was no sign of his earlier sickness. He waited for one and a half hours in the tent assigned to the contestants. He ate some ham—he had to replenish his missed breakfast.

He knew that he would be called soon, and he would have to fight again, and of course he would win. His good mood was only overshadowed by the morning's events. *What could have happened? What had made him ill? Why had they not woken him up in time?* As he pondered these questions by railings around the tent, he spotted the hooded priest who he'd been drinking with the night before. He approached him and spoke:

"What are you doing here? Are you following me?"

"I told you you're in danger. But you're still here. The question is not why I am here, but why you haven't left the city yet?" the priest said ignoring Ponga's question.

"Crazy old owl! This is the greatest day of my life. Why would leave on the world of a fool?" Ponga said enraged.

"You are the fool, my son! I want to save your life, and you insult me?" the priest leaned in quite close to him. This disturbed Ponga, and he stepped back.

"What's it to you?" he asked roughly.

"There is no point talking sense to some people. You are such a person. When you realise I am right, it may be too late," the priest answered.

"Wait a second!" recognition dawned on Ponga. "Did you put something in my drink last night? I'll kill you, you hooded rat!"

"You want to kill me when you can't even take care of yourself, you blustering boil?" the priest answered, then turned on his heels and hurried off.

Old idiot, Ponga fumed. *If I see him again, I'll throttle him.*

"Sir Didier to the arena," came the call. The next opponent was the favourite, the German

Hans von Basil. While they were introduced, Ponga felt like it was time to show everyone what he was really capable of. The combatants were awaiting the whistle when Ponga finally sized-up his opponent. Basel was a heavy, muscular blonde man with long hair in bun, so it would not interfere in the fight.

His downturned hanging lower lip made him distinctly unlikeable.

"Not another peasant!" Basel said towards the crowd. He had had to fight three commoners in the seeding rounds the day before.

"Soon you'll be whining in the dust, you idiot!" Ponga replied.

Von Basel charged at him, as he would have felt a long battle to be embarrassing against a peasant. Ponga stepped to the left, making sure not to do it at his normal speed, but much slower than the German could react to his movements. Basel followed him, adjusted the direction of his attack, and Ponga, at a speed that almost made him invisible, moved to the right, and the German broke through the barrier with all his momentum and fell amongst the crowd.

Apart from the few unfortunate people he hit, the crowd greeted the action with great appreciation. The French King also approved.

"Bravo! Bravo!" Lefebre clapped his hands in dramatically big arcs. He looked more like he was swimming through the air than clapping. "Isn't out French knight just wonderful," he turned to Perrier.

"Naturally, my lord, though I would like to mention that the Marquis Philippe Bertrand's son, Auguste, is still a contestant, and he—how should I say this—is a nobleman; this knight is nobody," the Councillor replied.

"Nobody, of course, yet he is French and entertaining," the King said in a tone that made it clear he would have the last word on the matter.

Meanwhile, the railings were re-erected; the injured spectators carted off, and the knights were ready for battle again.

"I'll kill you for that, you little worm!" the German fumed.

"You won't be too popular if you kill the spectators, Basel!" Ponga agitated him.

The blonde colossus charged him foaming at the mouth. Ponga moved around the back of the German at his usual speed. He made the half-turn before Basel could even change direction. With a smooth precise movement, he stuck his sword between the charging German's legs, smacking the knight in the balls. The German tossed his sword and shield and collapsed on the ground screaming. Though there was no blood, it was clear that Basel would not be able to continue the match.

"Ponga! Ponga! Ponga!" the crowd cheered as the victor bowed.

"Long live the French champion!" Lefebre shouted and looked rebelliously at Perrier.

"Aren't you celebrating, Councillor?"

"Yes, my lord," Perrier answered moodily and stood up to clap.

"Ponga to the round of four!" the master of ceremonies announced.

During the next match, Archbishop Cain Leroy approached Councillor Perrier.

"Councillor, a word if you would," he said impatiently causing quite a stir.

"Now?"

"Yes, now. It is very important," the priest insisted.

"Alright," Perrier replied, and taking the priests pendant, he dragged him out of earshot of the King's balcony.

"What is it that it can't wait?" the Councillor asked. Looking around, he saw that several people were staring at them.

"The French knight, Ponga, I think…" as the priest spoke, he gesticulated hurriedly.

"Cool yourself, my friend, if you don't want the whole world to be watching us," Perrier interrupted him.

"So," Leroy whispered, "that knight is a mutant, it is not natural to move so fast. I thought, before I captured him that I'd let you know."

"Dear Cain! If you dare do that, you will spend the night in the torture chamber for more reasons than one. Firstly, if you do anything behind my back, I will not forgive you. Secondly, the King is enjoying the knight, so you cannot do it anyway."

"But the church demands it…"

"Are you really this stupid, Archbishop, or just acting? If it is the latter, then please spare me!"

Leroy was speechless. His tongue was paralysed by fear and embarrassment. By the time he collected himself, the Councillor went on,

"But, of course, I will take the matter into my own hands—have no fear. Oh, and one more thing, if Marquis Bertrand wants something from me, tell him not to send his hound next time."

Not waiting for the astonished priest's answer, Perrier returned to the balcony. Before he took his place, he sat down next to Head Liquidator Luc Moreau and whispered in his ear,

"Send your best men to the winners' tent and do as we agreed. I don't want Didier Ponga to be here for the next round."

"Yes, sir!" Moreau nodded.

Ponga felt that he could allow himself a glass of wine alongside the ham and cheese. One cup would not hurt his performance. His next opponent sat opposite him—the dark-skinned, black-haired Bulgarian, Dimitar Borkov. After the matchups were decided, they were led back to the huge tent and had to remain there while the other fought.

"I like you," he said to Borkov, "but I have to defeat you."

"We will see. I think you will go home crying, and then I will feel a little pity for you," the Bulgarian answered with a smile.

"Let's drink to any outcome!" Ponga raised his cup and took a sip.

As he put the cup down, he spotted a hooded-figure on the other side of the barrier that surrounded the tent. *Was it the poisoner priest?* He was about to spring up to chase him off, and put him off poking his nose around, when the figure pushed his hood back. "That's not the old priest," he ascertained and turned back towards Borokov. As he turned, he felt that something was not quite right. Perhaps it was the hooded-figure's glance, or the sudden movement he sensed from the corner of his eye, that made him look back again and see the tiny flying object headed straight towards him. He barely had time to move his head back slightly. But that minute reflexive movement was enough to avoid the missile. As it narrowly missed his face, it burrowed deep into the Bulgarian knight's throat.

Borkov grasped his throat in surprise and began to twitch. Ponga leaped to him and saw the feathered arrow sticking out of his opponent's throat. The twitching and drooling suggested that the arrow was poisoned, or it would not have caused that much damage to anyone.

"Doctor, quickly! My friend has been poisoned!" he shouted holding the Bulgarian's head in his hands. Borkov died within a few minutes. By the time the doctor arrived, all he could do was confirm that the knight was dead.

"There was nothing to be done," he told Ponga. "If you had immediately removed the arrow, and I had been here, and would have known right away the type of poison they had used and could have administered an antidote right away, we still could not have saved him. Such a strong powerful poison works immediately before the antidote can neutralise it."

The murder had caused a large commotion in the tent. Soldiers and liquidators blocked off the area, but all this proved to be futile as the assassin had attacked from the outside and had long ago escaped.

The head liquidator accused Ponga,

"The murdered knight would have been your opponent and sat at one table with you."

"And what did I fire the arrow with? Or did I just spit it at him?!"

Ponga defended himself.

"It would be enough to stab him with it, you know as well as I," the liquidator went on, "and anyway, it's better if you say nothing. With the death of your opponent, you go straight to the finals, as you win by default. In whose interest was the death of this unfortunate soul?"

said the liquidator nodding at the corpse.

It seemed like Ponga was in serious trouble, when to his great fortune several witnesses appeared.

"I saw it; it was a hooded-figure with a blowpipe," said an old weapons-master.

"And I saw that this knight," a young stable-boy said pointing at Ponga, "was drinking wine when the knight was hit. This one," he pointed at Ponga, "has done nothing wrong."

"Commander," said Ponga turning to the liquidator, "I will have to fight the finals soon; can you not postpone the investigation till later?"

"You do not give orders around here! If you keep it up, I'll have you in chains!" the commander said losing his patience, with which he tried to mask his increasing uncertainty. When he'd arrived, the case had seemed clear, but the witnesses were muddying the waters.

Ponga didn't dare push him further; he didn't want to be arrested, so he stayed silent. As the liquidators questioned the witnesses, he stood to the side.

"A royal messenger! A royal messenger!" came a cry from the distance.

Soon a young messenger arrived, pushed his way through the crowds and approached the commander directly.

"Commander! Escort Sir Ponga before the King immediately!" The messenger waited for a second and then spoke again, "Unharmed!"

Lefebre was beside himself with rage. He sprang from his chair and shouted to the Councillor.

"Perrier, what's going on? Can't you even organise a tournament properly? Explain yourself."

"Your Highness," the Councillor began and also stood up because he could not allow himself the indignity of remaining seated in opposition to the raging monarch before him, "according to the newest information, someone committed murder due to a wager. Someone would have won a lot of money if Sir Ponga did not win. I promise we will catch the assassin today, and I will give you a detailed report of the proceedings."

As he explained himself, he glanced sideways at Head liquidator Moreau who was visibly embarrassed.

"Alright, report to me!" the King commanded the Councillor and then turned to Ponga.

"Sir, are you able to fight in the finals in your current state?"

"Naturally, my lord!" Ponga replied with simpering confidence.

"Go to it then! How long must I wait? Let the fight begin!" Lefebre announced and sat back down. Secretly, he was happy he could hold the Councillor to account for something. Unfortunately, such opportunities were rare as he was annoyingly perfect most of the time.

In the finals, Ponga's opponent was Marquis Bertrand's eldest son, Auguste Bertrand, who had fought the semi-finals while the commotion was taking place. Auguste gave the impression of a typical, spoiled noble boy; his loose posture and demeaning glance made Ponga feel disgusted. A nobleman, probably one of Bertrand's friends, shouted:

"What's up, Auguste, won't you greet Sir Ponga?" Bertrand turned towards the voice and loudly, so that everyone could hear, announced:

"A man does not talk to dogshit!"

"You'll be whining in pain soon, you conceited wart!" Ponga could not leave the insult unanswered.

Up on the King's balcony, the Marquis hissed audibly and unable to restrain himself exclaimed:

"What terrible times we live in! How dare you insult my son, you nobody?!"

Ponga shouted back at the Marquis:

"What is it, my lord? Do you talk to dogshit?"

The audience greeted his response with a standing ovation. Everyone liked that a common knight would talk back to such an established lord. The King approved of Ponga's guts and rose to his defence:

"Dear Marquis, your son was first to make offence, please do not be unjust."

The audience opposite greeted this with loud applause. Lefebre accepted the applause with a wide, contented grin; he liked to bask in his popularity. Bertrand Senior hissed a "Yes, my lord" through gritted teeth, but his scarlet face showed his true feelings.

Now Ponga did not merely want to win, he wanted to humiliate his opponent, and in a way that would not only hurt his body but also his soul.

After the whistle, they began to circle. It transpired that young Bertrand had seen his opponent's previous matches and did not want to make the same mistake as the others. So, he did not charge. With a swift movement, Ponga sliced at Bertrand's sword-holding hand. The young nobleman wanted to deflect with his shield-bearing left hand leaving it open. Halfway through the movement, Ponga switched direction and stood on the other defenceless side. The aristocrat did not shout, though blood flowed from his fresh cut wound. The master of ceremonies immediately shouted:

"A hit! Sir Ponga wins!"

"Blatant lies!" Bertrand shouted, "I cut myself with my shield, there was no hit."

King Lefebre interjected, "Sir Ponga, how do you see it?"

"Your Highness, if the noble knight says there was no hit, then I believe him."

"An elegant and spirited response," Lefebre replied, "the fight goes on!"

The nobleman charged forward having lost his patience, and Ponga stepped aside swinging his sword with all his might at his opponent's side. Bertrand let out an ear-splitting shout as he collapsed; his new wound spewing blood. Then Ponga approached him and asked loudly,

"Noble knight, do you think I managed to hit you now?"

The king stood to applaud him. "Bravo! Bravo! Sir Ponga shall rest in the palace tonight!" Lefebre turned to the Councillor.

"I will make arrangements," Perrier replied and glanced once more at the head liquidator.

Chapter Five

Perrier sat in his chambers awaiting Sir Lemmy Black.

"Dammit! What a cursed day is today!" he burst out towards Vincent Farall who sat in his usual simple little chair.

"I will have to report to the King in the evening about the assassination of the Bulgarian knight. We have to find an assassin and a person who hired them by then—they will have to be dead, of course. The head liquidator messed up, but I don't want to hurt him because I like him. Of course, the point is that he may still be useful to me."

"I assume you've already taken steps in the matter," Farall asked gently.

"What makes you think that?" Perrier asked.

"You would not just complain about something and not do anything. I don't mean to be disrespectful; it is a compliment of sorts," Farall backtracked and fidgeted as if he were sitting on pins.

Perrier looked at his aid more with pride than rage.

"You don't have to explain yourself. You are right on one count; on the other hand, we are alone, and you are right to be candid."

"What about Ponga?" Farall looked questioningly.

"He must be killed as soon as possible. Unfortunately, the King likes him a lot."

"He cannot be allowed to live?"

"Really, Vincent, the Church would accuse him because of his supernatural speed anyway. They would say he's a mutant. But if we finish him, we'll be doing Marquis Bertrand a favour too."

Farall swallowed hard and then collecting all his courage asked,

"Since when do you care about the Marquis' opinion, Alain? You never considered his interests; in fact, you opposed him wherever you could. And now he's suddenly become so important to you that you're doing him favours? Also, the Church is under the control of the council; so if the church is chasing mutants, then that means that the councillors want to be rid of them."

"If you see the situation so clearly, then why are you asking question? You want to hear a confession from me?"

"I didn't mean to be disrespectful. I just wanted you to know that sometimes I can read between the lines. Perhaps more than I should."

"Nonsense, no, it's good that you see more and more. The reason I insisted on your presence for the meeting with Sir Lemmy is that I expect your help. I want to find out what motivates Black."

Resting his elbows on the table, and leaning his fingers together, the Councillor stared forwards and asked, "Do you know why I care about the strategist's motivations?"

"Of course," Farall replied eagerly. "The second lesson in the councillors' training: Everyone is motivated by something: if you know the motivation, you can predict their actions as you know the direction of their intent."

At that moment, there was a knock at the door.

"Yes," Perrier said sternly glancing at the door and then leaning back in his chair. He knew the play was about to start, in which he would be one of the leads. It would be a performance written by none other than life.

The door creaked and in-stepped a skinny, short officer, and behind him appeared the thin, muscular figure of Sir Lemmy Black. He looked around without moving his head; only his eyes revealed how he was assessing the situation. *He was a real soldier, one who always did reconnaissance in enemy territory. It was probably instinctual for him to scan unknown places,* thought the Councillor as he smiled at his guest—because he surely would not think of being attacked.

"Excuse me for not coming alone, but Commander Caroll follows me everywhere," the strategist said as he walked to the table.

"Greetings, Sir Lemmy, please, take a seat!" Perrier indicated the comfortable chairs on the far side of the table. The chairs had been made in consideration of the expectations of the aristocracy. Besides having feather cushions, the golden-laced fabric emphasised the expectation of noble-born rumps to be placed therein. The armrests were lavishly carved, forming bears heads at the end, leaving no doubt as to the skill of the carpenter.

"I am not alone either, allow me to introduce, Vincent Farall, my aid."

Farall stood and bowed; Black nodded to the aid.

"You are very considerate to have brought me such an expensive special chair, though I am not a fan of such elegant furniture."

"How do you know I had it brought for you?" Perrier asked in surprise.

"I just had a look around your chambers, and this piece does not match the rest of the room, so you must have had it brought for this meeting."

"Right you are," the Councillor replied curtly, "Unfortunately, I did not expect the Commander."

"That's alright, he does not sit; he will stand behind me."

"Rumours have it that Commander Caroll is your bodyguard, and he follows you everywhere except for meetings with the king," Perrier scanned his adversary incessantly as he spoke.

Black wagged his head.

"Councillor, you say that as if you'd heard it on the market. Why don't you say, 'My spies told me'?"

Perrier smiled and crossed his legs; he was beginning to enjoy the conversation.

"I just wanted to be polite, but as you wish, let's get to the point. And why not? So do you think there will be war between our kingdoms?"

Farall's head jerked up, and Caroll's eyes went wide, but Black did not react. He sat in his chair with the same straight back as before, and his face belied no emotion at all.

Farall remembered the councillor's tenth lesson, saying: provoke your enemy, make him blunder. Those who act instinctively will usually not make the best decision. This can be equally true of a conversation or on the battlefield. *But Black had not won all his battles out of luck, he would not be confused by such a cheap trick,* Farall thought.

"You confuse me with King Mortimer. How could I know?" the strategist responded looking fixedly at the Councillor.

"Let's be honest with each other, Sir Lemmy! I know that you have great influence over King Mortimer's decisions," Perrier withstood his guest's harsh stare.

Farall could not believe his ears. This kind of insensitive questioning was too much, even from Perrier, but he could discern no reaction from the strategist.

"That is not quite true: King Mortimer does indeed ask my advice on some matters, but I do not control the kingdom; I merely help him. In short, he has not told me of such intentions."

"Would you tell me if he had?" asked the Councillor directly.

"Of course not. Though, truth be told I do not care. War—as is peace time—is just a situation to be solved. Peace brings its own set of challenges and war another: that is the only difference. True, I have not had much time for peace. You've been interrogating me constantly, do not be offended if I ask back now. What makes you think there will be war?"

It was Perrier's turn to wag his head.

"Strategist, let us not play games! My spies have reported." He put a mocking emphasis on the word 'spies', "that over the channel, the Royal English forces are assembling, and the fleet has united by the shores of La Manche. Furthermore, King Mortimer's provocative behaviour towards Marquis Bertrand is clear."

Farall was finding it hard to appear nonchalant, even though the Councillor had told him many times that it was important to show no emotions during meetings. He also knew that if he could not comply with this expectation, Perrier would surely punish him, but he was shocked that his master was so transparent before the enemy. *True,* he thought, *the councillor does everything for a reason; he knew him well enough for that.*

"Councillor," Black stared incessantly at Perrier as he spoke, "you're imagining things. What could England gain from attacking France? A war between two equally matched forces would lead to heavy casualties on both sides. Military manoeuvres are common place in England as we are almost always at war with someone."

"I'm not convinced, but I didn't think you would. Let's change the subject: I heard a lot about Commander Caroll," he looked at the motionless soldier, who completely ignored the fact that his person had become the next topic of conversation. "I've heard…well, how should I put this…that his movements are faster than normal, almost supernatural. Do you accept mutants in England?"

This was the point where Farall could no longer control himself. He jerked his head towards Perrier with a terrified look in his eyes. Such insolence was outrageous even from the councillor. He would not have been surprised if the guests had left without a word. But Black remained just as calm as he had till now. Farall wondered at the man, could nothing disturb his calm?

"You claim to be polite while accusing your guests?" Sir Lemmy expressed his discontent in the same tone of voice he would have used to chat about the weather. His perfect calm made the Councillor feel uneasy. "You know that mutants are not tolerated in England, and yet you accuse Commander Caroll of being one. Are you saying King Mortimer and I are supporting criminals? It follows that you think we do not value religion, that we are heretics. Besides, Sir Ponga, your new champion, is much faster than the Commander."

"I did not mean to be impolite, Sir Lemmy," Perrier said, "I just felt like we could be honest with one another; as you know, mutations and helping them are capital crimes."

"Is your idea of honesty threatening your guests?"

"Don't be so touchy, but if it makes you feel better, then I apologise," the Councillor switched to a conciliatory tone. "Don't you ever threaten your enemies?"

- No, no I don't," Black looked at Caroll for a moment and then went on: "I have no need for threats; my opponents fear me enough without them. Anyway, now that we're on the topic of honesty, would you answer me one question, Councillor Perrier?"

"Of course," Perrier raised his eyebrows.

Black waited a bit and then asked the Councillor,

"Why did you want to kill Sir Ponga?"

The silence, as the saying goes, was palpable in the councillor's chambers. Perrier greeted the question with a laugh, and he showed no sign of fright. Farall thought the Councillor would get a little of the insensitivity he showed back now.

"Because he's a mutant. Which was further complicated by the fact the Lefebre likes him. A mutant, adored by the king, as they say, is not the most fortunate situation. How did you know?"

"It wasn't hard, just a little observation. I saw that you did not approve of Ponga's success, even though the victory of a French knight should have brought you joy. You spoke to the bishop and then your head liquidator. And afterwards—surprise, surprise—there was an assassination attempt. I also saw that you could barely contain your rage over the failed plot. It was not hard to figure out what had happened."

"Strategist, the assassination was against the Bulgarian knight!"

"Councillor, please, spare me the games. Keep the excuses for your king. And now, if you don't mind, I must go, the jousting is about to begin."

"I'm glad you accepted my invitation. I hope we will meet again soon."

"Perhaps sooner than you'd like, Councillor," Black replied and then stood up and headed towards the door with a confident stride.

Sir Lemmy Black was at the door when Perrier called after him,

"Well, well, strategist, that sounded like a threat."

"Not at all, just a statement," Black said without bothering to turn around and then closed the door behind him.

Perrier leaned back contentedly in his chair and looked at his aid.

"That little chat was quite entertaining. I now know what motivates the strategist. I'm interested in your opinion. Let's have it!"

"Well," Farall scratched his chin, "Sir Lemmy's powers of observation are astounding. He can reach conclusions from the smallest signs. He immediately noticed that you had just had the expensive chair brought in and deduced from your behaviour that you tried to have Sir Ponga killed. I think he learned a lot about you from this conversation too. I think you shared information with him that it may have been better to keep secret."

"And? What else?" Perrier ignored Farall's concerned observation.

"Yet on our side, we have learned little that is nothing. He did not reveal whether there would be war, we did not learn what the point of war between two equally matched kingdoms would be. Sir Lemmy is not the kind of man to act without reason, so I don't know what he really wants, but I know we didn't learn anything from this meeting."

"You are right on all counts, but you have missed the point. It is true that black received information, which he will probably interpret correctly. Also, we do not know what is behind the conflict between the kingdoms. However, Sir Lemmy revealed much more about himself than I could have hoped. I think it was worth revealing some information to him, because what I received from him makes up for it in spades. In short: we made a good deal."

"Don't wind me up, Alain. If you want to tell me, please do. I won't get it on my own.

Sir Lemmy said, 'Have no need for threats, my opponents fear me enough without them.'"

"And?" Farall looked at his master nonplussed.

"Don't you get it? What have I taught you? Motivation is the second lesson of the councillors. He said, 'opponents, not enemies.' That means that the strategist is interested in the game; the process motivates him. Not money or power, faithfulness or truth, or even revenge, just the game of chess; the solving of the problem attracts him. Enemies are hated, opponents respected and not to be underestimated. Also, Sir Lemmy will only start a game that he knows he can win."

Farall furrowed his brow and was silent for a few moments. Then he looked the Councillor in the eye.

"You are right, as always; you are closer to solving the problem of his character—the problem is that this fills me with fear, not joy."

Chapter Six

Didier Ponga sat with his legs crossed smoking a pipe in the chambers that had been prepared for him. The extravagance of the royal palace had astounded him from the moment he stepped in. Elegant lords and ladies, expensive dining sets, rare delicacies and much laughter. He felt like he was in a dream. The lives of those who gained entrance here were filled with entertainment; no one was in danger, and everyone was happy. Now that he was alone, he had time to think about the events of the last few hours.

The King and Queen had personally congratulated him on his victory and had even gifted him an expensive sword. Perrier promised him a job as commander of the guards and the rank of captain and then introduced him to many influential people whose names he could not remember—they were so numerous. No one spoke of the English champion of the jousting tournament, only of him as he was French, and everyone felt complicit in his victory. The Councillor even offered to send him a beautiful courtesan in the evening. He did not reject the generous offer. Why would he? The chambers were lavish with paintings on the walls, a friendly fire in the grate and comfortable furniture everywhere, but he was most intrigued by the large, four-poster bed surrounded by curtains.

There was a knock at the door. He quickly knocked the ash from his pipe and with an elegant 'enter' invited whoever it was in. A servant entered bearing a tray heavily laden with food.

"Sir, I've brought your dinner."

Ponga was disappointed because he'd been expecting the courtesan the Councillor had promised him.

"I'm expecting a guest. I don't know if this will be enough for two." He enjoyed bossing around the staff. He had already ordered pipe tobacco and wine earlier.

"I'm sure it will be enough, my lord, but if it isn't, ring the bell, and I will bring more."

Suddenly, he lost the desire to nit-pick. These people almost enjoy being insulted. There was no inn where the barkeep would not have poured the drink in his face for speaking in this way.

"Alright, put it on the table, you may go!" he said relaxing. As the servant left, Didier approached the table and tore a thigh from the roast chicken there.

He was about to take a bite when he heard a scratching noise from the door. He stood up to see what it was. Carefully he opened the door and saw a small white dog wagging its tail. Surely it was someone's favourite pet, as there was no way that stray dogs were roaming the castle halls.

Ponga carefully stuck his head into the hallway and looked around. He was happy not to see the owner, because this way he could invite the dog inside. He loved animals, and dogs were his weakness.

"Hey you! Come on in!" he said lovingly.

By the time he'd said it, the dog was in the middle of the room staring longingly at the tray of food. Ponga laughed, closed the door and then stroked the dog. He'd never seen such a strange creature—on top of its head, between its ears was a black triangle of fur that looked like it had been drawn there.

"Don't tell me you're jealous. Here!" He threw the chicken thigh from his hand to the dog and took the other thigh from the chicken.

"I have to eat something too," he said to the dog as if it understood.

There was another knock at the door. He threw the meat back on the tray, and for lack of a better option, wiped his hands on his trousers. He did not want to hold a perfumed woman with greasy hands. He quickly sat down because he felt it was more elegant to greet a woman seated than nervously standing there.

The door opened, and two guards burst in.

"I did not say enter yet!" he complained. The older guard peeked into the hallway and then closed the door, then turned to look at Ponga.

"Who cares? Idiot!" the newcomer said. Ponga jumped up and ran to the guards; in his confusion, he even forgot to punch the guard in the nose.

"What? What did you say? How dare you! You burst in here and insult me?" he blustered.

"Don't you recognise me? Look at me closely!" the stranger leaned forwards.

Ponga saw and then spoke in disbelief, "You! Are you the hooded poisoner priest?"

"Speaking of poisoning, I hope you've not eaten from the food. If you have, we're too late."

"No. Why?"

"Liquidator Azor rarely dresses as a servant to deliver food, but if he does, I certainly wouldn't eat of it."

Ponga look at the dog in fear. Poor thing lay motionless on the ground. The poison had finished it quickly.

"Dammit! He was so cute…I've never seen a dog with a triangle like that before," he groaned and then knelt next to the dog and stroked its lifeless body.

"Are you really so dumb? Stop feeling sorry for the dog and worry about yourself! And now we must go immediately! They'll have discovered the dead guards by now, and they'll be on their way to take your corpse."

"What dead guards?" Ponga asked.

"Where do you think we got our clothes from? There's no time, let's go," the other replied and began shoving him.

You look much younger than in priest's robes, Ponga thought. He did not allow himself to be shoved; he just stared at the man who had been a wizened priest the day before and was now a young guard.

"Stop messing around, let's go," said the mysterious stranger ignoring the observation.

Ponga stood rooted to the spot; no matter how they shoved him.

"At least tell me your name!"

"If that's so important to you, my name is Jules."

Then Jules grabbed Ponga by the arm and dragged him into the hall while other man pushed from behind. As they exited the room, the flickering light of the torches did not make the hallway seem as inviting as it had a just a few hours ago—it was an intimidating view. Ponga knew that if they were caught, they'd find themselves in a torture chamber in a matter of seconds. He'd heard a lot about the Councillor's ruthless nature, and there was no way they could explain the murdered guards.

"Look!" Jules whispered, "We have to walk slowly and confidently; we're only going to run if we're spotted. Got it?"

"Yes, right you are," Ponga stammered. He still had not fully comprehend what was happening to him. The sound of shouting came from the distance—the dead guards must have been discovered.

Luckily, there was no one in the hall, so they could proceed undisturbed. After a few turns, they reached a spiral staircase.

"Do you know which way we want to escape?" Ponga asked.

"What do you think? Is that a normal question? How do you think we found you?"

They headed up the stairs. Ponga didn't know exactly how many levels they climbed, but it was only a few. Then they emerged into a hallway. Here there were no traces of elegance—probably only servants used this way. After a few steps, they ran into a guard.

"What are you doing here?" he barked at them.

"Didn't you hear?" Jules asked.

"What?"

"Two guards were killed, and the palace is being searched. The order is to patrol in pairs. I think you should report to your commander immediately."

"And how come the new champion Sir Ponga is with you? I saw your fight."

"Well..." Ponga began, but he could not finish because Jules' companion stabbed a dagger into the guards throat, whose blood spurted all over them.

"Pull him into the staircase, hurry!" Jules ordered.

After many turns, they reached the royal kitchens. The chefs were hard at work; kitchen hands milled around. The air was heavy with the smell of food and the heady scent of hot grease. The nauseating air did not seem to bother the workers; they'd had time to get used to it.

As they entered, one of the chefs turned to them:

"What are you doing here?" he asked with some suspicion.

"No time to explain. We're not hear for our own please, alright?! Someone poured poison in Marquis Bertrand's drink, and we have to investigate. So, control yourself, cook!"

Ponga had never seen anyone lie as convincingly as Jules. He almost believed what he was hearing too. Meanwhile, they reached the centre of the kitchen, the exit was only a few metres away when liquidators stormed in and saw them escaping, and their leader shouted,

"Catch them!"

"Now run, follow me!" Jules said.

They ran like crazy, pushing people out of the way. Soon they were out of the kitchen; the cooks had not posed much of a threat. Outside, Jules turned to them.

"We're almost there, Henri, go!"

They reached a little wooden door and through that a little closed off courtyard. It was dark, so the people coming opposite them could not see their blood-spattered clothes.

"Slowly, naturally," Jules whispered. It was hard to restrain themselves, because they knew that their pursuers would gain the courtyard at any minute. Luckily, they crossed the square without a problem and entered some stables. The horses greeted the strangers nervously.

They crept silently to the end of the stables. Henri opened the paddock of the last horse on the right, stroked the horse and went past the animal. The others followed. By the wall, after a brief search, he found a handle barely raised off the ground. He turned it, and a little door opened, barely half-a-metre high. All three of them slipped through it; and Jules who came last, closed it behind them. It was pitch black inside. Ponga heard a rustling. Henri was searching through his bag that he had been clutching in his hands throughout the escape. Soon there was a sound of sparks, and a few moments later, they all held lit torches.

"Now please, remain quiet. I will answer your questions in good time," Jules calmed the knight. At first, Ponga counted the steps they took, but after a while, he lost track of the distance. Even in the semi-darkness, he could sense that the tunnel in which they went was much higher than a mineshaft. Sometimes the hallway became so narrow that they had to pass the torches to one another and crawl through; then it widened out and became just as high as before. A few times, they reached large, dark cavern and then continued down the tunnel. After half an hour, Jules broke the silence,

"We can talk freely now. Ask me anything!"

"Who are you? Why do they want to kill me? And why did you save me?"

"One at a time!" As they kept moving, their footsteps reverberating off the tunnel walls. "I already saw in seeding rounds how quick you are. I knew the Councillor would try to kill you, as the kingdom persecutes mutants."

"I'm not a mutant, just fast. Is that a crime?" Ponga waved his torch in outrage.

"You'll have to ask the priests about that one. So, I tried to talk you out of it. In fact, I even put a sleeping potion in your drink at the inn and paid the innkeeper to not wake you up the day of the tournament—but alas, you still went. They wanted to kill you in the break, and yet you still did not feel endangered. After that we entered the castle to save you, and you were almost poisoned there. That is all I can tell you now."

"Alright, but who are you, and why did you help me?" Ponga turned to block their way. He was determined that they wouldn't continue till he saw the situation clearly, in which, unfortunately, he was playing the leading role.

"Later, when the time is right, I will tell you. For now, you will have to make do with this, let us pass. We cannot stop now."

With that he swept Ponga out of the way.

"What is this place?" Ponga asked as they went on.

"Do you always ask this many questions? Alright, one more answer. This tunnel was built by the ancient people, we don't know why. They drilled so many holes like this that the whole of Paris is full of them. Most of them collapsed long ago, but we've restored some sectors. We had to drill through in places where it was too narrow. You'll see how many giant halls these tunnels connect."

"Just one last question!" Ponga begged. "How do we get through any of the city gates? Not even a mouse could get through undetected."

Jules answered presently,

"We don't. We will pass underneath." One cannot sense something they were given at birth. He only considers something important when there is an absence of it. If he has to fight for it, then he will protect and guard it till his death. This is true for the councillors—they do not value security, well-being and free elections, even though they know the people of the known world lack all of these. John Neville never understood why, but he knew it was so. He observed how many youngsters from Atlantis longed for the known world. For them, adventure and the unknown is more important than a quiet life. They want a challenge, because it is missing from their lives; it is what they do not receive at birth. Neville had been leading Atlantis for ten years, and he knew well that the passion of adventurous youth helped avoid lethargy, it was their energy that kept the closed world working and helped form their current civilisation. How could one give up everything forever? He wouldn't do it, that's for sure. He looked at the young man sitting opposite him and said shaking his head,

"What name have you chosen?" Neville asked rubbing the bridge of his nose.

"I will be called Alexandr Petrov," the tall, thin man in his 30s, with the searching eyes, replied, "more precisely Councillor Alexandr Petrov."

When Atlantis sent a new councillor to a country, the candidate had to choose a name that would fit in the kingdom they were assigned to. Though the common tongue was spoken throughout the known world, but the names remained in the old tongues. Kingdoms welcomed new councillors much more readily if their name seemed familiar. But there was another perhaps more important reason for the name change stemming from Atlantis-tradition.

Future councillors would leave as a new man, and begin a new life, and that came with a new name that signified that they could never again set foot in their home country and now belonged to another world. Irreversibly.

"President Neville, is there something wrong?" asked the new councillor.

"No, nothing, just…Well, are you sure about this? Because, as you know, once you set off, there is no way back. You will have to live your life far from Atlantis, in a strange, wild, barbaric world. The others who work as informants and contacts may return home and can live another life. But being a councillor is a lifetime obligation."

"Of course, President. You know that I know all this. In fact, you know that I've spent my whole life preparing for this, and I've also spent three years in the Russian kingdom, so I know where I'm going."

"True, but do not forget, Councillor Alexandr Petrov, that many young people are prepared to be councillor, and we send many out on field trips, but only a few of them become councillors. I now appoint you councillor, there is no way back now."

"True, but all the candidates want to become councillors, so I am not surprised when the goals of my life come to fruition."

"Working in the Russian kingdom is one of the hardest tasks."

"President, you speak as if I had won the kingdom, I'm going to this by a lucky draw. Everyone knows that the best man for the job of councillor is chosen when a post opens up."

"Alright, I just wanted to be certain of your determination again."

Neville opened a drawer and took out an ornate ring. Holding it before him, he looked at it for a few moments and then handed it to Petrov,

"Take this ring; as you know, the poison it holds never loses its potency and will be just as effective in decades. The structure with the needle on the end can be activated with the hand it is on. It is important that you know how to use it, in case you have to. It is not because of the possibility of betrayal that you must wear it; Atlantis would survive that, this is how we want to protect you from terrible torture. I know you know this, but when I hand such a piece to someone, then I must say all this," the young man nodded impatiently. He was bored of the old…man's fussing.

"Councillor Petrov, do you want to talk about the Russian kingdom? If you like, I can describe the current political situation."

"I mean no disrespect, President Neville, but I think I know more about the subject than you. If this were not so, my training here on Atlantis would be worthless. If there were something I do not know then…well…how should I put this? The whole system of councillors would be worthless."

"You're right, but you know how hard it is for me to say farewell. Although we barely know each other personally, I was constantly informed of your process, and it is not easy to let you go."

The president stood up and walked around the table to shake Petrov's hand, who also stood up.

"Good luck, my friend!"

"Thank you," Petrov said and left the office.

Neville sat back down and felt contented. It was always the same; the last part of training was the farewell. Today's conversation would come back to him often, as it was an important, fateful moment in his life and the future of Atlantis.

Neville played the benevolent father's role, even if all the emotional acting made his stomach churn.

Chapter Seven

Claire Mallory looked out the kitchen window. She could not have imagined a more beautiful view. From beside the fireplace where she was busy, she could see the most beautiful corner of her garden. The garden was not beautiful in conventional suburban sense, but in the way Claire liked it. There was no sign of flowerbeds or well-manicured hedges or elegant trees. It closely resembled a dense, wild, untouched jungle. Beyond the veranda of thick planks began the empire, where she felt truly at home. A wild rose bush growing in all directions caught her eye. It was April, and the bush bore an army of pink flowers. The vines from the walls had spread onto the bush too which made it seem even thicker. Claire knew that she would have to free the rose bush from the vines sooner or later, or it would strangle it, but she didn't want to break the beautiful green disorder. *It can wait, maybe in a week or two*, she decided as she sniffed at the boiling food. The kitchen was not large, but she liked it this way, because it kept everything within arm's reach when she cooked.

The food needs at least another 20 minute, she observed. Her father, Commander Mallory, would be home for lunch in half an hour, so she had a few more minutes that she could spend in the garden. She put on her slippers and was out in the open. It had rained not long ago, and the air was fresh a clean, and she inhaled the scent of wet plants joyously. Then a voice spoke in her head; a voice she loved the most.

"When will we meet, my love?" Claire smiled and answered without words because he was not near her.

"My father will come soon, but I have time in the afternoon." She walked past the rose bush; it swayed gently in the spring breeze and seemed to turn after her as she went. Meanwhile, she awaited his response.

"Alright, then I will get leave from the castle too. I have something for you." Claire suspected that she would receive a present as she turned 18 that day, but she acted surprised.

"A present, Roy? How come?"

"Are all girls so false, or is it just you? You know very well why, little witch!"

"Alright! Don't be angry!" Claire answered as she arrived by her spice plants and plucked a strand of lemongrass to smell—she loved the scent. She had planted these warmth-loving plants not long ago and was delighted to see that they were flourishing outside as there was no more cold to come.

"I have to go now Claire, I love you!"

"I love you too, Roy, see you in the afternoon." After their silent conversation, she ran back to the kitchen as she was afraid the food would burn.

Adam Mallory arrived home earlier than usual. The London Royal Palace was 10 minutes' walk from their home, which stood by the castle wall. He was the commander of the guard, so he could afford to go home for lunch. These meals were the highlight of his days. Here, he could be with his adopted daughter, Claire. Of course, they met during the day too, or in the evenings for dinner, but the shared lunches had a special magic to them, and the moments were made even more special by the knowledge that his daughter was caring for him, as she always cooked lunch for them. The servants thought it strange that the young mademoiselle of the house would not let them into the kitchen, but the adolescent girl rendered them compliant with her adult determination. At first—and quite often—the lunch turned out terribly bad, but Adam still ate it and never told Claire the truth. Later, the meals got better and better, and the Commander did not care about the food much anyway. He knew that his daughter wanted to repay him for the care with which he showered her day by day. He thought fearfully of the day when a young man would up and take her away. This feeling came to him with increased force on this day she turned 18. He may not have many shared lunches left, and so he would value those he received all the more, which was why he had hurried home so fast.

When she heard him fussing in the dining room, she threw her arms around her neck shouting,

"How come you're home early, Daddy? The food is not ready yet."

"That's alright, I can wait. You just do your thing, I'll just sit here and watch. Won't you ask what I got you for your birthday?"

"No, I won't, I'll wait until you tell me!" Claire stroked her father's face and then turned back to her cooking. Mallory sat down and watched his daughter working in the kitchen through the open door.

He remembered the day they met. It was a cold October morning when the young, newly appointed Commander Lemmy Black fought his first battle against the rebelling Northern Lords. He had been entrusted to protect Black. In command of a six-man force, they followed Black everywhere. They had their work cut out for them, because the young leader liked to throw himself into the thick of battle. On that day, they had to siege the rebel base in Sheffield. They were winning when the overzealous Black was the first to breach the castle gates. Arrows, rocks and boiling water rained down from the walls. Black got ahead of his team and could not be held back. It had been him who ran after the commander and caught up to him a few metres from the gate.

"My lord! Stop and let us surround you; this is too dangerous," he begged desperately.

"Let me be, Mallory, I'm not a child. Take care of yourself!"

Meanwhile, the enemy soldiers advanced, and the chaos became too great to see who was fighting who. Mallory could not find his own men, but he did not want to leave Black alone. He racked his nerves to protect him and spot the looming dangers in time. In the castle courtyard, there was a bloody battle raging; there were no more arrows—just swords, shields and axes.

The horrors of man-on-man combat cannot be imagined by someone who has not experienced it. Soldiers murdered in uncontrolled rage. Mallory had seen men not even notice when their arm had been cut off, just charging forwards, killing with the sword clutched in their remaining arm. Newcomers would go into shock in their first experience of combat, and sometimes they just stood there till someone came and killed them, or they ran panicked back towards camp ignoring the shouts of the veterans that anyone turning their back to the enemy would not survive the fight. Most sieges ended in close quarters combat, the marks of which the soldiers carried on them to the end of their days. The wounds to the soul would never heal, the death cries, the disembowelled friends, and the accusing glares of innocent people would haunt them forever. The old men in inns always spoke of heroic acts, but they carried the nightmares within them, and every night they are forced to face the battles of their past.

Mallory suddenly spotted a soldier on the corridor that ran along the castle wall. From there, a bow could be used to great effect. The soldier was just taking aim at Black. Mallory did not think; he acted from instinct pushing his commander out of the way, but meanwhile the arrow burrowed into his own shoulder, finding a way between his shoulder and chest plates. Both of them crashed to the ground. Mallory barely felt the pain, he cared only about the Commander's life. He stood up quickly and helped Black up and looked around. The enemies had surrounded them; the two of them would not survive for long, especially if he could only use one of his arms. Fortunately, they spotted the green and black banner of their own troops not far off. It was not the first time Mallory had experienced the importance of uniform. In close-quarters combat, it was vitally important that everyone knew who the enemy was and who wasn't. The sea of rebels wearing blue-and-red armour approached quickly.

Mallory and Black collected all their strength to fight because they saw they would not have to hold out for long. And hold out they did. Black did not want to stop fighting, but he finally conceded that there was no point in being heroic, and they were rescued from the ring of enemies.

In the city by the camp, Mallory's wound was dressed. Luckily the arrow had now penetrated too deeply, so the siege could continue in the afternoon. By the evening, they had defeated the rebels, but skirmishes went on the towns surrounding the castle, because some of the enemy soldiers had managed to break through the siege ring. The next day, Black's men had to comb the town to find any hiding rebels. They were spread out, exploring the enemy territory one by one. The worst part of war is when the battle spreads to homes of innocent people. At these times, multitudes of defenceless people suffer the cruelty of soldiers. The enemy butchered anyone they came across. Mallory saw corpses everywhere, weeping, dishonoured women, and what was worst of all, crying children, looking for their parents. He was searching the yard of a house when he spotted a woman lying on the ground. He approached her. The woman was bleeding heavily, and she was dying. *Perhaps she had not let them rape her, or she had been protecting her family, and so they had hurt her*, Mallory thought. He knelt next to her, took her head in his arms and looked into her eyes. The woman, covered in mud and ready for death as she was, enchanted him with her beauty.

"Listen!" she whispered. "You soldier of the enemy, but perhaps you are a good man. I cannot be picky; either I beg you for help, or no one at all. My daughter is inside, please do not leave her alone, and care for her. I want to die knowing she'll be safe. It is no small thing to ask, but what can I do. Will you do that for me?"

"Yes, of course, I promise," he stammered. By the time he said it, the woman spasmed and then breathed no more. He wasn't even sure that she had heard his response. He let the dead woman's head gently to the ground and then entered the house. The door opened into a larger space that was at once a kitchen and a dining room. Further back he found two doors. A faint moaning came from behind one of them. He opened it. The little room was sparsely furnished with only a bed, a closet and two chairs. The girl crouched on one of the chairs.

"I'm going to take you now." He felt the harsh impact of what he said, but he had struggled to express his feelings his whole life. He'd failed again.

"Are you going to kill me like Mummy?" asked the trembling, skinny, round-eyed little girl who was about eight.

"Of course not, I did not kill your mother either. I have to take you, and that's all." He felt like he was unable to say more, so he grabbed her and took her to camp. She did not resist, but she obeyed him mutely.

In the evening, Black called for him. In the central tent, the Commander was surrounded by his officers. He sat on a chair with his legs spread wide and a straight back as if he were sitting astride a horse.

"Commander Adam Mallory, come in!" Black invited the intimidated soldier. "Sit down!"

"I'd rather stand, sir."

"As you wish. You saved my life in the battle there, and you almost died in my stead. You know I value my life highly, and I owe you. I would like to settle my debt today. You may ask me for land or rank. Which do you choose?"

"Well, my lord, the thing is…" He wasn't able to finish the sentence.

"Don't be shy! As the old saying goes: you reap what you sow."

"So…I found a little girl."

"So, marry her!" Everyone in the tent laughed, but Mallory was more and more flustered.

"Not like that, my lord, a child. There was a dying woman by a house, and well…I promised her to raise the child. She has no one and the promise…The point being, my lord, that I would like to retire. That is my request. Not land or rank. I have some money."

Black did not answer immediately; he just scratched his chin.

"I see, but I cannot let a faithful soldier go just like that. I think the London Castle needs a man like you. You will be commander of the guard and will receive a little house not far from the castle where you can raise the child. Will that suit you?"

"I am very grateful, my lord." In that moment, he felt that there was no greater man than Black. His opinion had not changed with time.

Ten years had passed since then, and had passed so quickly, he had barely noticed. *The girl fussing around in the kitchen was almost a woman, and soon he would be a lonely old man,* he thought bitterly.

Claire served the food and then sat down opposite him. Mallory took a little box from his pocket and placed it on the table.

"This is your birthday present." He look shyly at his daughter and stopped eating as he watched her open the box.

"Daddy, this is a key! Just like the key to our house."

"That's because it is."

"You gave me a spare key as a present?"

"Well, it's not exactly, well, errr…the house."

"Daddy, I don't get it."

"When you marry, you will have to live somewhere with your husband. I'm giving this house to you. This will be your dowry. No one will say of my daughter that she's a penniless nobody."

"But, Daddy, you can't! I want to live with you, even if I do marry."

"Silly girl!" Mallory smiled, but her words pleased him. "If you marry, it must be so, and anyway, we will still be close to one another. I will live in the castle and will visit you often."

Claire jumped up and sat in his lap whispering in his ear:

"My marriage is so far away yet, but thank you."

They hugged at length. Both of them had tears in their eyes. They knew their parting would take place in the not-so-distant future.

The meeting room of the English Royal Palace was not one of the discreet places of the known world. There were no decorations on the high walls, only the lines of torch holders adorned them. The torches were always lit, because the light had little chance of penetrating through the narrow windows. Seven people sat around the rectangular table—the King and the six members of the council.

King Arnold Mortimer sat at the head of the table. He sat there as if he wanted to spring up at any moment. He touched only the edge of his chair; his legs spread, and hands gripping the table top.

To the right of the knight, the King sat; Sir Lemmy Black eyeing the others with an impenetrable expression. He waited for the meeting to begin with straight, stiff posture.

Next to Lemmy sat James Horan, head liquidator—his skin was just as black as Sir Lemmy's leather clothes. The known world was populated mostly by white people, ebony-skinned folks, like Horan, were rare. If someone looked at him, the whites of his eyes flashed. He rarely spoke, and only as much as necessary when he did. At these times, his snow-white teeth seemed to flash. He had previously been Sir Lemmy's officer, who had recently promoted him in the place of the mysteriously disappeared head liquidator, William Barn. Councillor

Wilder had opposed his appointment, but he could do nothing because the King had supported Black as he did in everything. At the end of the right side sat the spokesperson for the nobility, Lord Christopher Millborrow. His noble features expressed great boredom, and he was generally bored by everything that did not involve war or hunting.

To Mortimer's left sat the old Councillor Ed Wilder, who had been appearing less and less confident of late; beside him sat Archbishop Eric Parker fidgeting in his chair—he could barely wait to find out why the King had assembled the council so suddenly. The Archbishop, with his watery, drooping eyes, hanging lip and pockmarked skin awakened antipathy in everyone. To his left at the end of the line sat an old, grey-haired, wrinkled man, Alf Kelly.

He represented the guilds.

"Lords," the King finally began, "I have called you here today because my best boat-builder has disappeared, who was leading the construction of our new battle fleet. I warn you all, if you know anything of the matter and stay silent, you will regret it."

"The situation, my lord, is that I wanted to mention master carpenter John Smith's disappearance as there is great concern among the guilds, and nobody know what may have become of him," spoke wizened, old Alf Kelly.

As he spoke, he fixed his eyes on the table and clenched his trembling hands before him trying to appear determined.

"My lord," Archbishop Eric Porter said, "I know the case."

"You do?! And may I inquire as to why you have not spoken of this yet?" Mortimer looked like he was about to explode. No one would have been surprised if he had sprung up and dealt Parker a blow.

"Your Highness, I had good reason to capture and question Smith," the Archbishop's confidence was waning.

"So, without even asking me, you seize my best carpenter, who is currently working on our new battle fleet?" The knight king couldn't nor did he want to restrain himself, as he shouted at the top of his voice,

"Your Highness, won't you even ask why?"

"I think you will tell me anyway," Sir Lemmy directed his words straight at Parker. He did not raise his voice in the slightest, yet everyone felt their gravity. "In your own interest."

"John Smith is justifiably accused of blasphemy. He wanted to build ships that could carry 500 men, even though everyone knows that normal ships carry exactly 300. This is the way in the whole known world."

"You stupid idiot!" Mortimer raged. "That is exactly what I needed. My boats could have carried almost twice as many men. What an advantage we'd have had."

"My lord, please, control yourself, you are speaking to a servant of God after all," said Ed Wilder rising to the Archbishop's defence.

"I cannot see what God has to do with my boats," the King growled a little more tamely.

The Councillor took a deep breath and went on,

"It is no accident that precisely 300 men fit on a ship. The councillors have long ago, after much experimentation, reached the conclusion that it is risky to build a boat to carry more men because it will sink. And this fact was recorded along with many other findings. And it is well-known that ignoring recorded council findings is tantamount to blasphemy. Besides religious matter, adhering to recorded facts is also in the Church's purview. So, I think Archbishop Eric Parker acted correctly."

"I don't understand why we cannot try new things," Lord Christopher Millborrow blustered.

"Interestingly," Wilder said looking around, "when the councillors stop a plague or increase produce, no one asked how they did it, and why not some other way. And yet, those are recorded facts too. I think the councillors deserve the faith of the King."

"Precisely!" Parker said whose confidence was returning.

Sir Lemmy scratched his chin and looking Parker in the eye said:

"I think the honourable gentleman enjoys hiding beneath the skirts of the council."

"Some seek refuge behind the council; some behind the king's robes," Wilder smiled.

Black laughed, which was a rare occurrence from him. "Councillor Wilder, I barely recognise you, have you discovered your non-existent sense of humour?" Then he turned to the Archbishop. "Don't forget what the robe you hide behind says on the insignia: 'Kingdom or Death!'"

"Is that a threat?" Parker asked Black.

"Of course not, I'm just saying what it says, here read it. What say you to all this, Head-liquidator Horan?" Black asked placing his hand on Horan's shoulder. Horan waited a moment. His two-metre tall figure of pure muscle commanded respect even when seated. Then he spoke,

"Kingdom or death! There is nothing more to add."

Roy Davis, Ed Wilder's ai could barely wait for the suddenly assembled council to begin. At these times, Wilder always let him go as he was not allowed to take part. Five minutes after the Councillor left, Davis went to meet Claire.

"I'm coming, my darling; a few minutes, and I'll be there at our place." They generally met in the park by the castle. They liked to go there; it was remote and perfect for a couple in love.

"Alright, I'm leaving soon too. I love you!" she replied.

Roy did not take the crowded stairways of the castle. He didn't want to run into some lord, who often stopped him to discuss council matters. They usually asked him to convey some message, as if he had any influence over old Wilder. No matter how he tried to explain this to them, they just smiled as if he were being modest. The worst thing was that the smile was always followed by a pouch of gold, which was so difficult to reject, though he had to. The last thing he needed was for the councillor to hear that he was accepting money for such things. So instead he took the servants' route which was uncomfortably narrow, but guaranteed an absence of noblemen.

The stairs led all the way down to the great garden that sprawled behind the castle. This is where supplies for the castle, mainly food, were brought. The way was crowded as usual, loaded cart arrived filled with wine casks, freshly butchered cows, pigs, and game, as well as fruits and vegetables. Roy enjoyed the hustle and bustle. This is where the best traders in the city came. People chatted jovially as they unpacked their wares. Kitchen boys took charge of the goods, with which they were mostly pleased, as who would dare come to the castle with bad products.

Davis crossed the yard and waved at a merchant with whom he was on good terms. He reached the gate and showed his badge which allowed his free passage at any time during the day.

"What's new, Tom?" he asked the head-guard standing at the gate.

"Lot of people; I've not had a chance to sit down all day," the officer complained.

"How much longer do you have?"

"Just an hour and then its change," Tom's face brightened.

"Keep it up!" Roy answered merrily and stormed through the gate. When he reached the huge oak in the middle of the park, Claire was already there.

"It's rude to make a lady wait like this," she said with her eyes.

"When we're together, we have to speak aloud as we agreed," he chided her.

"But no one is here apart from us," she said out loud.

"True, but I don't want a bad habit to form, because then we might use the voice in public and cause suspicion."

"Are you sure it's such a crime, Roy?"

"Oh yea! I've told you a thousand times, to other people we, as mutants, are enemies; if they found out, they would kill us!"

Claire approached Roy, stroked his face and then kissed him.

"You said when I turned 18, you would tell me how you realised you could speak without words."

"I did, but it's a sad story, and today we should celebrate! Here's your present." Roy took a little box tied with a ribbon from his pocket and handed it to her. Claire delicately unwrapped it and then shrieked quietly,

"Oh, it's beautiful! Can I try it on?"

"Of course! It's yours, you do what you want with it."

Claire took her present from the box, which was a pretty chain and medal with the letters 'C' and 'R' engraved on it.

"Roy, this must've cost a fortune! Why would you spend so much on me?"

"You silly, who else would I spend it on?" he smiled with pleasure as he could see she liked the gift.

"Now let's sit down, and you tell me what you promised." Claire took Roy's hand and pulled him onto the cool grass. She glanced down at the medallion glinting on her chest and then looked up at Roy and waited.

"So be it then," Roy conceded. "It happened four years ago. I was 22 at the time and had been serving Councillor Ed Wilder for a year already."

Claire listened silently. She was determined not to interrupt, not for all the riches in the world, so that Roy would not change his mind and stop the long-awaited story. "The councillor commanded that they go to the torture chamber because they had caught a mutant who had to be interrogated. Since he had been called by the King, I would have to do the questioning. You know how I hate torture, but if I had revealed that I'm sure he'd have sent me to the stocks to get used to it. So, I did not resist. And he can't be argued with anyway. When I reached the dungeons, there was a man tied to the table, and the hangman was burning his stomach with a branding iron. The prisoner screamed, but the red-hooded torturer did not care. His heart, if he had one at all, was coarse and steeled.

'Stop it! Stop it! It hurts!'

The prisoner reached the brink of losing consciousness, but his real trial was still to come. The hangman went to the other side of the room for some torture implement, and then it happened. I heard a voice inside my head,

'My friend. Do not say a word, and do not be scared.' In that moment, I thought I'd gone crazy, but I did not have time to think before the voice spoke again.

'It's me speaking to you, on the torture table here, without words, with thoughts. You can answer me. Try it!'

'Me? But how?'

'Like this! You see?' he answered. In that moment, I was shocked and afraid at once.

'Please, do not let them torture me further! Kill 'em quickly! I'm afraid, and I cannot hold out much longer!'

I took a good look at the man. He was no more than 30, and his eyes were drenched with fear. As he lay there naked, I pitied him. I felt some sort of kinship towards him, and yet I was still in shock. The hangman returned with a sort of hook which he jabbed into the man's right arm who screamed again, and then he kept pleading inside my head.

'Stop him, and I'll tell you what's happening in your head. Do not believe you've gone crazy. They're torturing me because I am like you.'

I felt like I had to do something. I could not leave him there alone, and I wanted to know what all of it was about. Suddenly, I turned to the hangman:

'Stop it! Can't you see he's about to die? Then what will you tell the Councillor?'

'Impossible, sir! I've tortured many people; I have a lot of experience in this, believe me! The man is young and in good shape; I can keep going till morning, so that he'll still be kicking.'

'How dare you argue with me? Every man bears pain differently. The way I see it, you must stop now. You can leave for at least half an hour, I will stay here.'

'Yes, sir, as you wish, sir!' the hangman said sheepishly. When he'd left, I approached the man and calmed him.

'I'm going to go get some poison, I'll be back soon.' He did not speak out loud, but in the way the man had spoken to me.

'Thank you!' the voice speaking in my head conveyed gratitude and fatigue.

I quickly ran to Wilder's room and chose vial from his poison closet that would kill the man instantly and make it seem like he had died a natural death. When I returned, the hangman was not back yet.

'This poison will kill you quickly and painlessly. But first, tell me what's going on!'

'There are people who can talk to one another through thoughts. You and I are such people. I've not met many, but there are a few. According to the councillors of the known world, this is a mutation. They are scared of us because it is invisible, so they've captured all of us and tortured us to reveal who else has this power. I only knew of two such people till now. You are the third. But rumours have it that there are many more in the known world. This is why what I'm telling you is important. Do not leave your mind open; other thought readers will recognise you instantly and may want to harm you.'

'I don't get it.'

'When you came in, I knew right away you were one of us. Because you did not hide your mind.'

'How can I do that?' I asked with growing fear.

'Practice, you will get a feeling for it, I cannot explain it another way. And now please, let's get this over with.'

Then I poured the poison into his mouth.

When Wilder arrived, he was very angry. Without a hint of guilt, I lied saying the hangman had tortured him to death. Luckily, the raging Councillor believed me and not the hangman.

Claire listened attentively. When Roy finished the story, he hugged him tightly.

"Maybe we will end up in a torture chamber too?"

"Never," Roy looked into her eyes, "I won't let anyone hurt you!"

They embraced one another, and in that moment, they felt like they could take on the whole world.

Chapter Eight

"Didier, get up! It's dawn; we have to go!" Henri said touching Ponga's shoulder. His had been the last shift on guard duty, so it was his task to wake the others.

"Alright, alright, I'm up, stop shaking me!" Ponga answered gruffly.

The April morning air was bitingly cool, and the thick forest air washed through their lungs. They got up and wiped their hands on the dewy grass of the meadow and then rubbed their faces with the fresh moisture. This was a novel way of washing to Ponga, but he enjoyed it thoroughly. He felt like he was being cleansed by the dew, not only on the outside but inside too. Later, they broke camp and set off through the forests that enveloped the hills.

They'd been on the run for a week now. When they'd left the tunnel leading out of the castle, they were well outside of Paris already. In the first village, they bought horses and dived into the woods. They had reached the hills two days ago and had let the animals go, as the difficult mountain roads and thick woods they were passing through were no place for horses.

Ponga hated the fact that they barely spoke; they just walked and walked. As always, he was the first to break the silence.

"Must we be quiet the whole way?" his question belied his impatience.

"Yes," Jules said turning to him. The grimace flickering across his face revealed that he was fed up with the knight's constant complaining. "To survive in the woods, one must listen. You have to keep quiet and listen, those are the two most important rules. You bluster around like a wild boar and always want to talk."

"I still want to know where we are going." He no longer cared who heard him at all.

"Calm yourself! We saved your life, and we expect no gratitude for it, but while you're with us, you have to accept my lead. I'm taking you to a safe place where you can decide whether you want to stay or leave."

"When will you finally tell me who you really are?" Ponga was very curious about his mysterious saviour. He almost certainly wasn't who he pretended to be. It annoyed him that he'd done nothing but obey for a week, and no one had even told him why he should be obeying.

Jules looked at him. It seemed like he was not going to respond, but then he changed his mind and said,

"We're escaping now. We can talk when we're safe."

"Alright," Ponga conceded. "Just tell me one thing: why are we moving at such a forced pace? It's clear we have a big advantage over our pursuers if they're after us at all."

"You clearly know nothing of Councillor Perrier. They are most certainly after us, and they are certainly ahead of us by no little distance. The Councillor has developed a courier system. When we escaped, mounted messenger were dispatched to the larger cities. When they arrived, they passed on the new. Then each city sends a courier on the highway, and many couriers go to the villages. This way, they always have well-rested horses and men to spread the news. The people escaping get tired, grow slower, but the fresh horses and people do not lose pace, so our descriptions are way ahead of us. This is the reason we are avoiding settlements."

"Perhaps I know nothing of the Councillor," Ponga said wagging his head, "but you know a remarkable amount."

Then they went on in silence. Spring has endowed the forest with especially livid colours. The leaves of the trees were still budding, and light could reach the forest floor. A myriad of wild flowers blossomed there. They only had these few weeks to grow—when the leaves took away their precious light, the flowers recede into the ground to await the next year when they could live for a few days again. The thick foliage was interspersed with occasional clearings, but they avoided open ground as they ran. It would have been so nice to get warm on the green grass for a while.

It was late in the afternoon when they sat down for breakfast by a fallen tree trunk in the thick of the forest. Jules had prepared for being away from civilisation while they escaped, so he had brought a large store of salted meats, sea-biscuits and dried fruit. Their packs became increasingly lighter as they went along. They would not go hungry for another day at least, but after that, they would have to do something. Either they would have to sneak into a village or hunt. But hunting would slow them down considerably. Ponga poked at his foot noncommittally, and he didn't even feel like talking. Sadness often overcame him now, which had only rarely happened to him previously. *Perhaps,* he thought, because the past week had robbed him of his goals. One week ago, he had known what he was doing and why, now he didn't even know where they were going. Self-pity ate away at him, and it showed on his face too.

"What's wrong with you?" Henri asked. "You escaped, you should be happy about that, no?"

"Happy? What about? I've wanted to be a famous knight ever since I was a child. All my life I hoped to find myself in royal chambers with everyone celebrating me, and before I can even believe that I'm not dreaming, I become a wanted fugitive. Well, I feel pretty rotten. Or do you think I should be happy about all this?"

"Surely," Jules joined the conversation "your life is a great success; you just can't see the why yet. You were marked for death, and now you are a free man. If you could ask the dead, do you think they would swap places with you?"

"If you look at it that way…" Ponga muttered, but he'd have rather bit off his tongue than tell Jules he was right.

Then they heard a noise. It was not the usual rustling of the woods, but something completely foreign. They silently gathered their supplies making sure to leave as few traces as possible and then headed towards the source of the noise. They'd covered about a 100 metres when they noticed a man lying on the ground. He was no more than 25, his clothes were torn, and he was wounded in several places. Jules signalled to Henri, who quickly left to scout the area, while Jules examined the stranger. He held the man's head in his hands and called to Ponga,

"Pass me the water!"

Interesting, Ponga thought as he obeyed, *that Jules can order me about in a way where I don't even consider resisting.* He didn't know where or whom to they were going, but he was certain that his saviour was an important leader amongst his men. Jules poured water into the moaning man's mouth.

At that moment, Henri charged out of the bushes.

"Quick! Five armed men are on their way! They'll be here any minute."

"We'll ambush them," Jules ordered. Ponga was in no mind to disagree. They quickly hid behind some bushes.

The men arrived with great clamour by the injured youngster.

"You blasted idiot!" A barrel-chested man shouted.

"You'll regret this!" shouted a fallow-haired man.

"We'll torture him so bad, he'll wish he'd never been born."

"Yes! That's right!" the others shouted.

Jules signalled to the others to prepare their bows. They prepared silently, signalling mutely to one another as to who would shoot who, and then the bowstrings twanged as one. The three hits were followed by screams. Ponga and Henri quickly jumped from cover and overtaking Jules flew at the remaining two men. Their enemies were not trained fighters, so the battle did not last long. Ponga moved so quickly that he was almost invisible, and the man before him didn't even have time to raise his sword in defence. Ponga thrust his sword up into the man's throat. Only a man whose guts were hardened from killing could do such a thing. He'd had ample opportunity to get used to the sight of blood, as half-sharpened blades were only in fashion among the dandy noblemen of the King's court. In real life, razor-sharp sword swung readily, and the lives of common folk were of no interest to anyone. Henri took a little longer to defeat his opponent. The charging muscular peasant swung his sword downwards with both hands, and Henri could barely deflect the blow. Then they began to brawl, and Henri managed to draw his dagger from his belt which was more useful in close combat. He held his sword in his right hand entangled with his enemy and stabbed the man in the stomach with the other.

The peasant doubled over, and Henri withdrew the short blade and swung down hard on the man's neck with the long one. The razor-sharp blade passing between his vertebrae quickly ended the man's suffering. Then they ran to the three men they'd shot who were not in battle-ready condition. They cut two of their throats, but when they wanted to finish the third, Jules shouted,

"Stop! I want to question him." He approached the terrified peasant who clutched at the arrow in his chest with both hands.

"Who are you, and why did you torture the boy?"

"Good lord, have mercy on me!" moaned the dirty, unshaven man as he spat claret foam between his lips. He was so scared, he didn't even comprehend that he was done for.

"Answer me!" Jules thundered holding his dagger before his victim's eyes.

"Well, Paul, the boy, was getting real palsy with the devil, and we're exorcists."

"What was his crime? Answer me!"

"Paul is a carpenter; he can make anything out of wood, and he invented many suspicious devices, which although were useful, had never been made by anyone before. It was surely the devil who whispered in his ear how to make them, he admitted as much to us."

"Who wouldn't have admitted it when being sliced by knives?" Jules said bitterly; then with a sudden movement, he cut the man's throat. Then he went to care for the unfortunate Paul. The young man's body was covered in cuts, and the image of the devil had been branded onto his shoulder. As he cared for the man, Jules quickly told them what they had to do.

"It is time for us to change clothes. See what you can salvage from the corpses, take everything that can be useful."

"Money, weapons, but only things we will definitely need; I don't want to carry anything useless."

Henri and Ponga began undressing the corpses. Meanwhile, Jules left the boy and looked around to see what he could scavenge.

"Isn't it immoral to steal from the dead?" Ponga asked dubiously.

"Don't pity these men," Jules began. "And I would like to remind you that we are on the run. We will have to enter a nearby village today. We will buy food, and the boy needs medicine. If we change, we increase our chances."

"Why the hell would we risk our skin for this?" Ponga asked pointing at the boy. "He doesn't deserve it," he observed with a self-satisfied, dopey look that always pushed Jules over the edge.

"How much do you deserve? Or have you forgotten what risks we took for you?" He stopped dressing Paul's wounds and looked reproachfully at Ponga.

"You're crazy!" Ponga waved his hand. "I would never do such a thing for anyone, except myself."

"It's good thing that Paul's fate is not in your hands then. Anyway, we need him alive," Jules replied ignoring the knight's selfish grumblings.

"Couldn't we hunt?" Ponga asked hopefully.

"Forget it! We don't have time. We can hunt when we reach our destination. And now get ready, because you and Henri are going to the village!"

As they walked towards the village, Ponga pondered his own behaviour. Why was he doing exactly as their leader told him? And what was worse was that Jules was always right. But somehow, he had a feeling of foreboding now, they should not be going into that damned village. And yet, they would—come what may.

Vincent Farall sat petrified in the Councillor's room. Perrier had said he would learn a very important lesson today. This, in and of itself, was not so terrible, but he had also mentioned that they would be going to the torture chamber, and he hated violence. More precisely, he loathed torture. He felt infinitely sorry for those poor people who had to suffer such horrible pains. The Councillor knew of his fear, and he had always spared him having to visit interrogations, so it was now strange that he would call him down into that disgusting cellar. When he waited for the Councillor, he usually took a book from the shelf and read; now he sat motionless on the chair.

He wanted to get it all over and done with. He knew that even if he suffered through the night, the memories would not let him rest for a long time to come.

Perrier entered the room. He approached the table and sat in the armchair. He moved as always—he glided over the ground with an ethereal lightness.

"Vincent, you're sitting on that uncomfortable hunk of wood again. I'm going to have it removed and have something better brought for you."

"Thank you, but there is no need. If you want to do me a favour, how about we skip tonight's lesson. I'm happy to learn, but I don't want to go down there."

"You know I'm familiar with your fear of the torture chamber, and I don't usually take you with me," Perrier's eyes revealed his compassion, "and I also know that you won't sleep well for a long time to come, but I will take you with me today. Believe me, I can do nothing else."

Farall kneaded his knuckles; sweat beaded on his forehead, though it was not warm. He took a deep breath before answering.

"I know you well-enough to know that you will not change your mind, so I will beg no more. Let's get it over with as soon as possible. Of course, unless prolonging my dread is part of the lesson."

Perrier shook his head.

"Of course not. I can hear the reproach in your voice, but I have no choice. Let's go!"

The trip did not take more than a few minutes, but it felt like an age. And yet, he would have liked to prolong it further, so that he would not have to enter there. The dark tunnels in the basement were all damp, and the blinking torches on the walls made the droplets seem black. It seemed like the whole cellar was sweating. He knew it was stupid, and yet he felt like those droplets were made of the blood and sweat of the prisoners tortured there.

And then they arrived at the torture chamber. The area consisted of several conjoined rooms. Every room was equipped with the tools required for interrogations, which Farall thought could only have been invented by twisted minds. On closer inspection, most of the tools were craftsmen's implements. There were hammers, pliers, tongs and needles. The tools which may have seemed harmless in a workshop were now terrifying. Luckily the torture tables were empty—perhaps by the Councillor's request—only the last room was occupied. They approached the prisoner directly.

The man was in a relatively good shape. He was still conscious, and he wasn't missing any body parts—he still had his arms, legs and eyes as far as Farall could tell from a quick glance. The half-naked hangman, wearing a red hood, greeted them mutely. Farall could not help but take a closer look at the prisoner. He was young and well-muscled, which would make him a soldier or a peasant—he observed. His eyes showed the unmistakeable terror that made its home here.

"You only worked him over as much as we agreed, right?" the Councillor asked the hangman, who nodded that he had indeed followed orders.

"I'll confess everything, great lord, just don't torture me anymore," the poor soul begged weakly. His stench was unbearable; he had soiled himself from fear and pain.

"Do you know how many times I've heard that? We'll find out the truth soon enough"

Perrier said to him, and then picking up a sharp knife, he rammed it into the prisoner's shoulder with a sudden movement.

The terrible scream cut Farall to his core. The Councillor's cruelty filled him with fear and rage at once.

"My lord! Don't!" the prisoner shouted. "I am not a mutant, I swear!"

"We shall see," Perrier replied icily. He grabbed the knife in the man's shoulder and twisted. The answer was another blood-curdling scream. Perrier's face suddenly contorted with anger, and he shouted,

"He doesn't know anything!" The Councillor's sudden change of mood after his emotionless, calm behaviour till now unnerved Farall.

"Disgusting fool!" the Councillor raged on, and he tore the knife from the man and rammed it into his heart with all his strength. His victim died immediately.

"Well, that's that," Perrier said with a nonchalance, as if he had just finished breakfast.

"Alright, Vincent, come, let's go upstairs."

Farall was in such a state that he couldn't even remember the way back. He only started to recover when the Councillor poured him a stiff drink.

"Here! Drink this! Then we'll talk."

Farall felt the medicinal effects of the alcohol and assumed he would now be able to think. Just to be sure he asked for another.

"Well, well!" Perrier laughed. "I see that really got to you."

"I don't see why that was necessary. What am I supposed to learn from it? I've always known I have no stomach for cruelty. And I also knew you did not relate to it the way I do. But the fact that you actually enjoyed it shook me. You know how I feel about you, but this one will be hard to swallow. To kill someone is one thing, I've done it before, but this...I don't know what to say."

The Councillor said nothing. He let Farall come to his senses, and for the drink to further overcome his aid.

After a while, he felt like it was time to explain the lesson.

"You know me well-enough to know that I don't do anything without reason. Never let fear take your mind! Why do you think that was necessary?"

Even in his far-calmer state, Farall was unable to find a suitable answer to the events that had transpired.

"I'm sorry, Alain, but I have no idea."

The Councillor never missed a chance to lecture when the opportunity presented itself to him.

"So be it. I see I'll have to explain it to you." He poured himself a drink, took a sip, leaned back in his chair and began. "What is the third lesson of the councillors?"

"Appearance and reality. Things are not what they seem."

"Precisely! You know, and yet you do not understand. Which is why tonight was necessary."

"How come?" Farall knew the lesson well, but he didn't understand the Councillor.

"Listen, you think I acted cruelly?"

"Yes."

"You think I am a notorious and widely feared councillor?"

"Of course, you are the most notorious in the Known World."

"Appearance and reality." Perrier always enjoyed surprising his student.

"The man was captured because they thought he was a mutant. I knew he probably wasn't one, but if I don't investigate the case, it may appear like I don't take such matter seriously. So the man was destined for a painful death regardless of me. I spared him the prolonged torture, and the hangman will spread the news of my cruelty, which grows the terrifying image I have cultivated. Hence the cloak and dagger of the madness and the calm to scare the hangman even more into not seeing the reality. So, the appearance is: The Councillor is very cruel, and the reality is that the Councillor is very humane. Which do you think is the right action? If I leave it or if I help?"

"You confuse me," Farall stammered. "I see it all differently now. But I could have understood it if you'd just explained it as well."

"True, but then you would not have felt the strength action requires. Knowing something is not enough, it must be applied. Besides, it is best you know that since I've been councillor, the number of torture interrogations in the castle has halved."

"How is that possible?"

"I often interrogate them personally. Usually it is enough to show them the torture implements, and they talk. And the executioners think I achieve this by being even more ruthless than they are. A fine thing it would be if I couldn't even outsmart these simple-minded people. Appearance: Councillor Perrier is the cruellest man in the known world—reality: no one has saved more people from being tortured to death than me."

"I get that," Farall replied a little more calmly. It felt good to know that the Councillor wasn't really so cruel, "but what I don't get is why you hid yourself from me. I know you respect me highly, but still."

The Councillor took a sip from his drink enjoying the moment and revelling in being what he loved to be best—mysterious. Then he answered with a smile,

"Appearance and reality. You know, there are a lot of things that are not what they seem. Today, I showed you one such thing, but only one."

Chapter Nine

Claire loved sitting around in the Two Lions. The nights were particularly entertaining in this suburban inn. People chatted and drank merrily, and those who were hungry could rest assured that the cook was a master of his art. The owner, Happy Jimmy, was not a greedy man.

A bender at the Two Lions could be achieved rather cheaply. But Claire appreciated the calm atmosphere of the establishment the most.

There were no brawls, drunken cursing or harassment of women. Tiny Tom kept the ship tight, though a calmer man was a rarity for sure.

Tom was none too bright, but his job did not require brains. If Jimmy told him to escort someone out, then Tom warned the person politely. If they were stupid enough to oppose him, they found themselves in the road in seconds. Tiny Tom as strong as a bear and looked a bit like one too. Claire called him 'My old bear'.

On that day, Roy and Claire were there to celebrate. After a long struggle, they determined to tell Claire's step-father about their love. And old Mallory, if not without some struggle, had given them his blessing. So from now on, there would be no more secret meetings, and they could bear their love proudly.

Claire called to Tiny Tom:

"My dear old bear, when you have five minutes, sit with us and have beer."

"Alright," he replied. "If Jimmy lets him, the old bear will come," he said grinning blankly at her.

Soon Happy Jimmy appeared at their table too. "What can I bring the young couple?" he asked, and his eyes sparkled as mischievously as if he were barely 20.

"Today we are celebrating, Jimmy," Roy began. "Bring us some good wine, and Claire would like a roast duck."

The old man pondered whether it would be polite to ask the occasion, and by the way, his curiosity overcame his manners.

"Alright. And what are you celebrating if I may ask?"

Roy had been expecting the question, and it made him feel proud to boast of the good news.

"From today, we are officially together. No more hidden dinners."

Jimmy greeted this with mixed feelings. For the one part, he was happy; on the other hand, he did not like to lose his customers.

"So, you won't be coming here anymore? As you will be able to meet inside the castle from now on."

"Don't be silly, Jimmy!" Claire looked at the innkeeper disapprovingly. "We will always come here, because it is the best place in the whole of London."

"Phew, I was getting scared there!" Jimmy clutched at his heart playfully.

"Which reminds me. We invited the old bear for a bear, provided, of course, that you allow him," laughed Claire.

"Of course, just be careful! You know he can't hold his drink," Jimmy said looking towards Tom. His eyes revealed the tenderness he felt. Jimmy had taken Tiny Tom in when he was just a boy and unable to take care of himself. Tom was a wandering orphan, and Jimmy had been living alone. He took pity on the little boy. Since then he'd grown into a giant with a matching appetite.

"We'll take care of him, Jimmy. You know we will," Roy said reassuringly.

"Alright, I'll bring the wine right away and giant beer. And, I almost forgot: Congratulations!"

All three of them laughed, and at that moment, Claire felt like the Two Lions was the best place in the world.

As the lovers waited for their meal, they did not talk. Somehow, both of them enjoyed the silence; they simply enjoyed the intimate moment together. Claire glanced at Roy, and she suddenly remembered their conversation from earlier when Roy had come to their house. They'd been meeting for half a year, strictly in secret, but the situation was becoming unmanageable. It was only a matter of time before Mallory found out. Claire was afraid of the moment when the two most important men in her life met. She was afraid because she didn't know if she could handle it if her father did not give them his blessing. Then she would have to choose between them, and she could not have given up on either of them. She'd talked Roy out of the meeting for a long time and made concessions to him instead. Such concessions, for example, were the nights they spent in the Two Lions when she could only get away from home by lying, or when she allowed him to kiss her. Meanwhile, Roy constantly asked her to speak to her father, because he wanted to make their love 'official'. Then the time of the long-awaited but also dreaded meeting arrived. Not many words were spoken, but each of them burned into Claire's soul. Claire led Roy in to meet her father. After greeting each other, they said nothing; they just sized each other up. After a long time, Roy took a deep breath and said what he had come to say:

"Sir! I am here to ask your permission. I love your daughter, and I would like your approval for me to woo her. You can expect two things from me: respect and honour."

Mallory did not reply; his expression did not reveal whether he was listening at all. Claire was so excited, but she didn't want to interrupt, she wanted to let the men decide her fate.

"Respect and honour," the old commander growled, "big words, pretty words. We will see what comes of them."

Roy did not reply; he felt he should keep quiet, and Claire was very grateful for it. She hugged Mallory. Silently, she held the man who never found words good enough to express his feelings.

The night passed quickly. Then the young couple noticed that the inn was getting empty. The old tower clock struck 11:00. They could stay a little longer now because Roy had promised Mallory that he would take Claire home around midnight. He had decided that they would be punctual—it was important that the Commander had trust in him. And if they were late the first time, their relations would sour.

"Errrr…Do you want to go outside for some air?" Roy turned to Claire. She pretended like she didn't know what he was thinking of. She wanted to finally kiss him too. When there were so few people walking the streets, they liked to go outside to a dark doorway where no one would see them. They could have done it in the inn too, but they were too shy for that. So, they were left with the doorway.

"I don't mind, it's hot in here," she conceded. In truth, she had been waiting for him to ask for a while.

"Jimmy," Roy said, "we're going out for some fresh air."

"Sure, Roy," the innkeeper smiled knowingly, "it is very hot in here."

They stood up and headed for the door. They were in no rush—it would have been impolite, though they were impatient to get to their little sanctuary. The doorway was some 20 meters from the entrance of the Two Lions. Standing there, one could see the whole street and yet remain hidden, because the moonlight and the few torches that illuminated the street did not reach there. An old woman lived in the house, and she had long ago gone to bed, so everything was ideal for the young couple. As they got there, they embraced and kissed one another. Roy stood with his back to the locked door, so he had a view onto the street. Though they had no reason to be afraid of being discovered, it couldn't hurt to be cautious. Truth be told, he was officially courting her now, but he still didn't want the news to reach Old Mallory's ear that his daughter was snuggling up with him in a doorway. Their mouths glued together; he was about to close his eyes when two hooded-figures appeared on the street. Their faces were hidden by their clothes, and they give the impression of being purposefully concealed.

Roy thought so and spoke to Claire without a word:

"Don't say a word! There's two suspicious figures on the street."

Claire withdrew her mouth in fright and looked towards the strangers.

"Of course, Roy, I'll keep quiet. They'll be gone soon." But the two figures did not go on but stopped just a few meters from them. One of them grabbed the others shoulder and spoke in a raised voice,

"Don't forget that you are not a nobody, your name is Hugh Jones!"

"Are you sure I can do it tomorrow?" the man called Jones asked in a nervous, strangled voice. The voice suggested a young man.

"I've told you he leaves the city tomorrow. He said so in the council meeting. I was there, I heard. Either tomorrow, or who knows. You won't get a better chance."

"I got it. I'll do what must be done," the young man replied.

"Alright, I'm trusting you. Don't forget that this will be no murder but a heroic act."

Then they went back the way they had come, and were lost slowly into the night. The lovers stood petrified for a long while yet, just to make sure the conspirators were not still around, and they may be discovered as eavesdroppers.

"Claire, wait a little longer and then forget about what happened. It's not our business."

"But, Roy, these men are up to no good, they're planning murder. Shouldn't we tell someone?"

"Of course not. Who would we tell? The Councillor? Who knows who those men were? You heard them. That was someone from the King's council. Whoever it was, it is better not to interfere. But now let's go."

They crept from the doorway and went back in the Two Lions Inn to pay. Then they ran through London, back to the heart of the inner district, the King's castle. They knew they would be late, but they hurried as best they could. Perhaps Mallory had gone to bed already, and they could get away with it.

They were not lucky; the old commander was waiting for them in the doorway. Mallory knew that a few minutes was not the end of the world, but he had been restless all night, and he was scared for Claire. Standing in the entrance, he tried to withhold his emotions, so that when the young couple arrived, he wouldn't mention them being late, but somehow he knew along that it would not work.

As they arrived, Roy was first to speak, "Good evening, sir! I am very sorry, it won't happen again."

"Daddy, don't be angry!" Claire begged.

Mallory was silent for a while, his fists clenched, and then he managed to speak one brief sentence, "A nice introduction indeed!" Then he turned around and went to bed.

Miranda Mortimer, the English Queen, was over 30, but she was still an attractive woman. The children she bore had left no mark on her body, her raven black hair was not flecked with grey, and her face was just as young and vibrant as it had been ten years ago when she'd married Arnold Mortimer, the King of England. She was a real woman and jealous too, as women usually are. Times such as these—when the King and his men went into the London night in disguise—she especially hated. Who knew what the men got up to? At these times, Arnold was just one man amongst many. True, the King could have cheated on her without a disguise if he'd wanted to.

The queen awaited Sir Lemmy Black, who would then accompany her husband on their evening adventure. Miranda knew that Black would take the conversation they were about to have as a sign of weakness, but a little humility was better than sitting in dread all night. She liked Sir Lemmy and knew that her husband could not ask for a better right-hand man than the strategist.

Mortimer's evening adventures were always preceded by the same drama. The Queen summoned Sir Lemmy to make certain of her husband's fidelity. The strategist never gave her a straight answer, he always lied to her face. More precisely, he never said untruths, he just twisted and turned his words until he weaselled out of his obligation. Miranda knew of no one who was as skilled with words as Black. He was able to oppose her, in a way that made her unable to be angry with him.

A servant entered the Queen's chambers.

"Your Highness, Sir Lemmy Black begs entrance."

"Bring him in at once!"

The strategist entered. He approached her in his usual tight leather suit and proud gait. Dancers moved in this way, with such a bent back spine, a too straight posture.

"My Queen, you called."

"Yes," she said kneading her knuckles, unable to mask her anxiety. "Do you know why?"

"Your Highness, how could I protect our king if I didn't even know this?" His voice was full of understanding and reassurance, there was no hint of mockery or distain. "You are worried about your husband's fidelity, because he is very important to you."

"Sir, you'd never lie to me, would you? Answer me truly!"

"My Queen, you always ask me this, and I always reply that the least I could do for you is to be honest in what I can be honest."

"So you would not lie?" Miranda knew she would not get a straight answer, and yet the vain hope stubbornly persisted in her that she could glean some truth from him.

"Your Highness, I could, I have told you, of course. I will always tell you the truth about everything, but that would have been a lie. I answered honestly, and that is much harder."

"What do you mean by what you can be honest about?"

"If my lord asked me to keep a secret, then I could tell to no one, but this is just an example."

"Alright, I understand. Sit down, will you! I hate that you always stand when you talk to me. It's annoying."

Black sat down. He knew that it was not his standing but his words that were annoying the Queen.

"Answer me, strategist." Miranda looked black dead in the eyes.

"Will my husband cheat on me with some harlot?"

"I don't know how much credibility my words carry with you now, but my answer is no."

"And if he cheated on me, would you tell me?"

Sir Lemmy pondered this for a moment and then replied, "No.

Sorry, no, I could not."

"You lying, two-faced man, I hate you!" the Queen shouted. These conversations always ended this way. When she realised she would get nothing from the strategist, she went into a rage and closed the argument with an insult. Black did not flinch; he was not the kind of person to be unhinged by a woman's hysterics. At that moment, the King appeared. He wore a simple soldier's uniform.

"Sir Lemmy, are you aggravating the Queen of England again?" his voice was jovial. He approached his wife, pulled hand to him and kissed it.

"My King," Black bowed, "I was only telling your wife the truth."

"Of course," Miranda interrupted, "Sir Lemmy's great truth is that he cannot say the truth."

"What's wrong, my precious?" Mortimer cooed.

"What is wrong? Well, it's this. Am I the only one?"

"My lady," said the King looking Miranda in the eye, "where could I find a more beautiful woman in this kingdom. Have I ever given you reason to distrust me?"

"True," Miranda blushed. "I'm ashamed of my silliness, but I still love you. Go, out of my sight the pair of you! Sir Lemmy!"

"Yes, my Queen!" Black turned around.

"Take care of him!"

"I can promise you that," the strategist smiled and then followed the King out.

Liquidator Hugh Jones sat alone in his room. It resembled a monk's cell. It was only a few square meters in size, and only the most essential furnishings were present. There was nothing decorating the walls, not a picture or a tapestry. He's become deputy commander a year ago and was hence allowed to have his own room. The others, liquidators without rank, live in a distant part of the castle in cold, shared rooms.

Being deputy commander was not a high post, but he did get his own room and in the somewhat more established garden side of the castle. He did not care about the rank, but it was useful that he would now be able to leave his room unnoticed. And he would make no stir at the city gate as off-duty liquidators were always coming and going.

Everyone considered him fortunate, as the post was rarely given to such a young person. For every 220 foot-soldiers, only 15 liquidators held rank. Initially he had been pleased with the promotion too, all until the mysterious disappearance of Head Liquidator William Barn. Then his faith in his profession faltered. Rumours had it that Sir Lemmy was behind the strange disappearance. Jones had not been one of Barn's favourites, and he wasn't sorry for the head liquidator, but he had a problem with the newly appointed James Horan. He felt like the strategist had purposefully gotten rid of the head liquidator and installed one of his own in men in his place. And that the liquidators were nothing more than pawn in his royal chess match. Jones had wanted to serve a real cause his whole life. As a child, his father had taken him to many celebrations in the castle. At those times, he enjoyed watching the saluting of the liquidators the most. The common folk were allowed into the inner courtyard of the castle, and everyone watched in amazement as the sun glinted off the red and black armour of the liquidators. The best was when the head liquidator turned to his men and spoke powerfully:

"We serve the King!"

The armoured men snapped to attention their heavy armour clanging in unison, and then they all shouted together,

"We are liquidators!" Jones pulled up his shirtsleeve and stared at his forearm covered in scars. When his family's benefactor, Sir Millborrow, had arranged for him to be accepted into liquidator training, he felt like he was the happiest child on earth. But he lost his enthusiasm rather quickly after that. The training eradicated all feeling from him. They cut his arm innumerable times and poured salt onto it. And he had not been allowed to talk or cry. The trainer had constantly shouted:

"We serve the King!"

And he had to shout back,

"We are liquidators!"

With that, he no longer adored those words, he learned to hate them. Later, he had to say it so many times that it was the only thing he could believe in.

Many years later, he was forced to realise that his whole life was pointless, and that all that suffering had been for nothing. Most children do not become liquidators because they fail at some point during the years of arduous training.

He'd persisted and achieved his goal, but he was unable to feel happy ever since his eyes were open.

He hated his new boss, James Horan, from the moment he laid eyes on him. He hated his dark skin most of all. "You can't trust these people," his father had always said when they saw a black person. It was true; they were all liars, but this one was his commander. Jones fumed as wrapped his poison-tipped arrows in doe hide.

He could never have imagined that life would change just because he'd accidentally stumbled into a secret religious meeting. The girl, Sarah, whom he'd met at the fish market a few months ago, told him that she'd been reformed, and that the world had taken on new meaning for her since. When Sarah had spoken to him, he'd thought she was just selling herself to him. An honourable woman would not approach a strange man like that. He wanted to chase her off, but it soon transpired that Sarah wanted to convey the true faith to him. Her voice was beautiful, and what she said enchanted him. Her clean, innocent light touched his soul. There at the market was the first time he heard that life can be lived without violence; later, when his new acquaintance offered to take him with her to a meeting, he accepted. What he heard there were real thoughts. The pastor spoke thoughts that were in all their hearts and were just waiting for someone to come and free them from their cells. He found out that Father, Son and Mother Moon send benign light towards people, asking only for them to live a peaceful life in return. His real life began from that day on; he found true faith and the peace it brought him. At one of the meetings of the sect, he met a man who convinced him that the greatest enemy of the faith was the King himself. The ruler was constantly at war and thereby in opposition to the will of the sun and moon gods.

Jones had been lonely his whole life. As a child he had played alone, and he hadn't many friends as an adult either. In the sect, he finally found people who were similar to him. He would have done anything for them, and it transpired that they wanted him to do a lot for them.

As he checked his weapons, he prepared himself mentally for his mission. This day may easily turn out to be his last, but his name would live on forever, he was certain of that. The worst part was that the others, with whom he shared a community, knew nothing of his mission. Bitterness overcame him when he considered that the only way for him to benefit his loved ones and the true cause was to do what he knew best—to kill. Fate seemed to have dealt him these cards. But if, by chance, he escaped that night, he would surely leave the castle and live among his new brothers in perfect peace.

He still had some time, because the King was only going out with his entourage at 8:00. He adjusted the bandage beneath his clothes on his right shoulder. Unfortunately, he had to hide the brand, so that no one could trace him if he did fail. When the mark was burned into his shoulder, he had not known he would have to kill for his new faith. If he survived, he would accept the mark of faith again.

He collected his weapons and put the wrapped-up arrows in a quiver. He stuffed his disguise and his other stuff into a large backpack and set off. He knew that between the King and himself, only one of them would see the dawn.

Chapter Ten

It was perfect spring weather. A blindingly bright sun shone from the damson blue sky. Ponga and Henri arrived squinting at the edge of the village. The whitewashed houses shone brightly in the early afternoon light. Well-ordered streets and front gardens revealed the work of careful hands. The windows of the thatch-roofed houses were all draped in dark blue curtains. The walnut brown boards of the fences all gave a uniformed image to the village. The birds chirping, dogs barking, hens clucking all vanquished the silence.

Despite the idyllic village-setting, Ponga had a bad feeling about it. He did not know what it was, but he was certain that something was not right.

"I don't like this at all," he said turning to his companions while he looked around constantly.

"This place is oppressive somehow," Henri acknowledged. "Perhaps it's the silence; there's only animal noises."

"That's it!" the recognition struck Ponga. "There's no children playing, smithies' hammer, no women gossiping, not a carriage or a rider, no old men sitting on benches before their houses. Where are the people anyway? This village is deserted!"

"Yes," Henri replied, "it's like a haunted village from a fairy tale." At that moment, it seemed like a curtain in a house moved.

"What a disgusting place!" Ponga said aloud turning to Henri. He hoped the villagers would hear him too. Let them know that they were not afraid.

"Quiet, you fool!" Jules said not to make a scene.

"How are we supposed to blend in with the crowd? I'm tired of being ordered about all the time."

Henri shook his head. Ponga was the most conceited idiot Henri had ever seen. It was a great shame that Jules wanted to save him at all costs, but if he thought it right, then it must be so. They went further into the village till they reached a main square; then an old man came out of a house and headed towards them—considering his age he moved quickly. As he reached them, he leaned in and whispered,

"Leave this village while you still can! They've no love for strangers here or locals for that matter."

"Who, Brother?" Henri asked.

"You don't want to find out," the old man replied, "they chased off my friend's nephew and out carpenter today." At the word 'carpenter', Ponga and Henri looked at one another. Henri put his hand on the man's shoulder and asked,

"What's your friend's nephew's name, Brother?"

"Does it matter, Son, you would not know him?!"

"What's his name?" Henri asked a second time. His voice had a hint of a threat in it. The old man did not hesitate; he replied,

"His name is Paul if you must know," and then just as fast as he had come, he left.

"Crazy old scarecrow," Ponga said lightly.

"How can you be so crude?" Henri said taking offence. "He wanted us well, he wanted to help, and you mock him?"

They arrived in the main square. It was not hard to find their way; there was a church in the centre of every village which could be seen from a distance, and there was also an inn in the centre of every village. At these inns, one could eat and drink and rest and do business. They were likely to find food here and find out where the doctor lived. Jules and the injured Paul were waiting just outside the village border—it would have been too dangerous to enter with him, it would have caused a scene. And yet, they hadn't even known at the time that this was Paul's village. It wasn't hard to figure out which house the watering hole was— a worn sign hung above the door. 'Good Buddies', it proclaimed.

"Can't say that's a fitting name," Ponga quipped. "I'd call it the Inn to the Cemetery myself."

"You will behave yourself inside, won't you? Don't forget we are on the run and wanted. There's no place for your stupid, uppity heroism. You know what Jules said."

"Oh, the great Jules, I almost soiled myself with fear. Of course, I'll obey, I wouldn't dare do anything else."

"Stop it, please! I don't want to argue with a man who has the brains of a five-year-old." Henri closed the subject. They agreed to disagree and entered the Good Buddies Inn.

The inn was packed. Ponga got the feeling that the village was empty because everyone was here. As they entered, everyone went quiet and stared at them— their looks were unfriendly and accusatory. It seemed as if they had all been waiting for strangers to enter the inn, so they could all spill their bile on them.

"Good day!" Henri said, as they took seats at an empty table, which was exactly in the middle of the room. No one returned his courteous greeting, they just stared at the two travellers.

"You're all very talkative today," Ponga took over.

"Innkeeper, wine!"

The innkeeper ambled over and smacked a pitcher of wine and two cups before them. Finally, a large, moustached man spoke to them,

"What are you doing here?" Suddenly the ring of people tightened around them.

"What's it to you?" Ponga asked starting to lose his cool. "And you could learn some manners."

"Well, well!" someone at one of the back tables said raising their voice, – "Recently crime has been increasingly infiltrating our little village."

The speaker was a small hooded priest. His little eyes were filled with cunning.

"Father," Ponga said with increasing anxiety, "you have the wrong door. Preaching is to be done one house down, in the church." As he said this, he knew he'd hit the mark—the tension became palpable.

"How dare you! You come here to offend our preacher?" shouted the moustached man.

Henri put his hand on Ponga's shoulder; he did not want the situation to escalate further, but Ponga was on a roll.

"Don't shout out me, you peasant, I'll wipe this inn clean with you." He could feel the pleasant excitement that preceded a fight spreading through his body.

"We're not going to fight one another! That is not what God wants," the priest said in a conciliatory voice. "You know, there was a royal messenger here not long ago, they're looking for a couple of fugitives. We have to be careful. You could be them for all we know. We don't know you, and so our lack of trust is justified. Besides, there have been more and more heretics around here recently. Which is why we are so impatient. I hope you can understand."

"Of course, Father," Henri replied as he dragged Ponga back onto his chair. "We just came in for a drink and to buy provisions for the long road ahead of us."

"We will help you, but first we have to know if you deserve it," the priest replied.

"Help is for those who beg. We will pay, so we have no need for pity, only service." Ponga was certain that the villagers were trying to start a fight, so he saw no point in wasting time.

The burly moustached man did not restrain himself either; he yelled so hard, his spit flew everywhere.

"How dare you, you heretic animals!" He could shout no further, however, because Ponga moved as quick as lightning. He leapt up, and wrapping his arms around the man's neck, he pulled him onto the table with all his strength. After a loud crash, the moustached man collapsed senseless onto the ground.

The inn suddenly sprang to life, as if a bag of fleas had been poured forth. Henri and Ponga, being experienced fighter, worked to protect their backs and jumped to the wall immediately. By the time they reached it, they'd both drawn their dagger. The villagers produced their home-made weapons. Peasants didn't usually walk around armed, but Henri and Ponga knew after the fight in the woods, what to expect in this region. A man lunged forwards, and Henri cut his wrist. Ponga sidestepped a hit and stabbed ruthlessly beneath the man's arm into his ribs. His opponent dropped down dead.

The villagers came to their senses by the death of their comrade, and their bravery turned to fear. Ponga used the moment of shock and shouted,

"Who else wants to see the afterlife?"

The villagers froze at the sight of death. Now the task was not torturing an innocent man to death, like Paul. This was not a helpless victim; their lives were at stake too. This fact significantly decreased their will to fight. Seeing the dead man, they ran, stampeding over one another to the door.

"Catch one, we need the doctor!" Henri instructed him. Ponga lifted a young man from the surge and held the bloody dagger to his throat.

"We won't hurt you if you help us." As he held him, he felt the boy shaking.

"Yes, sir, I'll do anything, just don't hurt me!"

"Henri, get whatever we need from the kitchen and then come back. I'll watch the boy till then."

Henri collected everything they needed in five minutes. Jules had said to only bring as much fresh warm food as they could eat in one sitting, because the rest would go off anyway. So, they should bring salted meats, smoked sausages, bacon because they wouldn't go off, as well as onions, dry wine and such things. But the most important things were: salt, pepper and paprika, because these spices were indispensable and made any hunted meat taste much better.

"Where does the doctor live?" Ponga asked the boy.

"Three streets from here, but he's with the others now. He was here in the inn," the thin, pockmarked boy blurted.

"Look out the window!" Henri said. "Leave the boy, let's go!"

The villagers were gathered in the square and headed for the inn. They were many, and everyone was holding some sort of weapon.

"Let the poor boy out!" Henri said.

"But…" Ponga began.

"Now!" Henri shouted. "There's no time to argue, my friend." The term softened his anger, and Ponga let the boy go. As the boy stepped into the square, Henri turned to Ponga.

"Quick, into the kitchen! The fireplace is surely lit. Let's burn this dump down."

They ran into the kitchen, and taking two shovels, they threw all the embers into a bucket. Then they ran back to the entrance and lit everything they could— curtains, spilled drinks, leftover clothes.

"Let's go out the back!" Henri ordered. "They had to escape, right away," the enraged mob was at the door.

They grabbed the food from the kitchen and headed towards the backyard. When they climbed over the fence, they saw that a few people had come around the building expect them to escape that way.

"Take the bag, I can fight better," Ponga said. "Stay behind me, we'll break out; once we've fought our way through, it's not a long way to the woods," Ponga instinctually took command. Henri did not oppose him; he knew that Ponga was a better fighter.

There were ten villagers holding sickles, straightened scythes and other hurriedly weaponised tools. They were loud and cursed the strangers constantly, but the two men suspected that their shouting was meant to conceal their fear. The knight, as always attacked suddenly and with superhuman speed. He stabbed the closest man in the belly with his sword; he didn't need to aim for his head or throat because the peasants wore no armour. The injured man screamed, like a stuck pig with its throat cut. Ponga did not stop; using the moment of shock, he cut left and right with his razor-sharp blade cutting both his victims from shoulder to belt. The horrible wounds spurted blood and intestines coiled to the ground. The sight of this shocked the villager, and they threw their weapons down and turned to run. Ponga had no intention of giving chase—they made their way towards the woods. Though they were slowed by their packages, they exited the village without further problems; and in a few minutes, they met Jules and Paul waiting for them by the edge of the woods.

"We brought food, but we have to hurry now, they're after us," Ponga quickly summarised what had happened.

"And the doctor?" Jules asked. His voice was fused with anger and reproach.

"We were attacked, we had no way to get a doctor or medicine," Henri replied looking disparagingly at Ponga, "perhaps we could have avoided all this if Ponga hadn't started a fight," he grumbled.

"Then he will die," Jules said sadly.

"No, he won't," said a hoarse voice from behind them. Reaching for their weapons, they turned as one. The man standing before them wore no sword, just a knife in his belt.

He looked calmly at the battle-ready strangers. His clothes were worn but clean. Though he was not old, his stubble was thick for his age.

"Who are you, and what do you want?" Ponga asked in a hostile voice.

"There's no time to chat, take the injured boy and follow me!" the stranger said, then turned around and walked off. The others went after him.

"Damn it! Another man giving orders. Just what I needed," Ponga raged to himself.

"Perhaps the problem is with you," said the stranger looking back. "I'd consider that if I were you."

When Perrier entered the King's council, he found King Auguste Lefebre IV with company. Marquis Philippe Bertrand and Archbishop Cain Leroy stood next to him. This surprised him, because the messenger had said that the King wanted to talk to him in private.

He pretended not to be disturbed and approached the large table indifferently and greeted the King:

"Your Royal Highness," he bowed; the ruler motioned for him to sit down. He sat, and in protest he ignored the presence of the others in the room.

"Won't you greet the Marquis and the Archbishop?" Lefebre asked annoyed.

"Oh," Perrier said looking around. "I didn't notice you two, probably because I was informed that the King wanted to talk to me in private, I didn't even look around." As he spoke, his cold eyes stared straight ahead. "Your Highness, perhaps I could come back later when the gentlemen won't be here."

The outright lie outraged the King.

"Are you messing with me, Councillor?" he raised his voice. "How dare you? You think I'll believe that you didn't notice the gentlemen."

"Of course not, Your Highness," the Councillor did not lose his cool even for a moment.

Bertrand and Leroy did not join the conversation; they just smiled mockingly.

"Well, they're not here by accident," the King began and then held a dramatic pause. The desired effect was somewhat dampened by the fact that he sat cross-legged on his throne.

"I am all ears, my lord," Perrier said crossing his legs and glancing at Lefebre curiously.

"The lords have had enough of your tyranny. They've told me their concerns, and I, as their king, cannot allow rivalries on my council."

"I see," The Councillor looked at the Marquis and the Archbishop. "Perhaps the lords would tell me about what ails them too. Naturally, only if they haven't taken vows of silence for today."

"There's no use in mocking us, my lord," Bertrand began. "I think you alone control the economy of our country, thereby curtailing the nobility, the church and maybe even the King."

"I second that," Leroy added.

"It's rude to throw accusations around!" Perrier leaned forward as he spoke. "May I know what complaint the lords may have?"

"It has reached our attention that the cost of the Knight's Tournament was precisely one hundred thousand gold pieces," said Bertrand glancing confidently at the Councillor, but he could not hold his stare for long and quickly averted his eyes. "As is well known, the chief source of the treasury is from the taxation of the nobility. So, Councillor Perrier took at once from the nobility and the King."

"So you have heard," answered the Councillor ominously, "as it is no secret. Any member of the council can ask for the exact accounts from the treasury. I take responsibility for all expenditure. What exactly is your grief? Was it the service provided to all the kings or the pay of the weapons-masters? Please, be precise in your accusations."

"We think the whole sum is too large in general," the Marquis stammered nervously.

"What do you mean in general, be precise!" Perrier almost spat the words; his accusers looked at each other in confusion.

"Alright, if you two cannot provide real information, I will supply you with some. Arch Bishop! Do you know how many churches have been built in the Kingdom of France since I am the councillor?"

"I've not had time to deal with that," Leroy said embarrassed.

"And you, Marquis, do you know what the yearly income of your estates is?"

"Of course," Bertrand replied suspiciously. He didn't know what the councillor was getting at.

"I even know why that huge fortune is not enough for you."

The King was beginning to feel uncomfortable and was crinkling the edge of the table cloth in his hand. The Marquis and the Archbishop were regretting setting themselves against Perrier.

"And you dare accuse me?" The Councillor was shouting now,

"Archbishop, since I've served the kingdom, there have been two cathedrals and 11 churches built in Paris. And the Church's income is constantly increasing." Perrier now turned to the King, "I'll also say why Marquis Bertrand hasn't enough gold. Because he lives a more lavish life than anyone in the King's court. We could speak of the orgies the Marquis organises, or Bishop Leroy's extra special attention towards young boys."

Bertrand and Leroy stood with their eyes to the ground. They didn't dare deny the accusations brought against them; they were certain that the Councillor was not making them up. He surely had proof. They figured it was better to keep quiet than entice details of the embarrassing subjects.

The King felt like he had to intervene before the situation got out of hand.

"Alright, I've heard enough. Dear Councillor, this is not an accusation, I just wanted to see things clearly. I think this has been satisfied. Sirs, please apologise to Councillor Perrier." The King looked at the frozen council members and chewed the corner of his mouth.

"Your Highness, I have no need for that. I'd be fine with the Lords just leaving us alone. I have something to discuss with you."

"Be gone! And next time think about your accusations, I don't want another embarrassing scene like this," Lefebre ordered them.

Bertrand and Leroy left throwing venomous glances at the Councillor.

"What did you want to tell me, Councillor?" the King began peaceably when they were left alone.

"The thought, my lord, of how sad Queen Josephine would be if she found out about your late-night adventures scares me." The Councillor's face seemed sad, but his grey eyes revealed a cold indifference.

"Are you threatening me?" Lefebre raised his voice, and Perrier felt the fear behind the King's anger.

"I wouldn't think of such a thing, I am the guardian of your secrets, I am your greatest confidant. Which is why I would not like for you to give the baseless accusations of other any credence. They just want you to control you, my lord."

"Why, what do you want?" asked the King accusingly.

"I want to help you to lead your country more easily."

Farall awaited the Councillor in his chambers. He sat on the usual chair when Perrier arrived.

Perrier swept across the room, looked at his aid and shook his head.

"How many times have I told you, I'm going to throw that piece of junk out!" He pointed at the chair with his index finger. He was very bored of this ever-recurring play, the centrepiece of which was this impossible chair.

"Please, don't...I like sitting on it. I couldn't lounge about in a big arm chair in your presence. You seem upset."

"As a matter of fact, I am. Those lowlifes, the Marquis and Leroy accused me before the King again. But the main problem is that King Lefebre is easily swayed. Of course, I handled the situation, but it's not a final solution."

The Councillor leaned back and thought with his eyes closed. Ten minutes or so passed before he spoke again. It seemed as if he were sleeping, but Farall knew that he was wide awake.

"Do you know, Vincent, what the fourth law of the councillors is?" Perrier kept his eyes closed as he asked this.

Farall did not understand what he was getting as he had memorised the law long ago. So why was he asking him?

"The fourth law states…" he began the answer, "always have a second plan."

"Exactly," Perrier said and suddenly opened his eyes. "If you are not satisfied with a situation, if things don't go to plan, then things must be changed, and the second plan implemented."

"I don't get it, Alain," Farall fidgeted in his chair. He usually did this when he didn't understand something. "The King's council and the King cannot be changed."

"Everything and everyone can be changed, but perhaps in this case, such proceedings are not necessary."

"So, what do you want to do?"

The Councillor scratched his chin and thought deeply. Farall was beginning to think he wouldn't get an answer when Perrier finally spoke.

"I think I need to bring the reigns in tighter."

Farall did not know what he was getting at, but he knew he didn't want to switch places with any council members.

Chapter Eleven

The Spanish Queen, Esmeralda de Aragon, carefully peeked out from her horse-drawn carriage. Holding her hands on her rounding belly, protecting her child-to-be, she proceeded to the agreed upon clearing where the King's makeshift camp had been erected. Her husband, old King Carlos Maria V, anxiously buzzed about her.

"You should not have come to the hunt, my lady, the child is due within a month. Why won't you take care of yourself?"

"Your Highness," Esmeralda answered stroking her stomach. She like to use every opportunity to rub the nose of those around her into the fact that she was the most important person in the kingdom, and that it was she who would bear the heir to the Spanish throne. "A wife's place is beside her husband, and queen's beside her king. You can see that I have two reasons for coming out, and it is a beautiful spring day; it's nice to get out a little."

"Of course, of course. You are right as always, my dear," Carlos replied. When he spoke to his wife, he almost gurgled as if he were speaking to a little child.

They reached the open royal tent and sat down inside. Esmeralda managed to use even this simple movement to draw attention to her pregnancy. She placed one hand gently onto her round belly and grabbed her old husband's arm with her other and sat down slowly.

Then she looked round victoriously, she could not get enough of the situation that after so many years she would be mother to the heir to the throne. They had met at a similar hunt to the one they were on now. The deceitful Councillor had done everything he could to stop her winning the King's heart, but she had won and wrapped the old goat around her finger. When she'd married Carlos, she could not have known that the old man was incapable of making children. How many years she had suffered till she'd realised. All the affluent young noblemen of the court had ended up in her bedroom, but none had been able to impregnate her. Finally, she was forced to allow a peasant between her legs, though he had at least given her a child, unlike many others. The hardest part was that she still had to get in bed with Carlos too because it was the only way to convince him that the child was his. Esmeralda spent years suppressing her disgust and pretending as if her old husband's feeble manhood were the most beautiful thing on earth. *No one knows how much I've suffered to achieve what I want,* she thought glancing at her stomach.

The King's entourage began preparing for the hunt. The riders and foot soldiers following the carriage went out into the fields where the King and the high nobility would practice their favourite sport. On single-day hunts, they usually shot small game, mostly pheasants. It was the same on this day. The hunters usually caught the game in traps, but if the King wanted to hunt, then he and the court's nobility would shoot with bows. Stalking their prey was too time-consuming, and the large horde of noblemen accompanying the King would scare away any prey, so they'd caught the animals the day before and would release them from cages to be shot down.

In order to maintain the illusion of hunting, the hunters placed the cages in thick brush, so that the King and his entourage would just see pheasants rising from the bushes like they would in a real hunt.

Soon Councillor Pedro Garcia arrived at the tent, escorted by the King's adolescent first-born, Teresa de Cantabria. Teresa, who'd been born of Carlos' first marriage was a thin, lanky girl with huge, warm brown eyes. She did not speak much, and the years spent in the King's court had only increased her reticence.

"My lord! My lady!" she greeted the ruling couple, bowing elegantly and then glancing, for just a moment, at Esmeralda. That glance contained all of her loathing; she saw nothing but the person it was directed at.

"Greetings, my royal father! And you my royal mother!" she squeaked in her high-pitched voice.

"Come, sit among us!" the King invited them, whose waving arms made him look like he was batting away flies.

"Thank you, my lord," Garcia replied for both of them.

As they sat down, Esmeralda began her favourite game, antagonising Teresa.

"A first-born should not slouch like that. The royal family must command respect, and you sit there on that chair, like a peasant girl."

"Sorry, Mother," Teresa mumbled grabbing the cloth of her dress so tight that her nails whitened.

"Don't be so hard on her!" the King pleaded with his wife.

"My dear," she snapped at him in a sharp voice "please, stay out of it! It is my job to unite the women of the court, and unfortunately, Teresa often sets a bad example."

"Forgive me, my lady!" Carlos interjected; he pitied her greatly, but the adoration he felt for his wife dampened all other emotions in him.

"If you'll allow me," Garcia said turning to the royal couple, "I promised Lady Cantabria that she could go pick flowers when we arrived."

There was something threatening in the Councillor's calm style. People rarely felt comfortable in his presence. Though he never raised his voice, one suspected that his soft measured tone was there just to suppress his explosive personality. Perhaps he didn't want to hide his real self any more than that, in this way at least he could keep everyone he met under constant pressure. Who could say exactly why Councillor does what they do?

"Of course, she may go," the King answered smiling at his daughter.

"Before you go, have some of this lemonade! It has mint leaves in it," Esmeralda said handing the cup to Teresa.

"My lady," Garcia said to Teresa, "do not drink from it!

The drink is iced, and you have a cold."

"Yes, sir," Teresa replied obediently and then turned around and headed to the nearby meadow. The Queen could barely contain herself from admonishing Garcia, but she controlled herself—the Councillor would not have put up with being lectured.

Meanwhile, the hunters finished up their preparations. The most important part was that everyone position themselves correctly behind the bushes. The task of the hunters was not without danger as the unskilled noblemen often missed their mark. The pheasants could only be released in the shooting range, so accidents were common. The royal hunters were highly paid, and if one of them did die, then their family would be taken care of by the treasury for the rest of their lives, so there was never a shortage of applicants.

Soon the head royal hunter arrived at the tent.

"My lord, everything is ready for the hunt."

"My lady," the King looked at Esmeralda embarrassedly, "do you mind if I leave you with the Councillor and go hunting?"

"Of course not, my lord, do what feels right, you are not only the King but also a man and real men always do as they see right," the Queen smiled sycophantically at Carlos.

Esmeralda waited for her husband to get out of earshot, then she looked Garcia in the eye.

"Councillor, how dare you oppose me?" her face contorted with rage.

"My lady, let us not play games! If I didn't protect Teresa, she'd be dead long ago."

There was no trace of the court etiquette left between them, but suddenly the Queen's expression changed; her enraged visage transformed into a kindly gaze.

"Alright, let's not be at each other's throats incessantly," she quickly changed pace, "it's futile. The thing is, if I bear a boy, he will be the heir anyway. Let's wait and see and not fight over it. Come, have some lemonade! If you don't trust me, I'll have some of yours too."

And so she did—she took a sip from the ice-cold drink and handed the goblet to Garcia. The Councillor took it, but he did not drink of it. Instead he stared rigidly ahead.

He sensed that something was not right. The Queen had never been so kind before. *What could be her motive? Teresa!* the recognition struck him. She wants to keep me away from her. In that moment, he stood up.

"I have to go now, my queen."

"You will go when I permit it!" Esmeralda was enraged again. But the Councillor ignored her and turned without a word running of in the direction Teresa had left.

Teresa took a deep breath of the fresh April air. It was filled with the scent of wild flowers. She loved these brief little hours when she could be alone. At these times, she imagined that she was not the King's daughter, just a little girl like all the others. She knew she would have to go back soon, but she decided to stay—the Queen was certain to scold her whether she was late or not. Holding a bouquet of freshly picked flowers, she sat down on a large rock and enjoyed the chirping of the birds—they sang so loudly that they drowned out the other noises—the rustling of the leaves, the gurgling of the nearby creek, the chatting of the hunters' preparations.

Poor birds, Teresa thought, *they won't have many springs in their lifetimes, perhaps that is why they are so delighted by it.* She glanced at the bouquet of flowers, which reminded her of her mother. Though she could not remember her features, there was a painting of her in a hidden corner of the castle. Teresa imagined her the way she was displayed on the wall, and she was certain that her mother had loved her very much. On that picture, her mother held a similar bouquet in her hands. A long time ago, the picture had hung in the royal chambers till Esmeralda had it removed. Teresa didn't mind that Mommy's picture had been moved, this way she could go see it without being disturbed. It became her habit to talk to the picture and tell it things she didn't dare tell anyone else.

Once, the Queen had caught her talking to the painting and had forbid her to do so again. The Councillor had warned her not to oppose Esmeralda, and her father had reminded her how badly the Queen felt at not being treated like a mother. Her father had also said that her step-mother had been so angry because she loved Teresa so much and didn't like her suffering over the past. Teresa knew this was a lie, but she was forced to promise to obey. After that she visited the portrait every day, but she spoke only without words to her mother. She felt like the two of them would be together forever through that painting.

Teresa didn't even notice that she was no longer alone. Suddenly something cracked behind her. Frightened, she jumped to her feet, but calmed down instantly as she saw Sir Demetri de Lopez, a member of the Queen's entourage.

"Greetings, Sir Knight! A lovely day, isn't it," she greeted him politely.

"It is for me certainly, but for you not so."

She sensed danger. The Councillor had taught her to pay attention at all time, as danger usually came when one least expected it. The knight was being disrespectful to her, and it was also strange that he had appeared so unexpectedly, as if he were stalking her. Carefully, she began to back away and forced herself to be calm as she spoke to him.

"I shall say goodbye now, my royal father is surely expecting me."

"You're not going anywhere, my dear!" Lopez said drawing his sword. He was advancing on her when a soft but all the more menacing voice spoke behind him.

"I'd put that sword down if I were you!"

The knight spun quickly, though his frightened movement closer resembled a deer bounding around. When he saw that it was the Councillor, he calmed down. *Just an old man, not even a soldier,* he thought, *I can take care of him easily.*

"Everything is alright, my lady, you keep your distance now!" Garcia called to Teresa, keeping his eyes firmly locked on his opponent. He goaded him on, like a snake goads a mouse.

"I'm sorry, Councillor," the knight's words expressed everything except regret, "but you will have to die here too, not just the wench." The knight understood the situation, as did Garcia; he could leave a live witness, especially not one of the Queen's greatest enemies.

Garcia slowly withdrew his word from its sheath, he did not want to make his opponent attack immediately. He knew he was at a disadvantage, his enemy was a much better fighter, in constant training and much younger too.

"I've never killed a Councillor before, I wonder what it will be like." The knight enjoyed being disrespectful to the notorious Councillor, as he could do so without consequence now. If he killed the Councillor, no one would know, and he would be in no danger. This thought brought a smile to his face.

Garcia could see clearly that Lopez was certain of his victory and so would attack unguarded. The knight didn't even assume a fencing posture; he did not turn his side to Garcia, but he stood with his legs spread waiting for the fight to begin. The Councillor knew that he could not fight straight up, he would have to take evasive action. And for this, he could not hand over the offensive to this opponent; he could only control the fight if he began the attack.

He went over the fight in his head, then took a deep breath a dove in. As fast as he possibly could, he attacked the knight's head. Lopez had no difficulty in deflecting the blow; he raised his sword and defended without even stepping back. Garcia knew that this was not a serious attack for a knight trained in battle, but he had only wanted to get within kicking distance. Almost at the same time as the cut, Garcia raised his right foot and turning it sideways he kicked Lopez's inner thigh. The move worked, he had struck the knight exactly where he'd intended to. The Councillor knew that the knee tendon was dislocated, which incapacitated his opponent immediately; he would not be able to use that leg, and the immense pain would make him unable to fight.

"No need to be afraid now, my lady," he consoled Teresa, but his words were made mute the unsettling sight of the screaming knight on the ground.

The Councillor took Lopez's sword and turned to Teresa,

"Run back, but avoid the Queen, tell Head Liquidator Marcos Sanchez to come here immediately with two men. Don't tell them what happened, just that I ordered it. Can you do that?"

"Yes. When will you come back?"

"Soon, just hold on till then, we'll talk later about what we are going to do. Hurry!"

Teresa ran off, and Garcia knew what he had to do. Lopez was one of the Queen's men. In fact, she was his lover according to court gossip, so it was clear to him that Esmeralda had sent the assassin.

When Sanchez arrives, they would have to secure the knight quickly. He could not be allowed to be put into the castle prison because the Queen would certainly have him killed before he confessed. He would have to get every bit of information out of that weasel. The Councillor knew that there was no point interrogating Lopez about the Queen; Esmeralda would just deny it and accuse him of trying to blacken her name. But the knowledge that Esmeralda would be terrified as the assassin was in his hands gave him no small sense of satisfaction. He looked down at the incessantly moaning knight, knelt down beside him and whispered in his ear,

"My dear friend, pull yourself together! The pain you feel now will seem like the high life compared to the conversation we will have tonight."

John Neville, the president of Atlantis, stared at the violin in the corner of his room. The instrument was housed in a glass cabinet that ensured a constant humidity, placed so that he could see it from where he sat at his desk.

Neville was over 60 but in good health—he certainly had a fair few active years left in him. Despite this, he knew he had to train a successor. The custom in Atlantis was for the sitting president to appoint and train the next president.

He ran his fingers through his imposing long grey hair and looked at James Mulligan his successor. Mulligan was more than 20 years younger than Neville. His pitch-black hair stood in stark contrast to the President's white mane. His bony face was hairless; he was always clean-shaven, twice a day if necessary.

And this pedantic attitude translated into his work too. *Another year or two, and he'll be ready to lead,* the president thought.

"Do you have any news of Councillor Aleksandr Petrov?" Neville asked.

"Not yet, but he will arrive in Moscow soon, and he's sure to send a message," Mulligan replied.

"Now, when the English and the French are on the brink of war, it is especially important that the Russian kingdom remain stable. Councillor Petrov will be responsible for reigning in a population of ten million." Neville had been particularly restless these last few months, the known world was beginning to slip out from under the control of Atlantis—at least he felt it was.

"But, sir, the Russians have peace."

"It is true, but a new councillor always brings uncertainty. Aleksandr Petrov will have to stabilise the situation quickly. I really have no idea what reason the English have for waging war. Sir Lemmy Black is a level-headed commander who has won every war. He's not the kind of man to act foolishly. If he's decided, there has to be a reason. But I have no idea what it is. What do you think, James?"

"It is true that King Mortimer would not start a war if Sir Lemmy opposed it. He trusts him blindly and does so wisely, I think. Black has made no mistakes till now, which makes it incomprehensibly why he would want war with an equally powerful kingdom. Perhaps he's just threatening, but I can't find a good reason for that either."

"Come, I want to show you something that you've seen many times before, but you don't know why I keep it near me." Neville stood up and escorted Mulligan to the glass cabinet.

"Do you know what this is?" the President asked.

"Of course, it's a violin. A musical instrument from the old times, nowadays there's something similar in the known world."

"It's a Stradivarius. Once upon a time in the old world lived an Italian violin-maker, Antonio Stradivari. He gave the Latin version of his name to his instruments. Every single violin was also named separately, usually the name of the person who bought it. The one you see here is called The Lady Tennant. The instruments he made were very expensive even when the master was alive, but after his death, wealthy people paid vast sums of money for them. The secret to his instruments was researched for centuries. Over time, human technology progressed in leaps and bounds, but no one could make an instrument like Stradivari. There were some who thought that Stradivari had used the roof beams of an old church for his instruments. Others thought the treatment of the wood was the secret. While others whispered that the master travelled to a secret place where he himself chose the pine he thought was best. Some violin makers think that he treated the wood with mushrooms. In fact, people even thought that his violins sounded so beautiful because he dribbled his blood into the varnish. No one ever discovered the truth. Why do you think this instrument is in my room?"

"I know your forte is the history of art. I'm sure you enjoy looking at this rarity."

"That's not what I mean," Neville smiled.

"Then it's because you like music."

"There's another reason, but it's not nice of me to keep you guessing an answer you could not know.

Come, let's sit back down, and I'll explain."

They sat down. Neville lent forward close to Mulligan.

"We control the known world, the current civilisation. Our knowledge is far greater than that of those we rule. And yet, we cannot be certain that we will not one day lose control."

"That's impossible!" Mulligan said in disbelief. "We have been in control for over two thousand years."

"Look! You will be my successor. You must understand what I am telling you now. Never underestimate the unique individuality of mankind. That is why the violin is here, to remind me at every moment that at some point in time, someone may come who will change the course of the world forever."

"But Stradivari was just a violin maker. What would happen is another such man were born? Nothing," Mulligan announced, "one person cannot change the course of the world!"

"Human unpredictability is not unique to masters. Your area of study is old history. You know how many inventors, politicians and despots created history on their own. Please do not underestimate human ingenuity. If you are wary of something, at least it will not take you unawares when it happens. I'm afraid that the man whose actions no one will be able to follow, not even us, will appear in my time."

"Could it be the strategist?" Mulligan asked in astonishment.

"Maybe. Who knows?"

Chapter Twelve

Hugh Jones really needed to relieve himself. He'd been lying on the roof of a house for three hours, right opposite the Wild Barbarians Inn. His situation was made worse by the constantly drizzling rain.

The news proved to be true, the King and his entourage were finishing their night's festivities in this watering hole. Jones had not dared to follow the group wearing civilian clothing from the castle because he knew how careful Sir Lemmy was, and there were certainly a multitude of hidden eyes watching over the King. So, he had chosen his observation post the day before, from where he had a perfect view of the exit.

His principal had been right—Jones remembered the conversation from the day before—he would not get a better chance to kill the King than this. Till the company had gone into the inn, he'd been plagued by doubt. He respected his informant, in fact he thought he was a great man, but it is one thing to respect someone and another to put one's life in their hands. Now he saw that he could blindly trust them, and it was his time to prove that he could be counted on.

He didn't want to do the deed when they went in, because this way allowed him to better observe the group. The damn strategist had dressed everyone in the same black clothes, but luckily he still recognised Mortimer, as he'd seen him in the castle many times.

He even checked if the two big torches either side of the door would be enough for him to be able to discern their faces properly. The raucous happy company entered the inn in single file. First went the immense form of Horan followed by the others. The King and Sir Lemmy entered last. Only when Commander Carrol stepped out and indicated that everything was alright inside, did Black allow the King inside and brought up the back himself. The strategist was almost inside when he turned around suddenly. He looked straight in Jones' direction as if he could see him through the darkness. The blood froze in Jones' veins, and it required nerves of steel to stay motionless. He knew it was impossible to see him, as he was completely hidden, yet he still felt like Black was staring right into him. For a brief moment their eyes met, yet it seemed like an eternity to Jones. Then the strategist turned back just as fast as he had looked back and went into the inn.

Then a whole hour crawled past. Jones could clearly hear the bell of a nearby tower clock. If only he didn't need to piss so badly. He felt like he couldn't hold on any longer, but he did not want to leave his spot. Suddenly, he thought of the solution. He turned onto his side, unbuttoned his trousers with his right hand and relieved himself there.

When he was done, he felt much better. But the relief only lasted a moment, and desperation came over him with brutal force. Was it possible that the company had left in the brief minute he wasn't watching? Would such a stupid moment of negligence cause his failure? What would his principal say when he told him what had happened? He wouldn't laugh himself to death, that was certain.

As Jones' sudden fright abated, he was able to think rationally again. That many people could walk down the street in such a short time. As they had been drinking all night, they were probably drunk and would be slower staggering; they could not have gone all the way down the street in just brief minute. He had heard no noise either—he pondered the situation—it was impossible for a drunken group to leave the inn in silence. After evaluating the possibilities, his fear was replaced with calm.

He checked his equipment again; liquidator training had taught him that preparation was the most important part of a mission. He gently lifted the greased deer hide tarp that protected his weapons from the rain. He was pleased to see how the rain beaded off the layer of grease, leaving the weapons beneath dry. Again, he felt the leather quiver that held the arrows. It was important that the arrows stay dry because if the feathers were wet, it would not fly straight, and he might miss. The arrow tips were poisoned, and the rain could have washed the poison off too.

Once again, he went over his plan of action. When the King stepped out—he would probably not be the first in line—Jones would shoot him. Then, leaving the weapons behind, he would slide down the roof to the other side, and clinging to the drain pipes, he would slide to the ground. He had opened the garden door when he'd come, breaking the lock meaning he could get to the next street quickly. From there he would have an advantage over his pursuers; by the time they came around the block, or broke the door down into the house, he would be several streets away. He'd bought the weapons from a foreign maker, they would not reveal him. Jones had completed many such missions, he'd never slipped up. A liquidator can only make one mistake, and that will cost him his life. Since he was still alive, it meant that his jobs till now had been completed perfectly, but the assassination of a King was far more dangerous.

He could not be certain of success. In case of failure, he had potent poison hung around his neck. It was much better to die quickly than to suffer torture at the end of which he would betray his principal and his new brothers. He thought of himself as a hard man, but everyone broke under torture sooner or later.

After he'd gone over all the possible scenarios, he was pleased to ascertain that he'd prepared for the mission perfectly. Now the dance begins.

The Wild Barbarians Inn was packed, there wasn't a chair to spare in the whole place. King Mortimer sat at a table to the side and was drinking his umpteenth cup of wine. To his left sat the huge, black-skinned figure of Head Liquidator James Horan, who drank far less than the others, except for Sir Lemmy on the right who drank nothing at all. They both considered themselves on duty for the evening, not out for a party.

Lord Christopher Millborrow, Lord Oliver Hamilton and Sir William Goldwin were only a hair's breadth away from total inebriation. The noblemen thought they could drink more than their King, but they were gravely mistaken. The company also included Commander Mark Caroll, to whom Black quietly gave orders.

"Go out into the yard and have a look around!"

"Yes, sir!"

"And stop saying sir because the Ki...well just don't say it."

"I'm not so drunk as to not hear your muttering. You know what will become of the man who calls me by my name?" the King asked.

"Of course, we know. Death. Hahaha," Sir Millborrow laughed.

"Hey, Old Ronny," Mortimer called to the innkeeper, "come sit with us and have a cup of wine with me."

"I would like to, my lord," Ronny replied, who did indeed seem old, but there is nowhere to sit.

"We'll fit you in. My friend can fit on half a chair. Right?" the King looked at Sir Hamilton. Though the nobleman was visibly displeased to share his chair with a commoner, but he knew it was not his place to argue. The old man brought a wooden cup with him, the only kind in the inn, and sat down among them.

"Meanwhile, Carrol came back in from the yard. His clothes were soaked."

"It's raining cats and dogs. If you'd not said a word, everyone would still know."

"You know what people say about London weather."

"What's that, innkeeper?" the King asked patting Old Ronny's shoulder jovially.

"In London it is either raining or about to rain."

Mortimer liked the saying so much that he slapped the table and roared with laughter almost upsetting the cups. Laughter is contagious, especially among drunks, so it did not take long for the whole table to be rolling with laughter.

"That's great!" Mortimer said wiping a tear from his eye. "You seem like a good man, brother. Tell me, what's your opinion of the King?"

The old man pondered this, then asked back, "Why, my lord, what should my opinion be?"

"Don't worry," the King understood Ronny's concern, "I'm neither a fan nor an enemy to Mortimer, I'm just interested in your opinion."

"The man is at war too much, and the women are left to cry alone!" shouted a fat woman from the next table.

"Be silent, you great hag! If you were my woman, I wouldn't even come home from the battlefield," Ronny said silencing her.

"So, my lord, my opinion is that a king, sorry for the expression, should have balls. And our king does. You know what I mean?—he's not a coward. Excuse the expression!"

"That's alright, I understand." The King enjoyed the complement. "Thank you for your honesty. Now go, the guests need wine, and you're not making money sitting here with me all night."

Mortimer signalled to Black to lean closer.

"Make arrangements tomorrow, send the old man ten gold pieces and say it's from the King."

Two tables over a man from a large group called out,

"Who's the idiot who wants to know what our king is like?" The man wore knight's armour and a sword. "I'll tell you—Mortimer is an idiot!"

"Who asked you?" Horan jumped up; his huge figure towering intimidatingly over everyone else.

"Leave him!" Mortimer held Horan's arm. "I'll take care of this."

"My lord!" Black pleaded, though he knew it was in vein.

"Enough! I won't say it again." He waved them all off.

"What's up, aren't you man enough without your backup?" the knight taunted. He was clearly an experienced warrior. He had well-worn clothes over his tall, muscular body, and his bearded face bore an old scar across it.

"Come here, and we'll find out if it's just your mouth or you can actually fight," the King retorted standing up from the table. He swayed a little as he did so; the wine was working its magic on him.

The knight did not need to be asked twice; he jumped over and smacked the King in the face with his face, who fell onto the table. Cups and pitchers went flying. His entourage sprang to their feet drawing weapons. The knight's company also lined up holding weapons. The pain sobered Mortimer up. He pulled himself up and wiped his bleeding mouth.

"Everyone, put your swords away! This is between the two of us. If you want, we can fight with swords—only if you're afraid of hand-to-hand, of course."

"Afraid? Of what?" the knight blustered, "Look at yourself, man!"

— "Put the swords away!" the King commanded the men standing with their swords drawn. Reluctantly, maintaining eye-contact, they slowly put their swords away.

"Alright, that's much better." Mortimer looked around pleased, then suddenly he swung his left hand as hard as he could into the knight's stomach. His opponent keeled over from the unexpected blow, and the King hit him on the chin with his right, so that the knight knocked people over as he fell backwards.

"Now look at yourself, man!" the King said laughing. "Do you want to keep fighting?"

The knight was helped to his feet. He was visibly shaken.

— "You win, sir, congratulations! No one has ever punched me like that before. Since I am the loser, I shall pay your night's festivities."

"Thank you," Mortimer replied, "I see you are an honourable man. Please, tell me, why is our king an idiot!"

"He isn't at all, sir," the knight replied, "I just wanted a little trouble. I regret it now. And not because you won, but because I had no reason to pick a fight with you."

"I see. Look! What's your name, sir?"

"My name is Sir George Silver."

"If you're looking for work, Sir Silver, go the castle. I have good connections there. Seek out Sir Lemmy Black and tell him Sir Alex sent you. He will take you into the army."

"I mean no offence, Sir Alex," Silver said meekly, "but I don't think the strategist will speak to a small fry like you or I."

"Well, you know," Mortimer said looking for words, "the thing is Sir Lemmy owes me a favour. So, go ahead and seek him out. Excuse us, but we must go now. I am certain we will meet again." Then, he headed for the door with his entourage.

High Jones was pleased to note that the rain had stopped—this would make his job much easier. He took his bow from beneath the tarp and produced an arrow. He would need no more, whether he hit or missed; he would have no time for a second shot.

Suddenly, an icy calm came over him. He felt that this was meant to be; if he failed or succeeded, he would go through with it, because his new brothers were more important to him than anything else in this life. When his parents had died, he was only eight. His father had served Sir Christopher Millborrow, but he had not accrued much of a fortune. Sir Christopher had arranged for him to join the liquidators. He had suffered much during the long years of training, but he'd always thought he served a good cause. This thought had given his life meaning. Then suddenly he was forced to realise that he and his companions were nothing more than puppets, disposable killing machines, in the dirty games of the Lords. In reality, he had not discovered this by himself, but had had his eyes opened by Glenda. The girl had also convinced him to go meet the community of brothers. Jones did not take his eyes off the inn-door, but the figure of Glenda appeared before him. When he'd seen her at the marker, it immediately became clear that she meant more to him than anyone else in life. He fell in love with her instantly, and the feeling was mutual. They'd grown close so quickly that she had allowed him that very night to embrace her. Naturally, he did not take advantage of the situation; he'd stroked her face gently, but nothing else had happened. His plan was, if he survived this night, to run away from the liquidators and spend the rest of his life with Glenda. Soon his fate would be in his own hands, and he could end the tyranny of the King who kept the Kingdom of England at constant war.

But Mortimer's greatest crime was not war, but that he persecuted those who thought differently, like his new brothers. It was not the King's job to hunt those who felt or saw the world differently. But tonight, he, High Jones, would restore world order and execute the tyrant.

Suddenly Commander Caroll appeared in the doorway followed by the others. When Jones saw Mortimer, he notched the arrow on the string, drew the bow, took a deep breath, aimed and then shot.

The bow twanged, and the arrow flew directly towards the King.

Commander Caroll looked around as he stepped out, but he had no chance of seeing Jones through the night. The King came next, and not looking where he was going, he stumbled over the threshold. He lost his balance and landed directly in a puddle; the poisoned arrow passed over him and burrowed into the chest of Sir William Goldwin who followed him. Goldwin shouted and grabbed onto Millborrow, who held him up as he collapsed. Black reacted instantly,

"Caroll! He's on the roof! Run around to the back street to the other exit. Go around the right! Sir Millborrow, take him inside the inn. Sir Hamilton, take the King inside immediately!" the strategist pointed at the gate of the house next to the inn; he did not want to send the King back inside the Wild Barbarians. He could not know if an accomplice or assassin was waiting inside. No one would have expected him to send him into the house.

Black liked to use the power of unexpected decisions.

"I won't go," Mortimer opposed him.

"My Lord, we have no time for this!" Black said in a tone that even the King would not argue with.

"Horan," the strategist turned to the head liquidator, "I'll go left, and you go through the door." He pointed at the gate of the house opposite the inn on top of which the assassin lay.

"Yes, sir," Horan replied and swung into action. The head liquidator, Caroll and Black had not drunk much, while the others had sobered up instantly.

Jones could see that he had missed, heard Black shouting orders. The moment after he loosed the arrow, he was sliding down the tiles to the attic window. He climbed in. The failed assassination shocked him. His mind was racing: if Caroll had gone around, he did not have much of a chance to get there first—Caroll was faster than anyone. But if he went out the front door, he'd run into the massive Horan, and all would be lost. Desperately he racked his brain. Then the correct solution came to him. He climbed back onto the roof. His only hope was to jump down into the street in from, and if he got lucky, Horan would be inside the house, and Carrol and Black would be waiting for him out back, and the street would be empty. By the time he thought this through, he was already down on the street opposite the inn.

Sir Millborrow helped Sir William Goldwin into the tavern, where he collapsed, foam bubbling from his mouth; his body twitching. From the symptoms Sir Christopher knew that his companion had been hit by a poisoned arrow. Goldwin gave one last jerk and then lay dead on the tavern floor.

Millborrow closed the dead man's eyes, then drew his sword and ran into the street to take part in the chase. As he exited the building, he came face-to-face with Jones jumping from the roof.

"Stop!" Millborrow shouted pointing his sword at the assassin. "If you move, I'll kill you!"

Jones stared frozen at the nobleman and heard somebody running at the end of the street. He glanced over and was shocked to see Black.

Sir Lemmy shouted from afar,

"We need him alive."

Jones knew he did not have much time to act.

"My Lord," he said to Millborrow, "I'm sorry if I've disappointed you." – Then he quickly opened the vial around his neck and drank the poison. He collapsed immediately, and by the time he hit the ground, he was dead. Then

Black arrived. He bent over Jones, but it was too late to save him. He stood up and turned to Millborrow:

"I told you we need him alive!"

"He poisoned himself, there was nothing I could do," the nobleman answered confusedly.

"We'll talk about this later. And also about whether you knew this assassin. I heard his last words clearly."

"What happened was…" Millborrow began.

"Not now! Go to the castle," Black interjected. He'd immediately recognised Jones, though he knew little of the introverted liquidator's private life.

Commander Carrol returned from the other street, and then the form of Head Liquidator Horan came through the doorway as well. No one wanted to speak.

They knew it was not a good time to disturb the strategist. Black looked at the Commander and then spoke,

"Carrol, run to the castle and bring back up. Horan! When the men arrive, take the King back to the castle and have the body taken there as well! I'll comb through the area with a few men, but until then, head liquidator, have a look around and bring any object that might have something to do with the assassination."

Then Black squatted down and looked into the corpse's glassy eyes. The others stood there rooted to the spot; despite the orders they'd received, they watched as Sir Lemmy leaned in quite close to Jones. Their faces almost touched.

"You died in vain, my friend, you cannot take your secrets to the grave."

Everyone was silent. No one would interrupt the strategist. Especially when conversing with a corpse.

Chapter Thirteen

The evening camp fire burned with bright red flames, illuminating the figures sat around it. Sometimes fire can bring a melancholy silence to those that sit around it, and sometimes it can cheer them into lively conversation.

This was one of the friendly kind. Perhaps the deer roasting over the fire had something to do with that.

Ponga whittled a stick smiling, Jules lay resting on his elbows, and Henri was helping their new companion Fabian to cook the meat. Only Paul sat in silence staring at the ground. They'd left the accursed village two days ago, so Jules thought it time to risk a late-night feast. They even had time to hunt, the result of which was spinning on a sizeable spit before them. Fabian was not lying when he'd said he could care for Paul's wounds—he proved his considerable medical knowledge. The boy's condition improved rapidly, and he could keep up with their pace. But he missed his family terribly. His physical wounds healed, but the ones on his soul would not heal over a whole lifetime.

"We don't even know who you are," Ponga broke the silence directing his words at Fabian.

"As a matter of fact, I didn't even ask who you are and who you're running from. But I have nothing to hide."

"A man does not live in the woods of his own free will," the knight stated.

"Yet, I myself chose this life. I've had enough of people's foolishness. While in the forest, I do as I please. If I get bored of one place, I go to another. The landowners don't give orders in the wild, there are no soldiers, and the King cannot tell me what I can and can't do. The wild has its own laws, those who stumble here will pay the price, but only the price of their own mistakes; they do not have to suffer because of the blunders of others. For me, this is an intoxicant feeling. The truth is that I had to move camp because of you."

"Why?" Jules asked.

"I know those people, and they know me. There are a lot of hunters in that village, and they would certainly have followed the tracks to me. In the end, they would have captured me too. Better for me to come with you."

"Look my friend," Jules said seriously. "If you come with us, just a few days is all, I will show you place I think will suit your needs. And if you do wish to leave from there, you will be free to go. It is a place where you can live alone in a nice house, but if you do feel like meeting people, then you can come visit us at any time."

"Nothing is free," Fabian answered. "What do you want in return if I agree at all?"

"We would only require your medical expertise at times."

"Well," Fabian said scratching his beard, "we will see. Perhaps I'll accept, maybe I won't. I've asked nothing from you till now, but after this offer, I need to know a thing or two."

He looked directly into Julian's eyes, and Julian felt that he would have to reveal some of his plan, as to the outsider's eye they must have seemed like a strange bunch.

"Three warriors escaping, carefully avoiding the roads. It's not that. That does not seem so strange to me," Fabian shook his head slowly as he spoke, "but that you are headed for a secret place, and want to live together there, that I cannot leave without question."

"I will go on," Ponga stated, but no one paid attention to him. Paul and Fabian eagerly awaited Jules' response.

"We are going to a normal village, where men, women, children and old folk live together. This place is special because no one knows it exists, only those that live there."

"How can that be?" Paul's eyes went 'round.

"I don't want to say more," Jules said finally, "when we get there, all your questions will be answered."

The deer was almost cooked. Fabian had salt, dry spices and paprika, which made for a wonderful feast. Everyone was in a good mood, and even Paul spoke a few words now and then.

Jules stared into the fire. He didn't even hear when the others spoke to him. The fire burned intimately, as they had a long time ago in Marquis Bastien de Caulmont's fireplace, back when he had been called Hubert de Godart, and Henri's name had been Edmond la Forge.

But Marquis Caulmont was the chief supporter of King Gaston de Bellehache. When the King and his family were killed by bandits during a hike, the Marquis retired to his estate near Bordeaux. No one from the royal family survived, though rumours abounded for a long time that the King's youngest son, Prince Fernand de Bellehache, was still alive, as his body was never found.

They searched for him for months, but they found nothing. The boy had been two years old and could not have survived alone. During the attack, Marquis Caulmont was also injured, but he managed to escape. Many considered him a coward. The Marquis was the biggest landowner in the Kingdom of France and also the richest. After the attack, there were fears of war breaking out in the kingdom. The tension developed between Caulmont, who supported the old King, and Marquis Bertrand. Bertrand was not a poor man either, and his fortune was only surpassed by his influence in the King's court. He was the apple in the eye of the Lefebre family and wanted the young Count Auguste to take the throne. De Caulmont hated Marquis Bertrand and the Lefebre family. The crisis was solved by Councillor Perrier, by convincing Marquis Caulmont to support his greatest rival Bertrand's suggestion, by making Auguste Lefebre the new King. In return, he arranged for Marquis Caulmont to retire from the King's court and assured him of his full support. What this support actually meant, no one, except for the two of them knew exactly.

When Caulmont returned to the family estate, he created an academy where young noblemen could learn art, humanities and history. The school made for the not-first-born children of the nobility was a good opportunity for the sons of small landowners who were not in the inheritance to receive a path in life suited to their rank. Caulmont recommended graduates to Councillor Perrier who then got them jobs in the court. There were not many students, because the Marquis educated them personally, so he could only teach a few youngsters at one time. Only two or three men made it to the court a year, and there were only ten to twelve students on his estate at any one time.

The Marquis did not have a family, so he was happy to have the young men to teach.

Hubert was also a member of the academy, where he got to know his future best friend, Edmond. Hubert was much older than the others because the Marquis had never sent him to the King's court. Caulmont always told him that he was so talented that he wanted to educate him further. But in reality, they both knew that this was not true; he just liked him more than the others and did not want to let him go.

Secretly, the academy, the Marquis and his disciples studied the past—more precisely, what had happened before the age of the councillors, and what could it be that the councillors were keeping secret. The Marquis and his disciples collected the scraps people found, of which they did not know the purpose. They also studied the old books that remained, which had naturally undergone many transcriptions over time. These books had been written in the old languages, so Caulmont taught the boys ancient English, ancient French and ancient German, which only a few scholars and enthusiastic noblemen could speak, as well as, of course, the councillors.

Often Caulmont left his home for some time, and no one knew where he went. On that certain day, the Marquis arrived home after a multiple day excursion. He sent the students to their rooms and told Hubert to stay.

But Caulmont stared at the fire in the grate for a long time, and until he finally brought himself to speak. This sort of indecision was not typical of him, so Hubert knew that they had something very important to discuss.

"Look, Son!" he always called him son. "The time had come for you to leave, but that's not all. Today I will tell you what the real reason for you all being here is. I will share a secret with you that the others cannot know, and no one else can know either."

Hubert began to feel uncomfortable. He was sorry that he would have to leave the Marquis, whom he loved as a father. And yet, it was not the imminent farewell that occupied his mind most. An uncomfortable feeling overcame him; he was afraid that Caulmont's secret would bear burden on him, and this undesired knowledge would act definitively on his life.

The Marquis looked 'round, not as if anyone could be eavesdropping there. He lowered his voice and leaned in close to his disciples' ear, speaking one sentence which instantly made the boy into a man.

"Fernand de Bellehache, the old King's son, who was the rightful heir to the French throne, was alive." As he spoke this, a huge weight fell from the Marquis' shoulders, but Hubert stared at Caulmont in shock.

"Wh–Wh–What did you say, sir?" was all he managed to stutter.

"You heard me. He was under my protection for a long time, then I had to part from him. Councillor Perrier himself has been taking care of him for a long time."

"Sir, is the Councillor with us?" he asked in disbelief.

"It's not as straightforward as that," the Marquis scratched his head. "When Lefebre took the throne, I made a deal with him. My condition was that we protect the Prince's life, and when the right time came, we would place him where he deserved to be, at the head of the monarchy."

"But, still…how can you entrust him to a man like that? Or do you trust him so much?"

"Not exactly, but I had no choice. Either I deal with him or the Prince dies."

"Then what we did was just a disguise?" Hubert asked in disappointment.

"Not at all. We research our past because it is how I wanted to get close to the Councillor. You can only defeat the enemy if you know them."

"Then Councillor Perrier is our enemy?"

"Not as we currently stand, but I could not hand a single child to an orphanage he controls with a clear conscience. Let alone our precious Prince."

"Sir," the boy asked with increasing confusion, "where is the Prince now?" He looked painfully at the man whom he loved more than his own father. He may have been the richest person in the kingdom, but his life was still a tightrope. At that moment, his robust figure seemed broken, and this made him sad.

"I don't know. The Councillor said that he'd taken him to a secure place. Somewhere no one would look for him, and no one could find him either. And you, Hubert, my son," the Marquis placed his hand on the boy's shoulder. "I'm sending you on a double mission to Paris. The most important thing is that you unite the graduated academics and those favourable to our cause living in the city. You will be their leader. They already know that someone is arriving who will be following my direct instructions."

"And what will my other task be, sir?"

"You will prepare the ground for the rightful King. Before he sits on the throne, he will require your help. Until then, try to be very carefully; find out where Perrier is hiding the Prince.

It is very import that the Councillor does not suspect you, because, although it appears that he is with us now, and more importantly, the fate of our true King depends on him."

"Aren't you coming to the court?" Hubert asked hopefully.

"It's too early, I'd cause suspicion. You will represent me. We will stay in contact through middlemen. When you arrive, report to the Councillor; I think he will offer you the job of librarian. You may go now!"

He was at the door when the Marquis called after him. "One more thing. You know I love you, my son, which is why it hurts to let you go. It is certainly not an easy situation for you. So, I thought you could take your best friend Edmond with you. Of course, you cannot tell him the true reason for you mission either."

"Thank you, sir," the boy replied gratefully.

One week later, Hubert and Edmond stood before the desk of the notorious head librarian Dexter Lalonde. Caulmont had warned them that their noble heritage and Perrier's commendation would not be to their advantage, because the lord of books—as he was often referred to—did not like people interfering in his business. Lalonde did not care for rank, he did not care where someone came from; for him, people were only worth the weight of their knowledge.

And the boys did not dare speak, they just stared at the old man ignoring them. Even seated, his hardy figure was obvious. His skin, the colour of parchment stretched tightly over his face, and his bald head was crowned by a few stray hairs. The chief librarian wore pince-nez on his sizeable nose.

They thought he would never look up from the huge stack of paper towering before him. After a long while, he nonchalantly glanced up at the young men wearing library uniforms.

"Now look here, I don't care who sent you here to pester me," he spoke in a grating voice, "in fact, I don't even care that my predecessor, Councillor Perrier, himself personally came to my office to recommend you. Disgusting!" he slapped the table. "Don't deceive yourselves. You will regret so impudently barging in on my presence. Looky, here's a book," he pointed at an old volume laying on his desk, "then we'll find out what you're worth. Don't come before me again until you've translated it."

The boys left the room quickly. They'd been told that the old man was insufferable, but they hadn't expected this. They went back to their quarters, which ten of them shared. The librarians lived in the castle, like the liquidators, their lives were controlled by serious rules. They could receive leave, days off or any other lenience from the lord of books. Hubert and Edmond spent the next weeks translating the hefty English language book into the common tongue. Apart from shared meals, they never left their room. The others were busy from morning till night in the library, and they translated incessantly.

When they were ready, they entered Lalonde's chambers, which was also his office, and gave him the original book as well as the translation. The old man immediately took their work into his hands and looked at it for a long time. After many minutes, all he said was,

"Alright, now get out of my sight!" Two days later, they received their own room and the right to go out at night. When they reported to the old man again, they were about to express their gratitude when Lalonde interjected crudely,

"Don't think you got it for your greasy faces, or the lords pushing your backs. You received it only for what's in your heads. Lucky that Marquis Caulmont had taught them so well, they thought gratefully of their benefactor."

Then, two long years passed, and Hubert achieved a lot with the handful of people entrusted to him. He established a route of escape from the castle, beyond the city limits. They made the huge tunnels of the old people passable, for which they built a hidden door outside the castle. In the tunnels they stockpiled food, weapons, water and healing herbs so they could have hidden out there for long time in case of emergency. They developed a secret ring of informers. If something important happened in the district, they knew about it almost immediately."

One day, much later, Perrier called Hubert to his chambers. When he arrived, the Councillor was flipping through the pages of an old book.

"Ah, Librarian Godart, please, have a seat. I've called you here because of this book. This is a very unique volume, and only one volume exists. I would like a copy."

"Then why don't you send it to the copiers, Councillor?" Hubert asked.

"Because I want you to copy it. This is a very important book that no one can know about. I trust you entirely. Because I know you and because my good friend Marquis Caulmont recommended you. Take it and copy it, and don't let anyone see it, or I will hold you responsible! Got it?"

"Yes, sir," he replied and carefully took the hefty volume.

They spoke for a few more minutes about library business; then he went back to his room and did not look at the volume till nightfall.

That night, he could not sleep, so he took candle and sat down with the book. Even the title seemed strange to him:

A Brief History of the Middle Ages. "What were the middle ages?" he asked himself and then began to read. The book was in English, and he found understanding the text difficult because the author had lived before the age of the councillors and mentioned many things unknown to him and did not explain what they were. It must have been natural for people back then to know what feudalism, serfdom or the church tithe were, but Hubert could only guess at what they meant from the context they were in. Though he progressed slowly, he thought that he was not sleepy, he would make it through a few pages. As he began to read, astonishment overcame him after the very first chapter, which was replaced by fear mixed with curiosity. He was holding a book that fundamentally hanged everything people had thought to be true of history and humanity till now. He was certain that reading the book would put him in mortal peril, but he also knew that there was nothing in the world more worth the risk than to somehow get his hands on that volume. Perrier had entrusted the knowledge of the past he kept hidden unto him. Did the Councillor know what this old volume held? If so, then why had he entrusted it to him? When he finished the copy, perhaps he would have him killed. If he did not know what he had handed over, he would be in trouble later. Sooner or later, Perrier would check the copy and fly into a terrible rage. Hubert quickly swept his fears aside and immersed himself in reading.

Time ceased to be, he could not have said if minutes or hours had passed since he opened the book.

There was a knock at the door—or more precisely a banging. Hubert found it hard to conceive of someone trying to come in. He stood up, went to the door and opened the latch.

"Finally!" Edmond said, as he crossed the room and sat on a chair. "I thought you'd never open up. What's up with you? Is something wrong?"

"No, nothing's wrong," Hubert answered confusedly, still under the influence of the book. "Why do you ask?"

"What do you think? It's noon, and everyone is looking for you in the library. You weren't there for breakfast, and if you could see yourself…you've rings under your eyes; you look like you didn't sleep all night."

"Because I didn't," he started coming to. "But that doesn't matter now. I was reading a book, you wouldn't believe!"

"Who cares about books now? Come, have lunch, you'll tell me all about it there!" Edmond shouted merrily, as he grabbed the armrests of the chair and prepared to leave.

"Look!" Hubert pushed his friend back into the chair, "Be quiet for a little, I'll tell you what's going on. This is no joke, my friend!"

Edmond fidgeted nervously in his chair, but he knew his friend well enough to know that if he was saying 'this is no joke', then something was wrong indeed. And this introduction did not bode well.

"Perrier called me to his office yesterday and gave me a book to copy," he began at the start. "He said that if anyone found out what the book contained, I would be done for. This volume," he pointed at the large book on the table.

"I began reading it last night, and I only stopped now when you knocked. It tells of times that are dreadfully similar to the times we live in now."

"What do you mean?" Edmond looked at his friend in disbelief.

"Could you please explain what you're blabbering about?"

"The age the book describes, that the author describes as the Middle Ages, is exactly like the known world, just without councillors. It only differs in a few details. For example, the Russians have a tsar instead of a king. But most details are unnervingly similar. People live in kingdoms in castles, warriors wear armour, and many things are just like they are now. Do you get it now?"

"I'm not stupid, I understand the meaning of your words; I just can't believe it."

"You must read it too!" Hubert said compulsively. "I need to make a copy that I can give to Marquis Bastien de Caulmont."

In the days following their conversation, Hubert was barely seen in the library. He even had Edmond deliver his meals to his room. They told the others that he'd caught a terrible cold, so he could not leave his room.

He was almost done with the copy, and the second copy too, when the problem happened. Misfortune appears in people's life, like lightning, suddenly, and it is impossible to prepare for.

This was no different, yet that calm summer's day started peaceably enough. He was progressing so well with the copy that he allowed himself breakfast in the canteen. He waited for Edmond for a while, but his friend did not arrive, so he ate alone.

He poured himself a cup of tea and slowly spread the butter from the tip of his knife onto a piece of toast. He liked hearing the knife's edge crackle on the hard, toasted bread. He hadn't even taken a bite when Edmond came running to his table.

"Big problem, Hubert! Come!" he said in a choked voice. He wanted to ask what the matter was because the fear was written all over his friend's face.

They ran along the corridor and sprinted up two flights of stairs. They didn't stop till they reached Hubert's door. Edmond ripped it open and shoved his friend inside. The sight staggered him. A man lay on the ground, a huge puddle of blood spreading around his head, which had not even begun to dry.

"What happened? Who is this?" Hubert asked trying to stay cool.

"This is Archbishop Cain Leroy's chief confidant, Gilbert Lacomb," Edmond replied.

As he leaned closer to the corpse, he too recognised Gilbert whom everyone in castle loathed and called him a fink behind his back. He was the King's chief informant.

"How did this happen?"

"When I entered the room," Edmond replied, "this weasel was rifling through the book entrusted to you. He must have had a key to the room. I shouted at him to leave, but he just kept repeating, 'Interesting…Interesting…' I shouted at him one more time, at which he stated that he was confiscating the book and taking it to Leroy, and that we should expect an investigation for stealing such an important book. He also said that we had kept the existence of this volume a secret, and that would be detrimental to our case.

I tried telling him we were acting for the Councillor, and that he would have Perrier to deal with; he said he served the Archbishop Leroy and not the Councillor. So, we began tussling; I didn't want to let him take the book. As we shoved one another, he grabbed the statue from the table you use as a paperweight and tried to hit me in the head with it. He almost managed to; I just managed to dodge the strike, and it just grazed my forehead. I didn't wait for him to strike again. I took the statue from him and hit him in the head with it. I was scared and hit him hard. You see the result here," he pointed at Lacomb's lifeless body on the ground.

Hubert did not answer immediately; he wanted to think the situation through. Edmond shouted at him impatiently:

"Well? What are we going to do? Are we standing here with a corpse till the liquidators arrive?"

"Open the chest and unpack it!" he replied firmly. "Then we'll take this maggot and put him in there. So it was. When they were done, they put the book and the two copies on the corpse, closed the lid and locked it. They took the carpet from before the bookcase and pulled it to the centre of the room to cover the pool of blood. They soaked the blood on the table up with a rag and threw it in the fireplace. Hubert looked around contentedly and then turned to his friend."

"Now we'll take the chest and go to the back garden. There we will go to the stable and take it into the secret tunnel. If we're stopped, I will do the talking. And if I shout 'now', then we leave the chest and run. Are you ready?"

Edmond sighed deeply, though it sounded more like a snort and peered sidelong at his friend.

"Up," was all he said.

They took the huge chest and began. To be safe, they peered out the door first, and when they saw the coast was clear, they crept out into the hallway with their dangerous burden. They made it to the spiral staircase easily. There was never much traffic there, so they began to believe their plan might work. When they reached the ground floor, they went out into a broader hallway leading to the back garden. They'd only gone a few paces when a voice spoke behind them.

"And where might you be going, good sirs of the library?"

They turned to see two liquidators coming towards them.

"We're just taking some trash down." Hubert replied coolly, as the liquidators reached them.

"Right," said the older one inspecting the chest. "And if you're taking trash down, why is the chest locked?"

"Just a silly habit," he replied, nonchalantly, forcing himself to be calm.

"Then open it and let us look inside!"

"The truth is that it contains secret documents that we must burn in the yard, which is why it's locked." He felt that this was a weak excuse, but it was the best he could come up with in the moment.

"Show me, I'll take the risk!" the liquidator said dryly.

"Here, take the key!" He handed it over and glanced sidelong at Edmond.

When the liquidator bent over the box, Hubert shoved him as hard as he could. The liquidator stumbled against his companion, and they both fell to the ground.

"Now!" Hubert shouted, and they both ran like crazy. They crossed the hallways in seconds. By the time the liquidators got off the ground, they were out into the nearby garden. Which is where the next stroke of misfortune befell them. As they barged through the door, they found themselves face-to-face with the chief librarian. Dexter Lalonde stared at them with his usual withering expression.

"What are you waiting for?" the old man shouted. "Run, before they get here!"

"Please accept our deepest grat–" Hubert was about to answer, but Lalonde did not let him finish.

"Run, you fools!" The boys took his advice. Like lightning, they crossed the courtyard and entered the stables. When they closed the door behind them, they heard the chief librarian talking to the two liquidators.

"Don't go towards the stables, they didn't run that way; they went through the gate."

The boys quickly opened the hidden door in the last paddock and disappeared down the tunnel.

From that day forth, Edmond la Forge and Hubert de Godart ceased to exist, but Henri and Jules were born.

"Jules, Jules," Henri said gently shaking his friend. "Come and eat, the meat is getting cold!"

"Thank you, just a second," Jules replied. He found it difficult to wrench himself from the shadows of the past. He took his portion and sat a little to the side, leaning his back against an old tree as he ate. Meanwhile, he listened to the happily chatting company. The dominant voice was Ponga's as usual.

"Can you imagine, I once saw a little dog that had a perfect triangle-shaped black mark on its forehead?"

"Where did you see that?" Fabian inquired.

"I can't tell you that," the knight's voice belied sadness. "And anyway, evil men finished that poor innocent creature."

This Ponga is unbelievable, Jules thought, *on the one hand, he's fast as lightning; on the other, he has a child's enthusiasm for animals.* Slowly their good spirits abated, and everyone was overcome by sleep. The fire was barely a flicker now, and Jules still stared mesmerised at the intimate flames that burned just like they had in the fireplace of Bastien de Caulmont a long time ago when he'd still been called Hubert de Godart and Henri Edmond la Dorge.

Chapter Fourteen

The Queen's knight was not in good shape. His hands were bound at the wrist, and the rope looped around abeam in the ceiling, while heavy manacles pulled his feet to the ground.

He could only whimper from the pain now. Councillor Garcia stood lackadaisically before the knight. What he had discovered was nothing new, but today's interrogation had confirmed what he had already known. Apparently, the knight was Queen Esmeralda Lopez's lover among other things. The Queen had sent him to kill Teresa, and Archbishop Oscar Martinez also served the Queen.

The Councillor had been interrogating Lopez for over two hours, and he had been transformed into a mass of bleeding flesh.

"Alright, that's enough," Garcia said to the executioner, "Kill him quickly!"

The hooded man hesitated for a moment.

The Councillor knew that some executioners liked to continue toying with their victims for their own satisfaction, even though there was no more information to be got out of them.

"Now!" he said firmly, and the hooded man quickly picked up a knife and cut the knight's throat with a well-oiled movement. Lopez gave a last gurgling squeak, which was more relief than pain.

There was a knock at the door. Without waiting for a response, Head Liquidator Marcos Sanchez entered. He paid no heed to the corpse or the executioner, he went straight to the Councillor.

"Sir, we must speak!"

The Councillor knew that it must be a very important matter, because Sanchez had not sent a messenger but arrived personally.

"Alright, let's go upstairs. We'll talk there."

"A carriage is waiting outside, sir. I'll tell you what you need to know on the way."

Garcia raised his eyebrows in interest, but he did not reply; he merely nodded. He didn't ask anything else, he would find out what he needed to know presently. He liked it if people acted individually, because nodding Norberts were useless for good work. He knew that the head liquidator would never be disrespectful towards him, and yet, he had made arrangements behind his back. Surely, he had a good reason for this.

The Councillor had not taken the knight to the central prisons in the castle, because he was certain that the Queen would fly into a rage and coax the King into releasing the knight. Garcia had arranged his second secret prison in a small village near Madrid, especially for cases like these.

The trip took at least an hour, which would give them ample time to discuss; the head liquidator seemed to the thing could not wait. As they got in, the Councillor looked questioningly at Sanchez.

"Sir, the Queen is enraged."

"So what? That was to be expected," the Councillor answered offhandedly. He looked out the window. The road was lined with olive trees. He like these plants, some of them were perhaps as old as Atlantis, and he wondered at the ancient gnarled trees who defied time.

"This is true, but we did not think she would call in the forces loyal to her and have Teresa kept in the castle, like a prisoner," Sanchez imparted the bad news coolly. He had not been hired to lose his head in a crisis. These were the times when he was most needed, and he was very much aware of that.

"And what does the King say of all this?" Garcia did not take his eyes from the row of trees as he spoke.

"Nothing, he does not know yet."

"Alright, assemble the liquidators, and we'll rearrange the power dynamic."

"With your permission, I've already made arrangements. I think 50 soldiers will be enough; it would be unfortunate to cause too big of a commotion."

The Councillor suddenly turned to Sanchez. He had ascertained many times that he made a good purchase with the head liquidator.

"I see, you acted correctly," Garcia replied. They sat in silence for the rest of the trip; they'd spoken of all they had to say. Neither of them was the kind of person to say more than absolutely necessary.

Teresa stood before Esmeralda; her knees trembling. The Queen sat in a comfortable padded chair, resting her hands on her belly. Beside her stood a monster of a man, Captain Urbano Gonzales, grinning disrespectfully at Teresa. Teresa felt that this time she would not merely suffer the usual ridicule, but that her life was at stake. Terrified, she glanced around Esmeralda's over-decorated chambers, as if there were someone else there who could help her.

"So, it is true, what they say, that your throat is so sick that no sound comes out your mouth?" Esmeralda asked mockingly.

Teresa nodded fearfully.

"Well, if you say so…Though I am certain that Captain Gonzales could do a thing or two to you that would get your tongue wagging. Isn't that right, my captain?" she turned to him smiling.

"Sure thing, I've an idea or two, my queen," the Captain replied constantly scratching his groin.

"You think you can outsmart me, missy?" Esmeralda went on. "I've had pen and paper brought. I will ask questions, and you will write down the answers. Got it?"

Teresa nodded and thought that Garcia's plan that she had a sore throat was all in vain. If she had to right now, then she would have to lie in writing, and she didn't know if she would be able to.

The Queen motioned to the Captain, and he immediately brought a little table and a chair onto which he roughly shoved Teresa. Then, he placed a piece of paper, ink and a quill before her.

"If you dare lie, you will not leave this room alive," Esmeralda said raising her voice.

"What happened to Sir Demetrio de Lopez?"

Teresa scribbled on the paper with a trembling hand, "I don't know, I haven't seen him."

"You lie, you little bitch!" Esmeralda shouted. "Don't you understand that your life is at stake? I'll ask another way then: what did the Councillor do to Sir Lopez?"

Teresa wept as she wrote, "I don't know, I was just picking flowers in the meadow. I didn't meet anyone."

"Gonzales, start treating her, but be gentle for now!"

Gonzales moved behind Teresa and began massaging her neck, and then suddenly he grabbed her breast.

"So, either you talk, or I'll rip the clothes of you right here and now and defile you!" he whispered in her ear.

"Leave me alone! Leave me alone!" she cried. "I didn't do anything, I didn't see anything."

"Well, well, Captain." the Queen smiled. "Did you hear that? It's a miracle, the little lady can speak again! She is certain to sing us the truth now."

Teresa knew that she couldn't deny it any longer, and that she would soon reveal everything. Of course, that would not improve her situation at all, but she felt her strength waning. All she cared about now was for this nightmare to be over as soon as possible.

Suddenly, the door was flung open, and Pedro Garcia stormed into the Queen's chambers.

"Your Highness! What am I to make of this?" His voice revealed not so much surprise but anger.

"I was looking for you everywhere, but you disappeared, so I was forced to ask Teresa what had happened on the hunt." The Queen's eyes radiated defiance, she didn't want to hide that she'd been interrogating Teresa.

"What do you mean what happened, my lady?" the Councillor said stupidly. "Did anything at all happen?"

"Careful, Pedro Garcia, I'm not in the mood for jokes. One of my most faithful men, Sir Demetrio de Lopez, has disappeared."

"And? How should I know where your man has wandered off to?"

"It seems you are more stubborn than I thought. In case you didn't know, Captain Gonzales is one of the greatest warriors in the kingdom, and if I order him to get the truth out of you, he will do it without question." Esmeralda looked contentedly at the Councillor, she felt that she had finally trapped him in a corner.

"Well, well, do you have a new pet?" Garcia turned dramatically towards the Captain.

"Councillor, if you don't watch your tongue, I will rip your head off," the huge captain said and placed his hand threateningly on his sword hilt.

"And it talks too," Garcia said acting surprised. "Though it says stupid things, it does talk! Now look here!" he switched tone, and his words became piercing. "Perhaps you can count too. Outside the door are Head Liquidator Marcos Sanchez and 20 of his best men. Anyone who tried stopping them on their way here is dead by now. In light of this, I would think twice what I do next, and what I say to the Councillor if I were your son."

"Well, my lord," Urbano Gonzales' bravery fell to pieces in a matter of seconds. "Well...So...I'm sorry...I didn't want to be disrespectful to you."

"You maggot!" Esmeralda hissed towards the Captain. "That's what your loyalty is worth?"

"My lady," the Councillor interjected, "loyalty in the bedroom has its limits; you of all people should know that." The brazen insult struck Esmeralda, like a slap in the face. After all, it amounted to the same thing; her face turned ruby red.

"How dare you...?!" she hissed. She struggled to recover herself.

"Teresa," the Councillor said, "will be leaving immediately. Teresa, Head Liquidator Sanchez is waiting for you outside; he will take care of you. Go!" Teresa looked gratefully at the Councillor, and then ignoring the rules of etiquette, she ran out of the room.

Garcia confidently approached Gonzales and stood with their faces all but touching.

"My dear captain, you may leave too now. And consider yourself very lucky that you are able to do so."

The soldier looked confusedly at the Queen, then slowly turned and headed towards the door.

"Come back immediately, you cowards, or you'll have me to deal with!" Esmeralda threatened, but the Captain was in no mind to risk his life.

As soon as Gonzales left the room, the Councillor approached the Queen's chair, produced his dagger, held it to her face and began gently moving the blade from one eye to the other. Then in a hoarse, restrained voice, he spoke,

"Do you see this?"

"Yes," the Queen forced the word out. She would have done a lot of things to be a bit further away from that blade.

"If you dare hurt Teresa again in any way, then I will cut the foetus from your body with this very knife."

Esmeralda could not speak in shock, she just stared at Garcia's razor-sharp knife.

Aleksandr Petrov dressed slowly in his grey Councillor's uniform. He had not used the uniform during his travels. He felt safer that way; he wanted to get a taste of real life anyway.

If he arrived in Moscow as a Councillor, then he would have to immediately report to the court with a military escort. In this way, however, he could spend two days in the inner district without anybody being aware of his presence. He lodged at The Old Fox Inn where the food was decent, and the beds were acceptably clean. Petrov stood up and examined himself in the dirty mirror in the corner of the room. The uniform suited him well; he had always aspired to wear it, and now his dream had come true. He knew that when he stepped out of the room, his life would change forever. Before he went upstairs to his room, he asked the Innkeeper Mihail Barov to come to his room. Barov begrudgingly promised that he would, but he never came. *No matter*, Petrov thought, *the uniform would teach him respect.* He wanted to interrogate the proprietor of the busiest place in Moscow as the Councillor because he wanted precise information, and who would dare lie to a councillor?

Soon, there was a knock at the door—not too quiet, but not banging either.

"Come in!" he said loudly and took a last look in the mirror before sitting down on the only chair in the room. As he took his place—as comfortably as he could on the uncomfortable piece of wood—the innkeeper appeared in the doorway. Astonishment showed on Barov's face, but by the time he spoke, he managed to collect his thoughts.

"Councillor Sir, you do me a great honour of lodging with me. If you'll allow me to…naturally you are my guest, consider your bill settled." The man bowed slightly as he spoke, subconsciously accepting his inferiority.

"Alright, come closer!" Petrov replied dryly. "Tell me, what are the rumours in Moscow nowadays?"

"Well, my lord," the innkeeper said scratching at his thick grey lick of hair, "mostly about you, or about when the new councillor will arrive, and what sort of man he will be."

"What do you mean what sort?"

"Well…How much tax he will collect, how ruthless he will be, and excuse me, sir, it's not me saying these things, just the people."

"Alright, I'll go down to the inn now, and you will collect my clothes. I will send somebody from the castle to collect them."

The Innkeeper nodded so vehemently, his head nearly came off. Petrov left him and went downstairs. As he entered the drinking area, the bar went silent, and everyone stared at him. He pretended not to notice the mute astonishment and sat an empty table saying,

"A cup of wine!" The silence persisted. He looked coolly around and asked, "What is it people, have you no tongues?"

Suddenly everyone began acting as if he weren't even there; they took their eyes off him and stared at the ground. Slowly people began talking again. The Councillor heard snippets of conversation from all directions,

"See, there's the new Councillor!"

"Isn't he too young?"

"Kurilov will eat him for breakfast."

"Better watch out. He's got such an evil stare."

Petrov knew that he had nothing else to do but wait. The news of his arrival would fly like the wind to the castle. He quickly drank his wine because he figured he had ten minutes at the most till his escorts arrived.

He was not wrong. Soon a liquidator officer and two of his men entered the inn. The officer immediately spotted Petrov, which was not hard to do in his uniform. He approached the table and saluted.

"Councillor Sir, Commander Igor Lermov at your service."

"I am Councillor Aleksandr Petrov. Is my chariot ready?"

"Yes, my lord, but how did you know…?"

"Commander Lermov," Petrov interrupted him, "I thought it likely that you did not wish to carry me to the castle in your arms."

"Excuse the stupid question, sir!"

They headed out. The chariot stood directly outside the Old Fox. The officer steeled himself and spoke to the none-too-friendly Councillor once more,

"Councillor Petrov, may I make a remark?"

"Out with it!" Petrov replied curtly.

"I think it is very dangerous for you to walk the city streets alone; my job is…"

"Enough," the councillor interrupted for a second time. "If you want to be on good terms with me, never question my authority. Your job is to obey me. I need liquidators, not babysitters. I am mature enough to blow my own nose or tie my own shoelaces."

"Yes, Sir Councillor!" Lermov replied obediently and determined never to warn his superior again, even if a house was about to collapse on him.

Petrov looked over the city from the carriage window. He liked Moscow. The Russians loved their land, their cities, and the royal capital most of all. And he felt more Russian than he did Atlantean. The years spend in service in the Russian Kingdom had tied him here forever. He liked this wild, raw, honest land. People here did not pretend; they loved madly or hated keenly, but lukewarm indifference was foreign to them. Moscow was completely different from the big cities of the known world. Even in the inner district, the houses were made of wood because they kept the cold out better than stone. The constructions of thick planks gave the royal city a fairy-tale atmosphere. Poorer people mostly painted their houses a walnut colour, while the wealthier residents preferred the far-more costly cherry brown hue, which seemed to contain a hint of light crimson in it. Petrov preferred the walnut brown because its infinite simplicity was closer to his heart. As the poor far outnumbered the wealthy, most of Moscow's districts were unified in colour. To his great disappointment, the journey was a short one. He would have preferred to look over the streets a while longer, but they arrived at the only stone building in Moscow—the huge royal castle.

A decorative welcome party awaited him by the gates. The court dignitaries stood in a half-circle. In the centre stood the crimson, broad-shouldered, middle-aged Commander Zahar Tihanov in full armour; next to him the sickly thin Archbishop Arkagi Simenov who naturally wore his ceremonial gold-threaded gown. There was also the robust, sharp-eyed Head Liquidator Nikolai Choronko in his red and black armour. Petrov knew them all, as he had served for several years in Moscow. After customary introductions, they headed for the King's Hall, where well-laid tables awaited him.

He was not surprised that they had prepared a feast of this scale at such short notice, since he knew that almost every day in the castle was spent in reckless decadence. After ceremonially greeting the King, they dug into the late lunch. When all were fed and watered, and many cups of vodka had been drunk, the King rose to speak. The ruler, Jurij Genisei, was around 50, and must have been handsome at some time, but the many barrels of vodka he'd consumed in his time had left their mark on his face. But his features still hinted at his younger self.

"Welcome Councillor Aleksandr Petrov! The motto of my reign is calm, and we all here strive to keep it. The much-respected late Councillor Oleg Voszinoj did the same. We hope that we can find a common voice with you too, and we can guard the peace together. To your health!"

The dramatic toast was followed by many more, and every one of them was followed by a drink. Later, Petrov went out onto one of the balconies to air his head out. He lit a pipe and tried to think of nothing, merely to enjoy this day. He'd not been out for two minutes when Queen Jelena Genisei joined him.

"I hope, Councillor, that you too are a fan of peace. Here in Moscow, we do not like unnecessary tension." She was not what one would call beautiful. Her thick figure was barely contained by her extravagant clothes, and her giant breasts were all but spilling out. Her round face, double chin and watery blue eyes did not make her more attractive either.

"Of course, my queen. You know that as a councillor, I am the King's servant. But would you tell me, why does everyone fear I will disrupt the peace, as if the councillor weren't here to serve the people's interests?"

"You're right," the Queen said combing back her thick blonde hair, "but you know, we were very pleased with your predecessor, Councillor Oleg Vosinoi, and there are so many terrible tales of councillors in other countries."

"Who do you mean, my queen?" Petrov asked innocently.

She tutted nervously. *Perhaps he's playing the innocent on purpose*, she thought.

"Well, let's see." She pretended to think a little. "For example, Councillor Perrier, who is a notoriously bloodthirsty man, who thrives on chaos."

"My Lady, you shouldn't believe every rumour you hear."

"You know," the Queen went on as if she hadn't even heard his response, "I am a mother, and it is very important to me that my princes grow up in peace. They are at a most critical age now; Pavel is 14, and Valentin is 16."

"And Ivan?" Petrov asked, though he knew well that Jelena did not like the prince born of her husband's first marriage. "He is 17 if I am not mistaken."

"Yes, of course he needs peace as well," she replied icily and then finished the conversation just as abruptly as it had begun.

"It was nice talking with you, Sir. I hope you understand me."

"Of course, my lady," he replied, though he understood nothing.

Late that night, Petrov surveyed his lavishly decorated chambers with pleasure. It was true that the ornate decorations were a little much for his taste, but slowly, gently he would shape the place into his new home. He especially hated the golden-coloured minutely carved furniture, though he knew they'd only been trying to please him by burying him under all this extravagance.

He poured himself a glass of water; he couldn't even think of any other drink after the amount of vodka he'd imbibed. All the experiences had fatigued him, and he wanted nothing but a warm soft bed. He was beginning to undress when there was a knock. *Who could it be at this hour and without an announcement?* he thought. He picked up his clothes and called out,

"Come in!"

A servant appeared in the doorway. The man stood there confidently; there was no mark of the servile slouch typical of servants. His figure was powerful, and his clothes were worn but clean. Petrov was surprised because only staff in decorative uniforms were allowed into his chambers. This man surely did some lowly job somewhere no noblemen could see him.

"My lord, I must speak with you," he said determinedly, showing no signs of shame or shyness.

The Councillor raised his eyebrows questioningly at the unusual guest.

"You know that it is a bold move to barge in here dressed like that?"

"My lord," the stranger went on without answering the question, "I am the man behind the man!"

Petrov froze. He needed a moment to recover his senses.

"Come in and sit down! Pour yourself a drink, my friend, and speak!"

While the stranger crossed the room, the Councillor's thoughts raced insanely around his head. Naturally, he knew who the man behind the man was, but there had not been a case of a councillor entrusting someone with something like this for at least a century.

Councillors had the right to choose someone from the Atlantean people working around them to help if they felt their life was threatened. At these times, they would tell the person who it was that wanted to kill them. With this, they helped those that followed.

Petrov was reminded of the famous tale of Councillor Normando Palacios. Palacios had not been in the Spanish castle for a week when an executioner in one of the torture-chamber spoke to him. He said that he was the man behind the man, and that his predecessor had entrusted an important secret to him. It was unusual for an Atlantean to infiltrate the tight circle of executioners, as it was an inherited profession. Back then there were so many people jailed, that more and more executioners were needed, so positions opened up to gain insight into the secret world of the dungeons. Palacios' predecessor had found out that there was a special prisoner in a hidden dungeon of the castle, who was a perfect double of King Serfin Arreola. The ex-councillor had spoken to him, but the prisoner claimed to be the King's twin brother, and he had lived there since he was a child. After the conversation, the Councillor did not feel safe now that he knew the King was keeping his own brother prisoner. He appointed a man behind the man, and two days later, he mysteriously disappeared. Hearing this story, Palacios decided that he had to remove the King who dared defy Atlantis. He organised a coup and placed the prisoner who was the rightful ruler on the throne. The new

King did not execute his brother, but locked him in the same prison cell he had been in. Serafin Arreola lived for many decades more. Apparently, his brother visited him daily and enjoyed listening to his pleading. "Brother, forgive me! Please, let me loose!" Serafin pleaded, but he never saw the light of day again.

Everyone in Atlantis knew the tale, but Petrov never would have dreamed that such a thing could happen to him too. He was not happy. Not least because the appointed man behind the man also had to report to Atlantis what he would tell the Councillor. *It's like being kept on a short chain,* he thought moodily.

"What did Councillor Vosinoi have to tell me?" Petrov asked with more than a little concern.

"He said to be careful because your life is in danger. The situation is that Oleg Vosinoi was afraid he would be murdered."

"By whom?"

"Unfortunately, he did not tell me? This is all I can say."

"I see. Where can I find you if I need you?"

"I work in the kitchen. Ask for Vassily the cook." Petrov nodded. He ended up pouring himself a vodka after all.

Leaning back in his chair, he sighed. *Well, so much for the much-commended peace and calm in the court*, he thought.

Chapter Fifteen

Roy Davis was still a little troubled by the ill-fated introduction of the day before. Commander Mallory had certainly not taken to him, in fact their relationship could not have begun more badly. True, it was not their fault they'd been late, but Claire's father had not even given him a chance to explain what had happened.

It was 7:00 in the morning. Roy noted that there was increased activity in the castle. At this time, the lords were usually still asleep, and only staff went about the corridors. But on that day, everyone was scurrying around like mad. Roy was late as Councillor Ed Wilder was expecting him at 7:00 sharp. The old councillor always went into a rage if he arrived later than agreed upon, but curiosity got the better of him—he wanted to find out what all the commotion was about. He stopped a guard he knew who was coming the other way.

"Hey Will! What's the ruckus?" Roy was in a good mood, but the smile soon waned from his face because he saw the guard was distraught and almost afraid. Before answering, the soldier looked around furtively to check if there was anyone else in the hall.

"Didn't you hear? Everyone's talking about it."

"About what?"

The guard looked around once more and lowered his voice to a whisper:

"Someone tried to kill His Highness, King Mortimer."

"What the…" Roy gasped. "And?"

"Thank God he escaped," the guard blurted and left hurriedly. Roy took the stairs two at a time all the way to the fool where the Councillor's chambers were. He was at the door when the clock struck quarter past. He shuddered. He knew that Wilder would be annoyed by the situation, and he would get a heavy scolding for his tardiness. When he entered, he saw that the Councillor was sitting at the table, and he wasn't in a bad mood at all. Quite the contrary.

"Come in, my son! Would you like a morning drink?" Wilder pointed at a bottle of spirits. Roy did not dare refuse lest the Councillor's good mood abate.

"Thank you, my lord," he replied and then carefully poured himself a little cup. He couldn't remember the last time the old man had offered him a drink.

"You've heard the rumours around the castle, my lord?"

He knew that he could not keep such a thing a secret, and he was certain the Councillor knew of it already.

"Of course. The event is most regrettable, but it has a silver lining."

"And what's that, my lord?" Roy asked and drank out the contents of his cup.

"The assassin was none other than Liquidator Hugh Jones. Now that whelp Horan is in trouble, in fact this is unpleasant even for the strategist. On one part, he appointed Horan head liquidator; on the other, Sir Lemmy himself is responsible for the King's safety." A mirthful smile spread across the Councillor's face. Roy's head was spinning. "So, one of the hooded figures from the night before had been the actual assassin...He couldn't keep this secret because the King might be attacked again, but he could tell either because he would get Claire mixed up in it."

Not to mention that he didn't know who to tell anyway as the Councillor might be responsible for the whole thing. One thing he'd learned during the years he'd worked in the castle was that no one could be trusted. If he acted, that was the problem; if he didn't, the problem was even greater. This was crazy!

"Is there something wrong, Davis, my son?" the Councillor asked noting Roy's expression.

"Of course not, my lord," he replied hurriedly, "I just don't understand who would do such a thing."

"Well," Wilder broke into a smile again and did not seem at all surprised, "who knows?"

The whole morning was a serious endeavour for Roy, making sure the Councillor did not notice how put out he was by the attempted assassination. That morning they had a lot to do. Wilder sent Roy to the royal scribe, who sent him back with a pile of reports. It took two hours to go through and organise them. Wilder ran an expansive spy agency in the castle and, of course, throughout the whole Kingdom, and on that day, he 'only' had to look through the past weeks material. Truly confidential information never made to the scribes, in fact those were never even written down. Roy was often witness to the reporting of one of the Councillor's informants, but the old man took care of the especially important conversations himself. He did not mind that Wilder left him out of political matters, as he knew well that it was not safe to know the secrets of great men. By the time they finished, the treasurer arrived, who gave an infinitely detailed account of the kingdom's assets and liabilities.

At noon, Wilder finally let Roy go to lunch, and he immediately ran towards Claire's house while silently talking to her.

"My dear, I have to talk to you," he began.

"Is something wrong, my love?" Claire asked frightfully.

"We must meet, I'm on my way over."

"It's no good." He heard the fear in her voice.

"My father will be home for lunch any minute now, and after what happened last night, it would be better if you two didn't meet today. He will forgive you soon, I know him."

"Look, Claire! There was an attempt on the King's life, and it was High Jones, the man whose conversation we overheard last night. We're in trouble. If we keep quiet, our life is not in danger, but we cannot do it because they may make another attempt on his life. I think we need to talk to your father. I haven't got a better idea."

"If you think it's the best solution, it must be so, but we have to stop talking now, he's home."

"Alright, but don't say anything to him, I'll do the talking. I'll be there soon."

Roy arrived presently at Claire's house. He took a deep breath and then taking the knocker rapped it on the thick wooden door.

Commander Mallory's grumpy face soon appeared in the doorway. He looked at him as if he were a cockroach, but he said nothing, waiting for Roy to speak.

"Good day, Commander Sir! Could we exchange a few words?" Roy groaned, hoping that Mallory did not notice his anxiety.

"If you want to apologise for last night, you had better be on your way." The Commander was impatient, not just because they'd been late, but because Roy had disturbed his lunchtime, which he could have spent with his daughter.

"It's not about that. Believe me, I would not disturb you if it wasn't vitally important."

"Grand words! What do you know about life?" Mallory barked, but he motioned Roy inside.

Claire waited for them in the dining room kneading her knuckles nervously.

Her father looked at her and said simply, "You knew he was coming?" She just nodded. The Commander sighed deeply and shook his head, and then begrudgingly offered Roy a seat. Roy did not dare speak till the old man gave him permission.

"Let's have it then!" Mallory said this as if he were having a tooth pulled.

"Sir," Roy began, "you remember that we arrived back late the day before last?"

"I told you, if you start making excuses about that, I will throw you out the door. I hate it when someone can't take responsibility for their actions!" the Commander shouted. Roy thought he was going to pass out at any moment.

"I don't want to make excuses, sir!"

"Daddy, wait for what he has to say and only judge him afterwards," Claire chided the irate Commander.

"So," Roy began meekly again, "the night before last we had dinner in the Two Lions in the suburbs."

"I know where it is," Mallory interrupted him.

"After dinner…well, I don't know how to say this…so we went to a place few metres from the inn where…well…" Despite his best efforts, Roy went red as a beet. "We go to kiss."

It's a doorway where people from the street cannot see us.

"Spare me the details, or I won't be responsible for my actions," Mallory growled, clutching the table with both hands. He could barely control himself, but he did not want to ruin his daughter's happiness. He knew that it would be difficult to grow to like the boy, but he hadn't imagined it to be this much of a challenge.

"It's not easy to say this, believe me! When we were there in that certain doorway, two men appeared. We could not see their faces, as they were hooded.

Not on purpose, but we were in earshot of their brief conversation. What they said is as follows,

'Don't forget that you are not a nobody, your name is Hugh Jones!'

'Are you sure I can do it tomorrow?'

'I've told you he leaves the city tomorrow. He said so in the council meeting. I was there, I heard. Either tomorrow, or who knows. You won't get a better chance.'

'I see. I'll do what I have to.'

'Alright, I'm trusting you. Don't forget, this will be no murder but a heroic act.'"

A short silence followed. Mallory feverishly racked his brain for a solution, as he had no doubt that the young couple were in mortal peril. Like everyone, he too had heard of the attempted assassination.

"Sir," Roy broke the silence, "we turned to you because we didn't know what else to do."

"You did well," the Commander nodded. "But you didn't tell Ed Wilder I hope?"

"Of course not. I don't trust him, and I didn't want to involve Claire either."

"Good. For now, go back to the castle and act normal. I will make arrangements."

"If I may be so bold as to ask what your plans are, sir?" he asked with concern.

"The castle is a snake pit where your lives have no value. There is only one person who can help us. I will go to him and organise a meeting. You will have to tell him what happened too. The truth is that you did the right thing in telling me; if you'd told someone else, you'd be confessing in a torture chamber now, and your lives would be brief."

"Daddy, will you tell us who you're meeting?"

"Of course, Sir Lemmy Black."

As the Commander spoke the strategist's name, the young couple shuddered and could read the fear in each other's eyes.

Sir Lemmy Black looked down on the naked corpse of the assassin Hugh Jones. The young man's thin, muscular body lay peacefully on a bench in a hidden cell of the dungeon.

The strategist was able to read from dead bodies. It was not black magic, just common sense. A body could tell a million stories; for example, it could say what the person had done during their life. If it was unkempt, if its hands were rough, then they were probably labourers, which meant they were neither nobility nor a priest. If the corpse was covered in scars, then they were a fighter or a liquidator; maybe a soldier, knight or nobleman. Many illnesses left their mark on bodies as well, in almost all cases they also revealed what the cause of death was. The strategist had been studying Jones for some minutes, who was revealing a lot about himself.

The assassin's muscular, toned body was typical of liquidators; constant training and fighting had carved every last ounce of fat from his body. The scar covering Jones' body were also common among liquidators. On his right shoulder a fresh wound. *A strange mark,* Sir Lemmy thought, as it was hard to identify what had caused it. It was not a like a burn, but scars caused by weapons looked different too. It seemed like a mark from torture, *but who had tortured him? And why only there? Anyway, who would dare harm a liquidator? Maybe Horan...No that could not be. Or maybe the Councillor? And why had Jones not mentioned this to anyone?*

The strategist had examined Jones' room and then taken all his things as well as his corpse to the cell. Liquidators had no personal possessions, just a change of uniform, civilian clothes and some hygiene items. What did he spend his spare time doing? He was certain that if he knew this, the motive would become plain. He personally interrogated the liquidators who knew Jones, but no one could provide any worthwhile information. They all said that Jones had been a recluse; he did not go drinking with them or visit pleasure girls. This was strange because liquidators commanded a lot of respect in the city and only rarely had to pay in inns, and girls often sought out their good graces. Presumably because the liquidators protected the girls, for which they received extra services. The castle turned a blind eye to these things because everyone knew that it was an amenity that made the job of liquidator especially attractive.

Black was so deep in thought that he didn't even notice Commander Mallory enter the cell. The old man waited a moment and then cleared his throat.

"Oh, it's you," Sir Lemmy said startled. "Did you bring them?"

"Of course. They're waiting for you upstairs."

As they left, Mallory questioned their agreement once more. "Sir, everything will be as we agreed, right?"

"You can trust me," the strategist replied. His voice was not harsh; he knew the Commander was very worried about his daughter, and he had good reason to be.

When the two men entered the strategist's office, Claire and Roy shuddered. The young couple awaited Black on their feet, though there were enough chairs in the room. The strategist humbly crossed his office and sat down. Then he looked at the old commander.

"Mallory, you may leave us now."

Three of them remained. Black knew that till he spoke, the youngsters opposite them would not open their mouths. He waited purposefully—increasing the tension. Not out of pleasure, but his years of experience had taught him how to get information from people under pressure. Those who were afraid had mostly honest gestures, and sometimes revealed more than their words could.

"Sit down," he broke the tense silence, "and tell me everything! Don't leave anything out, not even details that seem insignificant to the point in hand."

"My lord," Roy spoke, "Commander Mallory said that our conversation would remain confidential."

"This is so."

"And, Sir, well, how should I put this. We also know that the Commander has told you everything we told him."

"Right, but I want to hear it from you now." Black leaned back and looked fixedly at Claire and Roy.

They began recounting the events of that night. First one of them spoke, then the other; they finished each other's sentences. After the first few sentences, it became clear to the strategist that they were telling the truth. He'd heard a lot of lies in his life and had almost always sensed the untruth. He was like a hound dog on a trail: he could just sense it. Black finished listening to the story; he didn't interrupt their narrative even once. When they had finished, he looked at them significantly.

"You heard his voice, so you would recognise it if you heard it again," Black asked looking sternly at them.

"I don't think we would, sir." Roy and Claire looked at one another. "They spoke in a whisper, and we only heard them for a little while. We'd thought of this as well, but we wouldn't dare take part in an identification. We couldn't say for certain who the perpetrator was."

"Then this is all you are able to tell me?" Black asked, who showed no sign of being disappointed by their answer. Whatever he thought, he kept to himself.

"Yes, sir," Roy replied; a drop of sweat beading on his forehead.

"Do you know what all this means?"

"Yes," Roy replied. "It means that the assassination was ordered by a member of the King's council."

"And can you deduce from that?" the strategist asked. His blank expression did not reveal anything.

"That our life is in your hands, sir," Claire spoke.

"If you tell someone about this, we're as good as dead."

"You're right, my lady," Black nodded, "but my silence will not be enough. You must also keep quiet about what happened, and then no harm will come to you. One more thing," he said piercing Roy with a strange stare. "Why have you told all this to me and not to Ed Wilder?"

Roy wiped his constantly sweating brow. He knew that his answer could define their future—in a good or bad sense equally.

"Because I do not trust him."

"But you are his aid."

"That is why; I've had time to get to know him well. I wouldn't dare place our lives in his hands. Furthermore, maybe he is behind all this."

"And if I was behind it?" Sir Lemmy inquired.

"Well, sir," Roy replied flustered, "then we're done for."

"And yet you still came here?"

"We had to take the risk. And we thought you were the least likely," he replied.

"Looks can be deceiving, the councillors are fond of saying," the strategist ended the conversation, with an expression on his face that may have hinted a benign smile, "but this time you were lucky."

The person who planned the attack is panicking. He waited all night for Jones to report to him on the outcome of the mission. By dawn he knew that something was wrong. He imagined fearfully as the strategist's men appeared at his door, and he would have to use the poison. If he had to, he would rather kill himself, so he would not be interrogated. But they did not come, so he began to hope again. Maybe everything went well, and the liquidator had not come for some other reason.

Later, walking the streets in the morning, he heard the talk of the town about the unsuccessful assassination attempt on the King. They even said that the assassin was dead. The news bore down on him, but it could have gone worse. He clutched the invitation to the King's special council meeting in his hand, given to him not long ago by a messenger. If they met, Sir Lemmy would be in the dark, as if Jones hadn't spoken, and the dead don't talk, the strategist could not get to him. But why was it that the most skilled person in the Kingdom, this Bloody Sir Black, served the wrong cause for the wrong person? But he would show how to defeat the Great Sir Lemmy Black. If not right now, then a little later, once the storm blew over. *Right now, the most important thing is to stay cool,* he thought as he passed through the castle gates. The guards parted for him respectfully, and they did not suspect him. They would not have let him pass so easily. He felt braver already; he was almost in a good mood. It had not worked, but the moment would come when luck would not be on Mortimer's side.

Chapter Sixteen

As they travelled, the landscape changed gradually around them. First, the mountains disappeared, and the vegetation changed. The forest of huge trees were replaced with thick brush and little saplings. The landscape became increasingly wet. Later they had to take their boots off because the water was up to their ankles. Mud sucked at their feet as they struggled to lift them with each step. Jules warned them that they would soon reach the swamp, and everyone would have to be careful because it could quickly swallow a whole man in places. The sounds of the wild changed too, and the chirping of the birds was drowned out by the croaking of frogs. They sat down on a reasonably dry meadow to eat a late breakfast.

"Shouldn't we hunt?" Ponga asked because their supplies were running low, and they hadn't enough for dinner.

"There's no need," Jules replied, "we'll arrive by nightfall, and there will be food a plenty."

"We will arrive by nightfall; we just don't know where," Fabian announced and looked significantly at Jules.

"Have patience for just a little while longer," their leader replied, "tonight I will explain everything. For now, all I can tell you is that the place we are going is very beautiful and safe too."

"We're going to a secret world where persecuted people can live in safety. It is not usual to reveal a hiding place."

"And what if one of us wants to leave," Ponga said contrarily. "If there is one among us, like me, who does not want to live like a hermit among the trees and bushes."

"If you want to leave, we will escort you off the territory, and you may leave to wherever you wish. Does that suit you, Sir Knight?"

"Yes," Ponga replied, "I'll only stay a few days to test, and then I'll leave this fetid swamp."

"I always knew you were a huge whelp, Didier," Henri said expressing the whole company's unanimous opinion.

Only Paul remained silent; his heart was still in that accursed village.

During the next two hours, the water level rose to their knees. The members of the party continued on their way with their boots around their necks, and trousers rolled up past their knees. There were no more paths or runs to be seen, so they had to cut their own way through the increasingly dense vegetation. They agreed to proceed in a single file, because the swamp was getting more and more unpredictable. The slippery mud beneath their feet seemed solid in places, and soft and gooey in others. Naturally, Jules and Henri went first; the terrain was familiar to them. In time, the water got even deeper up to their waists. The field of reeds that replaced the bushes made the going even harder. Where the reeds grew thickly, they had to go around; they could only chop the plants above water, and the stems below the surface made it impossible to pass. As they went deeper and deeper, the swamp showed them yet another face.

From the connected bodies of water, a multitude of little islands emerged. These little bits of dry land where only a few square metres in size, but almost all of them were covered in a blanket of vegetation. Tiny bushes and trees, mostly alder. The strange, exposed alder roots seemed to take well to the water they reached into, this world being too wet for most plants. Jules suddenly raised his hand indicating that they should stop.

"Nobody make any sudden moves, and definitely don't reach for your weapons. It would be best if you didn't speak; I'll do the talking."

In the next moment, someone shouted at them from behind the cover of the bushes.

"Stop! Who are you, and what do you want here?"

"It is me, the leader, and Henri. We've brought people, please come here to me. If you like, then leave the other in cover."

"Are there more of them?" Ponga asked in a whisper.

"Stay calm, Didier!" Henri warned him, who'd had ample proof of Ponga's hot bloodedness in that damned village. "There are many bows trained on us from the thicket, and you can be certain that we are totally surrounded."

"And we just walked into a trap, knowing that this would happen," Ponga complained.

"These people are the guards of our territory, it is their job to keep strangers away. You'd best keep quiet." Henri closed the conversation.

In the meantime, a man appeared and approached them. His clothes indicated that he lived in the woods, a lot of leather and not much cloth. Despite his long hair and scraggly beard, he was clearly very young. As he came near, he recognised Jules and shouted to the other guards,

"Stand down, the leader has returned." Then he embraced Jules and Henri like brothers.

"I'm glad you made it back safe; a hundred more steps, and we'll reach the boats."

"How come? Are we taking boats from here?" Fabian asked in surprise.

"Yes," Henri replied, "from here on the water is deep enough to use boats from transport."

The guards escorted them to some small boats and said goodbye—their duty was done. They occupied two boats because only four people could fit comfortably in one, and they had bags too. Jules, Ponga and Fabian got in one boat, while Henri and Paul along with all their luggage, weapons and clothes got into the other boat.

The following one-hour long boat trip left a lasting impression on all of them. They had never seen anything so beautiful in all their lives. The water formed into little rivers among the dense vegetation. In some places, the trees touched over their heads, and they felt as if they were passing through a fairy tale tunnel that softly leaked sunrays. As they rowed deeper into the area, they saw that the islands had become larger, and that people had built houses on them. These tiny homes surrounded by water made the majestic view even more magical. The houses were built of straw and wood, and each one had its own little garden, and the occupants of the island had made sure to preserve the natural vegetation, so that every house had some bushes, trees and reeds. People got around with boats, so everyone had a little dock where they kept their boats. They wound between so many islands that they completely lost their sense of direction.

The land formed a huge idyllic labyrinth, in which it was a pleasure to be lost. The view stunned all of them, and even the eternally dissatisfied Ponga was rendered speechless until,

"Not too bad, not too bad," he muttered, "but in just a day or two, I'll be gone."

After about an hour, they arrived at a relatively large, almost 500 square metre island that held several houses and a large grassy area.

"This is Central Island," Jules explained. "Here you will get to know many people from our tribe. Later, I will assign you places with families. Those who wish to be alone will be hosted on uninhabited islands, though there will be no roof over their heads there. Oh, and most importantly: there is another larger piece of dry land not far from here; the Happy Island where we drink and talk. Tonight, I will take you there, and I'll be happy to answer your questions over dinner."

By the time they docked, some 50 people had gathered around to greet the newcomers. Jules introduced Fabian, Didier and Paul by their first names. It was not customary to ask people about their past in the swamp. They did not use surnames, and noble heritage did not mean anything. Everyone had equal rights, and everyone had to take part in the shared tasks. Only Jules, their leader was above everyone. After the introductions, the lodgings for the three newcomers were arranged. Several people volunteered to host them in their homes, hoping for hearty conversation. But the introverted Fabian and the consistently dissatisfied Ponga wanted their own islands, accepting the discomfort of sleeping beneath the night sky.

Paul did not want to offend the locals, who were almost fighting over who would host him. Jules had to appoint one lucky family who immediately took the quiet boy home. Ponga was placed on a little island close to the thick flat marsh. Whichever way he looked, all he saw was green, not another island in sight. He was little pleased about the sudden solitude because the past weeks had all happened very quickly, and he hadn't had time to digest it all. Not so long ago, everything had been fine, and he had achieved his life's dream; and then in heartbeat, he'd become a fugitive. He didn't want to stay in this strange village for long; he had no intention of living the boring life of the locals. He wanted victory, gold and pretty women to make his days exciting. Comfortably, he lit his pipe and felt sorry for himself as he stared at the water.

In the weeks they'd been on the run, he'd thought about his father often, who had always been jealous of his extraordinary speed. In fact, it had been the reason he's decided to leave his parents. He never understood why his father was not pleased that Ponga could outstrip him in something. He would certainly be happy if his son achieved more than him. True, he couldn't imagine ever settling down with a family. When he was five, he realised that he was not like other boys. He'd been playing in his favourite spot by the ditch with his friends. They were looking at the little critters in the water—frogs, leeches and insects. He liked the croaking hopping frogs. He became so immersed in play that he didn't even notice the miller's son, Eric, approaching.

"Look what I found, Didier!" the much older boy cried with a malicious smile.

Didier looked up in fright. Eric held an arrow on which many still wriggling frogs were impaled.

"Give me a few of yours too!" Eric said, and then kneeling down he picked a frog from the water.

Didier acted instinctually; he didn't consider that he had no chance against the much larger boy. He jumped at Eric so fast that the boy had no chance to even stand up. Once there, Didier kicked the boy as hard as he could. And Eric tumbled screaming into the ditch.

"Leeches, leeches!" the miller's son screamed and crawled out of the water and ran home crying. The news of Didier's lightning quick attack spread rapidly through the village. Children told their parents, and soon everyone knew about it. There are no secrets in tiny villages.

That night, his father shouted at him. Didier didn't understand why he was so angry at him, as he had done nothing to deserve it.

"If you dare to fight again, I'll disown you! Do you understand?" he yelled besides himself. Didier had never heard him shout before. He'd always been kind and patient with him till then, but after the incident, everything changed. From that day on, Didier often flaunted his special skill, and his father became more and more hostile towards him. Their relationship soured.

Only when they'd been on the run did he understand what had happened between him and his father. When Jules had told him that he was no different in the eyes of the world than a monster, a mutant, then he understood that his father had only wanted to protect him. He had forbidden him to fight because he did not want to lose him. His poor parents did not deserve what he'd given them, but there was no changing that now.

He did not know how much time had passed; he only realised that a boat was arriving at his island. The young boatman took him to Happy Island, which was a half hours ride from his place. The sharp laughter of people could be heard from far away. When they docked, all eyes turned to him, and he quickly made for the only house on the island, which was considerably bigger than the other houses he'd seen. When he entered, everyone went quiet. He looked around. Jules and Henri were not there yet. The house was actually a large inn, full of benches where people drank and talked. He wanted to get a drink in him too, so he headed for the far side of the hall where he saw what resemble a bar. The locals turned back to their conversation, but he felt that they were still watching him. Finally, he reached the bar where a woman stood with her back to him. *She must be the barmaid*, he thought and gently touched her back.

"Greetings, can I get a strong drink please?" he said politely.

"Who do you think you are?" the woman replied. "Everyone serves themselves here."

Ponga instantly flew into a rage and was about to say something truly nasty to the impudent wench when she suddenly turned around. The words stuck in his throat, and he could not say what had happened to him, but his rage suddenly subsided, and he wanted to quickly express something kind, something witty, but he couldn't get a word out edgewise.

"Well, I, the thing is, I didn't know that," as he said it, he knew he'd made a fool of himself.

"Now you know," the girl said sizing him up; then she turned on her heel and sat down at a table from where two men were eyeing him suspiciously.

Ponga quickly looked behind the bar where he found two demijohns and several wooden goblets. He sniffed the first, and the scent of a pleasant fruity spirit reached his nose. He poured himself a triple shot; he didn't want to come back for the next round any time soon, and then he sat down at a table from where he had a clear view of the girl. He took a sip of the strong drink, but he could not take his eyes off the sharp-tongued damsel. He had no idea what was wrong with him, all he knew that she was the most beautiful thing he had seen in his life. "What has come over me?" he asked himself, "I've seen plenty of pretty women in my life, held enough of them too. This girl is pretty, but there are many others more beautiful than her. So then what?" He stared at her thick, cascading, dark brown hair, her full lips, gently curving, slightly round face, shapely figure that bulged subtly beneath her simple yet pretty dress. He kept staring until an old man beside him spoke to him:

"Is something wrong, sir?" his voice held warmth and a hint of mischief.

"Oh, nothing," he replied, but he could not take his eyes off her.

"I see you've taken a liking to our Fifi," the old man laughed.

"Who?" Ponga looked over his manhood offended.

"Well, Fifi, that auburn beauty."

"Oh, so that's her name; well, she's not my type, that's for sure. Imagine, she scolded me not a moment ago, though I gave her no reason to be rude to me."

"Fifi needs no reason to scold anybody."

"She's no beauty," Ponga tried salvaging his remaining dignity.

"Lucky for you," the old man replied, "imagine how you would be staring at her if you actually liked her."

Ponga thought it better not to answer. Then they sat in silence, and Ponga watched Fifi, and the old man did not want to antagonise the stranger further. Half an hour passed in this way, and in that time, all he could think of was what reason he could find for speaking to her. With great difficulty, he steeled himself. He stood up, approached her table where the two young men also sat talking.

Producing his best manner, and the most polite tone of voice he could muster, he said,

"Excuse me, please, my lady, I meant you no offence back there; I just wasn't aware of the customs here."

"No problem," Fifi replied and then turned back to the two men to continue their conversation, but Ponga spoke again.

"I'd like to introduce myself. My name is Sir Didier Ponga," and with a move he'd seen in the King's court, he bowed elegantly.

For a moment Fifi was confused, and she was just thinking of what to reply to the impudent whelp when the larger, more muscular of the two men in her company spoke.

"Get the hell out of here! Can't you see you're bothering us?"

Ponga's blood boiled, but he did not want to make a bad impression on Fifi, so he steeled himself and did not beat the man senseless. He simply replied:

"Do you think I was talking to you, maggot?"

The young man leapt up and leaning in so that their faces almost touched, said:

"Don't take advantage of our hospitality, outsider; no one cares who you are!"

"Leave him, Jaques, you're not going to beat him up here?" Fifi chided the man who was good head-taller than Ponga.

"Don't fear for me," Ponga said producing his most seductive smile, which he had used to great effect on many women, "you should be worried about this walking comet here."

"I'm not worried about you," she replied, "I just don't want Jaques to get in trouble for stomping their guest into the ground."

"No one had ever stomped me into the ground, because I am the greatest warrior in the kingdom, my lady," he announced grandiosely.

As he said this, Jaques' fist was already on its way towards his face. The blow was not slow, but it was no challenge for him to move his head to the side, and grabbing his opponent's arm, he pulled the man. Losing his balance, Jaques fell forwards onto the ground.

"Now you'll get it, you bastard!" Jaques shouted springing up.

Faster than lightning, Ponga placed a punch on his opponent's nose, which broke with a loud crunch, and then, just to make sure, he placed another powerful blow into his stomach. Jaques bent double and sprawled out on the floor.

"What have you done to poor Jaques?" she raged.

"Me?" He started the fight, and I warned him that he shouldn't fight me.

"It's easy to beat the weak," said a man from another side of the room, who then stood up and walked slowly towards Ponga. As he approached, people moved aside and took their chairs and tables with them, clearing a space for the fighter, because everyone was certain that the brawling was just beginning.

"You won't get away without fighting me," said the new challenger who was no giant; in fact he was bout Ponga's size, and his confidence indicated many victorious battles.

"One more lamb to the slaughter," Ponga joked, but Fifi was clearly not taken by his humour.

"Sir, you don't know what you're doing! Please leave while you still can," Fifi pleaded with Ponga.

"Are you worried for me, my lady?"

"Not in the least, but if Felix beats you, which he will, it will be his problem to deal with later."

"It's not enough that you do not worry about me, you underestimate me too? Didn't you see what I'm capable of?"

"Felix is different, believe me, you have no chance." Fifi was visibly worried.

"Enough of this whining," Felix said arriving before them.

Before Ponga could answer, Felix was striking. Ponga was surprised by his opponent's speed. He could barely move his head in time, and the blow grazed his skull. He'd never seen such speed before; Felix was the quickest he'd ever seen, but he wasn't as fast as him of course. The first blow was followed by a second, but Ponga was expecting this one. He knew that he couldn't take this opponent lightly. He grabbed Felix's hand, and even compared to the speed of the strike, struck back faster at Felix's head. Felix collapsed immediately; he wasn't prepared for being struck. His undefended head remained a perfect target for Ponga to strike. Ponga had never fought anyone like himself before; he thought he was the only one who was this fast, but the knowledge that, even in possession of such skills, Felix could not compete with him filled him with joy.

"Well, so much for that," he said looking around, "if anyone else would like to fight, speak now before I sit down."

"But not at my table, that's for certain," Fifi announced loudly.

Before Ponga could answer Jules, Henri, Fabian and Paul appeared in the doorway. Jules looked around and said:

"Dear Didier, can you not be left alone for a single minute? Come, let's find an empty table, and you can ask me all the questions I did not answer you on the road."

And so they did; the companions sat together, and order was returned to the inn. The injured were helped out, and the chairs and table moved back.

"Before we start talking, let's have a drink!" Jules said merrily.

"Then we have to go to the bar because everyone serves themselves here," Ponga said.

"Not necessarily," Jules smiled and called over to Fifi, who was sitting moodily two tables away.

"Fifi, bring us five goblets and flask of spirit please!" Grudgingly she rose and brought it for them and then sat back where she'd been.

"Well, I had to serve myself." Ponga's eyes went 'round. "I tried asking Fifi, but she gave me scolding."

"Well, she'll bring it for some people and not for others," Jules laughed, "after all, I'm the leader here."

"Did you know that Felix, well, he's something like I am, just a lot slower?" Ponga asked rubbing the place where Felix's blow had grazed him.

"Yes, he is a mutant just like you. It's a shame I didn't get here sooner; I could have stopped the fight."

Then the questions began to cascade, while the plum brandy decreased rapidly.

"Who lives in this village, what's it called, how many are there?" Paul was the first to ask.

"There are 200 of us, mostly families chased off their lands, some mutants and ex-nobility make up the tribe. Here everyone must learn to use a weapon. Only we can protect ourselves; there's no one else to count on."

"Excuse me if I ask something you don't want to answer," Fabian said, "but I think a village cannot be maintained without outside help. I'm thinking of basic materials that can only be bought from the outside."

"You are right, I cannot tell you the source, though we need a lot fewer things from outside than you might think. We buy only metals, spices and cloth from the outside; we make everything else here," Jules said with some pride.

"How did you end up here?" Fabian asked the question on everyone's mind. Jules did not reply immediately; he looked into their eyes one by one.

"I won't lie to you, which is why I've told you nothing about myself. If I spoke of my past, then I'd have to reveal other people's secrets too. And that I cannot do. This is true for Henri too."

The questions would not abate, but Ponga was not paying attention any more. He was watching Fifi, who sat straight-backed and tight-lipped all night ignoring him.

Chapter Seventeen

Councillor Alain Perrier was in no hurry. After waking, he took a bath and ate the breakfast brought to his chamber slowly and comfortably. Then he got dressed and even allowed himself the luxury of enjoying the view from his window for a few minutes.

The gigantic trees, the bushes and the lawn showed a continued change of the spring that gifted the royal gardens an abundance of life. The birds sang raucously as if they were trying out the noblemen's children playing in the yard. The gardeners watered the recently planted flower which brought with them the scent of imminent summer.

The Councillor thought sadly of how it had been a long time since he'd last walked, aimlessly, lackadaisically around, and not rushing from one place to another taking care of some business or other. Soon Vincent would arrive, and they would go into the city together. Maybe they would find a good inn and have a hearty meal. *Yes, so it will be,* he decided. He hadn't even figured out what they could do in the afternoon when his aid arrived.

"Oh, I was beginning to think you'd gotten lost, Vincent. We're going for a stroll in the city today, are you game?" he turned away from the window towards Farall who was taking his place on the small simple chair.

"Good morning, Alain! Of course, I am, but my lateness is no mistake." Farall was silent for a moment; he didn't want Perrier to think he wasn't in the mood for a walk, and that he was looking for some excuse now and had only come up with made-up reason now. The Councillor raised his eyebrows.

"Will you tell me, or do you wish me to get on my knees and beg."

"Sorry," Farall replied abashed, "on the way here I came across a greater than usual commotion, so I asked a servant what had happened."

"Get to the point!" Perrier interrupted. Somehow, he got the feeling that his planned excursion was in jeopardy.

"So, apparently King Lefebre is very ill," Farall said.

"And you're telling me this now?"

"Sorry, but…"

"Yesterday, he was fine, I don't get it," the Councillor said wagging his head, "we're going to see the King immediately."

Farall could barely keep pace as he glided towards the King without a word. They almost ran along the way and saw people whispering excitedly throughout the castle. The corridors were filled with fear and hopefulness. Those lords who were close to the King or his closest associates were worried. If the new king was not from their circle, then they would be shunned or worse. Dishonour spread like the plague. Those noblemen, merchants, soldiers and servants in the King's favour now could all fall. Those who'd been in the shadows till now, who'd been barely tolerated till now, were hopeful because if the new king was favourable to them, their golden age would be upon them.

It was hard to look into people's eyes now; it was clear who was on which side.

Farall stared at the people they passed and suddenly felt sorry for the King. For the court, the King was nothing more than the embodiment of power. Everyone wanted something from the foremost person of the kingdom: gold, rank, land, but no one love them. *Ruling must make one lonely,* he pondered as they wound their way through the huge building, *the King has no real friends.*

In the anteroom to the King's bedchamber stood Archbishop Cain Leroy and Marquis Philipe Bertrand who were in a fierce competition of compassion about 'who is more distraught about the King's condition'. The councillors did not slow his pace as he passed them and did not return their greetings but entered the King's chambers forthright.

The King lay moaning on his four-poster bed surrounded by an army of doctors. Perrier approached him directly, meanwhile one of the doctors felt duty-bound to describe the affliction.

"His Highness was taken ill this morning, yet yesterday afternoon he was happily walking the gardens. In fact, he even sunbathed an hour, and..."

The Councillor quickly took the King's pulse looking at the speaker. This silenced the doctor immediately.

"You may go now, wait in the anteroom, and when I'm done, I will tell you what to do."

The doctors left hurriedly; they knew that the Councillor was better-versed in medicine than any of them. During the plagues, they had experienced the extent of his medical knowledge. They would have been completely lost without his useful advice and efficient potions. They didn't understand why the Marquis had called them before he'd notified Perrier.

The King's pulse was beating rapidly. His forehead hot with fever. His ragged breath was interspersed with violent coughing fits. He'd sweated through his nightgown and was rambling incoherently.

"Councillor Sir! When is the next King's council? I don't want to be late...I don't want to be late...I don't want to be late..."

"Relax, my lord! You must rest now! We will hold no council till you recover."

"Alright, alright," Lefebre replied, and in that moment he fell into a deep slumber.

Perrier told the doctor waiting outside what they had to do. Besides constantly keeping a damp towel on his forehead, he was not to be exposed to old air, and all the servants should heed this when airing the room. He told one of the doctors to report to his chambers in an hour, he would make a potion by then, and they would discuss dosing then. Furthermore, one of the doctors was to report the King's condition hourly. When he finished with the doctors, Marquis Bertrand and Archbishop Leroy barred his way.

"Dear Councillor," Leroy began completely ignoring the presence of Farall. They spoke about the future of the kingdom as if he weren't even there. "We understand that you are depressed by the King's condition, so we forgive you for not greeting us. Believe us, we too are most concerned, but at these pressing times, it is our duty to remember the kingdom. We expect you in the Council room for a meeting at 12:00 sharp."

"Why was I not informed of the King's condition sooner?"

"What do you mean?" the Marquis asked.

"It's a simple question. You told the doctors before me," Perrier's voice was so icy that Bertrand immediately defended himself.

"Excuse me, but we were suddenly confused, which is probably why we forgot to tell you, and we were about to send for you when you arrived. Can we count on you at noon?"

"Of course," the Councillor replied, then turned on his heel and left the two gentlemen staring after him.

Perrier slammed the door to his chambers with such force that Farall shuddered.

"Those meddling, conniving snakes! This is what they set their mind to?" the Councillor raged. Farall had seen the Councillor angry many times, but he usually avoided vulgar expressions. Truth be told, the present situation was far from usual.

"The King was not in good shape, and this brought the subject of an heir into light with regard to the kingdom," the Councillor went on a little more calmly.

"What could be wrong with him?" Farall asked. He hadn't wanted to bombard the Councillor with questions when he'd been examining the King.

"Probably pneumonia," Perrier replied, but his thoughts were elsewhere.

"Will he survive?"

"Maybe. The next few days will decide. Vincent! Go down to Head Liquidator Luc Moreau and Commander Azor. I want to see them immediately."

Farall left quickly, and the Councillor was left alone with his thoughts. He was no longer in the mood to stare aimlessly out the window at the resplendent gifts of spring. He closed his eyes and tried to think through the situation rationally.

It was clear the Marquis Bertrand and Archbishop Leroy had not warned him because they'd wanted to waste time. In this way, they had time to send envoys to the noblemen loyal to the Marquis and also to mobilise their soldiers. Another fay or two, and a significant army would arrive at the gates of Paris. Not least, the later they warned him, the greater the chance of the King dying would be, as he would lack his immediate care. They would use the council meeting to discuss the question of an heir.

The situation was not encouraging—he came to his final conclusion—but not without hope either.

About 10 minutes had passed, and Farall stood in the doorway with the two liquidators.

"Come in and sit down," Perrier began. "I'll be brief because time is of the essence. Have you heard of the King's sudden illness?"

The men nodded.

"Then you know how delicate the situation is. Soon troops will arrive at the city, who will all support Marquis Bertrand and Archbishop Leroy. If this happens, and the King dies, then, Luc, you must not oppose them!"

"I don't understand, Councillor," Head Liquidator Moreau said, "our job is to support you in everything."

"This is true." Perrier smiled, who welcomed the head liquidators unwavering loyalty despite that fact that he'd never doubted him, but the most obvious action is not always the best one.

"Could you explain?" Moreau did not understand what the Councillor was getting at.

"If you resist, then their numbers will crush you anyway, and I will not be able to use you further. So, you will surrender; in fact it would be best if you requested a meeting with the Marquis and gave him your support."

The head liquidator listened to this increasingly unsavoury plan with tight lips.

"Look!" said the Councillor looking Moreau in the eye, "there are difficult tasks in life which must be completed. Can you do it?"

The answer was a mute nod.

"So, you let them know you're switching sides, and in the meantime you will help me leave the city. Commander Azor and a few loyal men will escort me to Marquis Bastien de Caulmont, and I will organise the counterstrike. Luc, you will await my message, and then you will see how useful it is if one has an entire division in the enemy's ranks."

Head Liquidator Moreau was beginning to like the idea, and he showed it by smiling slightly, though he was not at all prone to such gestures.

"That's it for now," the Councillor said finally, "and one more thing," he called the liquidators headed for the door, "Luc, I would like you to speak to the Marquis immediately."

"Why so urgent, Sir?" Moreau asked.

"Because I want to go to the Council meeting with the Marquis already thinking the liquidators are on his side."

"And why is that good for us?" Farall asked.

"If this happens, then Bertrand will become over confident, and those with too much confidence tend to underestimate their enemies and make costly mistakes more easily," the Councillor said this with such ease, he could have been talking about the weather. He was visibly in his element.

At 12 o'clock sharp, Perrier appeared in the King's Council room. Everyone was already at their seats. Only the throne towering over the end of the table stood empty. To its right, Marquis Philippe Bertrand's face was ablaze with confidence. Beside him sat Head Liquidator Luc Moreau. He looked as if he'd just bit into a lemon, and his usually grim appearance was moodier than ever. To his right sat the young General Marcel Durand, behaving as he always did, that is, in no way at all. On the other end to the right shivered old Raymond Petit, the head of the guilds avoided eye contact with the other, revealing, despite his intentions that he was not among equals. On the left, the first empty chair was the councillors. Beside him sat the widely grinning Archbishop Cain Leroy, bearing no sign of the anxiety he had displayed by the King's chambers earlier. To his left sat Treasurer Leopold Dubois looking left and right from one council member to the next.

Perrier swept over to the table and sat down, speaking only after he'd taken his place.

"Gentlemen! I am eager to hear why you have convened this council. I hope that the condition of our beloved King has not inspired you already to flock about his corpse like vultures."

"Perrier could not resist any opportunity to provoke the Marquis or the Archbishop. And he'd achieved the desired result. Bertrand's head turned beet red, and Leroy out a stifled snort of derisive laughter."

"Councillor Sir!" the Marquis attempted to respond calmly. "Do not pretend that you don't know that our job is to deal with the King's affairs. Even if we are torn apart by worry as we do so. I am certain that His Highness will recover, but if he does not, then we have to do our jobs."

"If the King dies," Leroy took over, "excuse the subject, but the throne passed by ancient law to the next male heir, who is the six-year-old Pascal Lefebre. In this case, a regent will have to be appointed. The majority of noblemen and my humble self would choose to appoint Marquis Bertrand to this post." Leroy looked triumphantly into Perrier's eyes, then suddenly averted his gaze because Perrier's cold, penetrating gaze was almost painful. He collected his courage and went on.

"I know that in many countries it is the Councillor's task to appoint a person to this post, but excuse me, my dear councillor, we would only accept the Marquis to this position. Our job now is to vote on the possible appointment of Marquis Bertrand. I would like to hear your opinions on the matter." When he finished, he leaned back in his chair, but carefully avoided Perrier's eyes, and he did not want to have to jerk his head away again.

"I agree with the idea that we should appoint someone; foresight is always wise. I also think that Marquis Bertrand is the most suitable person for Regent," Head Liquidator Moreau said clearly; then he stared out the window so as not to have to confront the stares of the others.

General Marcel Durand answered in outrage,

"How dare you, Head Liquidator. You speak as if the King were dead already. In war, we do not choose a new commander while the old one lives."

"But if the old one becomes unable to lead, someone takes their place right?" Leroy grinned complacently trying to protect his new ally from challenges of politics.

The opinions of Treasurer Leopold Dubois and Raymond Petit did not matter much. So, when they gave skirting answers, no one bothered them. And the Councillor purposefully waited to give his answer last of all. When everyone was staring at him, he felt it was time to express his position.

"I find your effort truly commendable, gentlemen, to find a solution to a problem we do not have as soon as possible. But King Lefebre is still alive. I find it tasteless to debate such a matter like scavengers 'round carrion."

"Councillor, take that back or…"

"Or what, my dear Marquis?" Perrier was polite, but everyone felt the deadly menace in his words.

"I don't think anyone here wants me to report back to the King, if and when he recovers, how you all wished him dead." The Councillor shook his head.

"That's a lie." Leroy snapped fearfully.

"It's not me you have to convince but our king."

"We're not going to fight one another, are we, gentlemen!" Bertrand said. "Perhaps Councillor Perrier is right, and the most important thing is that we have a united King's Council. What do you suggest, Councillor?"

Perrier noted with a pleased expression, that things were once again going his way, that is he had gained a little leeway. He looked around dramatically before speaking,

"A cart pulled in two ways at once will go nowhere," he said significantly.

"Could you speak more clearly, sir?" Leroy asked the Councillor.

"For the weak of mind in the room, I'll say it another way." Perrier looked at Leroy. "Marquis Bertrand is right, we need to be unified. I will forget today's discussion, in the case the King recovers. And you will only raise the question of the throne again when the time comes."

They agreed on this.

John Neville, the president of Atlantis, was exhausted as he ran his hand slowly through his thick grey hair. He hadn't been able to relax even for ten minutes all day, and it was almost 9:00 in the evening. Opposite him, on the other side of his desk, sat his potential heir and student, James Mulligan. Recently he had felt that they were losing control over things. He suspected that many considered him a dithering old fool, maybe even Mulligan did, but he knew that this unfortunately was not the case.

The known world was in turmoil. Soon the winds of change would sweep the lands and upend everything they had built till now. He felt that he could not relax even for a moment; there was still a chance to grab the reigns.

"James, I know you haven't stopped all day, but we have to discuss matters." Though Mulligan did not show it, he was sick and tired of being worked late into the night day after day.

"The messenger had finally arrived from the Kingdom of Russia with Councillor Petrov's message saying that everything had gone smoothly. Though it was strange that everyone was manically preaching peace and calm. I think it strange as you know nothing particular has happened there in recent years."

"Strange," Mulligan replied, who always wanted to please the President as best he could. "It is as if they were trying to hide a serious problem. How can they believe that they can hide anything from the Councillor? Despite all that, it is an encouraging beginning. According to Petrov, the introductions had gone well. It seems the Russian Court has accepted him."

"I think so too," Neville replied, "but the English-French situation is becoming increasingly worrisome."

"Councillor Perrier is an experienced man, and he is not worried at all," Mulligan said impatiently. "The two countries have not fought for a long time; they've had enough experience to know what happens when two equal military forces clash. The end result is peace without victory and a long recession."

"I still don't understand what the strategist wants, but you are right. We can trust Perrier," Neville replied, whose gaze had wandered off for moment. He was looking at the Stradivarius. The instrument stood in its case.

"The Spanish situation is far more critical," the President went on, "according to Pedro Garcia, Esmeralda, the Queen had lost her mind."

"She's a crazy woman, but the Councillor will sort things out," Mulligan replied massaging his temples.

"I know many people think I'm not what I used to me. Believe me it is not so," Neville stared into his student's eyes. "You too have to learn the practice of questioning everything. Many great empires have fallen because after centuries of rule they thought their power would last forever. If they hadn't lost their focus, then they could have prolonged their reign. The order of the world is change; everything passes."

"If that is so, then we have to bow before the inevitable," the student drew the conclusion.

"People are mortal," Neville replied staring into space, "but we always think in term of eternity. We cannot make do with less."

Chapter Eighteen

Ponga spent the night awake on his tiny island. It was dawning, but he remained sitting there listening to the frogs' croak. Some people are annoyed by the night-time song of animals, but he loved it.

Maybe it was because he had grown up around here. He couldn't say if his village was close to this swamp, but it was certainly no more than a few days ride. Their area had been filled with lakes of all sizes, so the night-time atmosphere of the swamp was not unfamiliar to him.

He scratched his head and thought through the events of the previous day for the hundredth time. There was no two ways about it, he had made a complete fool of himself in the inn the day before, though Fifi had played a significant role in it too. How could he have messed it up? What had he done wrong? If he could start it over again, what would he do differently? These were all questions that made no sense. What had happened, happened, and could not be changed. He knew that it was pointless to get hung up on the past, but it is one thing to know and entirely another to feel it. The problem wasn't what the people around him would think of him. He didn't particularly care that his new-found friends, Henri and Jules, thought he was a conceited idiot, because they had thought that of him before the fight. The issue was that he had messed up so badly in front of Fifi. They had not even begun their relationship, and he'd buried himself at the introduction.

Sitting there on the island, he couldn't quite understand what was happening to him. The world was full of women, who mostly appreciated him, so what was he getting worked up about. He mulled over this for a long time until it suddenly became clear to him—he would do anything for that girl. Even after what had happened, he couldn't wait to meet her again; despite their brief and stormy encounter, he missed her terribly. He saw no sense in it. How could someone who he didn't even know and who he'd seen not long ago leave such feeling of want in him? He imagined that he knew what love was. He'd felt it, not often, but he had. But since his encounter with Fifi, everything had changed; until that moment he'd seen her in the inn, he had not known exactly what love was. But he knew now, and the knowledge filled him not with happiness but with desperation. Until then, his life had been, if not calm, but in a certain sense, peaceful at least. There was no connection, or person whom he had to worry about, and now he had it; instead of sleeping peacefully, he was awake and in turmoil over this woman. If this was love, he didn't want any of it, thank you very much. The problem was no one had asked him what he wanted. Finally, he came to a decision. In the morning, not too early, say around 9:00, he would get into his little boat and go to Happy Island. And then, somehow, he would set things straight. Fifi would certainly be there because the others had said that she basically ran the only inn on the islands, though she received no money for it because everyone worked for the community on the islands. *It was a strange inn, that's for sure,* he thought of the island, *who ever heard of an Inn where you didn't have to pay for drinks.* Fifi did not live on Happy Island, but she was working there from early morning so as to be ready to open in the afternoon. He found this out from his friends.

He had no idea what he was going to say to her, but he was certain that things could not be worse than they were currently.

Fifi was up early as was her custom. She was used to dragging herself from her warm bed around 5:00. Quietly, she crept out of the house. As the exit opened from her room, she never woke her parents who slept in the back room. She crept silently, like a cat, because the thin reed divider only served as a visual barrier. She was barefoot, and the dewy grass softly stroked the soles of her feet. She changed hurriedly and put on her sandals and untied one of the boats. She used the oars carefully and lowered the paddles carefully into the water pulling softly. When she was further away, she rowed with more force. In ten minutes, she arrived on Happy Island. She liked the long morning hours because there was no one around the inn, and she could be alone. Fifi undressed comfortably and bathed herself in the cool water. She could do this without fear as the reeds behind the house provided a perfect cover. She'd cut the plants from around the shore herself, giving her a few square-metre bath, where even those passing close by the island in boats could not see her. After bathing, she had breakfast, but she was still early for the day's chores, so she made herself a tasty refreshment. The lemonade was from her own recipe. She added a lot of lemons, fresh mint leaves and finally sweetened it with honey. Taking the drink out onto the front porch, she sprawled out in one of the chairs. She stared at the swamp glinting in the early morning sun and could not get enough of its beauty. The rays of light seemed to slide along the surface of the water and weave themselves among the myriad shades of green foliage.

Sometime she was haunted by the dark shadows of her past; at these times, memories broke upon her unexpectedly. Then, there on the porch, she remembered that accursed day, two years ago, the horror of which would torture her for the rest of her days.

On that day, she had been tending to her flower garden. Back then, she had not simply been called Fifi but Sophie de Montfort. She carried a flower-patterned flowering can, stepping carefully among the flowers, watering each in turn. She didn't care that the hem of her pretty dress got muddy, worst that could happen was that her mother Lucille de Monfort would scold her, and she would listen silently to why an 18-year-old girl shouldn't behave like a child. When she was going towards the well to refill her watering can, the sound of shouting came from the house.

"Although a nobleman is not obliged to pay tax to another noble, I would still do it, but the harvest was so bad last year, and there is nothing left." She heard her father's desperate words.

"I don't care about your excuses," Marquis Gilbert de Bilon's son, Julian, threatened, "the army my father keeps for the King is expensive, and every nobleman must contribute. I've warned you several time, if you've no money, what did the peasants sow in the spring? And the villagers here are too fat anyway. Starve them a little, and then the little tax my father asks of you won't be a problem."

"I cannot do that. If the people can't sow, then we can't reap, and there will be famine in the villages."

"Don't contradict me!" Julien thundered. "I will be back in the afternoon, and if you don't have it by then, I will take what is mine by force."

Then the Marquis' son stormed out the door, followed by his men. Julien spotted her. Sophie was speechless with shock.

"You'll see how strict I can be," he said as he strode away from their house.

She ran panic stricken into the house. Sophie found her parents in the living room. She had never seen her father as distraught as he was then. Leopold de Montfort sat collapsed on the chair, and he seemed much older than the 45 five years he had seen. His wife stood by his side stroking his head when Sophie appeared in the doorway.

"What's wrong, Daddy?" Sophie asked scared of his response.

"Oh, nothing serious, just the usual scuffle between the Marquis and myself," said Leopold trying to downplay the issue.

"Daddy! I'm not a little girl any more, and I heard everything anyway. What happens when he comes back in the afternoon?"

"Nothing," her father smiled, but it was a weak and uncertain expression, "we will argue a little, and then they will leave. Go to the kitchen now; your breakfast is ready."

"Yes, Daddy," she said, but she was in no mind to obey him. The moment she closed the door, she pressed her ear to the other side.

"Leopold," her mother said, "what are we going to do?"

"My dear, there is nothing beyond these five villages, and the people are very poor here. I cannot let them starve to death just because all the money in the world is not enough for the old Marquis' lavish exploits. You know this is not about any kind of army, but I, who am much weaker, would still give if I had any to give with."

"And if he does burn the villages, if he does as he promised? He was angrier than usual today. He never said he would come back in the afternoon before," Lucille flustered.

"My dear, we have nowhere to go; we are nobility after all; he cannot do as he pleases with us. Please, calm yourself, everything will be alright, I promise."

To this very day, she didn't know how she could have believed her father's financial optimism. Perhaps she'd been too young or truly wanted to believe what he was saying, or maybe it was her mother's acceptance of her father's calming words that convinced her. Who knew, but somehow, she believed what her father said. She ate breakfast and then went out into the garden to flowers once more. She didn't even notice that her mother had forgot to scold her for her muddy dress. Soon, she forgot about the morning fight and did as she usually did on a bright spring day—spent the day in the garden and only went inside for lunch.

In the afternoon, she heard a great commotion and shouting from the house. She ran inside quickly and found her parents waiting for her in the living room.

"Look, Sophie," her father said placing his hand on her shoulder and looking sternly into her eyes, "I will have to go now; you will lock yourself in the house with the servants. I will be back soon." His voice was full of worry.

"Leopold!" Lucille's voice shrilled, "you're only stepping out of this house if I'm going with you. I won't let you do anything stupid."

At that moment, one of the servants barged in screaming,

"Help me, my lord! Julien de Bilon's men are burning the village. Many are dead, hurry!"

Her parents looked at each other, and her mother nodded visibly.

"Alright," Leopold said to his wife, "I'll be very careful."

"I will be taking care of you, let's go!" Lucille replied and then turned to Sophie. "Sophie! Stay in the house, we'll be back as soon as we can," she said hurriedly kissing her daughter and then running out of the house.

Sophie was terrified, but she was certain that the house, surrounded by the thick oaken fence and locked door, was safe. She was left alone; though her father had ordered the servants to guard her, they had all run home to take care of their houses and loved ones. The terrible noises did not stop, the shouting crying, death rattles came through the walls, and she tried plugging her ears but could not strike the horror from her mind. After a while the commotion abated, and she went outside and stared at the garden gate. She really wanted to see her parents again. Suddenly the latch opened, and she almost squealed with joy, but when the door did not open, there was a loud banging.

"What the hell?" She heard a man's rough voice. "This is locked."

"Since when has a lock stopped you?" another voice asked, and she recognised Julien de Montfort.

She wanted to run inside, but the men broke the door down with one kick and entered the garden.

"Where are you off to, pretty one?" Julien asked with a mocking smile, "our company does not displease you, I hope."

She tried to run away, but one of the men caught her arm and pulled her powerfully to him. She felt the sour stench of his sweat.

"Do you remember what I told you?" Julien looked at his prey with watery eyes, "I told you I can be very strict."

"Throw her to the ground and hold her fast," he ordered his men.

She tried to protect, but the four men held her tightly. They lay her on her back; two men held her arms to the ground while two others held her legs. They caught her knees and pulled her legs up and apart towards her head leaving her groin exposed. Julien tore her clothes off with sadistic delight; he took off his belt, pushed down his trousers and roughly penetrated her.

She struggled vehemently, but they held her steady and punched her too. When she felt Julian's manhood inside her, she began to squeal with pain. But the worst part was that from now on she would be a shunned woman who was no more than a slut. Julien enjoyed his dominance; he enjoyed lording over her, doing whatever he wanted. He was so excited by the situation that he ejaculated quickly which made him angry. He stood up and spoke as he pulled up his trousers.

"I think the girly has a big appetite, one is not enough for her. It's your turn now." He pointed at one of his men. "I'll hold her." The man lay on top of her and then a third. Her strength was gone, she could resist no further, she just wept quietly and let the violence be perpetrated upon her. When she thought it could get no worse, the last man climbed atop her; he was called Spotted Mike because of his face.

"Come on, spotty! Give 'er hell!" They encouraged him. The pockmarked man seemed to lose his mind at the sight of the naked prostrate girl.

Sophie felt such disgust that her stomach churned. The ugly man's bad breath and the pain in her groin made her swoon. The worst was yet to come. The man must have been bothered by his comrades' raucous encouragement, he could barely shove his half-erect member into her.

The others began to ridicule him,

"Do you need some help, or can you manage it alone?"

After a long while, the man began to relax, and his member stiffened in her chalice. He leaned over her, but he did not kiss her; he just twisted his tongue in her mouth.

"Enjoy it, you bitch! Enjoy it, you bitch!" Michael shouted as he climaxed.

The men left, but she just lay there in the dust, feeling like her heart had been wrenched out, and she was just a chewed-up piece of meat in the dirt. She didn't remember how long it took till she could get to her feet. Somehow, she staggered into the street, and half-conscious she searched for her parents. This is how Jules found her—naked, bloodied and glassy eyed. She kept saying she had to find her parents. Jules had gone to the village with some of his men to collect supplies. When they arrived, the Marquis' henchmen were nowhere to be found. Jules helped Sophie find Leopold and Lucille de Montfort. Fortunately, they were alive, though they had been beaten senseless.

Meanwhile, Sophie collected herself somewhat, she was clothed and could wash the blood and dirt from her body in a nearby yard. She asked Jules that he keep her shame a secret when her parents recovered their senses, and that he was to mention it to no one. Later, Leopold and Lucille told the swamp people exactly what had happened that night. Jules promised them that he would take them to a place where they could begin their lives anew, although their rank would not matter there. Her parents didn't need long to decide; a few minutes later, they were on the road.

Two years had passed, but she, who had once been Sophie, now Fifi, could not accept the advances of any man. Julien de Bilon had exiled love from her life forever.

Ponga thought that the time would never arrive when it would not be embarrassing to go to Happy Island. He figured it was about eight o'clock. He collected his few belongings and sat in the boat and began the journey. If he had known exactly which way to go, it would still have taken him more than half an hour to row there, but without knowing where they are, he arrived well after nine o'clock. He could see Fifi busying about on the large balcony, and she had spotted him well before he reached shore, but she pretended not to notice him. From the dock he went up the hill to the inn, yet he still had no idea what he was going to say.

"Good morning, *mademoiselle*!" He opened, none too originally, though the niceties must be observed.

"Good morning!" She almost apt towards him, with no intent of masking her distain.

"Why are you here, when you know full well that I only open in the afternoon?"

"Well, so, you know, how can I put this? I'm here—you've done it now, you stupid cretin," he said to himself, "because I wanted to speak to you in private about last night."

"There's nothing to speak of, Jacques and Felix got the sharp end of your foolish heroism. It's easy to hurt the weak."

Ponga was upset by her words. He had not begun the fight, in fact he'd tried to avoid it. How could she accuse him when it was a downright lie? But at the same time, he felt that this was not the time or the place to argue, or he would have come here in vein.

His mind raced over what to do with this vicious cat of a girl.

"Anyway, I have no time to listen to excuses," Fifi went on, "I have a lot to do."

"And if I help you," he asked pouncing on a last thread of hope, "then will you listen to me afterwards?"

For a moment, Fifi pondered this. "Alright, we have a deal, but don't come whining to me that you have to do a woman's job."

"I promise I won't complain," Ponga laughed.

They quickly got to work; first they took the chairs on the balcony and put them on the tables. Then Fifi brought two buckets of water and started mopping thick floor planks. Ponga had clearly not done much mopping in his life as he constantly upset the bucket.

"Sorry, it wasn't on purpose," he said after every blunder, "I'll wipe it up right away."

Fifi giggled quietly and helped the hapless Ponga. When Ponga slipped over in his eagerness to help, they both laughed out loud. When they finished the balcony, they went inside and did the same with the inn floor. They laughed so much, their tears began to flow. They washed up the dirty goblets and cleaned the backrooms. By the time they were done, it was passed noon. Suddenly she turned to him and said,

"It seems we are done with everything. I need to go back to my parents because lunch is surely ready. You kept your word, and you can tell me why you are here."

Ponga had almost forgotten why he was there. He had never felt as good as he did that morning with Fifi. The question caught him off guard, and suddenly he didn't know what to say. He only knew one thing—he didn't want to ruin the day by saying something stupid.

"Forget it, I don't want to start making pointless excuses. I'm new here, and I don't know the customs yet. I'll come back in the afternoon and try to make peace with your friends. Will you help me?"

Fifi smiled gently.

"I can try, but now you should go before someone sees the two of us here and misunderstands."

Ponga was a little hurt that she didn't want to accept being seen with him, but he did not show his disappointment.

"Of course," he replied and went to leave, but he turned back after one step. "Fifi, can I help you tomorrow too?"

"Alright, me at the same time," she replied and then headed towards her own boat.

Ponga felt happiness the likes of which could not have imagined before. He hadn't even left, and he could barely wait to return to Happy Island—to Fifi.

Chapter Nineteen

Vincent Farall locked the door to his room behind him and crossed to the room to his one and also favourite chair and sat down.

The dawning spring sun cast its last rays through the window providing him with enough light to light a candle. If it were pitch black outside, he thought, he would have to bring a torch from the hallway to light a candle and then take the stinking smoking piece of wood back into the hall. Luckily, he escaped this predicament. He took a book from the little table by the chair which he had begun reading that morning. His enthusiasm for books was his only passion. The Councillor knew of this and so had arranged for him to have access to the royal library. He considered himself very lucky because not many people were allowed among the King's books. Unfortunately, only the Councillor and the King were allowed in the restricted section, and it held the most exciting books. When Perrier really wanted to spoil him, he smuggled him a book from there. It was such treat he had been reading that morning, and he'd been waiting all day for the night to come, so he could throw himself at the book. Before he began reading, he remembered that Perrier had warned him to be very careful as Marquis Bertrand had become completely unpredictable. He'd made Farall promise to lock his door for the night. He always closed the latch, and he seemed to remember doing it just now, but he got up anyway and went to the door to check.

On the way back, he took a bottle of wine from the shelf. *There is no greater pleasure,* he thought, *than drinking wine while reading or reading while drinking wine.* He smiled at his own word joke and curled up in the chair pouring himself a cup. He enjoyed how the pleasant nectar soothed him. After a few minutes of daydreaming, he could resist the book no longer and was about to immerse himself in the sea of letters when there was a knock at the door.

He was startled. No one ever came by at this hour except the councillor, and he always announced himself after knocking. After a few moments, they knocked again. More forcefully and impatiently now. He quietly stepped to the door and listened with bated breath.

"Well, what is it? Knock louder!" He heard the tense whisper, which was soon followed by more clattering at the door.

He seemed to recognise the voice of Cain Leroy. He was frightened if Leroy was ordering people about; it followed that there were several persons out there. And Perrier had warned him to be careful of the Marquis whose greatest ally was the Archbishop. He ran back to his chair and tried to think, but nothing came to him. He could not escape through the window, as he was on the third floor, and there was no point in shouting, as no one would hear him. Terror paralysed him entirely. He had no idea what he was supposed to do. If they wanted to, they could easily knock down the door. He had to find some excuse, but what could he say not even knowing why they were there. That's it! He'd talk to them without opening the door.

"Who is it?" he asked forcing a note of confidence into his voice.

"My Lord! Councillor Perrier's called for you," came the reply.

"I've gone to bed, tell him I need some time to get dressed."

"My lord, the Councillor said it is an urgent matter. I must escort you to him at once. I'll wait for you here, hurry!"

"Then wait!" He shouted through the door, afraid that if he protested, they would suspect him and start breaking down the door. At least this way he had a little time, though he had no idea what to do with it. Suddenly he grabbed a quill from the table, dipped in ink and opened the precious book he'd been reading. On the first page he wrote,

"Alain!
Archbishop Leroy is in front of my door with his men.
If something happens to me, please help!
Vincent"

He closed the book and approaching the window and opened it. When he looked out, he felt dizzy, but the fear had imbued him with strength he could never have imagined. By the time he knew what he was doing, he was standing outside on the ledge, inching slowly along towards the next window with his back to the wall. As he crept along, he heard his door being broken down with great force, and he quickened his pace. Reaching the neighbouring window, he tried pushing it in. He knew that if he failed, he was done for. On the third push, the window moved, and taking courage from this, he leaned against it with all his weight, as a consequence of which he fell into a room. He heard shouting, but he didn't care much. He crossed the dark room with a few bounds, opened the door and ran down the hall.

From behind him, he heard his pursuers leave his room and give chase. He also heard the Archbishop shouting to his men,

"I want the bastard alive!"

He didn't even dare look back, and his mind raced feverishly. He had to reach the Councillor's chambers, but he might even get help from a liquidator on one of the hallways, assuming that they weren't supporters of the Archbishop. Soon he reached the spiral staircase. He ran down at a crazed pace, but he knew that his advantage was waning. He could almost feel the panting of the men on his heels. He as almost on the first level where Perrier lived when he tripped and fell. He did not sense pain; fear extinguished all other feelings. His pursuer caught up with him and began to beat him. He instinctively protected his face with his hands, and all the while he could not believe this was happening to him. Soon Leroy arrived with three more men.

"Stop hitting him, you idiot!" the Archbishop said. "I want him in one piece in the dungeons. There he will tell us all, I'm sure of it."

Hearing of the dungeons, Farall fell into a blind panic. He cared about nothing but escaping that predicament.

"Help! Help!" he shouted as loudly as he could.

"Quick, gag him," Leroy ordered. "One of the men took a dirty rag and stuffed it in his mouth. The others tied his hands behind his back and blindfolded him with a cloth."

"So, take him to the village as we agreed. If the Councillor suspects me, the first thing he'll do is check the church dungeons.

But he will be disappointed, this little maggot won't be there. I will leave in the morning; I need to speak with the Marquis first. No one touches him till then. Understood?"

"Yes, Father," they replied.

They lifted him like a sack of potatoes, and no matter how hard he struggled, strong hands held him firmly, and he had no chance of escape. After a short while, they left the castle. He knew this because a soft spring breeze swept into his face. He was in no state to appreciate the kindly caress of nature's most pleasant month. They must have been going for about ten minutes, and he was exhausted from his futile struggling. Then they stopped, and he heard the neighing of horses. They threw him down, and the carriage started. Soon the horses were galloping at an insane pace.

Farall was deathly afraid, and the torture he knew awaited him seemed to have paralysed his mind. He had no doubt in his mind that Leroy would treat him as cruelly as he possibly could. He would take out all his hatred of the Councillor on Farall. Horrible images haunted him; why was all this happening to him? With him, who hated violence more than anything, him who felt such pity for those that suffered, and now he would have to endure would couldn't even bare to watch.

Half an hour went by till he was able to assess the situation somewhat rationally. He listened, but aside from the thundering of the carriage and horses, he heard nothing. Maybe he was alone? Because if someone were there, they would surely speak to one another or at least move, but he heard no such noise. If this was so, then he had to try and escape, and if they were there, he would take a few kicks at the worst. He lay on his back, and he began rubbing his head on the floor of the cart. He was hoping that he could get the rag off of his eyes in this way. If he could see, he would be able to assess his situation far better.

He lost sense of time, and he couldn't tell how long he'd been struggling to remove the rag without getting anywhere. His head was bloody from the effort, but the rag would not move. He had to change tactics; with his legs he pushed himself to the side of the carriage and tried to find something sharp to help take that damned thing from his eyes. His effort were crowned by success. Suddenly, he caught on something, and he quickly began moving his head up and down, up and down and presto—the rag was off. Quickly he looked around, he was certain that there was no one guarding him, or they would have intervened. He was in the passenger area of a carriage and could see from his seated position that the door was locked from the outside. These carriages were used for transporting high-ranking prisoners. He could not have broken down the double-latched doors even if his hands and legs had been free. Suddenly, he felt terrified. How long had he spent taking the blindfold off? What if they arrived and his minute success had been for nothing? If he did not hurry, he would die in terrible agony. He tried to calm himself. He knew that if he didn't come up with something he was done for, and fear was not getting him anywhere. He looked around once more; the windows were heavily barred, he certainly would not break through those, and there was no other chance. The Councillor had once told him that if a person really wanted something, then they would eventually get it. He wanted to leave this carriage more than anything. He stared fixedly at the door and then suddenly remembered that he had found a letter opener in the hallway earlier that day. It was highly decorative, the kind Perrier used. He'd picked it up and put it in his trouser pocket, as he's wanted to return it to Perrier.

If he could get it out from there with his bound hands, then maybe he could move the door latch too. He had to try. The very thought that he had a plan filled him with energy. Farall began trying to get at the blade. With great difficulty, he stood up; it was not easy to remain standing because his bound legs wobbled under him with the movement of the carriage. He leaned against the wall and carefully pulled out the knife. His hands were cramping as he twisted his hands, and the rope cut into his flesh. Meanwhile he took care not to drop his only hope because he would lose precious minutes. When the letter opener was in his hand, he hobbled over to the door, turned his back to it and shoved the knife between the door and the doorframe. It was no easy task; he could only access the gap by holding the knife in his right hand and lifting the door as best he could with his left, all this with his hands bound together. He kept struggling till something caught, and he placed his whole weight on the knife. The letter opener slipped from the crack, and for a moment he was afraid the blade had broken, but it had not. He tried again, and this time he felt the door move. Collecting all his strength, he lifted the door again, and with a loud crash it tore from its frame. He thought the driver would certainly have heard him, or the people in the back if there were any there. He waited a little, but nothing happened, and the carriage sped on. Then he realised it was foolish to wait as he would have to jump quickly if they had noticed him or not. He turned and looked numbly into the knight and saw nothing. They were certainly in an uninhabited area, perhaps it was the silhouette of the woods he could see in the darkness.

It is no mean feat to jump with bound hands and legs from a thundering carriage into the unknown darkness. Then suddenly, he remembered the torture that awaited him, and the leap became far more appealing. He jumped, gathering momentum, as he did not want to land on the road as his captors would surely notice him. At first, he felt nothing and then a great deal. He more rolled than fell, and every summersault was painful. He could not protect his body with his arms, nor could he dampen the blows. When he stopped rolling, he remained motionless for a few minutes, and then slowly tried to stand up. It was hard going, but he managed. He was covered in wounds, but it seemed like nothing was broken. Perhaps they had not noticed his escape, and he had a little advantage, but he knew that he would move very slowly bound as he was. If he was lucky, they would not know where he had jumped, and it would make their pursuit of him much more difficult. He knew that he had to go as far as he could because they would look for him around the road at first. By the time he thought this through, he was on his way, jumping along, falling often, but not giving up for a second. It was impossible to navigate in the dark woods, he just tried to go in a straight line so as to get as far away from the road as he could.

He'd been going for hours, suffering, exhausted, but with hope in his heart. Perhaps he would escape, he thought. Then he tripped on a tree root, fell and his head smacked something very hard—the world went dark around him.

The clock in the royal palace struck 7:00, and Alain Perrier leaped impatiently from behind his desk. *Where is that boy?* he thought as he left to check on the condition of the King. On the way, he was troubled by Farall's tardiness. His aid had never been late before. They had agreed on 7:00 in the morning, and he was always sitting on that lousy chair at the agreed upon time, yet today, he was late. *Maybe there's something wrong with him,* the only possible solution came to him. *When I'm done here, I'll go to his chambers and find out the truth,* he determined.

In the King's anteroom, Marquis Bertrand and Archbishop Leroy stood about bemoaning the King's condition as usual. When Perrier entered, Leroy whispered something in the Marquis ear. As they spotted the Councillor, they flitted apart like kissing lovers at the sight of a priest.

"Good morning, Councillor!" they greeted Perrier sycophantically. Their eyes belied some confusion.

"Good morning, gentlemen," the Councillor hissed, but he did not slow his pace as he swept by them. In the bedroom, King Lefebre was surrounded by a host of doctors. The Councillor approached them, and instead of a greeting them, he got right to the point,

"Have you followed my order? How is the patient?" he asked in quick succession.

"Well, Councillor Sir," the elder doctor said, "his condition had not improved; in fact, it may have gotten worse. He had cold sweats, we cannot lower his fever, and what is worse are his coughing and trouble breathing. Of course, we've treated him by your instructions."

"Alright, keep treating him as you have been and continue to report to me," the Councillor replied as he checked the King's pulse and fever.

Then he left the room without saying goodbye.

Outside, Leroy took his arm gently, and Perrier glared at him at which the Bishop withdrew his hand as if he had been burned.

"My lord, is there still hope?" Leroy's smile was in stark contrast with the question.

"You are the priest, not me." Perrier's stare was murderous, "so you should really know that there is always hope."

Then Perrier headed straight for Farall's room; on his way out, he could still hear Leroy's response,

"How true. How true, Councillor."

Perrier quickened his pace, as an ominous feeling was coming over him. He did not like Bertrand and Leroy's confidence. He was worried about Lefebre's condition, but most of all he was worried about Vincent.

When he arrived at the room, he knocked. No answer.

"Vincent. It's me, Alain, open up!" No answer.

He opened the door and found no one inside. He went to the bedroom in the back, but it was empty too; in fact no one had slept in the freshly made bed that night. He walked around the room but found nothing suspicious. The book he had brought from the restricted section was there on the table. He found it strange, as Vincent would never leave precious books lying around. Perrier wagged his head. He did not like it one bit, and there was no logical explanation, and a feeling of foreboding overcame him. It was becoming more and more apparent that something had happened to Farall. He took the book and headed for the exit, but he noticed that the door had new hinges on it, and the wall around them had been mended too.

"Dammit!" she exclaimed aloud.

This door has been broken down recently, he assessed observantly, and he almost ran back to his chambers, telling the liquidators on his way to immediately summon Head Liquidator Moreau and Commander Azor.

He sat nervously in his chair and threw the expensive book onto the table. The old, dusty volume fell on its spine, peeling off the front cover revealing the first page. Perrier immediately notice the writing inside and snatched it up to read it.

"Alain!
Archbishop Leroy is in front of my door with his men.
If something happens to me, please help!
Vincent"

He felt as if he'd been punched, his hands clenched into fists, and unbridled rage and desperation overcame him with equal force. He knew he only had a chance to save him if he did not allow his emotions to overcome him. But this attack had found his only weak spot. *Everyone has a weakness, the first rule of the councillors, yes...well, it is you, Vincent,* he thought sadly. He looked at Vincent's uncomfortable little chair and spoke aloud,

"I will help you, Vincent, of course I will help you," he said to the empty chair.

In that moment, the door opened and Head liquidator Moreau and Commander Azor entered. They approached the Councillor's desk and stopped there without a word, paying their respects with a bow of their heads.

Perrier took a deep breath to calm his mind, and in a few moments, he felt ready for the fight. With an emotionless face, he looked at the liquidators before him and simply said,

"Gentlemen, today we hunt down Archbishop Leroy."

Chapter Twenty

Sir Lemmy Black stood rigidly; his spine almost bending backwards before King Mortimer. He clasped his hands behind his back and waited with his eyes fixed on the King to be granted permission to speak after greeting him.

"Well, what is it?" Mortimer asked who was stuffing his pipe sitting with his legs spread wide. "I hate these formalities. You asked to meet before the Council meeting. In fact, come to think of it, you were the one who wanted to have the meeting in the first place. And then you expect me to beg you to speak?"

"My lord!" the strategist ran his long, almost-effeminate fingers through his thick black hair, trying to organise the locks falling over his eyes. "I would like you to appear together with me in front of the lords, and it would be best if we made them wait too."

"What the hell? Do you want to start new customs? I don't even recognise you. You want to brag about our friendship? Showing off your power? So be it, as you wish." He drew on his pipe and looked at Black with a mischievous smile. He knew that the strategist had good reason for asking him this; he did not do anything without reason, but it felt good to goad him on a little.

"You don't mean that seriously, Your Highness," Sir Lemmy answered, purposefully ignoring the joke. Mortimer deserved a little back talk.

"Of course, I have a reason for asking. I would like to put pressure on the council."

"And why would you want to do that? Do I have to draw each word from you like an arrow?" the King snorted.

"Well, my lord, because the person who planned the assassination will be sitting right in front of you."

"Dammit!" Mortimer shouted and slapped the table with such force that it hurt his hand. "You bastard, you're doing this to me on purpose. You're all secretive and tell me barely half-truths and let anger overcome me, but worst of all you always manage to make me beg. You will tell me everything immediately! Got that? Got it? Everything!"

Black told him about the conversation between the two hooded figures. He told the King that one of them, the later assassin, was Liquidator Hugh Jones, and while the other's identity was unknown, he was a member of the King's council.

Mortimer listened attentively, and his anger abated rapidly. When the strategist had finished, he spoke,

"Have the witness brought to me!"

"Unfortunately, I cannot do that, my lord, I promised him…" He used the singular on purpose so as not to reveal there were two of them, because that would make looking for a coupe much easier. "…to keep their identity a secret. Since confrontation would yield no results, since they did not see the assassin, I would only be signing their death warrant."

"But you can still tell me," the King replied somewhat offended.

"My lord, how could you trust me later if I did such a thing? How can a person who cannot keep a promise to a commoner keep his word to a king. I trust you more, my king, than my own self, but I cannot break my word. I would only do such a thing if it served you, my lord."

"Treacherous snake," Mortimer replied in disappointment, "you worm your way out like you always do. You know the lords will be furious if you accuse them without hard evidence?"

"Of course, my lord, but I have to scare the rabbit from the bush."

"Speak clearly, man, or I'll throw this at you." He raised the finely carved pipe in his hand.

"We must put pressure on the perpetrator and force them to act, and those who act hastily tend to make mistakes. Briefly, as I have mentioned, I want to scare the rabbit out of the bush."

"Well then, let's at it. If I remember correctly, the tower clock has struck 4:00, and the Lords have been waiting for a while now. Let us go see this rabbit!" Mortimer was beginning to like this game.

When the King and Sir Lemmy Black entered the council room, the lords were all seated and fidgeting about nervously. The strategist had asked the King that he send ten liquidators into the room before him and have the weapons of the council members taken by force if they resisted. When they were seated, Black kept his hand on his sword's hilt, knowing that this gesture would further increase tensions."

Mortimer sat down languidly, and the other sat down after him. After greetings, the lords all scrambled to gain the right to speak.

The usually calm Councillor Ed Wilder nervously fidgeted with his shirt sleeve. Archbishop Eric Parker chewed his lip. And old Alf Kelly stared into space, though he always did so, and the current situation could raise his nerves no higher. The usually lackadaisical Sir Christopher Millborrow had a sparkle in his eye and was furious at having his sword along with his rights as a nobleman stripped away from him. Only the obsidian-skinned Head liquidator James Horan sat with perfect calm.

"Gentlemen!" Mortimer began. "I am sure you have all heard of the attempt on my life. I have relieved you of your weapons because of this. I ask you all to accept this."

"A nobleman without his sword is like a woman," Sir Millborrow burst out. "I, like my ancestors before me, have the right to bear arms. Even before the king."

"This is true, Dear Sir Christopher," Black replied impassively, "but we are living in dangerous times. And this measure, I ordered, is only temporary."

"You ordered?" Archbishop Parker could contain himself no longer. – "How dare you? You are in no position to give us orders!"

"You are wrong, Archbishop," Sir Lemmy replied with a grin that suggested he thoroughly enjoyed flaunting his power. "I have all the power for such a measure and for much more unpleasant ones besides. So, I suggest that you do not question my decisions because I will be forced to take harsher measure."

"Your Highness!" Councillor Wilder interjected. "We want an explanation for Sir Lemmy's behaviour and the whereabouts of our weapons. We do not understand why we cannot be armed in your presence, and why the strategist has the right to be?"

"Gentlemen!" the King replied, "this morning I assigned Sir Lemmy Black to investigate my attempted murder. My protection is in his purview. I hope that my life is important enough to take priority over archaic customs. From this day forth, I have given Commander Black complete power because otherwise the case will never be resolved. So, from now on, Sir Lemmy can act of his own accord."

"But today's actions are just bullying. I don't see the point," Sir Millborrow announced.

"I promise I will explain soon."

"What is your opinion of the case?" the King asked. It had been a long time since he'd felt this good in council. He enjoyed debasing the great lords.

"I, my lord," Kelly said in a shaking voice, "will question the masters and traders. Maybe someone can give information."

"And I will question the lords," Sir Christopher said pompously.

"I will join," Archbishop Parker said, "I will investigate among my own circles and the believers."

"Naturally I will do what can too, and that is a lot for a councillor," Wilder said finally.

"No one will do anything!" Black interjected harshly. He stood up and placed his hands on the table looking around seeking out everyone's eyes. "Only I can investigate here; you would only mess things up despite your best intentions, and you would scare the perpetrator off."

"But the most important reason is not this, but that the perpetrator is a member of the King's council."

A huge commotion broke out; everyone was speaking at once.

"Silence!" Sir Lemmy quieted them down. "I will tell you something now, and I would like to say it uninterrupted."

Then he told them of the conversation that had taken place between Liquidator High Jones and the hooded perpetrator. When he finished, everyone sank deep into thought. Ed Wilder was first to speak,

"I demand that you produce the witness because without them these are all just blind accusations."

"I would be mad to do so," Black replied, "you heard me say that the witness did not see the perpetrator because he wore a hood, and I will not put their life in danger. Head liquidator Horan, you've not yet spoken today. What is your opinion on the matter?"

"The life of the King is most important. Until we find the perpetrator, everyone will follow your orders."

"Of course, Head liquidator Horan is on your side; he is your man," Parker spat, "and I am not even certain that you were not the one orchestrating this whole thing to get rid of your political opponents, us! Besides, the assassin was a liquidator, and this does not bode well for yourself or Head liquidator Horan."

"Look, priesty!" Black began. The name struck the lords, like a slap in the face. Not even the King would have dared to address them like that. "I will tell you briefly, once more. There is nothing more important to me than the King's life, so I will gladly trample over everyone and everything is necessary."

"And I have just been granted the power to do so. Is there anyone among you who would like to see how far I will go?"

Sir Lemmy looked around; all the eyes radiated anger towards him, but at their depths he could see the fear in them.

Later, when the council members had left, Mortimer, laughing, asked the strategist,

"Well, my friend? Are you satisfied?"

"Well, as a matter of fact," Sir Lemmy said scratching his chin, "I think we may have scared that rabbit out of the bush."

Roy Davis waited for Councillor Ed Wilder to return from the special council meeting impatiently. *When the old man arrives*, he thought, *maybe he will let me leave early, and I can go see Claire.* He looked around the dark, dusty room. He spent the better part of the last few years in this disgusting hole. The councillor did not like sunlight, and when he couldn't avoid it he sneezed all day. His chambers were north-facing for a reason, and even the little light that did seep through the windows was caught by curtains. The torches in Ed Wilder's domain burned constantly, and Roy could always smell their strong scent on his clothes. The worst were the days when it was sunny and warm outside, and he had to rot in this dingy mouse grey hole.

The councillor arrived in a fit of emotion. He slammed the door closed, threw his sword into the corner of the room and sat down to his desk.

"The strategist manifested his own interests with regard to the assassination," Wilder raged.

Roy did not dare nor did he want to interject; he had never seen the councillor this angry. Wilder told him in a few sentences about what had happened and peppered his report generously with swearwords and expletives.

"But despite all the bad news, there is a little good, my son," he looked significantly at Davis.

"What would that be, my lord?" he asked politely.

"The olden people had a very wise saying they used them they were forced to overstep certain rules or laws. Briefly put, if they had to do bad, but somehow this bad was in the interest of the greater good. So, the saying goes, 'The ends justify the means,'" Roy nodded enthusiastically, what else could he have done, but he hated it when the Councillor came up with old sayings, and it happened often.

"The situation fits another old saying," the Councillor went on, "I need hardly say that it too is lost in the fogs of time. It is as follows: 'Hair of the dog.'"

Davis received an enthusiastic nod again.

"But I won't drone on much longer," Wilder went on, "I will introduce you to someone who will be a great service to us in our fight against mutants. The most dangerous mutation of all is communication through thoughts."

Roy shuddered; his stomach clenched, and he had to use all his force not reveal his fear.

"It is the most dangerous," Wilder went on, "because there are no outside signs. The situation is made worse because if we do find one, the interrogation usually reveals that they only know a few other like them. There are some telepaths who can keep their gift a secret from other telepaths too; somehow, they block their brains.

Since I've been serving the Kingdom of England, I only managed to catch a few such mutants over the years. But from now on it will be different! Come with me!" the Councillor said standing up and heading for the door. Roy followed him with a feeling of foreboding.

They went all the way to the ground floor, then Wilder stopped at a door before which a priest stood. Davis found it unusual that a priest would be guarding a door, but he knew that the Councillor and the Archbishop were close allies. It seemed, Wilder did not trust the liquidators, so he had used the priests instead. They entered—only a young man stood in the empty room. Roy did not like him; there was a fox-like cunning in his eyes.

"My son, I will introduce you to someone who will help us in the fight against mutants. Meet Mick Taylor. Mick, this man is my aid; he obeys me in all things. He is Roy Davis."

They stood opposite each other and nodded curtly, then Mick smiled,

"Greetings, my friend, I've been waiting for us to meet!" Roy's hand flew to his head as Mick's voice spoke in his head.

"Pull yourself together!" He heard Mick say. "Don't blow your cover! We will do great things together!"

"My son, do not be surprised at what I'm about to tell you," the Councillor said, "Mick is a mutant who can speak in thoughts."

Roy was still shaken, and he stood silently before the stranger.

"I know this is hard to accept, but he himself offered to help me," Wilder patted Roy's back, "we will make an exception for him, and he will help us find those like him. Roy, you can tell no one what Mick is; this is our secret."

"Yes, sir!" Davis replied, not taking his eyes off of Mick.

"You may go now," Wilder said to Roy, who nodded and walked out. Mick speaking in his head as he left,

"Oh, I almost forgot. Give my regards to your little girlfriend!"

Roy closed the door feeling fain and headed straight for Claire. He had to speak with her, personally, only in voice. Suddenly, the recognition struck him that he couldn't tell her any of this because though he spoke in words, his thoughts would betray him. He did not know how to get out of this horrible rat trap, but he had to find a way. As he went through the city's corridors with his head bent low, another old saying the Councillor was fond of popped into his head, 'Birds of a feather flock together'. *Well*, thought Roy as a faint smile flitted across his face despite the situation, *sometimes the olden people were wrong too.*

Chapter Twenty-One

Aleksandr Petrov sprawled out luxuriously on the huge bed in his room. Beside him a naked young woman sobbed quietly. The Councillor looked at the girl, whose body was riddled with bruises and seeping wounds. *Perhaps I went a little further than necessary,* he thought. But the sight of her aroused him again, though he knew he had a lot to do that day. *And anyway, the wench would not withstand another round.*

"You may dress and leave." He let the bedraggled beauty go free. "There's a pouch on the little table, take it! If I require your services again, I'll let you know. If you dare tell anyone that you were here, our next game will be in the torture chamber."

"Yes, my lord," the girl sobbed, and gingerly but quickly, she put on her clothes. On the way out, she picked the pouch up from the little table.

"This is true power," Petrov observed, "when a man can possess a woman completely without limitations. This would be unimaginable in Atlantis. There women had the same rights as men. People chose partners freely, of their own will, and if they get bored, they simply move on. Back home, there is none of the exploitation that makes love-making truly exciting."

Everyone has a weakness, he'd been taught along with the other prospective councillors. He was not stupid, he knew the answers they expected of him, and he said precisely that. If he'd told the truth that he wanted to serve in the known world because he could debase and abuse women to his heart's content, his teachers would surely have failed him. Naturally, he had enough cunning to know what they wanted to hear. Like saying that he wanted to be a councillor because he was attracted by the adventure and wanted to benefit mankind, and that his only weakness was his adventurousness. What lunacy! He was the top of his class, so tricking a few old men was no challenge to him. He achieved what he wanted; he could beat up as many women as he wanted while he made them his own. This was real life, life that could be lived only here in the known world if one had enough power, and a councillor had plenty.

He dressed, and the games he'd played last night played on his mind. He was satisfied; other people were pleased by other things, but for him, this was it.

There was a knock at the door; his servant entered and told him that Lord Boris Kurilov was asking permission to enter. Petrov was surprised; it was not customary to burst the door down on a councillor in this way. But he did not send the unwelcome guest away; he was determined to make him wait, returning the impolite gesture. He entered the waiting room, which was also a study a good quarter hour later. He saw that Kurilov was deeply offended; his eyes glistened with anger, and his hands clutched the armrests. He looked like he would like to jump up and spring at the Councillor's throat. The Councillor crossed the room with measured steps and sat down at the writing desk opposite his guest.

He did not speak but waited. He acted just as he had been trained: Do everything you can to upset your opponent's calm. A long silence was just the thing to use in this situation. He watched the man seated before him. Kurilov was not exactly handsome. His stocky build was accompanied by a wide round head with little piggy eyes. His head was covered in sparse hair and a thick beard. Kurilov could not have been over 50, but his constant revelries had left a mark on his body. When Petrov felt that the lord was about to explode, he spoke,

"To what do I owe this flattering visit, my lord?"

"You made me wait," Kurilov said ignoring the question, "I'm not accustomed to this."

"I could say that a councillor comes and goes when he pleases, but I, unlike you, will be politer. So, I would like to remind you that it was you who barged in on me without prior notice. And I had more important matters to attend to, which is why you had to wait a little."

Boris Kurilov's head turned beet red at the unrelenting insult.

"I'll teach you who the most important person in this kingdom is!"

Petrov waited to respond, annoying the lord to no end.

"My dear sir, listen to me now because I'm going to tell you something that I will not repeat again. You are not the most important person in the Russian kingdom, King Jurij Genisei is. And my badge says: *Kingdom or Death!* not *Boris Kurilov or Death!* I do not serve you, I serve the King. You should thank me if I do not mention to him that you are the most important person here. I will not mention it to him yet, but if you don't reign in your arrogance, I will speak of it to the King."

Kurilov was visibly stunned by the young councillor's firmness. He admitted that threats would get him nowhere. In fact, if Petrov were actually to tell the King, then he would have to explain himself, which would be extremely embarrassing.

"You know that's not what I meant, Councillor Petrov, I'm not here to argue with you."

"Well then?" Petrov smiled making it clear that he was prepared to be friendly.

"I wanted to pay my respects to the new councillor. Further, I would like to personally invite you to my palace on the night after next. I would like to commemorate your appointment with a splendid feast."

The Councillor was in no mood to enter the lion's den, but he knew that he could not refuse the invitation.

"It would be my honour, Lord Kurilov," he replied as he remembered that someone in Michael Barov's tavern had said that Kurilov eats councillors for breakfast. *Well, we will see who eats who,* Petrov thought. In any case, his money was on himself.

When Kurilov left, Petrov wanted some fresh air. He knew the park around the King's palace already, and he wanted to have good walk around it. He got dressed with many layers because spring in Moscow was still nippy.

Petrov went down the decoratively carved stone corridors, where the lords lived. Stern liquidators guarded the doors. He was about to leave the castle when a servant spoke to him:

"Councillor Sir! Someone would like to meet with you in secret."

"How dare you disturb me? Don't you know you're playing with your life peon?" Petrov raged at the servant.

"Of course, I know, sir, but the person whose message I bear hold much authority. The issue for which I disturb you is very important to you."

"What is it?" the Councillor asked; his curiosity aroused.

"Well, if I, an insignificant servant, knew that, it wouldn't be much of a secret. I was only told that it was vitally important to you." Listening, the Councillor was certain that the servant was no simple person. His words and logic indicated a well-groomed mind. With regard to the case, this was clearly important, but he took note of it.

"Alright. Lead me, but if you are wasting my time, you will pay for your insolence."

"Yes, sit, my lord, you will be the judge of whether your time was wasted or not."

After that they did not speak. Petrov followed the bold servant silently.

In the annals of the castle, they were crossing the service quarters when the servant spoke.

"We are here. Please, go through this door. I will wait here and make sure you are not disturbed."

Petrov passed through the simple, plain door. In the dark room, his eyes adjusted slowly to the dim light of a few candles. The frigid room barely held a few roughly hewn pieces of furniture. The centre of the room was occupied by a table and two chairs, on one of which a young man sat. When the Councillor entered, the young man stood up to greet him.

"Thank you for accepting my invitation, Councillor Petrov."

"You're welcome, Prince Ivan," Petrov replies, who recognised the boy as the King's son from his first marriage.

"I've not been fortunate to receive much of the kindness granted to children in my life. So, I no longer require it, please, call me Prince Genisei," the boy replied.

As they sat down, the Councillor had a good look at the Prince. He was muscular and thin indicating good training, and his pretty, shapely face was framed by long, straight black hair. But the most striking thing about him were his eyes. His gaze indicated the type of person who has experienced more in his brief years than most will in an entire life. And Petrov suspected that these experiences were none too pleasant. The eyes that stared back at him were those of an old man living in a young man's body. The Councillor shuddered despite himself, though the room was pleasantly warm.

"My dear Prince," he tried taking over the conversation, "why did you want to meet with me in secret?"

"Councillor," Genisei replied rather curtly, "stop this condescending blubbering! Maybe I've not been alive for long, but if you consider that there's been a price on my head since I was an infant, perhaps my 16 years are not so few after all. You could not know, so I do not blame you, but please do not mistake me for a child again."

"Many men, who no longer live, did not take me seriously. Of course, do not take that as a threat, as we are not enemies."

"Excuse me, I was fooled by your young age," Petrov answered peaceably. After all, why would he want to offend a child, especially a Prince? At the same time, he was growing bored of the conversation with this spoiled, self-important brat. "Let me ask you again, why did you call me here?"

"No matter, you will learn to take me seriously," the Prince said. "I want to make a deal with you."

"So, make your offer, Prince Genisei!"

"Don't you think it strange that the body of Councillor Oleg Vosinoi was never found?"

An alarm went off in Petrov's head with resounding force. *This boy is truly not what he seems. He did not know yet who he really was, but he was certainly not to be taken lightly.*

"I've been informed that he went hunting in the nearby forest and was lost. Such things, if not too often, do happen around here. Perhaps he met a bear," Petrov stated the widely known facts.

"Of course, he was murdered. By your greatest enemy no less, who also conspires against you, the perpetrator is Lord Boris Kurilov."

"But Prince! You cannot expect me to believe that."

"I've not finished yet!" Ivan raised his voice. Petrov was surprised to note that the boy had a great impact on him.

"You surely must know that Commander Vladimir Niachev is the newest inmate of the castle prisons."

"Certainly, I know of it," the Councillor replied. "Niachev was the notorious commander of the whole region, who allegedly denied a royal order, for which he will be executed."

Getting rid of that notorious commander is not such a bad thing, Petrov thought, *in Russia he is known only as the White Terror.* Niachev was well-known for his ruthlessness and free will.

"I was certain you knew of the case," the Prince ascertained, "so here is my offer. Firstly, I will prove to you that Vosinoi was murdered by Kurilov. Secondly, you will complete my request, and then I will be willing to kill Kurilov."

"These are heavy words you speak, Prince," Petrov replied in a measured tone.

"Did you think I requested this meeting for some passing fancy? You thought I want to discuss my birthday celebration? Look! If I prove the murder, then you will believe me and then it is your turn."

"What do you want from me?" Petrov asked.

"I want Commander Vladimir Niachev! I want you to help me free him. I need your help because he's guarded by the liquidators. Otherwise, if you do not help, Kurilov will kill you too, as he did Vosinoi."

Petrov's mind raced feverishly; if the kid was right, and he could prove the murder, he would come out on top. But to free that beast was too risky. On the other hand, if he entered the deal, he could always sidestep later. It was worth a try, because he had much to gain from such a bargain.

"What will become of Niachev when he is freed, provided you can prove the murder? The King will never let him live. And why would you murder my enemy? I could do that too."

"Good questions," the Prince nodded, "the Commander is my business. I will let him free. And I will kill Kurilov because I still have servants who are in his service and will help, and no one would suspect me. Now it is my turn; I do not expect you to accept immediately, but if I keep my word, and show you the proof, then do we have a deal?"

"Yes, Prince Genisei," the Councillor said shaking hands, "then we do."

Vladimir Niachev sat sadly in his cell. It was not his imminent death that upset him, a soldier is always ready for that, but the fact that everything he had fought for was for nothing. He felt betrayed. He'd fought for many long years in the motherland against the yellow-skinned tribes and had learned to respect them along the way. At the end of the seemingly infinite wars, when they surrendered to him the White Terror, he receives an order which makes no sense. According to the order, he could not make the peace treaty that would be so beneficial to Russia, but had to upset the previous agreement and destroy his already defeated opponent. He did not do so. He returned to Moscow to speak with the King and request adherence to previous agreement by which a peace treaty with the surrendered tribes would be possible. He was not allowed before the King, but he was arrested. He looked around the small cell—the last place he would ever see. The grey walls glistened with damp.

Beside him lay a liquidator who lost his life when six men wanted to chain him at once. Finally, they managed, but he, Vladimir Niachev, had not relinquished his freedom easily. He did not release his victim during the fight, even when he knew he was dead. He needed him, because he used his blood to write on the wall, 'Nobody come near me!' The gruesome text had the desired effect, and the jailers treated him with fearful respect. He did the same thing in battle too—he terrified his enemies. All this happened two days ago. Since then, they had only dared enter his cell so that he could not reach them, and only to give him food and water. Niachev knew that the food or the water, or perhaps both could be poisoned, so he touched nothing. He still felt strong, though he'd been fasting for 48 hours. He had no doubt that as soon as he lost consciousness, he'd be jumped and murdered after a fake trial. Niachev determined that when he felt weak, he would pretend to faint, and then he would kill as many of the men that approached him as he could. This thought calmed him, even though he knew that his real enemies were the traitors Kurilov and Jurij Genisei, the King of Russia. He stood up to stretch his numb limbs a little. The stench of the two-day old corpse alongside his unwashed body were quite a repulsive combination.

Suddenly, the iron door screeched, and a man appeared in the doorway. He held a tray in his hands, on which roast meat, a pitcher of water and a flask of wine were laid. The unknown person approached the soldier.

"Halt kid! Can't you see the writing on the wall?" Niachev thundered. "If you come closer, I will write something else with your blood."

"Greetings, Commander Vladimir Niachev! My name is Prince Ivan Genisei," he said slowing his steps.

"No further, or I'll kill you. At least your treacherous father will suffer a little."

"You're wrong about that, my lord. There is no greater favour you could do, my royal father. When my mother died, I was only a year old. Since then, there have been many attempts on my life, mostly by my own relatives. Therefore, if you want to cause my father joy, then go ahead." By the time he said this, he stood directly in front of the disgraced commander.

"Well, you're no coward, Prince Genisei," the prisoner opined.

"And if you'll allow me a remark," the Prince said looking the notorious inmate dead in the eye, "a real soldier kills his enemies, not his allies."

"You're still breathing, Prince," Niachev said in a hoarse, quiet, almost muffled voice, "but don't get cocky. You know, the difference between life and death is only a second sometimes."

"I did not come here to trade insults, or to chit-chat, but to make an alliance, which could change the history of the Russian kingdom."

Niachev would have considered these words empty boasts from anyone, but somehow the way the young prince said rang true.

"Pretty words, my prince, but why try and convince a dead man of your mission?" asked the soldier, whose voice was filled with a mocking mirth.

"I am here to discuss our shared future."

"I'm listening," Niachev replied, "but don't forget that I will never do or promise anything that goes against what I believe in.

I will fight the enemy with valour, but also with respect. And the yellow men are straight people. I will not exterminate them just because Moscow orders it so!

Today I brought you food, tomorrow I will free you, and one day you will be the one to help me regain the throne. And when I am king, we will vanquish our shared enemies and reinstate the kingdom's former glory. And you can make peace with the leaders of the inner territories. Are you with me? Will you be my right-hand man when I bring it down upon those treacherous knaves?"

The Commander said nothing, but he slowly took a morsel of food from the tray, and when he'd swallowed, he spoke,

"I am with you, my king!"

Chapter Twenty-Two

The company who had escaped from Paris sat drinking on Happy Island. Paul was enthusiastically telling the others how he would solve the changing water levels of the swamp.

A medium-sized river ran into the territories, and sometimes, in the rainy season, the water levels got dangerously high. He would build a dam, with which they would divert the majority of the water flow, and when they needed it, they could let all of it flow into the swamp. According to loose lips, the real cause for his high spirits was not the construction but the daughter of one of their hosts.

Fabian watched the group in silence. He was satisfied with his new home; it was far enough away from everyone, and if he did feel like talking, he could come out from his hiding place. He took care of medical needs to everyone's satisfaction.

Jules and Henri, like everyone else, knew of Ponga's afternoon exploits. Nothing could remain a secret here. It was the talk of the town that Ponga was buzzing around Fifi for the third day running and completing all sorts of womanly tasks, just to be close to her.

"Listen, Didier! I don't remember what you said? When are you leaving us?" Jules asked and winked at Henri when the knight wasn't looking. Henri could barely keep a straight face, but he somehow managed to suppress the laughter that welled up inside him.

"Well, so," Ponga began awkwardly, "so, the thing is, that I might stay here for a while. The area is surely overrun with the Councillor's men, and it would not be safe to leave now."

"I see," Jules nodded, "but you surely won't stay here long enough that I need build you a house?"

"Well, you know, maybe that's a good idea," Ponga blurted, who would have given an arm and a leg to change the subject.

"What's a good idea? To build a house or not to? Maybe it can't be built," Jules said winking at Henri again.

"You want to kick me out? Why did you bring me here?" Ponga looked around in outrage, to see if anyone would come to his aid. Sadly, he acknowledged that everyone sat in silence.

"Not at all, I'm just asking if you want a house or not. We won't build you mansion for just a week or two," Jules said with as straight a face as he could muster.

"So be it," Ponga said nonchalantly. Meanwhile, he turned his head nervously, carefully avoiding people's eyes.

"So, you will be staying with us for a longer while then, little knight?" The address was mocking, as only first names were used in the swamp, and only Jules as leader held rank.

"I'll stay," Ponga raised his voice, "are you happy now?"

Then Henri took over landing the fatal blow.

"Listen, Didier! Won't you come over to my place too to do the dishes?"

Suddenly, the joke became clear to Ponga.

He answered going scarlet in the face,

"You can all go to hell!" he said finally, and none too elegantly, and everyone nearly fell from their seats with laughter; even Fabian laughed.

"Get off my back; I'm just trying to be useful, now that I'm here," Ponga said. But this remark brought forth even more laughter.

When everyone had laughed themselves silly, Jules turned to more serious matters. His face reminded the others that they had walked a dangerous road to get there.

"My friends! Soon I will leave on an important mission. Who will come with me?" The leader looked slowly and significantly from one to the other.

"I," Henri said raising his hand. There was no question in his mind about accompanying his dear old friend. They always faced danger together, and this was not about to change.

"Me too," Fabian said seriously. He surprised even himself at volunteering for such a thing without any knowledge of the dangers involved.

"I don't want to be left out either," Paul said enthusiastically.

"They need you here, Paul," said the leader to the boy, "the dam must be ready by autumn."

"And you, dear knight?" He turned to Ponga who sat with his arms crossed over his chest.

"If you say knight one more time, I'll wallop you. You know I'm faster than you. And how could I say yes to something without even knowing what the mission is?"

"True. We have to steal a book that is well guarded."

"Is that so dangerous? Come, let's do it now!" Ponga interrupted. "Where is this book?"

"In the King's castle," Jules smiled.

"What did you say? You mean in Paris? But we just escaped from there. That's lunacy I won't go," Ponga announced. He hoped that someone would agree with him, but he had to join.

"Alright," the leader summed it up, "so we are as follows: Henri, Fabian, myself and Fifi."

"What!?" Ponga shouted smacking his goblet on the table. "That cannot be it is too dangerous for a woman."

"Look!" Jules raised his voice. "One! I say who goes and two we will need Fifi because she knows things that we do not."

"You want to use her like a slut! I won't allow it!" Ponga raged. People at the neighbouring tables looked over at the raised voice.

"Are you always this stupid, or are you just having a bad day? The thought never crossed my mind. And don't interrupt from now on; in fact it would be best if you sat at another table while we discuss these matters." Jules turned away from Ponga who shoved him roughly in the back.

"I'm staying! This involves me too," he said bitterly.

"You just said that you wouldn't do it," Henri goaded him on.

"Me? Don't even think of leaving me out of this! Of course I'm going," Ponga announced. "What book is it?"

"A volume in ancient English over a thousand page. The title is, *A brief history of the middle ages*."

"Brief, sure, at a thousand pages, how long would the long version be?" Ponga observed.

"So," the leader went on, "this volume is guarded in the restricted section of the royal library. We will not enter the city through tunnels because Didier and I will apply to be librarians, and for that we must enter through the main gates."

"What tunnel?" Fabian asked.

"I'll tell you later," Henri waved.

"And why would they accept us; there's no shortage of learned people there," Ponga interjected.

"But not many people like me," Jules went on, "I speak English, French and German too."

"Well, well! That's something, my friend!" Fabian nodded in admiration.

"I only speak the common tongue," Ponga muttered under his breath.

"That's alright, it's enough! My knowledge will be enough for both of us."

"You think they won't recognise us in the castle," Ponga said hesitantly.

"That's where Fifi comes in. We will arrive with a big carriage as travelling actors. And Fifi will make disguises for us. Do you remember when we first met I was an old priest. I did that. Fifi is much better at it, no one will recognise us."

"Actually, where is Fifi? She should be sitting here too." Jules looked around.

"As far as I know, she left to the nearest village a few hours ago because she need some supplies for the Tavern from the market," Henri replied. "She took two guards with her, but she's not come back yet. It's very strange, she should be back by now."

"Give me a few men who know the way, and I'll go find her!" Ponga said springing up.

"Wouldn't you like a few warriors to go with you? You'll manage alone?" Jules asked. Ponga looked him sternly in the eye.

"What do you think?"

Fifi was happy as she set out for the market. She sat in her dinghy, and at the edge of the swamp, Claude and Gustave were waiting to escort her. As she rowed, she thought about the past few days and more precisely of Didier and the hours they'd spent together. She'd rejected all his advances till now because she could not forget that fateful day when a piece of her soul and her innocence had been lost forever. But this boy was not pushy; if anything, he seemed shy. Fifi hoped that their relationship would grow deeper over time, and then perhaps they would live together like people who had not spent their lives in hiding. Not as if she wanted to go back into that world. The swamp was the safest and most beautiful place she'd ever seen. *How stupid of me,* she thought, *maybe he doesn't even love me, as he never said anything to the effect, and here I am dreaming about our future.* Anyway, she would have to tell him what had happened to her two years ago. She could not live in a lie, and if Didier found out, then he may never speak to her again. Who could want a common slut like her? Yes, that is what the men had shouted as they defiled her one after the other.

"I have to get over the past, she said to herself, "otherwise I'll never live a normal life. Meanwhile, deep inside, she wanted Didier to help her, to tell her that he still loved her even after what had happened to her."

Fifi also suffered from the fact that the only educated people in the swamp were Jules and Henri. Though she like her kind, simple friends here, she could not imagine her partner being an uneducated person.

It was true that Didier was not particularly learned, but at least he could read and write. She could tell from their conversations that he was not stupid. She could teach him what he did not know, provided they got that far.

She'd been rowing for half an hour, and her thoughts did not once stray from Didier. She had not verbalised it to herself yet, but the fact remained that she was hopelessly in love with the boy.

The two guards, Claude and Gustave, stood waiting for her in knee-deep water. When she arrived, they helped her moor the boat, and they passed through the increasingly shallow water for some ten minutes. The guards had hidden a cart not far from the swamp. Since there were only few horses kept near the watery hiding place, there were none left to spare for such a small, two-wheeled cart. But this was not a problem since two people could easily pull it along even if it was fully packed. Gustave offered for Fifi to sit up on the cart, and the two of them would pull her as the cart was empty anyway. Fifi politely declines and laughingly said that she was not a princess who was not able to walk.

It was slow-going with the cart, so the trip took more than an hour.

By the time they arrived, the market was in full swing. The pleasant hubbub of people filled the otherwise bleak village with life. The merchants shouted out their wears loudly, people haggled vehemently to lower prices, and drunken anecdotes filled the main square of the village. At these times, people from all the surrounding villages flocked in. Often, there were so many of them that they filled not only the square but also the surrounding streets.

Fifi produced a piece of paper on which she had written all the things she needed to buy. They produced most things themselves, and the things they did not Jules and Henri procured from the outside world. Here, at the market they only bought plants which they could grow in the damp earth of the swamp.

Firstly, as was her custom, Fifi wanted to survey the market. She wanted to assess which merchants were selling what, and how much they were asking. She asked her escorts to wait for her while she looked around; one pass through the thick crowd with the cart would be more than enough. Fifi went through to the other side of the square and was about to turn around when a commotion struck her ears. Riders were galloping through the crowd overturning the makeshift stands as they went.

"If anyone talks too much, I'll cut their throat!" someone shouted. "Don't you know who I am, you ignorant peasants!" Fifi wanted to quickly return to her guards, but she was too late, and two horsemen stood in her path. She looked up and saw in terror that one of the men was Spotted Michael, who had been the most disgusting of the scoundrels who'd raped her.

Unfortunately, he recognised her too.

"Come over here, my lord!" he shouted. "Look who we have here!"

The crowds ran away from the riders who surrounded Fifi.

"It isn't who I think it is?" She heard a voice from behind her back, and she quickly turned around. She knew that the person she was about to see was Julien de Bilon, the Marquis' son. "Dear little Sophie de Montfort."

Meanwhile, Bilon signalled to two of his men who jumped off their horses and grabbed the terrified Fifi.

"Well, boys," the Marquis said to his henchmen, "it was worth making the trip to this godforsaken shithole."

Then Bilon got off his horse too. And approaching her he whispered in her ear:

"Did you miss us very much? If you enjoyed our little game last time, do not fret; you'll get another taste of it very soon. But we'll be much more thorough this time; we'll keep stuffing you till you can't even move any more. And you're going to enjoy it, you little slut."

Meanwhile Claude and Gustave broke through the dense crowd that had formed around them.

"Leave the lady alone immediately," Gustave said; his sword drawn.

"Lady?" Julien laughed mockingly. "Did you hear that boys? A lady!...Kill these two cretins!"

The two men were no match for the riders. They stabbed them in the back, and they had no chance of defending themselves.

Sophie was tied up, a bag pulled over her head, and she was hoisted onto a horse.

"Where shall we take her, my lord?" one of the riders asked.

"I saw a barn up the road, we'll take her there," Julie replied.

Soon they arrived at a somewhat run-down, rotting wooden building. They looked around, but saw no one near them. The Marquis' son dismounted and turned to one of his men,

"Gilles! We will go collect taxes because if we wait too long, everyone will be hiding. And if we don't return with enough gold, my father will kill us. You stay here with the girl. But don't you dare lay a finger on her, or I'll cut off your prick!

The first round is mine, and then you can have your share of her too."

Julien and his men rode back to the village. Leon took Fifi inside the barn and threw her roughly to the ground. He looked at the dusty, ruffled but beautiful girl with yearning, but he did not dare touch her. He liked his manhood too well for that.

Ponga had never felt as afraid as when he set out in search of Fifi with his guide Remy. They rowed with such force that their arms ached. When the boat hid ground, they rushed through the knee-deep water towards the village. They reached the only stables in the swamps, where two horses, indispensable for long journeys, were kept. There, people worked in shifts, because the animals could not be taken into the swamps. They chose two horses and then galloped as hard as they could.

Ponga realised that; until now, he had had no idea what real loss was. Not long ago he had been sad about falling from the rank of honoured knight to wanted criminal. Now he knew that that was nothing, but if he lost Fifi, then his life would be bereft of meaning. He would do anything to see her safe again. *Anything, just don't hurt her,* he prayed to god, though he was not a believer. But if she turned up alright, he may yet convert. It would not be fair to lose her before he even gained her. Maybe she wouldn't accept his advances, the thought struck him, but he would be satisfied just to remain near her. They made the trip quickly, though it felt like an age to Ponga. In the village, his fears multiplied.

Terrified people ran through the streets, and dead bodies lay strewn about them. The market more closely resembled a battlefield. When they arrived there, people jumped away from them in fright thinking that the Marquis' horsemen had returned. But they soon realised their mistake when they saw that the newcomers bore no threat, they went about their business and ignored them. Ponga noticed that the bodies of leather-clad swamp people lay in of the houses, he dismounted and ran over to them. Gustave pushed himself up on his elbows, a large pool of blood beneath him.

"Claude is dead; the riders took Fifi, and they will be back soon to destroy the village."

"Where did they take her?" Ponga asked in desperately.

"I don't know; they stabbed me before that and poor Claude too." He looked pityingly at the body beside him.

"I heard they took her to a barn by the main road," said a boy who'd been hanging around them.

"Thank you," Ponga said gratefully. He placed a hand on the boys' shoulder, and with the other he fished a silver coin from his pocket and gave it to him.

Meanwhile, Remy also arrived and noted his comrade's condition with horror.

"Take the injured home," Ponga ordered him, "I'll go after the riders."

He jumped on his horse when the boy called after him.

"My lord, don't you want to know how many there are?"

"It doesn't matter," Ponga clenched his teeth, "they're all dead."

Fifi lay tied up on the dirty barn floor. She could not accept her fate; she simply could not accept that the same thing would happen to her twice, and just when she had met someone who could change her life. She tried to move her hands and feet, to see if the ropes might loosen, but the knots were tight. Gilles, who was guarding her, could not restrain himself. He went over to her and flipped her over.

"Enjoy it, you little slut," he said sweating with excitement as he undid her blouse; then he began to roughly grope her breasts.

His hands hurt her, but the shame was far more painful. She knew that soon all the men would rape her, but she did not want to accept her fate.

"If you don't stop," she warned Gilles, "I will tell your boss you touched me. And he will cut off your prick."

"Well, okay," the man pondered the situation, "you are right. I can wait a little longer, but you had better know that I will mount you many times, you little bitch."

He buttoned up her blouse and walked away from her, but in doorway he turned around and spat:

"I've been inside you before, I know you enjoyed it. You haven't got long to wait, and you'll be enjoying yourself again."

Then he slammed the door, and Fifi was left alone. Hours passed until the sound of hooves broke the silence. She knew that this sound meant that she had nothing left to hope for. The riders arrived and dragged her outside; they untied her and held her tightly.

Julien began unbuttoning his trousers, and he grunted at his men.

"Tear her clothes off." With a few rough movements, they freed her of her garb.

Fifi stood there naked in front of five men, and she couldn't even move in their strong grips. In a hopeless rage she broke into tears, though she had determined not to utter a sound and to not show her emotions.

"Throw her to the ground," Julien said; his trousers around his ankles, his erect member protruding conspicuously. Then they held her down, and the Marquis' son lay on top of her and pushed his manhood into her. Julien looked at her with eyes glassy from pleasure as he moaned.

"Stop it, you maggots!" A voice came from behind them.

The men suddenly let her go, and she quickly slid out from under Julien. They reached for their weapons while the Marquis' son fumbled lamely with his trousers shouting at the stranger,

"You'll die for this, you bastard!"

Fifi looked into the stranger's face. She recognised Didier, and she was overcome with a terrible feeling of shame. Not only was he seeing her naked, he was witness to her rape.

"Well, death there will be," Ponga said in a furious, icy whisper. The men were frightened of him, though they outnumbered him.

"Get him," Julien shouted, "what are you waiting for?"

Ponga held a long dagger in his left hand, and his sword in his right. He knew that this time he wasn't going to play around like he usually did, he would kill as quickly as he could.

Gilles was the bravest and launched an attack. Ponga stepped to the right, deflected a blow with his sword and plunged the dagger into his opponents exposed chest. He did all this with incomprehensible speed. The others stood frozen, but Ponga was in full swing. He lunged forward and found a sheath for both his blades in two men's throats. The fourth henchman turned and tried to run, but he quickly received a sword in his back. Julien sprang in terror onto his hoards, but Ponga caught his leg before it reached the stirrup and pulled him to the ground.

"I am the son of Marquis Gilbert de Bilon," Julien blubbered.

"Right," Ponga said sinking his dagger into the man, but he did not want to kill him outright, so he only dipped the point into his flesh. He wanted the man to suffer.

Julien screamed and began writhing in the dust.

"Take up your sword!" Ponga said; he knew he would enjoy toying with this beast who had been between Fifi's legs not so long ago.

"No, don't, I can pay you a lot of money," Julien tried reasoning with his torturer.

"Raise your sword!" Ponga shouted.

The Marquis' son saw that he had only one hope left: a swift attack. He ran desperately forward, hoping in the element of surprise. But Ponga deflected his blow easily and sunk his dagger into his opponent's groin. Julien gave a blood curdling shriek and fell to the ground dropping his weapon.

"Please, don't! My god, it hurts!" Was all he could say.

"Take up your sword!" Ponga said again; an evil smile appearing on his face.

"No!" Julien resisted. Then Ponga pierced his thigh. The strike was followed by another scream.

"Take up your sword!" Ponga repeated.

Despite the excruciating pain, Julien reached for his sword because he did not want to be stabbed again.

"Didier!" Fifi said, "I know he deserves it, but I can't watch this."

"Sorry," Ponga said catching himself, "I was thinking only of myself when I should be taking care of you."

He looked at Julien kneeling before him and stabbed his neck with such force that the blade came out the back of his skull.

Then he ran to Fifi and tried to hug her, but Fifi pushed him off ashamedly.

"Excuse me, I'm very ashamed."

During the fight, Ponga had thought about what he would say when he held her in his arms. He wanted to talk about how worried he had been, and how he would do anything to see her whole and healthy again, but he just stood there, and all he could say was,

"I love you!"

Fifi embraced him, as she was naked, dirty and dishevelled.

"I love you too," she replied.

Chapter Twenty-Three

Farall opened his eyes. He felt like his head was about to explode from the sudden pain. He was in a room, and he could a see a slim woman wearing a floral-patterned dress standing with her back to him.

Before he could speak to her, the stranger turned around and dropped a damp cloth from her hand in surprise.

"Are you awake, my lord?" her voice chimed pleasantly.

Farall sensed that something was not right, but he could not tell at once what was amiss. Slowly he realised that she expected an answer from him. He looked at her. In fact, he had not been able to take his eyes off her since he'd opened them. He'd seen red-headed beauties before, but nothing like her. Her thick, wavy hair fell in locks over her shoulders. Her pretty white skin was decorated with freckles around her nose, and Farall suddenly realised that he loved freckled. Strange that he had never known this before. But the most beautiful thing about her were her light green eyes with which she watched him awaiting his response.

"Well, I think so, yes." Something was not right, but he still did not know what the matter was; only that something was wrong, of that he was certain.

"Are you ill, my lord?" The green eyes looked at him with concern.

"No, not really," he said and stood up quickly. The thin sheet that covered his body fell to the ground, leaving him standing there naked. Ashamed, he leapt back into the bed lifting the cover from the floor.

"Why am I naked?" he asked going red with embarrassment.

"I'm sorry, my lord, but I had to wash your clothes; they were covered in blood and mud. And I had to check if you had any other injuries as well. Somebody tied you up, but you must have escaped them."

"Why, where am I injured?" Farall asked lifting the sheet with one hand to check himself. His body was covered in bruises and scratches. He made absolutely certain that his nurse could not peek under the covers.

"Well, you've a cut on your forehead. You looked pretty bad, but don't worry, I've dressed the wound. And I'll bring you your clothes now," as she said this, she ran from the room. Carefully, making sure the sheets covered his privates, Farall sat up. He couldn't understand what was going on. But he didn't have much time to think, as the girl reappeared with his clothes.

"Here." She handed him his clean, washed clothes. Then with a small smile in the corner of her mouth, she stood before him.

"Thank you," Farall replies shyly; then he looked at her. "Would you mind going outside while I dress."

"Who do you think undressed you and washed you with a damp cloth, who cared for you? But if you're so shy, then I'll go outside,"

she said turning around and marching out in mock offence. Farall surveyed the freshly washed uniform. Maybe she hadn't brought him his clothes.

His feeling of foreboding intensified. He dressed quickly and noted a badge on the shirt. Then he went through to the other room. When she saw him, she stood up and introduced herself.

"My name is Amelie Chanel; what is your name, my lord?" She stretched out her hand politely.

Farall was completely confused, and he realised that he couldn't really remember anything—he couldn't even remember his name. He panicked, who was he? He tried hard to remember his past, but there was nothing. Suddenly he did not know what to tell her. He just stared at her outstretched hand, but he didn't dare take it because he would have to tell her name to go with it, and he had no idea.

"Sorry, is there a mirror in the house?" He grunted. Maybe he could recognise himself and realise who he was.

"Oh, how vain," she laughed, "believe me your face has not been ruined; a few days, and your scar will disappear."

"You misunderstand me, that's not it. I'll explain in a second, but now bring me a mirror!"

Amelie was surprised, but she said nothing more, bringing the stranger a mirror.

Farall stared at himself for a long time and saw that he was quite handsome as best he could judge. His black hair reached his shoulder, his eyes were dark brown, and his face was framed by a short beard. But he had no idea who this stranger was staring back at him from the mirror.

"The situation," he began telling the shocked girl, "is that I don't know who I am. I don't remember anything of my past. I feel like my whole life began just a few minutes ago."

"Are you joking with me, sir?"

"Do I look like I'm joking? Help me, Amelie. You're the only person I know in this whole world."

"You know, we live a solitary life here with my parents," she began, "but my father is scientist. I'll call him here, but you should know that he is not at all pleased about my bringing you here."

"Thank you, you are very kind to me," Farall replied gratefully. Amelie stormed away, and Farall sat desperately on the bed. What if by tomorrow he forgot today too? Who was he anyway? How did he get injured? What uniform was he wearing? The storm of questions made his mind reel, and he couldn't answer a single one of them. Soon Amelie returned with a thin man, with a high forehead and searching eyes who looked at him distrustfully.

"Good day, sir!" Amelie's father began, gesticulating like a spider as he spoke. "My name is René Chanel. And you, if you are telling the truth, are unable to introduce yourself."

"That is right. I could lie, but I have no intention of doing so. The truth is that I am very miserable. Have you heard of such a thing before?"

"Yes, though it is not too common, but I have heard of such instances, though I've never met anyone it has happened to." Chanel looked at him as if he were staring at a rare and infinitely interesting scientific problem, which, for Farall's host, he was.

"How could this have happened?" Farall stood up and looked Chanel straight in the eye.

"I think you lost your memories because you hit your head," he said pointing at Farall's forehead.

"And when will I remember again?"

"Who knows, perhaps you will stay this way, you will excuse my honesty."

"Daddy!" Amelie interjected heatedly. "How can you say such a thing to him? He's in no condition to put up with your blabbering. If you cannot help him, at least don't hurt him!"

"You are right, my darling, better if our guest has something to eat and then comes to my office to discuss what to do next," Chanel said blushing at his daughter's chastisement. The moment René Chanel mentioned food, Farall realised that he was starving, and his stomach began to rumble. Amelie brought him ham, some cheese, fresh brown bread and a pitcher of weak wine. After a hearty meal, he did not see his situation as being so bad. It was true that he knew nothing of his previous life, but it was likely that his past had not been as splendid as he had been found tied up and hunted.

Perhaps it was better never to find out what had happened to him.

He stood up and went to seek out the lord of the house. He passed through two tastefully decorated rooms and came to a closed door. Before he could open it, he heard heated voices from within:

"He cannot stay here," he heard René Chanel's hoarse voice, "he'll endanger us."

"But, Daddy," Amelie objected, "we cannot just throw him out; he doesn't even know who he is. You cannot toss him into the unknown. Someone tried to kill him, and he doesn't even know who they were. He could easily wander into their trap once more."

"You should not have brought him here," said an older female voice.

"But, Mother, I could not just leave him there bleeding and unconscious."

"You are right," the head of the family muttered, "I will speak with him. Maybe I can solve the problem."

Farall did not want to eavesdrop further, so he took a deep breath and opened the door. The room suddenly went silent; René Chanel stood up and approached Farall.

"Please allow me, sir, to introduce my wife; my daughter you know already." An attractive woman stood up and approached Farall; her hair glistened red like her daughter's.

"Yvette Chanel." She offered her hand.

Farall kissed it and felt instinctively that she was a woman aristocracy. How he knew what the correct behaviour in the situation was, he had no idea. He must have been among rich people before, perhaps he too was well-off.

"I'm sorry I cannot give you my name, my lady," he replied sadly.

"I know, and believe me I am very sorry," her eyes displayed genuine pity.

"I do not want to be a burden to you; I was witness to your conversation despite my best intentions," he admitted.

"Come, sit down, we'll figure something out," René said and sent his family outside. He only spoke again once the women had left:

"I owe you an explanation," he began, "you must find it strange that your presence caused such a commotion here. You will understand once I've told you our story. Once upon a time, I was a rich nobleman, who was relentlessly drawn towards science.

This was to be my downfall. I came into increasingly heated debates with the priest who lived on my land, who did not appreciate my reading old books, or that I did not blindly accept the church's often pointless principles. I did not believe that my family could get into trouble for my bad relationship with the church. I will not bore you with my feud against the priest—there's no time. Sufficed to say that I now know that I was stupid when I thought I could defeat the church. My mistake almost cost my family their lives. I cannot forgive myself my irresponsibility till my dying day. The priest went to the city and reported that I had denied God. Luckily for me, a faithful servant reported that a small army was headed to my estate to seize me and my family. I had time only to collect as much gold as I could carry and escape to the far side of the kingdom. This was many years ago, and we've lived here since, and we only go into the nearby village when we must. I do not want the locals to get suspicious, so we live here alone. I've been honest with you, because I have no other choice than to trust in your understanding. If you betray us, we are done for. The fact that you do not remember your past further endangers us because if you regain your memories, you may turn against us. Even if you now promise not to do so."

"I understand you worries," he replied, "but I can do nothing more now than to assure you that I will not hurt you or your family. I will keep this promise even if I remember again since you saved my life. I thank you for your kindness, and I will be going at once."

"You're not going anywhere," Chanel said firmly, "leaving will not help any more. You'll stay here a while, maybe you'll remember, and if not, you can live with us. Provided, of course, that you accept that you cannot go among other people, we will be safe here."

"Thank you for your kindness, and I accept your terms," Farall replied, while thinking that he could not image a more pleasant incarceration than being locked up with Amelie.

Night fell. The French Royal Castle was silent as a crypt. The ruler had been fighting for his life for days, and in such a situation, no one was permitted to make a sound. Councillor Perrier was just exiting the King's bedchamber when Marquis Bertrand gently touched his arm.

"Excuse me, Councillor, do you know anything of Archbishop Leroy? The thing is, I agreed to meet him, and he is never late." His voice was lacking his usual pompousness. The Councillor sensed a slight tremor in his touch too.

"I'm coming from the King now, and you are worried about Leroy, not our grace's condition?" Perrier did not want to contain himself. He was certain that the Marquis was involved in Farall's disappearance, since the Archbishop did nothing without the marquis' consent. He would have like to impale the man where he stood.

"Errrr, you misunderstand me, I'm looking for the Archbishop because I wish to pray for our king's recovery," the Marquis stammered.

"I see," Perrier said frowning, "but why are you asking me? Send a servant to fetch him."

"I have. If you hear of something, kindly let me know."

"Of course, but you'll excuse me now, I have a lot to do." Without waiting for response, the Councillor left.

Perrier was filled with worry. Farall had disappeared about 24 hours ago, that is, he'd been kidnapped by the Archbishop. The chances that he was not a piece of ground-up meat by now were slim. *Poor Vincent,* he thought. He was almost at his chambers when he spotted Commander Azor approaching him.

"Sir." The liquidator bowed. "We've completed the task; the prisoner is upstairs."

"I see," Perrier said somewhat relieved, "then let us go! I will begin the interrogation immediately."

Upstairs, the Councillor had a secret interrogation room. When he did not wish a prisoner's presence to be public or did not want the jailers to blab about what they'd heard, then he used the 'upstairs room' where his own people did the dirty work. He was so sick with worry that he bounded up the stairs tow at a time throwing his dignity to the wind and then ran along the corridor to the room.

When he entered, Head Liquidator Luc Moreau saluted him, but Leroy could not speak a word as he was bound and gagged. The windowless room was lit by torched. There were four of them inside—the two liquidators, the Councillor and the naked Archbishop tied to a chair. Perrier lent down and looked into Leroy's eyes. Secretly he hoped that fear and the situation would be enough to break his victim, but the priest's eyes seemed to hold a glimmer of hope in them yet. The Councillor had no time to break his victim nice and slowly because Vincent was probably in some other torture chamber going through hell and being crippled forever.

There was no time to waste; he needed immediate results, and so he had to make this bird sing quickly.

"Cut off one of his fingers," he said nonchalantly as he took a step back. He did not take his eyes off Leroy; he watched him the whole time while Azor raised a pair of scissors, bent over the prisoner's bound hand and completed the order in the blink of an eye. The gagged pleased could only groan, but he soiled himself from the pain and fright. The Councillor watched all this like snake watching its prey, with unmoving eyes, indifferently.

"Water him down!" the Councillor said off-handedly.

Commander Azor poured a bucket of cold water over the half-conscious priest. Perrier leaned over him once more and examined his eyes again. He was pleased to see that there was only a terrible fear of death remaining in those eyes.

"Listen," the Councillor almost whispered, "what just happened to you is just an innocent little game compared to what comes next if you fail to cooperate with me. I will ask you questions, and you will answer them, but if you dare lie to me, I will be truly rough with you. Only answer my questions, nothing more. Nod your head if you understand!"

The terrified priest nodded vigorously. Perrier didn't want to torture him further, he'd seen it too many times how tortured people began talking nonsense after a while. They'd admit to anything, even things they had not done, and he needed useful information only, so he motioned to Azor to take the gag from the priest's mouth.

"Where is Vincent Farall?"

"I…I…kidnapped him. On the Marquis' orders, but…"

"Careful what you say because the next thing I chop off will be your manhood!"

"I'm telling the truth! I'm telling the truth! I wouldn't dare to, I swear it, I swear it!" Meanwhile Leroy looked in panic at his fear-shrivelled member dangling between his thighs.

"Where is Vincent Farall?" The Councillor could tell instinctively that the priest was telling the truth.

"I kidnapped him and took him to Beauvais, but he escaped on route. I'm telling the truth, my lord; I took two goof men, but they swore on their lives that the boy jumped from the carriage though his hands and feet were tied, and his eyes blindfolded. They only noticed he was missing when they arrived in Beauvais, and by then it was morning. I only found out what happened not long ago."

"Should I cut off your prick, or will you tell me the truth." Perrier knew the priest was not lying, but he wanted to be sure.

"I swear I'm telling the truth," Leroy sobbed. "The two men are called Pierre Surau and Lucien Noiret."

"Why did you kidnap him?"

"The Marquis wants to know all about your plans; he considers you his enemy, my lord. He was afraid that you would try to stop our plans after the King's death, provided he does die."

"Put the gag back in his mouth!" the Councillor ordered. "Find these two men immediately and interrogate them. I will be in my room awaiting your findings. And you," he said turning towards the priest, "pray that they confirm what you've just said."

He turned on his heel and left the room.

Perrier stayed awake and awaited the news with dread. He vowed to be much more honest with his aid when they met again. There were so many things he had to tell him, maybe he would never get the chance. This thought bothered him the most. Dawn broke, and he sat behind his desk unable to distract himself. He was in no mood to go about official business, nor did he feel like reading. He just sat there and stared at the door, waiting for his men who would bring him news of the life or death of his aid.

Around three o'clock in the morning, there was a knock at the door, and Commander Azor entered.

"What news?" Perrier demanded in lieu of a greeting.

"The priest spoke the truth, sir," Azor said curtly.

"Don't make me draw it out of you," the Councillor grunted, "tell me everything!"

"Sir, Surau and Noiret said the same thing as Leroy, I interrogated them separately. Farall was placed, bound and blindfolded into the carriage, and they left for Beauvais. Only when they arrived did they notice that the carriage was empty. That was this morning they headed back for Paris immediately, to tell the Archbishop the bad news."

"Are you sure they were not lying?"

"Sir, their held their stories till their ends. I am certain they were telling the truth."

"Alright, then take a few of your men and start combing the area around the road. Vincent cannot have gone too far from there," Perrier said springing up and pacing his office, like a caged animal. His helpless rage seethed inside him.

"Sir, this could take a long time, the road is at least 20 miles long."

"Did I ask how long it would take? Go at once!" Perrier rarely shouted at the Commander, who showed no emotion. If he was offended by the Councillor's behaviour, he gave no sign of it. It was true that he was in no position to do so either.

"Sir, what about Archbishop Leroy?" Azor asked calmly, as if his superior had not just shouted at him.

"He told the truth, he deserves a quick death and get rid of his corpse immediately!" Perrier replied, then dismissed the Commander with a wave.

Leroy is a lucky man, the Councillor thought, *because if Vincent had not escaped that carriage, the Archbishop would have been under his claws for weeks on end.*

Chapter Twenty-Four

Heiress Teresa de Cantabria spent the happiest week of her life in the little village near Madrid where she had moved on Councillor Pedro Garcia's orders.

She lived under heavy guard in a little house on the outskirts of the village. Her days were spent simply and pleasantly. A little gardening after breakfast, a walk after lunch with her escorts and reading till she fell asleep in the evening. *Being away from the Queen makes life wonderful,* Teresa thought. The Councillor had said that she would only have to stay there till the Queen gave birth, and then things would settle down. But she would have been happy to stay in the village for any amount of time. The house she was staying in was not too elegant, but it had a friendly atmosphere. The house's whitewashed walls glistened blindingly in the sunlight, and the walnut-brown shutters and door stood in stark contrast to the walls. Most of all, she liked the cascade of flowers blooming on the windowsills. The fenced-in garden was like a wonderful roofless room, with little, gently babbling fountain in its centre. She liked to spend her time in a hidden corner of the garden surrounded by dense bushes where she had had a little bench placed. Teresa was just like a cat, hiding manically anywhere she could to disappear from the world.

On that day, which further confused her already complicated life, she was sitting in her favourite hiding place feeling like nothing from the outside world could touch her behind those bushes. She was watching a blackbird hiding in the nearby branches when an ominous sound reached her ears. There were sounds of shouting in the distance and the clashing of swords. She dared not move, as she felt invincible among the green plants even if, logically, she knew very well that this was not the case. *If only I could be a bird, like this blackbird, then no one would ever find me, and I could fly wherever my heart desired,* she thought.

She was jolted from her dream by Liquidator Alonso barging into the garden. She liked him best of the men who guarded her. She'd grown to like him, and even thought that he was the most handsome man she'd ever seen. The liquidator ran to the bush because he knew Teresa always hid there when she was in the garden.

"My lady! We must flee at once! Hurry!"

Teresa quickly exited her hiding place and was shocked to see that Alonso was bleeding heavily.

"What happened to you? You're bleeding, we must dress your wound at once," she blurted and reached to mop the blood flowing from the liquidator's chest with her handkerchief.

"My Lady, pay me no heed," Alonso replied and gently pushed her hand away. "Here's a purse. There's enough gold in it for you to get back to the castle."

Meanwhile, the noises of battle had reached the house, and the smashing of blades and blood-curdling screams were nearby.

"You cannot leave through the house," the liquidator said bleeding profusely – this was the first time he did not add "My Lady" to his sentence. She would have liked him to speak to her so informally at other times too, but she knew there would be no other times.

"We're going to go to the fence and I'm going to lift you over it," he panted, and he led her over as he spoke. She had no time to answer as she found herself on the other side of the fence.

"Take care, Alonso!" she sobbed and began running.

"Yes, My Lady," the liquidator answered, and Teresa heard a warmth in his voice, but she might have just imagined it. What she definitely heard was Alonso's shout, which would be his last.

She ran in terror and fear drove her legs rapidly beneath her. Her mind lazed feverishly as she went. If they were in the garden, then her only chance was to reach the woods next to the village. She looked ahead and saw that she had a few hundred meters left to run, and she heard shouting from behind her.

"There she is, get her! I want her head!"

Teresa did not believe she could run any faster, but she could. Her will to live gave her a power she could not have dreamed of. Her legs carried her with a speed more akin to a horse than a person. She did not dare look back, but despite her pursuers being slowed by their armour, she could hear from their sounds that they were gaining on her.

What if, the thought crossed her mind, *they start shooting arrows?* They would have to stop for that and the woods were very close now, she might make it before the arrows reached her.

They probably knew this too, because they were still running.

Teresa reached the cover of the trees, but her relief did not last long, as the thick undergrowth slowed her down. Her frilly, elegant dress was not designed for running through bushes, and though she tried holding the hem up, the thorns tore at the cloth. She could almost feel her pursuers' breath on her neck, but the dense foliage also offered her cover. Teresa could feel her strength waning and she quickly jumped behind a bush just in time, because the soldiers appeared rushing past the bush she was hiding in. She tried breathing quietly, she didn't want her panting to lead the soldiers to her. Then she heard someone shout, "Stop. Two men turn around because the little bitch might be hiding somewhere."

Teresa knew she couldn't stay where she was too long. Sooner or later they would find her there. Then she remembered how, after begging Alonso to go for a walk with her, they had gone to the banks of the nearby river. It was somewhere nearby. Perhaps, if she could make it there, she could cross over and her pursuers could not track her there. As she lay hidden, she could even hear the gurgling of the water, and though she was not certain, there was nothing to lose so she set out in the direction of the sound. The gurgling increased and in a few minutes, she found the rapid little brook. As she watched it, she was forced to accept the fact that she would not be able to cross as the flow was too rapid.

She'd not been on the riverbank more than two minutes when her pursuers caught up with her.

"There she is! Come on! You gave us a good run around, little wench!"

Teresa quickly tied the pouch Alonso had given her and gritted her teeth. She would sooner die in the water than in their hands. She flung herself into the water. The cold water chilled her to the bone and the current dragged her along so powerfully that she was out of sight in a moment. She heard the soldiers fling themselves into the water after her, but she could not know that the men in heavy armour were dragged down beneath the foam.

Councillor Pedro Garcia sat behind his desk. He liked watching the rays of sunlight that leaked through his window illuminating the specks of dust floating off the books and carpets. The sight filled him with a calm, peaceful sensation. But that morning, the sunshine and dancing dust were lost on him—he was restless and nervous. He did not like what had happened in the royal castle in the past few days, he knew very well that Queen Esmeralda was plotting something. If it had not been so, she would not have asked King Carlos to live together in the royal suite till the birth of their child. There Esmeralda was untouchable, he could not get to her when she was with the King. Since then, she'd been increasingly condescending towards him. He was worried about Teresa, because he thought that Esmeralda's behaviour was certainly connected with the Heiress. He had threatened that bitch firmly, but to little effect. A woman who would sleep with anyone just to bear a royal heir would do anything to get what she wanted.

The Councillor felt hopeless, and this was an unfamiliar feeling for him. He'd hidden Teresa from the eyes of the court, but it was just a temporary solution. The problem would have to be solved somehow, but at the moment, there was nothing he could do – he had to wait, and this was the hardest part.

There was a knock at the door. He'd not even said "Yes," but the door was opening and Head Liquidator, Marcos Sanchez, entered and hurried directly to the Councillor's table.

"Excuse me, Sir, but this cannot wait."

The Councillor sensed that there was something wrong. He gave no outward signs, but worry consumed him inside.

"Speak," he said curtly, as he looked Sanchez in the eye.

"The Heiress' house was attacked. They were outnumbered, all our men were killed. Lady Teresa escaped, but we have no information on whether she succeeded."

"Dammit, that stupid bitch won't get away with this!" Garcia hissed, looking at the Head Liquidator. "Do you think she's still alive?"

"If I were them, I would not hide the body, because people might question her death, leaving the question of inheritance open."

"Send men to the scene and search everywhere, maybe you can find a trace of her."

"I've made arrangements, Sir."

The Councillor liked the Head Liquidator's independence, though he knew this trait sometimes did more harm than good. But Sanchez had never made a hurried mistake.

"Alright," Garcia said as he stood up and started towards the door. He did not mention that he should be informed of any news, because he knew it would happen anyway. "Now, I will go see the royal wife."

When the Councillor entered the King's chambers, he was somewhat relieved to see that Esmeralda could never hide her feelings. This made it easy to guess that she was very angry, her eyes flashed, and her hands drummed nervously on the armrests of her chair. Carlos greeted his arrival with jovial calm, "I'm glad you've come to visit us, Councillor. Is there some reason for your visit?"

"Nothing special, My Lord," Garcia bowed, "I'm just here out of curiosity. I wanted to know how our Queen and heir-to-be are doing."

"Oh, thank you, for your kind question. Everything is perfectly fine," Carlos replied, while Esmeralda could barely contain herself. Watching the Queen, the Councillor knew for sure that she had not managed to capture Teresa. This was precisely the information he had come for. *If only all my enemies were as easy to read* he thought.

"My Lady," Garcia smiled, "you are very quiet today, though the King has just told me that everything is perfectly fine."

"So it is," Esmeralda replied, barely keeping it together. She'd just recently been told that the wench had somehow escaped. But how could she have? How could a small army of men armed to the teeth fail to capture one teenager? Speaking with the Councillor was difficult for her now. The rat was probably laughing behind her back. She spat her words as if she were being sick, "I just feel a little weak today."

"Then I will bother you no further with my presence," the Councillor replied, his voice containing a little mockery, "if you'll excuse me, I'll take my leave. I have much to attend to."

On the way out, Garcia savoured the sweet taste of revenge, *you will pay for everything my Lady, and I will have no mercy on you. It's not in my nature.*

Teresa woke shivering. Dawn in the woods offered never before seen visions to her. Her situation was desperate, but in that moment, in the heart of the forest, she felt like she had never done before. Birds hopped around in the dew-specked grass, their chirping washed over the meadow and the cool spring air softly caressed her skin. For a short while, she was engrossed in the bounty of nature, and then, she remembered the last few hours.

When she'd thrown herself into the river, she'd thought she was going to die, and the icy water had chilled her to the bone. She was a strong swimmer, her body did what it needed to and the she only had to make small movements as the current took her. She knew struggling would only drag her to the bottom. After a brief rest, she continued her escape into the woods. The night had been terrifying, she thought she would not be able to sleep, but fatigue overcame her fear and overcame her as she sat.

Her stomach rumbled. Standing up, she checked if she still had the pouch Alonso had given her, and then went down to the stream where she had drunk the day before. After a long refreshing draught, she headed out. If she reached a village, she could get something to eat there. Then, she would find someone to take her to the castle where she would be safe.

She walked all day and her clothes were torn and soiled, as if she'd been wearing them for weeks. She was becoming desperate when she spotted a church spire in the late afternoon.

By the time she reached the settlement, night was falling. She was glad she did not have to spend another night in the woods and she could not have kept going without food for much longer.

Nobody paid her any heed in the village. People came and went about their own business. Her dirty clothes made her look similar to the villagers, and in the dark, no one noticed that she was wearing a noblewoman's dress.

She turned into a side street and spotted three armed men. She noticed that they were not wearing uniform like her pursuers and this calmed her a little. She was almost past then when one of them caught her arm.

"Where you off to, little lady?" he asked mockingly.

"What's it to you?" Teresa replied, and tried to free her arm from the soldier's grasp.

"Don't struggle, little lady!" he was enjoying his power.

"Let me go! You're hurting me!" she was almost in tears with hopelessness. *She could not fall victim to a few drunken scoundrels when half an army had failed to catch her before*, she thought desperately.

"Now, we're going to play a little game," her attacker grabbed her with two hands and pulled her to him. "Looky here, what's this?" he spotted the pouch on her belt and tore it off in a swift motion.

"It seems we're going to have a party tonight, boys," he said, turning to his companions.

"But first, we're going to play, my dear!" Teresa struggled in vain, she could not break the man's grasp.

Suddenly, someone stepped out of the shadows, she could see only their silhouette in the settling dusk. He wore a hood, but he was no priest as he wore tight fitting clothing and held a sword in his hand.

He approached them slowly.

"That's enough," he spoke. His voice was perfectly calm, but also grated unpleasantly, "let the girl go and go home while you still can."

"Leave it out, you idiot!" the man holding Teresa replied.

"Get the hell outta here!" another added.

"Fine by me," the stranger replied.

Then he swung into such a speedy attack that Teresa could barely follow him. She had seen many knights battle in the King's court but she had never imagined that such speed existed. The figure jumped from the shadows, pulling a dagger from behind his back and thrust forwards with the two weapons at once. Both blades hit their mark. His victims didn't even have time to defend themselves, because only the man holding Teresa was left standing, while his two comrades lay moaning in pools of their own blood. They did not have long left to live.

"One more move, n' the girl's dead!" the soldier shouted desperately, holding a dagger to Teresa's throat.

"If someone is so stupid that they cannot see their options then they deserve to die," the hooded man said and pierced his enemy's throat with such speed that he had no chance of hurting Teresa. The mysterious man then lent over the body, took Teresa's purse off the corpse.

"This is yours," he said, handing the purse full of gold to her, "now we must leave the village quickly, they will discover the bodies soon."

Teresa was still in shock from what had happened and she allowed the man to lead her along. Soon, she was riding through the night with her saviour.

She'd never travelled this way before, with two on a horse – but she was not scared, the man held her tightly and he was a good rider.

Neither of them spoke on the way, and she looked sidelong at him, illuminated as he was, by the moonlight. He was not young, and the slip of the hood as they rode revealed long, greying hair, a short beard and the scar that crossed his face. Despite his wild appearance, she was not afraid of him, because his eyes radiated kindness and intelligence.

They'd been travelling for about an hour when they reached another village. They soon found the only inn, which was also the local tavern. The man paid for a room and then ordered food, telling the innkeeper to bring it up to the room. The owner did not ask why they would not eat downstairs, though he had no reason to, he had been given enough gold not to have questions.

They finished dinner and still not a word had passed between them. Teresa was so confused by the horrors she'd experienced that she was glad of a little silence. And the stranger, for some reason, did not ask anything. When they had their fill, the man packed his pipe and smoked, letting the smoke roll luxuriously from between his lips. Finally, Teresa broke the silence.

"You are not from the countryside, sir. you must be a noble, the way you speak."

"If you say so," the man replied grimly.

"Will you tell me your name?" Teresa inquired. "If you tell me yours, I'll introduce myself also."

The warrior smiled, he liked the informal banter of this little teenager. It had been a long time since anyone had been kind to him.

Wherever he went, his road was fraught with terror, but this little girl was attentive of him.

"Your name is Teresa de Cantabria, if I am not mistaken," he smiled, expelling a plume of smoke. He took a little pleasure in her astonishment.

"Are you a mind reader, sir? How do you know? Will you tell me?" Teresa asked in one breath.

"Many questions, little lady. Let's see – your speech and garb are of royalty. Who would have clothes where the embroidery is worth more than a villager's house? Then, if a man listens about in taverns, one hears many things. Like, for example, that the Heiress is being kept in the area, and that her house was attacked not long ago. If I also add that the Archbishop's soldiers are searching for a well-dressed girl in every village, then it is not hard to find out who you are."

"True, though I must say, nobody has noticed me till now."

"People are stupid and don't pay attention to details," the man said, drawing hard on his pipe, and languidly expelling the smoke.

"But you are a very strange man," she said. She was beginning to enjoy his company more and more, "you are not too young, yet you fight like none other. Your speech is refined but your clothes are ragged. And nothing escapes your attention, and you help strangers. Will you tell me your name?"

"My name is Alejandro," the man replied curtly.

"Those who will not reveal their surname are keeping a secret," Teresa frowned.

"Look at that! Interrogation in exchange for my saving you," Alejandro said, frowning playfully back at her.

"Excuse me, sir, I was ill-mannered. I did not want to hurt you."

"No matter. Now, what is our next step? Archbishop Oscar Martinez, wants to capture you at all costs."

"Well, regarding that," Teresa replied, "if you could take me to Councillor Pedro Garcia in the Royal Castle, we could escape."

When she mentioned the Councillor's name, Alejandro scowled.

"You're not the only observant one," Teresa said with a furrowed brow, "I am too. You do not like Pedro Garcia."

"Why?" the man laughed, "does anyone in the kingdom like him?"

"Yes, I do, he's always taken care of me."

"That's different," Alejandro said, changing tone. He didn't want to offend her, "then he's done something good in his life too. Now let us rest. Tomorrow, we will figure out how we'll get to the castle." The man made a bed for Teresa, and he lay down beside the fireplace. Teresa slept badly, her dreams were restless and she tossed and turned as she relived the events of the past two days. Suddenly, she woke up. She was afraid that if she fell asleep again, she would re-dream all that had happened to her. She got up and went over to Alejandro.

"I'm scared to sleep alone, can I cuddle up to you?"

Alejandro sat up and looked at her. He covered his embarrassment with a smile.

"Come here, don't be scared. You'll be safe with me."

She cuddled up to him, took his hand and pulled it to her. Alejandro's heart was filled with a warmth he had never felt before. He knew he would take Teresa back to the castle even if their road would be lined with corpses along the way.

Chapter Twenty-Five

"I'm very pleased with your attitudes," Ed Wilder said to Roy Davis and Mick Taylor. The two boys stood in front of the Councillor's desk. He jovially filled his wine goblet, "we caught three mutants this week."

"If we continue like this, we will get rid of all the maggots in the Kingdom." Roy would have liked to kill Mick who stood grinning beside him, but he couldn't because he was scared for Claire. He felt like he could no longer stand the slaughter of innocent people, who had the same ability as him and that damned Taylor.

"My Lord," Mick answered sycophantically, "may I ask you something."

Wilder looked at him suspiciously. He did not like people asking favours of him.

"Spit it out, son! Then I'll see what I can do for you."

My Lord, I would like to celebrate our success with Roy. If you would allow us to have this afternoon off, you would afford us a great pleasure."

The Councillor was relieved, because he had secretly been afraid that Taylor would ask for something bigger, like money or rank.

"Go ahead, you've earned it," Wilder replied. Then he searched in his pockets till he found some change and threw it on the table, "here, have a drink on me!"

"Oh, what generosity, Sire," Taylor continued his disgusting flattery, "Thank you!"

Then they left the Councillor's chambers. As they entered the hallway, Roy burst out, "I can't take this any longer, I'll be off now."

"Let's not discuss our matters where the servants can hear us, but if you can't hold it in till the tavern, use telepathy, like I do," Mick's icy style was in stark contrast with the weaselly flattery he used for the Councillor. This good he felt in his telepathy too. "You're coming with me or you'll end up in a torture chamber with your little darling along with the people we captured."

There was nothing Roy could do, but he also knew that he would not help hand another man to the hangman.

"Alright, let's talk, but I cannot handle telepathy like you do. If I speak in my mind, others like us could hear it too," he told Mick.

They left the castle in silence, Taylor did not say a word till they reached the tavern. They ordered two beers, and Mick took a long draught, wiped the foam from his mouth, and then started what he had to say.

"Remember, one talks about important matters when no one else is around, or when surrounded by a lot of people."

"What do you want from me?" Roy asked as he looked around nervously. *This maggot is right*, he thought, *the tavern is packed and no one is paying attention to us.*

Everyone was focused on their own table. *Maybe he can sense all my thoughts?* He looked nervously at his companion. *It cannot be*, he calmed himself, because telepathy required predefined thoughts in his mind. *In any case, I have to pay close attention to what is going on in my mind,* he determined. Not as if he hadn't known this till now.

"Look, there are two types of people," Mick began his lesson. "One group are people I can use, and the others, I cannot. I do not care for the second group, but I value the ones I can use greatly. It is up to you which you want to be. We can go far together."

"You want to gain rank in the Court?" Roy asked. He didn't understand what Roy was getting at. But it was becoming increasingly apparent that Taylor loved showing his intelligence. He was vain about his mind, like a girl about her breasts.

"True power is not given to you, it is gained for yourself," Mick replied condescendingly, "the two of us can lead Ed Wilder by the nose. I've already made quite a lot of gold by not handing over some people to the Councillor. Of course, I gave him one or two mutants, since we have to show something for our work. But it's not only mutants who pay, but others too."

"How come?"

"Look!" Mick leaned close to Roy. "If I say someone is a mutant, then they will be taken. Of course, they will deny it at first, but after being treated by the jailers everyone will admit to anything. Got it? We decide who lives and who dies. This is true power, and it is very lucrative."

As Roy listened to this insipid worm, he racked his brain as to how he could end this situation. The biggest problem was that Mick could sense his thoughts as well as Claire's. He could not even tell her what trouble she was in because she may have revealed it despite herself, since neither of them was able to block their thoughts. He just listened to the gratuitous boasting of Mick, until he realised the only real solution—just in time, because Taylor finished what he was saying.

"Well, let me hear it, will you be my partner or are you against me?"

"You know," Roy said, collecting all his thespian abilities, because he knew that Claire's and his lives depended on his behaviour, "you've convinced me. I didn't think you had it all so well planned. I have only one fear."

"Tell me! I'm sure I can come up with a solution," Taylor said pompously, and patted Roy on the back, condescendingly.

"If we start this wonderful venture, then I will be vulnerable to other mutants since they can see into my head and so may betray me to the Councillor. Of course, I can deny it, but if it happens several times, the old man will certainly discover who I really am. He accepts you the way you are because he wanted a mutant to work for him, but I've deceived him for many years and he won't accept it. Besides, I cannot control my thoughts. You can speak to me without words without another mutant noticing anything."

"No problem," Mick replied confidently, "I will teach you how to block your thoughts and even how to control them. I can train you in just a few minutes."

"Let's shake on it," Roy replied, reaching his hand over the table which Taylor took gleefully.

Roy was very careful not to let his thought form into words, because if the monster sitting opposite him knew of his plan, he will kill him on the spot.

Sir Lemmy Black sat at a round table in the liquidators' hall. Above this huge room was where the liquidator slept, so if someone was not on duty, they sat in the company of others in this common area. The sight of the Strategist was not uncommon there, he often walked among the liquidators. No one dared bother him, as his persona commanded a mix of fear and respect.

Black felt as if the mission to discover the King's assassin were stagnating. He had tried provoking the King's Council in vain, he could make the perpetrators make a mistake, in other words, he had failed to scare the rabbit out of the bush. Sitting in the hall, he was, for the umpteenth time, going over what he knew about the case. It was certain that the true perpetrator, the one who'd sent the assassin, was a member of the King's Council. The motive could be anything, all the members had good reasons for killing the King. Perhaps Head Liquidator, James Horan, was not suspect. He was certain of this not only because Horan was in the embarrassing situation of the assassin being one of his men, but because only he had nothing to gain by the King's death.

If the assassination had been successful, then all the King's confidants would have fallen, including himself. And the others? Naturally, he had interrogated the Council members one by one already. Councillor Ed Wilder had a thousand reasons to hate King Mortimer. The King, and of course, he himself, had almost openly opposed the Councillor's power. If Wilder was behind it then it was certain that Archbishop Parker was not innocent either. He could not imagine that the Archbishop would act on his own accord. The most suspect was Sir Christopher Millborrow, because he had known Hugh Jones previously – in fact, he had brought him to the Court. At the time of the assassination, Millborrow had been there, and though Black had shouted at him to keep the assassin alive, Millborrow had let him kill himself. On the other hand, it was also true that no one could have stopped his final deed. But Jones' last words were still ringing in his ears: *"I'm sorry, I disappointed you."* Sir Christopher had sworn that these words referred to the shame he's brought on his benefactor, and not to messing up the assassination. There was also Alf Kelly, the head of the guilds. The guilds suffered heavy losses due to the constant wars, but they had enough gold to hold power, and old Kelly could not be judged based on his behaviour as the guilds themselves chose their leader, and so Kelly was not on the Council by mistake.

The case was at an impasse, Black determined; he hated nothing more than unsolved mysteries. He hated nothing more than not knowing the answer to a question. A slight murmur ran across the hall, Black glanced up and saw two liquidators escorting a third towards him. They were far from the table but he could see that the man was none other than Sir George Silver, the man who had fought the King, and who the King had told to seek out the Strategist if he wished to become a liquidator.

Followed by all the eyes in the hall, the group reached Black's table.

"My Lord! This man said to lead him to you, because some Sir Alex recommended him," one of the liquidators said.

"My Lord, it is you," Silver said, recognising Black. "Sir Alex did not say you would be in the castle too. Are you going to take me to the Strategist?"

When the guards heard the stranger speak so insolently to Black, they flew into a rage.

"How dare you! You bastard!" they shouted.

"Leave him! It's alright, if I have a problem I will call you. You may go now!"

"But, Sir Lemmy," one of the guards protested.

"Enough! Leave!" the Strategist raised his voice. The two soldiers left at once.

"My Lord," Silver stammered, "my Great Lord, I had no idea…"

"Enough! It is not your fault. I was there in the tavern in disguise, pretending to be someone else. Now come, I'll take you to the storeroom, where you can put on your uniform and get to know your commander. If you haven't changed your mind, that is."

"No, my Lord, we can go."

They left the building and were crossing the gardens when Silver spoke, "Permission to speak, sir?"

"Granted."

"I just remembered how lucky I am that I smacked Sir Alex and not you."

"If you say so, though luck is a matter of perspective," Black replied as he barely suppressed a smile. He didn't want to ruin King Mortimer's game. As he spoke, Sir Lemmy spotted the King and Queen Miranda walking in the garden, and they were headed right towards them.

"Look," Black said to the knight, "here comes the Royal couple. I will introduce you to them. Be respectful, and only speak when spoken to!"

"But Sir! I am just a speck of insignificant dust, how come I to be introduced?" Silver said in fright.

There was no time for further whimpering, the royal couple were close. Black and Silver fell to their knees and bowed their heads.

"My Lord! My Lady!" Sir Lemmy greeted the ruler and his spouse in the correct fashion. "Allow me to introduce a new member of the liquidator team, Liquidator Silver."

"Greetings to both of you. Stand!" Mortimer replied. Silver looked at the King and could not stop himself from speaking—he didn't want to, but it slipped out.

"I'm done for!" was all he said.

"Why do you say that?" the Queen asked in surprise.

"My King, take my life! I deserve it," he threw himself on his knees.

"Stand up and answer! The Queen asked you a question, and if my Queen asks then no one can deny her a reply, I would not dare to myself," Mortimer could take it no longer and burst out laughing.

Silver stood and answered the Queen embarrassedly.

"Well, my Lady, the thing is that I hit his Highness in a tavern, though I did not know who he really was at the time."

"And what did he do?" Miranda asked, laughing.

"He hit me so hard, my Lady, that I fell over a table."

Miranda shook her head, laughing, "Will you never grow up? You're like a big child."

"Maybe, my Lady," Mortimer replied and then turned serious.

"Did you scare the rabbit from the bush?" the King looked at Sir Lemmy.

"Unfortunately, not yet, but the time will come sooner or later," Sir Lemmy replied, and left along with the shamed knight.

Directed by a sudden thought, the Strategist changed his mind. He did not take Silver to the liquidators, instead they rode to the scene of the crime by the Wild Barbarians Tavern. They only took two liquidators with them because Black did not want to cause a scene. He wanted to see the place by day, maybe he had overlooked something before. And Silver would come in handy as he could be sent un-surreptitiously into Old Ronny's Tavern, maybe he could gather some quality rumours, and Black would examine the house opposite, where Jones had hidden on that night. On the way, he told the new liquidator about the details, but made him swear that he must pretend like he knew nothing once in the tavern.

When they arrived, one of the liquidators left to tie up the horses and Silver went inside to drink something, and Black headed for the assassin's hiding place. The third soldier came with him. They entered the building and climbed through the attic onto the roof.

Black determined that Jones had chosen a perfect place for the assassination. The tavern door would be clearly visible, even in the pouring rain. He looked around but saw nothing. In truth, he did not expect to find anything, but he could not accept that the case was not moving forward. He climbed off the roof and was headed for the tavern to get Silver when six men in masks, armed to the teeth, appeared opposite them. Sir Lemmy acted immediately, he turned and began running, while shouting at his companion, "Run!"

The soldier was momentarily confused and did not understand the situation and this cost him his life. Black only heard the liquidator shout and turned to see the attackers hack him to shreds. Several blades penetrated him at once, and he hadn't even time to pull out his sword. The Strategist knew that he could not help the man, so he ran on as fast as he could. He saw that he could not shake his pursuers so he jumped over a low fence and ran on through gardens and over more fences. Meanwhile, he threw off his unnecessary weapons as they were only slowing him down. Soon, he found himself in a street once more. His pursuers were a little way behind him now, but they had not lost him from sight, so he was still far from safe.

Quickly, he ran through an open gate. If he got them in single file then he could fight then successfully, he had no better idea. When the first masked man ran through the gate, Lemmy thrust his only remaining weapon, his sword, forward. The sudden attack was successful and the man crumpled over, dead. The attackers were confused and suddenly did not know what to do.

Black heard their leader barking orders, "Two men stay at the gate, three go around the back!"

The Strategist did not want to wait to be attacked from two sides, so he charged out of the building. He trusted in the element of surprise, and he was right, because as he broke out, he laid one of his opponents down for good. And he could fight the other one on one. Black was a good fighter, he trained daily, and this was clear on his performance, and he defeated the man before him. Just in time, because the other were arriving through the gate into the street. There were three of them and Sir Lemmy was beginning to tire. He charged at the closest one who reacted slowly to the attack and was stabbed, but another soldier thrust his blade through Sir Lemmy's sword arm. The Strategist dropped his weapon and he stood there defenceless against two men. Disgruntled, he ascertained that if he had brought more men with him, then all this would not have happened, and he also figured that this hidden enemy must have spies in the castle, as the attackers knew that there were only few of them or they would not have dared to attack him. Black heard the frantic thumping of boots from behind him and saw Silver charging towards them, his sword drawn, accompanied by two other men. Black collected his remaining strength and began running towards them. The opponents did not like these odds and escaped in the other direction.

Black was bleeding heavily, he needed care immediately, so he went back to the castle with silver, and left the other liquidator to bring reinforcements and bring the bodies back to the castle to be examined.

In the liquidator barracks of the castle, they had just finished dressing Lemmy's wound when Silver entered the room.

"How are you, Sir?" he asked ,concerned.

"Thank you, well, you arrived just in time. Did you find out anything in the tavern?"

"No, Sir, but there is something that may be important, maybe…"

"Spit it out!"

"Well, with your retroactive permission, I examined the bodies and found something strange."

Black did not interrupt him, he could sense there was a lead in there.

"All the bodies had a sun and moon tattooed on their shoulders, and I know what these two things mean."

"Let's have it!"

"There was once a wench in my bed who had the same mark on her shoulder. I asked her what it was and she said it was God's sign. She was a member of some sect, and its followers all have the sun and moon tattooed on their shoulders. I don't know if this matters, but I thought you should know."

"Liquidator Silver! You will be promoted for this," the Strategist said ceremoniously, forgetting about his freshly stitched wound.

"Sir, I've not been in your service a whole day, and you're promoting me? If I continue to move up this rapidly, I will be commanding you in a few weeks," Silver said laughing.

"In that case," Black replied, who could also not contain his laughter, "I had better watch out for you."

They both laughed when King Mortimer stormed into the room.

"May I know what's so funny that you're both laughing about?"

"My Lord," they both said. Silver fell to his knee and the Strategist began climbing off the bed.

"What are you doing, idiot? You're not about to kneel in front of me when you're injured? Don't you dare! Instead, tell me what happened!" Mortimer said, pushing Black back onto the bed.

"Well, my Lord, I scared the rabbit from the bush," the Strategist answered mysteriously.

"And?" the King thundered impatiently.

"The rabbit almost bit my throat."

Chapter Twenty-Six

Councillor Aleksandr Petrov sat at his desk, with Vasili, the man-behind-the-man, sitting opposite him. The old Councillor's entrusted secret-keeper waited patiently for Petrov to tell him why he'd been summoned. He found it strange, because he was the cook in the castle and it would have been less conspicuous to meet somewhere other than Petrov's office. The Councillor poured them each a cup of wine and then spoke, "Vasili, I trust you, you were one of Oleg's best men. I need your alliance, even if I cannot know for certain who among our people is cooperative and who is merely pretending to be. I am so suspicious because your message, that is, Oleg's message, warned me to be cautious."

"I am at your service, Aleksandr," the cook replied, and raised his cup to his lips.

"Then let us drink to our cooperation," the Councillor said, also raising his cup.

Vasili sipped his wine, and only he noticed that the Councillor had raised his cup to his lips but not drunk any of it. In that moment, he knew he was a dead man. Only half a sip went down his throat, he spat out the rest, but even that little amount was enough to finish him. He clutched at his throat and his whole body went into a spasm. He looked accusingly at Petrov and fell from his chair.

Now I have cut the umbilical cord that tied me to Atlantis, Petrov thought. Vasili, as the man-behind-the-man, reported directly to the president, and this was a constraint the Councillor could not tolerate.

Petrov watched Vasili's brief death struggle impassively, then he raised a little bell from his desk and rang it. Almost in the same moment, the door opened, and Commander Igor Lermov entered with two men.

"Commander Lermov!" Petrov said nonchalantly, "clear away this garbage."

"Yes, Councillor Sir," the liquidator replied and said no more, merely motioning to his men, who lifted the corpse. The Councillor left the room calmly, as if nothing had happened.

Petrov had planned to visit the King while Lermov and his men put his chambers in order. As he walked along the corridors, lords and ladies greeted him, their eyes glinted cautiously, which gave him a pleasant sensation.

Suddenly, someone gently touched his arm. He was startled because he had not noticed how this impudent person had gotten near him. He was about to shout at the person when he recognised the man who had escorted him to Prince Ivan Genisei. The hooded eyes had something unsettling about them. He felt as if the man standing before him was prepared to sacrifice his life at any time for what he believed in. He had never liked fanatics because they were hard to control, and their stubbornness frightened him.

These were the people you could not break in the torture chamber.

"What do you want?" Petrov glowered at him.

"My Lord would like to meet with you, Councillor," the man's impassive calm upset Petrov.

"Why doesn't he tell me ahead of time if he wants something?" the Councillor raged, letting his emotions loose.

"My Lord, not all times are suitable for such a meeting to be held. Please, come with me and believe me, you will not regret it." The crass words seemed not to affect the Prince's faithful servant. He only cared to complete the task entrusted to him at any cost. The Councillor nodded and followed the man towards the servant's quarters the way they had gone for the first meeting. The man stopped at a door and spoke, "Please enter here." As he spoke, he disappeared down the hall. Petrov entered.

Genisei was waiting for him in the dark room, wearing a ragged, hooded coat.

"Greetings, Councillor. Please, put on this cloak, we are leaving the castle and it is very cold outside."

"My Prince," Petrov bowed, "why must we wear such soiled rags?"

"I do not want to be recognised," Ivan said, and looked at Petrov as if he were a little dim.

"And this will make us invisible?" Petrov asked.

"Councillor, Lords do not see commoners. If we bow our heads, no one will know who we are. Come now, I do not want to be away for long, our absence would be noticed."

Petrov put on the worn cloak and hood just as the Prince did. They left the Servant's quarters and moved to a busier area of the castle where commoners could feast without a servant's uniform. Sometimes, a noblemen passed them but paid them no heed.

After a few minutes, they exited the castle through one of the backdoors into a huge courtyard. In fact, it was more like an estate than a courtyard. The King's castle was surrounded by a well-kept garden, but if one went further, the land became increasingly wild and unkempt. As they exited, the cold wind hit their face, though they were well into April, the weather was stern and bracing. Spring always came late to Moscow. Gradually, they left the well-manicured, mostly evergreen garden and headed towards a pine forest which was about a verst from the edge of the park. They reached the little forest but they kept going, deeper and deeper into the shade of the trees. Petrov could not judge how long they had gone. At first, he counted the steps, but he stopped after a while and could only think of when he would return to the warmth of the castle. Suddenly, the Prince touched his hand.

"We're here," Ivan said, "do you remember I promised to prove that Vosinoi was killed, and even who did it. You remember, Councillor?" His ice-cold stare penetrated Petrov's brain. The Councillor felt particularly uncomfortable in Ivan's company.

"Yes, but I don't understand why you dragged me into the woods," the Councillor took a few steps back despite himself.

"Look!" the Prince said, and then began kicking at a pile of leaves and branches beside them. He soon finished and he motioned the Councillor over to him. When Petrov got there, he looked down at the ground and froze solid in shock. In a small pit in the ground, lay the body of Councillor Oleg Vosinoi. The cold had kept his body quite recognizable. His clothes were torn to shreds, and his body was covered in reddish brown congealed blood.

"Examine him," Ivan said, "it does not look like the work of a bear. Besides, there are no bears in the gardens. He did not die here, probably in the castle and he was brought here because they did not want to smuggle him through the guards. But they could not leave him in the castle either, revealing that he had been murdered. No one could find him here except for me, I often walk these woods, but no one knows of this habit of mine. I like being alone."

"How did you find him, he's in a pit, or did you dig it?"

"No, I was here with my dog and he dug him out. The perpetrators could not dig too deep in the frozen ground."

"How do you know who killed him? It could have been you. You'll excuse the idea."

The Prince smiled and took a piece of a paper from his pocket that he handed to Petrov.

"Councillor, do you know Vosinoi's hand?"

Petrov had often seen the ex-Councillor's letters when he had worked here, and he'd often had to transmit Oleg's messages to Atlantis.

He usually had to take the messages to the outskirts. He had opened and read each one of them despite the protocol. He had resealed them with a stolen stamp and only then given them to the messenger.

"I know it," Petrov replied. He took the paper and begin to read it:

"March 15.3 pm
Meeting with Boris Kurlov."

Petrov knew that it was Vosinoi's habit to write what he had to do on slips of paper to carry around in his pocket. This was opposed to Councillor training. Lesson ten: 'never leave a trace'. But Vosinoi could not get rid of the habit.

"Where did you find this?" the Councillor asked, still staring at the piece of paper.

"It was in his inside pocket. Do you know when Councillor Oleg Vosinoi disappeared? I'll tell you, on that very day he was seen in the palace in the morning, but not after that. Then the rumours began to circulate that he had gone hunting. I never believed them, because when a person goes hunting they leave early in the morning, not in the afternoon with only a few hours of daylight left."

"You searched the body?"

"Naturally, to stay alive in the castle I needed as much information as I could gain. I completed my half of the bargain, now it's your turn."

Petrov was beginning to think up a good excuse to buy himself some time when the man who'd escorted him to the Prince appeared out of nowhere.

He simply appeared standing there, staring at the Councillor, and his suspicions that the man was a warrior increased. His slow deliberate movements hid a predatory instinct, and animalistic nature that could switch from perfect calm to attack in the blink of an eye.

"Allow me to introduce Captain Sergei Giakin," the Prince pointed at the man, "I know you've met before. He will escort us to Commander Niachev now."

Petrov did not dare oppose Ivan, he had no doubt that Captain Giakin was there to enforce his side of the bargain.

"Alright, I cannot openly release the prisoner held by the King," he resisted gently, "furthermore, I cannot let Head Liquidator Nikolai Choronko in on the plan as I cannot know for certain if he would oppose the King's will."

"That is not your problem anyway," the Prince said in a voice as if the Councillor were his inferior. Petrov did not dare argue, fearing an attack from Giakin. "But you will get a key that opens Niachev's chains, and you will get a key to the cells too, which I will take to him along with weapons. The Commander will wait till nightfall, then he'll open the door, take care of the two guards while the guards in the corridor will be silenced by Captain Giakin. If Commander Niachev makes it out of the castle, I will be waiting for him in the garden and shall take him supplies and horse. This will be enough for him to escape. You, Councillor, can be accused of nothing, since you did not organise the guarding of the prisoner, you arrived after his imprisonment."

Petrov was forced to accept the deal. In fact, he was not taking much risk at all, and in return, he had found out who had killed his predecessor. In fact, he would get Prince Kurilov out of the way too. Besides, Prince Genisei's alliance may come in useful alter on.

"Well, I think that is all," Petrov tried, at least, to maintain the semblance of control.

"I think, Councillor Petrov," Ivan replied, "that you are the kind of person who is able to make the right decision. And I value such a rare trait highly."

Petrov sensed mockery and threat veiled in the Prince's tone. He began to perspire suddenly, though he should have been shivering in the cold.

When Councillor Petrov arrived at Boris Kurilov's palace, he enjoyed a King's welcome. He had barely exited his carriage when an army of servants escorted him through the huge front doors where the host himself awaited him with his pretty, young wife, Natasha, and his not insignificant number of children from previous marriages.

"Please enter, Councillor, my humble abode, but first have a drink with me of the water of life," Kurilov greeted him kindly, though the phrase 'humble abode' was more of a boast than humility. As the host finished greeting his guests, a servant appeared with a tray lined with shots of vodka. Kurilov took one and Petrov grabbed one too.

"If you enter here," Kurilov began the obligatory toast that accompanied every shot, "your rank will be greater than the host's."

"You do me a great honour," Petrov replied in kind, then finally, they entered the building.

They went through to the giant entrance hall where servants gently helped the Councillor remove his coat. Petrov was always surprised when he entered a nobleman's house; how the Russian's could build such huge structures out of wood. They passed through to the, also monumental, dining hall, where the other dignitaries awaited him. When he appeared, he was greeted by a storm of applause. Kurilov took his arm and guided his guest to the chair reserved for him, which was at the centre of the long side of the massive rectangular table, opposite the exit. He could not even be seated, when he had to endure another toast with a hefty dose of vodka. Petrov had lived in Moscow for years, so he was not surprised by the river of liquor that accompanied such a feast. He knew, that in the beginning they watched who was drinking, but later on it would be enough to raise the glass to his lips, because the increasingly drunken company would not be watching his every move. The two strong drinks on an empty stomach numbed him a little, and a pleasant dizziness came over his body and he sat quickly down.

Petrov felt as if he deserved a little relaxation, his day had been rather fatiguing. By the morning, news of Niachev's escape had broken and the whole castle was in uproar. King Genisei immediately summoned him, and questioned him furiously about what had happened. He, of course, defended himself, by saying that it was not in his power to check the conditions of the prisoner, and he had believed that Head Liquidator Choronko was well prepared for the task. In fact, he got away with the whole thing quite easily, and now all he had to focus on was enjoying his evening.

The army of servants scurried about among the guests, constantly refilling their glasses. He asked for another cup of vodka, which he drank in one gulp. Why not? He deserved a bit of relaxation that day. Petrov leaned back and felt his muscles relax, the tension of the day passed. He was just considering what kind of food he should choose, when on the other side of the table his eyes met those of one of the servants and he saw that it was none other than Sergei Giakin. His high spirits turned to nervousness immediately. Surely, he didn't want to kill Kurilov here in front of everyone? Why didn't he wait at least until the storm of Niachev's escape passed? And why did he need so many witnesses to the murder? *This was insanity, he cannot do this*, the Councillor panicked as he felt himself sober up instantly.

Not two minutes had passed since he spotted Giakin when someone leaned over to him.

"Don't turn around," they whispered in his ear. He recognised Giakin's voice immediately, "when I'm gone, ask for venison loudly, so that everyone around you can hear. But do not eat any of it!"

By the time the Councillor turned around, there was nobody behind him. Soon another servant approached him and respectfully asked, "What type of food would you like, Sir?" The noise around him ceased suddenly, everyone wanted to know what the Councillor would choose.

"Oh," Petrov hummed in confusion, he had not yet digested the shock the appearance of Giakin and the impending murder would mean. "Venison," he finally grunted.

The host, sitting at the head of the table, heard Petrov's words.

"A great choice my friend, everyone knows I love venison, and I eat it at every meal."

Kurilov laughed.

"It's a good idea," he turned to the large guest at his side, "I will eat venison too."

Petrov heard from many places on the table that people were now inclined towards the venison. He looked around in fright, *could all the venison be poisoned? It could not be, they could not kill this many people just because Kurilov had to die.*

The multitude of servants began serving the food, and they placed the first plate in front of the host, laden with meat and potatoes, the Councillor was served next and only then, the others. Petrov slowly and deliberately drank another cup of vodka and then asked one of the servants to bring him some water. Meanwhile, people received their food and began eating among cheerful chatter. *When would the poison start to work?* Petrov asked himself, he couldn't come up with any more excuses not to eat. Suddenly someone, maybe Giakin, shouted, "The venison is poisoned!"

In the next moment, panic broke out. Those who'd eaten venison stuck their fingers down their throats trying to throw up, others jumped from their seats and stared in terror at those who had eaten the meat. Then nothing happened, and the guests stood around nonplussed. Kurilov was the quickest to recover, though he had just been throwing up himself. He stood up, clinked two glasses together to gain everyone's attention and then spoke.

"Ladies and Gentlemen! It seems someone is making a fool of us, but have no fear, I will find out who it was and they will pay for their crimes."

"And now, everyone, please sit back down and enjoy yourselves."

As he finished, his body spasmed and he fell to the ground, foam seeping from his mouth. Then, all the other guests who'd eaten venison were sick too. People ran out of the hall, and about twelve people went through a death struggle with the poison. Petrov stood in astonishment, watching the terrible scene unfold. A horrible thought crossed his mind, *I've unleashed a beast. A mere teenager, acting like a monster.*

"Who do you think you are?" John Neville, the President of Atlantis, shouted at the five students before him. "You think because you are the best in your class that you cannot be wrong? You all failed the test prepared just for you! Get out of my sight!" The young men left the President's chambers hastily, their faces red with shame and anger. In the background, James Mulligan, vice-president, shook his head.

Neville sat down at his table and turned towards Mulligan, "Come, James, sit down. But first, please bring two mint drinks, my throat's gone dry from all the shouting."

The vice-president took over the drinks and sat down opposite his boss, who looked feebly into his eyes, "John! Why do we need this? You know the problems are impossible to solve. They had no chance, their failure was not their fault and yet, you trampled over them. Why?"

The President sipped his drink, then smiled.

"Anyone who aspires to be a Councillor someday must know that they are no infallible. They have to be able to handle failure, otherwise, they will make mistakes in the field. Consider it a part of their training."

Mulligan shook his head again, he could not resist chastising the President.

"Why could we not explain it to them, they would surely understand."

"You know why the Councillor's order is arranged the way it is, with our men being second-in-command behind the King? They could have been Kings and then we would not have to manipulate the rulers constantly, and it would be much easier for us to manifest our will on important matters. But our men are second-in-command. Why do you think that is?" Neville leaned back and took a great sip of his cool beverage.

Mulligan was very surprised by the question. Was his mentor trying to change the subject on purpose, or had the preceding scene been a pre-planned admonition. He couldn't decide, so he admitted his uncertainty.

"I have no idea."

"You know, power corrupts people, their original goals change, and ruling brings the worst out of everyone. If there are no limits, inhibitions are lost along with rational thought. The Kings are our natural barriers, standing between the Councillors and power."

"And who are you? We have far more power than the Councillors. Who will hold us back?" Mulligan still did not understand what the President was getting at.

"We are in a different situation entirely. If one feels power on one's own skin, then they fall into temptation. We do not have an army of servants awaiting our orders, the world does not bow before us, and we cannot do as we please. We direct – we do not rule, we serve and do not corrupt. We are not in contact with the outside world, which could make us feel the magnitude of our power. Therefore, our personalities are not as distorted as, say, a ruler's."

"I still do not understand why the students must be given unsolvable problems."

"Because," the President replied, "they must feel the power over them, because it will be so in the Known World too. In fact, even you are not omnipotent, as you know, I rank over you."

"I understand," Mulligan scratched his head, "and over you? Who stands over you?"

"Unfortunately, nobody," Neville replied with a bitter smile.

"Then who protects you from the corruption of power?"

"Again, I have to say, nobody."

"And what gives you power if there is no one above you?"

Neville looked significantly at his heir before answering, "My deepest belief in my own infallibility."

Chapter Twenty-Seven

The team made the trip to Paris much faster than when they had been escaping from there, as this time they could use the roads and did not have to cut their way through the wilderness.

It was morning, and they were eating breakfast at their last campsite from where they could see the city. Jules said that he would meet with his man in Paris, who would bring them clothes, costumes and a great big carriage. They would dress like travelling comedians, and simply walk through one of the gates of Paris. Ponga, as he had often laid his eyes on her, during their travels, watched Fifi, who was headed for a nearby stream to wash. He crept after her, because they had barely gotten a chance to be alone together during the trip. She had insisted that they not share their emotions with the others so as not to disturb the mission. Ponga suffered greatly from this as he wanted to spend every minute with Fifi, and he was worried about her dangerous mission too. When he caught up with her he took her hand and pulled her to him.

"Stop it, they will notice us," she tried pushing herself away from him.

"This is the last time we can be together," he looked balefully into her eyes, "soon, we will enter the city and Jules and I will live in the Castle. And you will be waiting for us outside for weeks, perhaps. Who knows, we may never see each other again."

Fifi moved over to Ponga and kissed him at length, then gently pushed him away.

"I have to go wash now," she announced, "I know you've seen me without clothes before and what happened there," she suddenly went silent. She could not find the right words, "well, I don't know what you think of me, but things should not have turned out the way they did between us."

"I will never ask you what happened," Ponga interjected, "if it hurts you and you wish to tell me someday, I will listen to you, but you must know one thing! I have never seen anything as beautiful as you lying there naked."

Fifi smiled embarrassedly, she kissed him again then turned and went to the river. Ponga stood there, watching his departing sweetheart, and thought that he was the luckiest man on earth.

Half an hour later, Jules briefed the company. They sat in a semi-circle on the grass in a meadow. Fifi, Ponga, Fabian and Henri. Their leader opposite them.

"Pay attention!" he began. "There is no wishy-washy stuff from here on out. Those who cannot accept this may leave."

He looked around, no one said anything, not even Ponga.

"Alright, then I will tell you the other rules. No one can cause a scene. You cannot get drunk in a tavern, you cannot order expensive food, you cannot fight, not even if they've offended you. We must blend in with out surroundings and become invisible. If anyone breaks these rules, they risk not only the mission, but all of our lives too."

"Soon we will receive the necessary supplies and Fifi will change our appearances a little and then we will sneak into Paris. There, we will find a place for our carriage, which will also be our lodgings."

"Why don't we rent rooms, it would be much more comfortable," Ponga asked.

"Because the whole carriage would be stolen by morning and our disguises would be shot."

There were no more questions. As they sided each other up silently, they realised that their fate was not in their own hands, but in the hands of their companions.

A few minutes later, three men arrived. They brought a carriage that was full of all sorts of clothes. They clearly knew Jules and Henri and they exchanged a few words. Then the strangers left hurriedly. They did not speak to the other members of the group. The team put on their new clothes, which were of bright resplendent colours, but made of cheap fabrics. After dressing, it was Fifi's turn to change everyone's appearance. With the help of paints, brushes and wigs, she changed them into completely different people.

"Now you understand why I looked so much older when we met?" Jules asked Ponga. Ponga looked in the mirror and did not recognise his reflection. He seemed at least ten years older than his age and his hair colour was different too.

"It seems that Fifi has enchanted us," he replied, staring in disbelief at his reflection.

"Especially you," Henri laughingly remarked.

"What do you mean?" Ponga asked sharply. When he saw the whole company laughing at him, even Fifi, he did not speak again. *Why should they keep their relationship a secret if everyone knew about it?* He asked himself, but he would not have told Fifi this for the world.

If she thought it right that they should not show their feelings, then so it would be, and that was that.

When they reached Paris, Ponga was assailed by strange thoughts. If someone had asked him, during their escape after the tournament where he would most like to be in the world, he would have replied Paris. And now? If he were asked now, he would reply, 'the swamp'. Maybe that is why fairies, if they exist, do not fulfil human wishes? Since they, themselves, do not know what they want.

The paved streets were buzzing with life. The traffic that had amused him not so long ago, bothered him now. He wanted to go back to Happy Island and be alone with Fifi. They found a less-frequented square and made camp there. They had already paid the necessary silver for this at the gate. By the time they had prepared their lodgings, it was dinner-time. They decided not to leave the carriage unguarded, so Fabian stayed behind to watch over their newfound home. They would bring him dinner later.

The White Horse Tavern was their destination for dinner, as Jules and Henri had eaten there many times and they knew from experience that Fat Jean's Tavern made the best food. Ponga was afraid he would be recognised, but his worries soon abated as Jean spoke to them.

"What would the fine thespian gentlemen and thespian Ette lady desire?" he asked them. Seeing their clothes, the Innkeeper knew straightaway that they were travelling comedians. He did not recognise the hooded priest and the champion of the tournament.

"We would like dinner," Jules replied, "provided you have cheap and good food, sir."

"Of course, we do! Have a seat there in the corner. A table is still empty there," he pointed at the far corner of the room.

While they waited for their food, Ponga stared over the thronging crowd. The densely packed circular tables were sat about by many people. He did not understand what people were enjoying about this crazy hullabaloo. The common features of the pleasure girls, their breasts spilling from their dresses and their raucous laughter filled him with disgust. Even more than the girls, he was annoyed by the pompous noisiness of the knights. *How could he have lived here? How could he have been just like these knaves?* He asked himself, but found no answer.

Half an hour later, Fat Jean and a serving girl appeared carrying plates. The company had ordered pork ribs with potatoes and sauerkraut, and watered wine to drink. They set about their meal, ravenously. They agreed with Jean beforehand that they would take another portion with them, as Fabian was waiting for his dinner. They did not speak much as they ate, though, truth be told, they had not spoken much before either. It was hard to relay when they had to be extremely careful of what they said.

They had almost finished eating when four men sat down at the table beside them. They had clearly visited a few taverns that evening, as they shouted half-drunken slurs.

"Hey! Barkeep!" one of the knights shouted. He must have been their leader because the others never joked at his expense and he was the loudest of the bunch. "Where are you, you fat idiot? We want to drink, now!"

"I'm coming, your lordships," Jean shouted from two tables away, and hurried over, "excuse me, but we are especially busy tonight."

"Who gives a damn!" the man said roughly. "Bring us wine immediately, before I kick your ass!"

Ponga bowed his head, he did not want to get the others into trouble. He could not contain himself, however, and he looked up for a moment, his eyes meeting those of the leader.

"Are you looking at me, you filthy commoner?" the knight sprang up from his table.

"Not at all!" Ponga forced the words out. Fifi, who was sitting beside him, took his hand to calm him. The drunken man spotted the movement.

"What's up, is your slut feeling you up there? She could feel me up too, you know, but not just my hand," the company laughed loudly at the callous joke. "Come here, my darling, I'll show you what real man's like!"

Fat Jean arrived in the meantime, holding carafes of wine in his hands. He felt the trouble brewing, put down the wine, wiped his ever-sweating brow and tried to make peace among the two parties.

"Kind Sirs! You're not going to…"

"Shut up, or I'll smack your mouth!" the drunken man snapped.

Ponga could barely contain himself, he'd killed far greater warriors than these and for a lot less provocation too. In fact, no man had defeated him. Yet now, he could not act. He felt like he would skin the bastard at any moment.

Suddenly, Jules stood up and interjected.

"Sirs!" he spoke to the agitator. "Excuse our crass behaviour, we are simple people, who do not know how to pay our respects to such great warriors," the man was suddenly rendered speechless by surprise at what Jules was saying.

"We would like to make it up to you," Jules went on, "allow me to pay for your wine there and right the wrong we have done you."

The knight hesitated for a moment but then his unbounded vanity won.

"Alright, I accept your apology."

Two minutes later, they were headed for the carriage and Jules patted Ponga on the shoulder, conciliatorily.

"You behaved grandly, my friend. I would not have believed you could resist such a provocation."

"I thought I would snap his neck," Ponga replied, still unbalanced by what had transpired.

"You know," Jules said, "those who cannot control themselves do not know how to control others."

Councillor Alain Perrier sat massaging his eyes with his fingertips. The King was in a tenuous state. He thought of the events of the past few days – he could die any day now. Marquis Philippe Bertrand knew this too, and his behaviour was becoming increasingly intolerable. He bullied Head Liquidator Luc Moreau and his men around, as if they were dogs. At least the case was flowing through the trough he'd dug, he thought, but the unpredictability of the Strategist vexed him more. The problem was that Sir Lemmy only appeared to be impulsive. In fact, his every move was meticulously premeditated. If this was so, then it was absolutely baffling, why he was cruising the French coasts with his fleet. The Councillor had had to send Commander Marcel Durand to the Normandy Coast for the eventuality of a landing by the English troops.

Durand had taken a large part of the army with him and the cream of the nobility too. Marquis Bertrand had, of course, backed out, claiming that he had to be by the King's side. The already complicated situation was made worse by the fact that Marquis Bastien de Caulmont, along with the noblemen loyal to him, had abandoned Commander Durand's army, and come to Paris, having heard of the King's condition. The Councillor looked at the clock on the wall, which showed half past nine. *The Marquis should be arriving now,* he thought, and in that moment, in stepped Marquis Caulmont and Head Liquidator Moreau. Perrier stood up and approached the Marquis and embraced him as Moreau discreetly left the room.

"My friend," Perrier said, "why have you taken such a great risk?"

The Councillor gently guided the Marquis towards his desk. The well-intentioned gesture clearly bothered the Marquis, so Perrier pretended not to notice his tension. Meanwhile, the Marquis shot murderous glances at his host. Such a glare was usually reserved for one's enemies.

"Let us not play games, Councillor," the Marquis nervously stroked his beard as he tried to force his large, robust body into the small chair. "I left the camp and came here secretly to you to see Fernand de Bellahache, the son of the murdered, true King. You remember, you promised to make a ruler of the boy?"

Perrier pretended to ponder this. But Caulmont was certain that the Councillor was winding him up on purpose, and he was probably right too.

"Of course, I remember, I gave my word. But I cannot bring you Fernand."

After speaking, Perrier crossed his legs with a nonchalant movement. He did not intend to give a reason as to why he was not keeping his promise. It seemed as if he were purposefully antagonising the Marquis.

"Why?" the Marquis did not need much to lose his remaining calm, and the Councillor was just the person to bring up the beast in him. He clutched at the chair's armrests as if it were the Councillor's throat.

"You don't think he's here in the castle where so many have intents on his life?"

The Marquis went silent for a moment. The wormy bastard was right again, he thought disappointedly, but the will to see Fernand would not let him rest.

"This is true," Caulmont conceded, and to conceal his confusion, he quickly changed topic, "how are things in the palace? Are you in control of the situation?"

"Have you ever seen me not be in control?" Perrier asked back, offended, with a superior expression that boiled the Marquis' blood anew. "Bertrand believes that Moreau is on his side. In fact, the Head Liquidator also convinced him to send all his armed men away from the palace, leaving only the liquidators."

"Then at least, complete your other promise now, give me Marquis Bertrand's head. Head Liquidator Moreau, that is you, are in command of the castle anyway."

But Caulmont expected Perrier to reject his request, but to his greatest surprise, the Councillor did not protest.

"Please, if you can contain yourself no longer, then so be it," then he rang the bell on his desk. Moreau appeared almost immediately.

"Bring Marquis Bertrand here, but not by force! Tell him I must speak with him urgently."

The liquidator left, and the Councillor turned to the Marquis.

"So what's going on in Normandy?"

"The Strategist is toying with us; he pretends to advance, then he retreats." When he spoke the Strategist's name, Caulmont's face twitched. He hated him, at least as much as he did Perrier. These two men never did what he expected them to. It was impossible to predict them.

"I think," said the Councillor, "that until Sir Lemmy joins his fleet on his vessel, the Dreadnought, there will be no battles waged. And according to my spies, Black has not left the Kingdom of England yet."

The Councillor poured himself a glass of wine, but Caulmont declined it with a wave and Perrier went on.

"What did Durand say that you and the other Lords left him there?"

"What would he have said?" the Marquis snorted. "I told him the future of the Kingdom was at stake. Oh, and by the way, as you very well know, his father and I are childhood friends. So he had no choice but to say yes. It's not possible for the Strategist to make a move on them, he couldn't even come ashore because of them. Durand will do just fine without me. You know, I'm needed here right now."

"True," the Councillor said, tiredly. His thoughts were really on Vincent Farall. They'd been searching for him for a week on both sides of the road from Paris to Beauvais, all the settlements and the woods, but there was no trace of him.

If he'd escaped then why hadn't he reported? Maybe he was afraid that if he entered the castle, he wouldn't make it to the Councillor. If it was so, then why didn't he send a message? There were only questions and uncertainty, he thought bitterly, and then, with a deep sigh, he looked at his guest.

"Please, go through to the other room," Perrier motioned towards a door. "I want to surprise our mutual friend."

"Maybe he is your friend, but he is certainly not mine," the Marquis replied as he walked towards the door. Before he closed it behind him, the Councillor called after him.

"I can see, my dear friend, that your sense of humour has not improved over these past years."

A few minutes later, Marquis Bertrand stormed into the Councillor's chambers, followed by Head Liquidator Moreau. He threw himself into the chair opposite Perrier. He didn't even wait for the host to offer him a seat.

"What do you want, Councillor? You know I've been busy lately. I don't have time to chitchat with you. And anyway, in the future, if you wish to speak with me, make an appointment and don't order me about," the Marquis said, pouting furiously.

"Just like that? Councillor?" Perrier asked quietly but threateningly. "Not long ago, I was Sir Councillor…"

"Times change, power balances shift. In your place I would take it back a notch before some misfortune befalls you for your crassness Councillor."

"Alright, I'll take that under serious consideration, but that's not why I called you here. I wanted to surprise you with something."

The Marki tutted dramatically, but he was visibly taken aback. It seemed like the Councillor could be easily tamed, he thought with some surprise.

"I wanted to have you meet a kindly guest who you've not seen in a long time."

Perrier rang the bell on his desk, and Caulmont entered the room. Bertrand sprang from his chair and turned in terror to the Councillor.

"What is this man doing here? And how dare you put me in such a situation."

Bertrand turned and spoke to the Head Liquidator, "Head Liquidator Moreau, take the Marquis to prison at once! I will have a serious chat with you later, Councillor," the Marquis poked his finger towards Perrier.

No one in the chamber moved. Moreau stood there as if he had not heard the words addressed to him, but Caulmont sized up his hated foe silently, and Perrier was thoroughly enjoying the situation.

"Did you not hear my order?" Bertrand still did not understand the situation.

"Dear Marquis!" the Councillor smiled, "the situation is that no will follow your orders here. What was it you said? Times change, power balances shift. You see, I learn fast, but it seems you do not."

Bertrand reached for his sword, but the Head Liquidator was much faster and held his blade to the Marquis' throat.

"Don't hurt him!" Caulmont growled in his deep voice. "And please, do not take his sword, I want to duel him, here and now."

"We could do this much more simply my friend," Perrier suggested.

"I want to take his life in legal combat," Caulmont replied as he produced his sword from its scabbard. "I have to get revenge for my own honour, we will fight man to man. My Lord Perrier!" Caulmont looked victoriously at his newfound old ally.

"If I were to die, let Marquis Bertrand free! Let the fight have a true wager. Respectably!"

"Of course," Perrier replied, though he knew Bertrand would not leave the room alive. But if Caulmont did not kill him, Moreau would finish the task. After all, chances in life did not come freely, they had to be taken by force.

The Councillor motioned to the Head Liquidator to let the two men fight. The Marquis began circling the chambers, their swords drawn. The room was too small for such a duel, but Caulmont kicked a chair aside without taking his eyes off his opponent.

"What did you come here for, you old fool?" Bertrand began condescendingly, but his voice wavered.

"You know too well! I will wash your evil past from history with your blood," Caulmont thundered.

Unfortunately, all over my carpet, Perrier sadly ascertained.

Bertrand could not hold back any longer and began his attack. Caulmont elegantly flicked his opponent's blade to the side and with the same momentum stabbed the Marquis in the throat. Bertrand fell to the floor clutching his throat; a gushing, bubbling sound coming from his throat. Caulmont watched his opponent's death struggle with relish. When Bertrand did not move, the Councillor turned to the victor.

"Why all this drama, my dear Marquis?" he shook his head watching the Caulmont like a troublemaking child.

"You think honour is drama, Councillor?" the Marquis was panting after what had been more exertion than his age would warrant.

"You are a hopeless romantic, my dear friend, but perhaps it is what I like about you most of all. They say opposites attract," Perrier smiled at his own witticism. The Marquis sensed the hidden irony in the Councillor's comment.

"What do you mean?"

"Well, it can't be your non-existent humour that attracts me," the Councillor replied, and then drained his wine glass.

"Now tell me, where is Prince Pernand de Bellehache, the son of the murdered King Gaston de Bellehache, the rightful heir to the throne," Caulmont asked, returning to their previous subject.

"I cannot tell you, yet," Perrier once again produced his condescending, dangerous style.

"Councillor," Caulmont said, raising his voice, "you are well-versed in winding me up! Why not?"

"It is true that the crown is rightfully his, and if King Lefebre were healthy then we could depose him because only he stands in our way, but..."

"But, what?" the Marquis interrupted.

"He is dying. It would look bad if we threw a helpless, sick man from the castle. Wouldn't it be opposed to your famous honour?"

The Marquis sensed that the Councillor was, once again, right.

"So what do you suggest? What shall we do?"

"You go back to the other noblemen and wait," Perrier's gaze had become deathly serious. All playfulness had left his voice. "The King will die soon and I will let you know. Then, we can rewrite French Royal history together."

Chapter Twenty-Eight

Vincent Farall had existed for one week. More precisely, he could now remember the past week of his life. But what a week it had been! He would not have traded that brief time for anybody's lifetime of memories.

He was in love with the most beautiful girl in the world, Amelie Chanel. True, he had not met any other young girls, or he did not remember meeting any. Despite that, he was certain that he would not want anyone else, even if he knew all the girls in the world. He felt that Amelie was reciprocating his feelings, but he was not so certain of this. Maybe, she was just being polite to him, and didn't want to offend him, so she spent most of her time with him even though she did not like him. This doubt cast a shadow over his happiness. He had wanted to admit his feelings to her on several occasions, but he feared rejection. He was also afraid that Amelie may be offended, and would start avoiding him. He determined to put his fears aside that day and tell her everything.

Spring had painted the trees green. A light wind gently brushed his skin in the sunshine. Vincent and Amelie were walking through the grounds to check on the workers. In truth, they needed no encouragement, they were all well paid, and René Chanel was no miser. The family visited the workers on the ground, so that they would feel valued.

The villages around Paris were better off than the other settlements in the Kingdom, but people here also appreciated the extra pay.

When they arrived, the workers doffed their caps and greeted Amelie with respect, and she returned their salutations. Farall noticed that Amelie called the men by name, who were very grateful for her kindness.

"Come, Yannick, let us go to the river. I am thirsty," Amelie said to Farall, who had chosen the name Yannick, as he could not remain nameless forever.

"Alright, let's go," he replied curtly.

"Is something wrong? You're so silent today," she said, with some offence in her voice.

"No, nothing. I just want to tell you something important." Vincent, that is Yannick, felt sweat dripping down his back, though it was not a hot day.

"Tell me!"

"At the river." *I'm a weak, coward*, he chastised himself, *why would it be better there than here? It wouldn't.*

Ten minutes passed as they walked. They moved in silence and Farall was so nervous it felt like an hour to him. He had never wished during the past week to not be near her, but he wanted to be somewhere else now. He noticed with terror that they had reached the water and he could not postpone the matter any longer. As they arrived, Amelie lay down and touched her lips to the water, drinking deeply. Her red hair fell into the water and she did not mind. Then she stood up and stepped closer to him, closer than usually, and stood and stared at him questioningly.

Farall watched and was not able to speak.

"Well? I want to hear what you have to say!" she said coyly. Her merry, sparkling voice confused him further.

"I don't know…Where to begin."

"What?"

"It's not true that you don't know what I want to tell you!" Vincent took a step back and stared into the stream.

"Yannick, are you mad at me because I cannot read your thoughts. How could I know what that crucially important thing is that you can only tell me here, or not even here?"

He began to feel that Amelie knew what he wanted to say and was winding him up. Desperately, he waited for her help, but to no avail.

"Oh, I don't know what a man is supposed to say at these times." She looked at him, her voice gentle and accusatory, all at once.

"You're not making it any easier!" Vincent blurted, finally.

"You're the man, not me! So why should I help?" she smiled kindly.

"The thing is…"

"Wait! Don't say anything!" Amelie embraced him and then, very slowly, she kissed him.

"Does that make it easier for you?"

Vincent looked into her eyes, his fear evaporated and he leaned close to her ear and whispered, "I love you!"

"Me too, silly," Amelie replied and they kissed at length.

No more words were needed between them now. They did not know how, but they found themselves on the soft grass somehow.

He leaned over her gently and kissed and caressed her. He didn't mind any more that he had been bold, or perhaps it had been Amelie who'd had the bravery he lacked. In any case, the point was that things could not have gone better. Vincent unbuttoned her blouse with gentle hands. Her snow-white breasts enchanted him, and he stared at them at length, before burying his face between them. Amelie's breath became heated and staggered and when he kissed her nipples, she moaned softly.

"Well, well! I always suspected that Lady Chanel was a no-good slut!" Came the sentence ruining the most beautiful moment of their lives. They jumped up suddenly and she hastily pulled her blouse around her. The rider stood before them. Amelie recognised him immediately. It was Gaspard Dessauge, the son of the richest man around. She had rejected his advances before, and he had been after her ever since, unable to accept his failure.

"How dare you behave so with nobility? Apologise immediately, you peon!" Vincent did not think about what he was saying, it just slipped out. He could see from the young rider's clothes that he was not a nobleman, so he was certain it would offend him to the core.

"What's that you mangy dog!" Gaspard said, jumping off his horse in a rage. Despite his young age, he had a soft, rounded figure, and a weak beard dotted his chin. He wore a sword by his side which surprised Farall, as he did not seem like a fighter.

"I'll teach you respect!" Dessauge's already red face turned redder. "And I won't marry your slut after this, that's for sure."

"Gaspard!" Amelie tried to interject. "I did not belong to you before, nor will I ever. Please, accept it! And now get out of here!"

"Shut up!" Dessauge barked at her, unable to tolerate the humiliation. "You will not forget this lesson!" he directed his words at Farall and reached for his sword with his right hand.

Vincent acted instinctually, he stepped close to his attacker and grabbed Gaspard's wrist with his left hand, stopping him from drawing his sword. At the same time, he bent his right arm and sent his elbow straight into the Gaspard's big red nose. Gaspard clutched his nose, screaming, and Vincent took his sword and struck the boy on the backside with the flat side of the blade.

"Get back on your horse and get out of here," Farall said sternly, "or I'll kill you right here and now!"

Gaspard did not need to be asked twice, he climbed, moaning, onto his horse and rising up in the saddle a bit, he rode off.

"Who was that?" Vincent asked.

"He tried courting me, but I rejected him," Amelie looked at him playfully. "He's the son of the richest man around here."

Leaning forwards, Amelie groped Vincent's muscular arm and looked playfully into his eyes.

"You're a trained soldier. Where did they teach you to fight like that?" her voice revealed that she was very impressed by Yannick's expertise in battle.

"You think I know that or anything else about my past?"

He embraced her as she looked with concern after the departing rider.

"This will lead to trouble," Amelie sighed, cuddling up to him.

"Nonsense, if he comes back, I'll chase him off again. What are you afraid of?" her closeness filled him with a bravery he had never felt before, though his experiences were limited to one week of life.

"I don't know, woman's intuition."

Vincent did not reply. What could he have said? Men could only oppose facts, never emotions.

Councillor Perrier came storming out of the King's chambers. Everyone hurried to get out of his way. It was never fortunate to bother him, but nowadays he was especially testy. His own men only approached him if they really had to. Yet, Commander Azor could do nothing else on seeing the Councillor, he approached him directly and stood in his way.

"What?" Perrier growled. "I hope it's important, otherwise I will be angry."

"I wouldn't dare bother you with trifles sir," the Liquidator withstood the murderous glare with an impassionate expression.

"Well then? Should I guess or will you tell me?" the Councillor gesticulated vehemently, though it was not his habit to do so.

"My Lord, if I may be so bold, if we could discuss it in your chambers."

"Pray that I think it prudent too!"

Azor was unfazed, he stood silently before the Councillor, who snorted and then motioned the Commander to follow him. As they entered the chamber, Perrier fell into a chair.

"Well?"

"My Lord, we found trace of Vincent Farall."

"Why did you not tell me at once? Where? When? Is he alright? Speak or I'll kill you," the Councillor almost exploded with nerves and he sprang from his chair.

"He's probably on a farm some two hours ride form here. I just got the information, I'm taking four men there immediately, to bring him back, if the news is true."

"What do you mean, if?"

"A man reported that a person appearing to be a nobleman had appeared on the farm not long ago. Such a thing is not too common, so I think it's almost certain that it is him."

"We need twenty liquidators and I'm coming too. Be ready in ten minutes."

There was a knock, and without waiting for an answer, Head Liquidator Moreau barged into the room.

"My Lord, the King is dead!"

"Really, right now!" was all Perrier said.

"What shall we do, Sir? Should I inform Marquis Bastien de Caulmont."

"Not yet. I need to go get Farall, we've found trace of him, everything else can wait."

"But, Sir," Moreau rarely opposed the Councillor, and this was one of the few occasions, "with your permission, I think the French throne is more important than an aid. Commander Azor can bring him back too."

"Head Liquidator! I know your intentions are good, but as far I know, I am the Councillor of this kingdom, and I determine the order of urgency. Or do you disagree?" as he spoke, Perrier sprang up and stood before Moreau.

"No, Sir, I'm sorry, sir," the Head Liquidator answered, but his eyes belied his disapproval.

"Very well then, I will leave with Commander Azor, you order a state of emergency and wait till we return."

Perrier was at the door when Moreau called after him.

"Sir, if Marquis Caulmont finds out, and the news will get to him fast, he will come here directly."

"So what? If he could wait so many years, a few hours won't kill him!" the Councillor replied and slammed the door with titanic power.

There was no room for opposition left.

The Chanel family were preparing for lunch. Vincent loved these shared meals in the family's heart. The servants brought in the food, but dishing it out fell to Amelie and Yvette. They both insisted on serving the men their food. These events were made perfect by the merry conversation that accompanied them. Vincent listened mostly, and the head of the family spoke on scientific matters, and the women discussed the events of the day. Vincent felt as if he had always belonged here. He no longer missed his forgotten memories. The present was perfectly satisfying to him.

They had just finished soup and the women cleared the table while the lady of the house waxed on about the spicing of the main dish when the liquidators barged into the house. Everyone was frightened, the men pointed their swords at the family and no one dared move. They sat in silence, waiting to see what would become of them.

Rene Chanel was the first to break the silence.

"What do the honourable sirs request? We are peaceful people, we've done nothing against the law."

The liquidators stood impassive, none of them answered. Soon, the Councillor arrived. His grey uniform and insignia on his chest indicated the presence of Alain Perrier. The level of fear intensified, the dreaded Councillor never brought good luck. Even Rene Chanel was silent now, and all eyes were on Perrier. The Councillor approached Vincent directly, embraced him and spoke.

"Vincent, I've been very worried about you. Why did you not come home to the castle? You could have, at least, sent a message."

Even the liquidators were surprised by the Councillor's behaviour. The notorious Perrier did not worry, especially not about a common aid, and it was unimaginable that he should hug somebody. Of course, they knew that Vincent was the Councillor's favourite, but this display of emotions surprised them. The family looked on with surprise and dread.

"My Lord," Vincent began stammering, "the thing is I don't really remember." His brain raced feverishly. He racked his brain. Maybe he would find something, some explanation, as to what these men were doing here. But despite his best effort, his memories spanned only the past few days.

"Don't play games with me, Vincent," Perrier raised his voice. "I've searched half the country for you and you play games with me?"

The Councillor's hand was still on Vincent's shoulder.

"It never crossed my mind, Great Lord," Farall tried to reply with the utmost respect and humility to the great man standing before him, who, he knew, would kill him at one false word.

"You're angry at me because I failed to protect you, is that why you call me Great Lord and not Alain?" Perrier looked at him with disbelief and disappointment.

"Well, errr…" Farall did not know what to reply in his confusion.

"May I speak, Sir?" Rene Chanel asked meekly. He knew he had to recount what had happened.

"Speak!" the Councillor replied curtly.

"We found this young man in the woods. He was unconscious and he was clearly running from someone, his body was covered in wounds and a great gash lay upon his forehead. When he woke, he could not remember his past. I think his head injury caused him to lose his memories."

Perrier furrowed his brow but did not say anything. In that moment, Gaspard Dessauge entered, flanked by two liquidators, a gleeful grin on his face.

"Lords! Do I deserve my pay?" he asked.

"Give him his gold!" the Councillor ordered, not taking his eyes from his aid. Dessauge was nothing to him, not worth looking at.

"You bastard!" Farall hissed. "You're even getting paid for your treachery?"

"Why," Perrier said, "would you not give him anything? He was the one who led us to you."

"I would only give him what a traitor deserves!" Vincent replied bitterly.

"Alright, as you wish," Perrier shrugged.

"Commander Azor, give him what a traitor deserves!"

By the time the others could understand what the Councillor had said, Azor sliced Gaspard's throat with a quick motion. The sight of the flowing blood shocked Farall and the Chanel family. Farall realised that Gaspard had died because of what he'd said. He was angry at him, but he did not wish him dead, yet he felt responsible for what had happened.

"Now, Vincent," the Councillor turned to him, "you're coming with me!"

"My Lord," he replied, "may I speak with you in private a moment?"

"No." Perrier could not allow any further delays. Every minute he was away from the castle increased the already significant tensions.

"In that case, you will have to kill me because I won't budge an inch," Farall replied. The Councillor could see his determination. He could have taken him by force, but he did not want to be rough with the boy.

"In that case, we can talk," Perrier motioned to the liquidators for everyone to go outside.

When the two of them remained, Vincent spoke.

"My Lord, I do not remember anything from my previous life, but I found a home with this family. I will only go with you if you promise they will come to no harm, and also promise that I can return for Miss Amelie Chanel because I love her."

"Well, these requests are easily satisfied," the Councillor replied and raised his hand dramatically to swear. "I give my word, but let's not waste any more time, we have to go!"

"I only ask for a few minutes to say farewell to the girl," Vincent looked hopefully at Perrier who nodded impatiently.

Vincent ran to the family and pulled Amelie aside.

"Look! I have to go now, but I will come back for you. Will you wait for me?" He did not care if her parents found out about their affair. There was no time for subtlety.

"Of course," she replied, her eyes filled with tears. She did not believe she would ever see him again, but she did not want to offend him.

"And your family will be safe," Farall looked at Rene Chanel. "I give you my word."

Meanwhile, Perrier exited the house, mounted his horse and shouted to Vincent.

"Time is pressing, we must go!"

Farall quickly embraced Amelie, then got on a horse and did not even look back. He was afraid that if he did, his heart would break in two.

They did not speak much on the road back to Paris. After a few questions, Perrier had to admit that Rene Chanel had spoken the truth. Vincent truly only remembered the last brief interval of time. So there was not much point to conversing, they both sunk deep into thought. The Councillor was desperate, he had found his aid, but it was almost as if Vincent had died. And Farall thought in fear of the tentative future that lay before him, his only hope was that he could return to Amelie.

After two hours of hard riding, they reached Paris. The buzzing city was unknown to Vincent, and the constant bustle bothered him, the rolling throngs of people disgusted him. Going along the city streets, he saw how people moved aside in fear as the red-black armour-clad liquidators passed, and when they saw the Councillor's grey garb, they sank to one knee.

Farall did not know who he really was, but he was certain he was no commoner since the procession was followed by a feeling of fear and respect. And the notorious Lord Councillor considered him an important person.

When they entered the castle, Perrier turned to the leader of the liquidators with a steely expression.

"Commander Azor! Bind Farall and take him to the torture chamber!"

The Commander did not seem surprised. He could never make heads nor tails of the Councillor's decisions – his intentions were always mysterious.

"Yes Sir!" Azor replied. There was probably nothing Perrier could have said which would have elicited a different response. Azor was a good soldier.

Before Farall knew what was happening, he was dragged from his horse. His hands were quickly bound, strong hands gripped his arms, and by the time he could speak, the Councillor was gone. He was dragged into the castle and felt the pitying glances of passers-by. People who were taken so were never seen again. No one spoke to him. He'd never seen a torture chamber but he was not an idiot, he knew he was in big trouble. He did not understand what was going on. Why had the Councillor been so friendly to him and treated him so? Who was he, an important person, or a complete nobody? If he were a nobody, why would such a great man come to get him? And if he was important, why was he going to be tortured? What was torture? What would it be like? Surely, painful, but what exactly were they going to do to him?

His mind raced as he was shoved along the cold, damp corridors. The clammy stones shone in the torch light, and the screams of anguish issued from behind the occasional iron doors they passed. His mind was paralysed by fear, he could think of nothing but the horror that awaited him. Then, a door was opened before him and he was shoved inside. Inside, men wearing red hoods grabbed him and chained him to kind of pole. Opposite him in the room, a half-dead figure was groaning. He'd never seen such horrors. The man was but a piece of mangled meat and he kept saying, "Kill me! Kill me!"

Besides his tongue, there was not much left of him. Farall realised that he would be such a pitiable wreck soon. He was so terrified that he felt he would die before the torture even began. Then he realised that fate would not be so kind to him. He must have done something that he could not remember. He must have been escaping from the Councillor when Amelie found him. He would admit to anything, that was certain, but how could he when he remembered nothing. The long wait drove him to the edge of madness. The hooded men watched him, but did not touch hi, they were probably enjoying his fear and did not want to finish him quickly. When the tension became unbearable, the iron door creaked and the Councillor himself entered. His gait resembled that of a predator who was preparing to swoop down on him, but would toy with him at length first, just like a cat plays with a mouse. Perrier went quite close to him and then quietly, dispassionately, asked him.

"What's your name?"

Vincent knew that he had no chance of a correct answer and if he gave the wrong response, they would impose unimaginable pains on him.

"My Lord, don't hurt me. I'll do anything, just don't torture me!" he begged like a man bereft of honour. The truth was that he had none left.

"What's your name?" Perrier asked again. Vincent realised that he would hear this question until he died and that would be a very long time.

"I don't know, what I remember is that they called me Yannick."

"Wrong answer. Fiery Iron!" the Councillor ordered. He said it nonchalantly, as if he were talking about the weather.

One of the jailers took some prongs from the fire and moved towards him slowly. Farall felt like his brain was going to explode. He tried feverishly to remember his past. He had to say something, anything to stop the hot iron on its way towards him. The effort made him feel like he was going crazy, then, the memories of the past struck his mind like a lightning bolt. Yannick was dead, and Vincent was reborn. He looked accusingly at the Councillor.

"Alain, why are you doing this to me?"

"Stop!" Perrier raised his voice. "Finally, you're back, Vincent," he said with such happiness that even the jailers flinched.

Later, they had gone up to Perrier's chambers and they sat in their usual chairs – Farall on his uncomfortable seat and the Councillor behind his desk. They watched each other for a long time. Finally, Vincent broke the silence.

"I don't understand why you did this to me. You knew how terrified I am of torture."

"That's exactly why. I knew you needed some strong emotional force to shock your memories back. At least, I really hoped it would work."

"And if I hadn't regained my memories, then would you have tortured me?"

"Of course not! But in order for my plan to be effective, it had to be authentic."

"Could another method have been successful?"

"I tried everything on our ride back. I asked you about our past, but nothing, so I saw no other option. You know, Vincent, I've told you many times, and there is always another way. You know the saying? If the river can't move the rock, it goes around it."

Chapter Twenty-Nine

The members of the King's Council sat silently in the hall. They'd heard of the attack against the Strategist and it did not bode well for them. The King's confidant had always taken advantage of his friendship with the monarch, but from now on, he was certain to take advantage of the present situation. Councillor Ed Wilder clasped his hands, thereby masking his nervousness. Archbishop Parker bowed his head and stared at the table. He looked ahead of him as if there were something interesting to see on the blank piece of furniture. Sir Christopher Marlow clasped the sheath of his confiscated sword. He still could not accept that after the attempt on the King's life, Black had ordered all their weapons taken from them when in the King's presence. Old Alf Kelly did not seem any more nervous than usual, though this was hard to judge since he was always tense and fidgety in his chair. Only the obsidian-skinned Head Liquidator James Horan sat with perfect calm. They waited there for King Mortimer and of course, the Strategist, who'd made a habit recently of arriving late and only in the presence of the King. This, of course, was to ridicule everyone and to show off his power. The silence was increasingly oppressive, yet no one seemed willing to break it. The calling of an emergency council meant that the Strategist had come to some determination on the assassination, and, if the perpetrator were indeed a council member, then someone would lose their head that day.

No matter who Sir Lemmy pointed at, they were a dead man, even if they were not the real perpetrator.

Finally, the door creaked and the Knight King entered with a stern expression, winged by the Strategist, his right arm in a sling. His face revealed nothing. When they entered, the others stood, because no one could sit in the presence of the King until he himself was seated. Mortimer sat, and signalled the others to do the same, he did not speak, though he usually greeted the others from the doorway.

"Lords," the King began deliberately, "as you probably know by now, Sir Lemmy was attacked. It seems that the despicable people who wanted me dead, did not feel safe. They were afraid that Commander Black would discover them and tried to get rid of him. But they've made a mistake now, and will finally pay for their sins. Sir Lemmy, you may speak."

The Strategist stood with a soft elegant movement, he did not hurry, he looked around very slowly before speaking. The hall was filled with the pungent odour of fearfully sweating bodies.

"It seems that someone is using their power to keep the honourable members of the Council in checkmate," Parker blurted out the words that were in everyone's heads. A soft humming filled the room after this outburst.

"If you're going to interrupt," Black replied softly, forcing their attention back on him, "then call me by my name. Anyway, the King gave me the right to speak, so control yourself, or I'll have you taken out."

This impudent answer shocked not only the Archbishop, but the Councillor too. Neither of them dared to speak.

"So," the Strategist went on, "to summarise what has transpired. As is well known, Liquidator Hugh Jones made an attempt on our King's life. His Highness' protection is my task, and I have to say that it was only due to blind luck and fate and God, to each their own, that the bastard failed. I have a trustworthy informant who was witness to the discussion between Jones and the perpetrator, who told me that the person is one of the King's Council. Unfortunately, they could not identify the person because they wore a hood. Yesterday, they tried to kill me as well, they sent a small army against me and my men. The attackers could only know that I would go to the scene from an inside informant. In fact, they also knew how many men I was taking. Thanks to luck or fate or God, I not only survived but found decisive evidence." Everyone stared rigidly, sweat pooling on their brows. Only Mortimer sat calmly, since he'd spoken to Sir Lemmy before the meeting.

"Now, we would really like to know who your informant is!" Councillor Ed Wilder said tensely.

"Unfortunately, I cannot tell you, and it does not matter with respect to the case, because I hope to soon unveil the perpetrator. But I ask you not to interrupt. When I've finished, I will answer your questions. So, let's get back to the attack on me. Four of the enemy's men were slain, whose bodies were examined by George Silver, one of my new liquidators. The proof is thanks to Silver because he found the tattoos on the attackers' right arms, depicting a Sun and Moon."

"Silver had a friend who also had this sign on his arm who said it was the sign of a secret sect. Then I remembered that Jones had a strange scar on his right arm, which I did not give great importance to at the time, but in light of the new information, I am certain that Jones was a member of this sect too. If our luck does not leave us, then the perpetrator must be a member of this sect too, so they too will bear this tattoo. So, I would kindly ask everyone to expose their right arm."

"How dare you? You think I, the Archbishop, will strip for you?" Eric Parker objected.

"I don't think, I know. If the security of my King is at stake then you may strip naked, if necessary. And what does it matter? There are no women on the Council."

"That was a bit harsh, Sir Lemmy," Ed Wilder noted, gently coming to the Archbishop's aid.

"Gentlemen!" Mortimer slapped the table, "enough of this. Everyone expose their arms."

Slowly, they all began undressing, peeking sidelong at each other's arms. They were embarrassed, but no one would oppose the King. Old Alf Kelly was last to undress, exposing the Sun and Moon tattoo on his arm. For a moment, there was deathly silence. The Strategist looked firmly into his eyes and simply asked.

"Why?"

Kelly answered with cool confidence. No one had ever seen him this powerful, the dithering old man was replaced by a defiant rebel. He spoke.

"King Mortimer has waged more wars than any other ruler, he's destroyed thousands of families. There's no end to the widows and orphaned children. The guilds which I control have become loss-making due to the constant warring. I've found peace among my brothers, but in the name of love, I determined to resort to violence."

When he'd finished, he took a little vial from his pocket and quickly drank it. No one had time to intervene, the poison acted instantly and the old man was dead in a matter of seconds. Black walked over to Kelly, grabbed his hair, raised his head from the ground and staring into his glassy eyes, the Strategist said.

"What sort of love requires the murder of a King?"

The Council members were more surprised by Black's behaviour than they were by Kelly's death. It was not the first time the Strategist had talked to a corpse. He had done the same with Liquidator Hugh Jones. Nasty rumours circulated in the court about the Commander who conversed with corpses. No one knew why he did it – maybe so they would be afraid of him, or worse, because he was crazy.

When the Council members had departed, only Mortimer and Sir Lemmy remained in the room. The King did not beat about the bush, he got straight to the point.

"Don't tell me you're seriously talking to corpses," he said pointing an accusatory finger at Sir Lemmy.

"I knew that Hugh Jones would continue speaking after his death. The scar on his arm put us on the right path. The dead never lie, while the living usually talk nonsense."

"Are you kidding me? Careful, I am your King!" Only the King's best friend, Black could wind him up so badly.

"I'm sorry, your Highness, for the jest. Naturally, I do not converse with corpses. The act was for the honourable King's Council, it is to my advantage if they're afraid of me. I've no use for their friendship."

"If you think it right, you can go to the cemetery for conversation. Just don't think I'm that stupid! Anyway, that was good work today, my friend! Now that we're done with this, tell me, why our fleet has to cruise up and down the French coast."

"Not for long now, my King. The danger has passed and the dance may soon begin!"

Roy Davis felt as if he had done everything in order to make his plan succeed. *Everything would be decided today*, he thought, thought it would only transpire later if it was for better or worse. He reached for his wine glass with a slightly trembling hand and drained it. Merry Jimmy's Tavern was almost empty in the early afternoon, people usually worked at this time and only began to amble in after seven. Beside him, there were a few old timers and a traveller or two wearing down the chairs. Roy thought over the events of the past few days again. The hardest part was helping the traitor mutant, Mick Taylor. Just in the last few days, they'd handed four unlucky people over to Councillor Ed Wilder. Davis knew that his actions would haunt him for the rest of his life, but he had to convince Mick that he was on his side. If he failed, then his life, as well as Claire's, was in jeopardy. Meanwhile, Mick taught him how to close his mind from telepaths.

The next step was to pass this knowledge on to Claire. Once they were both able to block their thoughts, he asked her to close her mind and then he could finally tell her who Taylor was and what he could do to them. They agreed to speak only of trivial matters in thought from then on, so that Taylor would not become suspicious. The past few days seemed like an eternity, and Roy was constantly afraid that Mick would see through him and all would be over. He was so nervous that he wanted to order another cup, though he knew he would have to drink with Mick too, and if he got drunk, he would not be able to focus on the task at hand. Finally, Taylor arrived, looked around, and quickly spotted Davis sitting in a secluded corner of the tavern, he slowly approached him and sat down.

"Well," Roy asked in lieu of a greeting, "are you in?"

"I don't know, it seems pretty rough. I think we should leave it, it's much easier to get gold the usual way," Mick said running a hand through his hair and then waving at the innkeeper. While the wine was brought, neither of them spoke, they sat in silence, or at least that's what any observer would have thought. In truth, they had switched to telepathy.

"Let's go over it once more," Roy goaded Mick, "if we blackmail Adam Mallory, I will get the house, and you will get his fortune. He won't give us any trouble, the girl is the most important thing in his life. I've spoken to him already and told him I'd be taking a close friend of mine over for a drink. Then we'll tell him that his daughter is mutant, and he'd better not mess around."

Mick scratched his head. He didn't like the plan, there was too much risk involved.

"What if he attacks us? I've heard he's a dangerous man. It would not be advisable to fight him. A further complication is that the Strategist likes him and he might turn to him for help."

"Look, he loves Claire more than his own life, he sacrificed his military service for her, though he could have gone far. And Sir Lemmy can do nothing. If someone turns out to be a mutant, even he cannot save them."

"It's still a stupid plan, why the risk?"

Roy knew Mick's weak spot already, his vanity, and he felt that this was his last resort.

"Well, if you can't help, I guess I'll do it alone. I know it's risky but I thought it wouldn't be a problem for you. I guess I was wrong, I'm sorry, it seems there are some cases that are too much for even you. Please understand that he will not let me marry Claire, and she will not oppose his will, but I want that woman."

"Alright, though I can't understand why that wench is so important to you. We can make enough gold that you can buy any woman you want."

"I want her! And I trust your skills, you just need to come along today, you can have a look at Adam Mallory yourself, and then you can figure out what you want. Help me, please!"

"Alright, let's go, but don't take this as a promise. I'm just assessing the situation today, then I'll see."

Claire carefully laid the table with wine and glasses. She adjusted the tablecloth, though it was not wrinkled. She adjusted and readjusted the perfectly laid table. Her father approached her, gently took her hand and smiled at her.

They didn't say a word, they did not speak without words either, not that Adam Mallory could, but they understood each other, because emotions were more powerful than any words.

A knock broke the silence. Claire shivered, Adam motioned to her encouragingly to go open the door and he sat down at the table. Soon, they entered the dining room and Roy introduced Mick to Mallory – the old man did not seem especially friendly.

"You know," Roy said to Claire, "Mick came to the castle not long ago, we've been working together since."

"I've heard of the work you do," Adam Mallory said, bitterly.

"That's flattering, sir," Taylor replied sweetly, "that means my reputation has proceeded me in such a short while."

The Commander stroked his beard and looked sharply into his guest's eyes.

"A reputation does not necessarily mean a good one. I don't think sending people to the torture chamber is flattering; it's disgusting."

"You should be more polite to your guests, especially when you know who the person in your house is."

"Who would respect you, you scoundrel?" Mallory raised his voice.

Taylor sprang from his chair and reached for his sword but the Commander was much faster than him and his sword was already at Taylor's throat.

"What's going on here Roy? Why aren't you defending me?"

"Why would I? I've been waiting for this moment since we first met."

"It's disgusting how you throw your own kind to the dogs," Claire added.

"I warn you, the Councillor's men are waiting by your door. If anything happens to me, you're done for!" Mick said in a shaky voice.

"Then I should be really scared now, right?" Mallory asked, and stabbed Taylor in the throat with such force that the blade went straight through his neck.

Claire screamed, she'd never seen a murder before, but Roy felt relief, while Adam felt only rage. Mick's struggle with death did not last long. Mallory turned to Claire, he knew from experience that at times like these it was best to give people in shock something to do, this would get them through the critical state faster.

"Claire, go on out of the house and have a look if the men are really there! Act naturally out there and then come back and tell me what you saw!"

Claire visibly recovered her senses, nodded and left. Mallory wiped his blade, shaking his head as he did so. Then he looked sternly at Roy.

"I should have known there was something wrong between you. You sat beside each other in silence too often, lovers are always chatting, but you just stared at each other."

"Are you angry at us, Sir?"

"Of course not, it's no one's fault how they're born."

Meanwhile, Claire appeared in the doorway, her eyes filled with fear.

"Unfortunately, that rat was speaking the truth. There are, at least, ten armed men outside."

"Then out the back we go!" Adam gave the order, "we've no time to waste."

"But where shall we go, Sir?" Roy asked.

"To the only person who can help us. He helped us out not long ago, I hope the Strategist has patience left for us, because he has other things to do than protecting your backs all the time."

Sir Lemmy sat in his chambers and listened attentively to Roy, Claire and Adam Mallory's story. At first, Roy spoke, then slowly Claire and Adam joined in too. The Strategist did not interrupt, many years of experience had taught him how to notice lies, and these people were telling the truth, and in that case, it was better to let them tell the story themselves. When they'd finished, the Strategist nodded, as usual he showed no outward emotions.

"Commander Mallory, you've more trouble with these two youngsters than I have with the entire Kingdom," The Strategist smiled. There weren't many people in the Kingdom who'd seen him this way.

"Excuse me, my Lord, but I could only turn to you," Mallory said, falling to his knees and bowing his head. He waited for the Strategist's judgement over his family in this fashion.

"You acted wisely. Stand! I am no King for you to kneel before me. I will help you, but this time it will come at a price. Not long from now, I will ask something of your daughter and Davis here. Now go, I'm expecting the Councillor now, and I reckon you would not be inclined to meeting him."

"My greatest gratitude, my Lord! May I ask what you will ask of my daughter and her suitor?" The old soldier never resorted to asking back when Black said something, but his anxiety overcame decorum.

"I will be going on a dangerous journey and they will have to come with me."

"I understand, my Lord," the Commander answered, though, of course, he understood nothing. But he didn't want to press the matter.

They were at the door when Black called after them.

"Commander Mallory, you are fortunate to have but one daughter. I loathe to think what would happen if you had more."

Interesting, Sir Lemmy thought, *sometimes fate made things more difficult and sometime things work out. As if fate were my ally*. He didn't have long to ponder this because Commander Caroll appeared in his chambers.

"My Lord, Councillor Ed Wilder has arrived."

"Bring him in at once!"

As they entered, Black noticed on the old Councillor's that he did not take being ordered about too kindly. Lately, Wilder had been less and less in control of his emotions, Black ascertained, though his training must have prepared him to control them. It seems age was not kind to him.

"Are you taking every opportunity to flaunt your power against me?" Wilder said bitterly, as he sat down opposite Black at the desk. Caroll remained standing as he always did.

"You misunderstand me, Councillor, when I tell you why I called for you. You will relent."

Ed Wilder's expression visibly slackened and his voice was fused with curiosity.

"Well," Black went on, pulling out a drawer and producing a letter, "you had to come immediately because I am at a loss. I require your help. Please read this letter carefully."

The Strategist pushed the densely written letter across the desk. Wilder was about to carefully pick it up when Caroll brought a battle-axe down with lightning speed. He aimed carefully so that the Councillor's finger that bore the poisoned ring was separated from its hand. He had to be certain, so the Councillor left four fingers in total on the table when he instinctively withdrew his hand. In that moment, the Strategist swept the fingers off the table with his right hand along with the ring. He did not want the Councillor to grab the deadly jewel with his other hand. After his initial shock, Wilder felt the dull force of unbearable pain spreading though his body. He thought he was going to faint, but his body was much stronger than he thought.

"Doctors, now," Black said to Caroll, who opened the door and let the two healers in. The Councillor screamed, writhing on the floor in pain, several men held him down as the blood flow had to be stopped. The doctors went about their job skilfully, they opened Wilder's mouth and forced a large amount of sedative potion down his throat. Then, they began stitching up his hand. The job took several minutes. By the time they were done, the Councillor spoke dopily, with fear in his eyes.

"Why did you have to do that, Strategist?"

"I would like to ask you a few questions, and I did not want you to think about using your ring. And now the possibility of torture has become very real. This fact should facilitate your honesty."

"What do you want to know?"

"Everything! First of all, tell me where Atlantis is!"

Chapter Thirty

Alejandro woke early, his left arm completely numb from Teresa's grip. She had slept all night, and did not wake when he peeled her fingers off him

Quietly, he crept out of the room and went out of the inn into the street. He preferred the calm peace of villages to the crazed bustle of cities. The shops were open, because the villagers preferred to shop early in the morning or late in the evening as they toiled on the fields by day. He entered a grocery store that sold almost everything. After a brief search, he found some men's clothes that Teresa could wear. Besides this, he bought a pair of scissors and some used boots. In the next shop, he bought bread and goat's milk, then he headed back to the inn. Teresa was waiting for him, crouching on a chair.

"I thought you'd left me here," she said disparagingly.

"How could I do such a thing, my lady? Is that how you've come to know me?" her distrust hurt him.

"No, but I've come across many lies in my life, and I was afraid you would betray me. I see you've been shopping. What did you buy?"

Alejandro could barely follow her sudden change of subject. One moment she was talking about lies, then the next she asked pointed questions. He decided to answer her question.

"We can't leave here till you've changed your clothes. Put these clothes on, your pursuers will not recognise you in them."

He handed the clothes to her and turned his back so she could dress in peace. When she was ready, Alejandro turned serious.

"My Lady, I have bad news. Unfortunately, we will have to cut your hair. There are no boys with such long, silky hair."

"Well, do what you must!"

Alejandro was surprised by her answer. He thought she would be disinclined to part with her beautiful, long hair. It seemed that Teresa was different from other girls. True, he knew that from the instant he saw her, but the thought only now cemented in his mind. As he fidgeted with her hair, she became talkative.

"Sir, I hope you will not be offended if I ask you something very personal."

"You've done nothing but ask me questions since we met. Why would I take offence now? The truth is that I am beginning to get used to it." In fact, he really enjoyed speaking with her.

"Don't you have a family? Because men who do, do not wander the world aimlessly and don't have time to just help people out."

"I have no family," Alejandro replied curtly.

"Did you once?"

"I never had anyone." As he said it, he realised that she had noticed something that he had worked hard to ignore. *What kind of life was it to be alone?*

"May I ask you more?"

"You're going to, anyway!"

"I don't want to offend you or confuse you."

"Spit it out, my Lady!"

"When you were fighting yesterday, well, it was hard not to notice and I was thinking…"

"What?"

"That you, sir, are you not a mutant?"

Alejandro stiffened, he suddenly stopped cutting her hair. He didn't know what to answer.

"Excuse me, I did not want to offend or expose you, but I've never seen anyone move so wonderfully, or so quickly."

"You know," Alejandro began his answer, "people cannot accept differences in others. Priests and Councillors most of all. Yes, I am not like the others, we could say that I'm a mutant."

"Do not be afraid, Sir, I will never betray you, you can trust me."

"Thank you, my Lady," Alejandro laughed. The clever girl was winding him around her finger, he would not admit it to himself, but he was glad to answer even the most awkward questions.

"You know, Alejandro Sir, I really like it that you are not like the others. I'm not just talking about your ability to destroy anyone in seconds, but I've never met anyone as kind as you."

"If you say so, but we must go now. My Lady, when we leave the inn, let us not talk anymore. Please collect your questions throughout the day, and ask me once we are safe!"

"I promise, I will obey you!"

They stepped out into the streets, the majority of people were at work already, and the few pedestrians still out did not notice the grumpy man escorted by a stable boy. Before they left the village, they acquired another horse because travelling on one animal would have been suspicious. They rode the whole morning, avoiding villages and main roads, since there were regular patrols there, and the Archbishop's men were always around, searching for Teresa. In the early afternoon, Alejandro decided they would stop at a dusty little highway inn.

Inside, there were only a few peasants who had stopped in for a cup of wine. The innkeeper brought them roast chicken and watered wine. They were almost done when soldiers entered the inn.

"Stay quiet. If need be, I will do the talking," Alejandro whispered in Teresa's ear.

As the uniformed men stopped in the middle of the inn, all eyes fixed on them.

"Have any of you seen a well-dressed young lady around here?" their leader asked in lieu of a greeting.

Everyone shook their heads, and the soldiers walked between the tables. One of them approached their table directly.

"Are you from around here?" he asked Alejandro.

"No, sir, just passing through. I have not seen a young lady who was well-dressed."

"And who is this beside you?"

"My aid, but he cannot respond on account of the fact that he's a mute."

Teresa nodded quickly, pointing to her mouth, indicating she could not speak. Though she was very nervous, she remembered that this was the second time she'd had to play a mute in a short time.

"His skin is so white," the soldier said, "as if he were a girl."

As he said it, he realised that it may even be true. He glanced at his commander, who nodded at him.

"Stand up quickly. I want to inspect your aid."

They stood slowly, Alejandro's eyes became slits, and his muscles tensed, reminding Teresa of a predator preparing to pounce.

"Show yourself, undress immediately," the man ordered. "That will reveal the truth."

Alejandro swung unexpectedly into action. His sword appeared in his right hand and his long dagger in the left. In the same moment, he was standing before the soldier, who had no chance of reacting to the lightning-quick attack. He died before he could even touch his sword. Alejandro dripped both his blades in the man's chest, easily penetrating the man's light leather armour. The three other soldiers ran towards them, Teresa hid behind her protector, who positioned himself to block the exit. She knew that he did so because he intended to leave none of them alive. Two of them attacked at once and Teresa could barely follow Alejandro's movements. His defence and attack blended as one, and a moment later, the two soldiers dropped dead onto the dusty floor. The last soldier dropped his weapon and begged for his life.

"Good Lord, have mercy on me. I have children."

"Why did you not think of them when you enlisted?" Alejandro replied, and killed the grovelling soldier with a single stroke.

They left in a hurry, and the shocked peasants dared not speak to the terrifying stranger and his escort. They ran to the stables for their horses and then rode quickly to the nearby woods. Alejandro was certain that a search party would be sent after them before long. From now on, they would not be looking for a well-dressed girl alone, but an ageing man and a stable boy.

"My Lady," Alejandro spoke after they had been riding through thick cover for half an hour, "from here on, we will go more slowly and you may get hungry a little too. If we'd followed the road, we would have reached Madrid in a day, this way it will take two."

"No matter, I don't eat much anyway, and I love the forest, there are so many birds living here. Do you like birds too?"

"Well, I've never thought about it," Alejandro replied in surprise.

What was there to think about whether he liked them or now? You know, it will be good here in the woods, we will have lots of time to talk.

And so it was, though it was Teresa who talked for the most part, Alejandro answering from time to time, but mostly, he just listened. Over the course of the afternoon, Alejandro was reminded several times of Teresa's first question on whether he liked birds. Probably he did, though he was not certain of it, but he was certain that Teresa's voice was far dearer to him than the chirping of all the birds in the world. By evening, they arrived at a small city. Alejandro thought they could rent a room without issue, he would take the horses to the stables alone, and she would quickly sneak into the room they booked.

Once they were there, he could go get food, and at dawn, they could leave without being noticed. So it happened, everything went to plan, and when Alejandro returned to the room with food, he was the one to ask a question.

"I hope, this time, My Lady, you did not think I was abandoning you."

"It is not nice to joke with a scared child, Sir!" Teresa's eyes glinted laughingly.

Later, long after dinner, she cuddled up to him, took his hand and looked at him.

"Alejandro, will you wake me at dawn when we must leave?"

"Of course, my Lady," he replied. He'd been waiting for her to cuddle up to him all evening.

They'd not been sleeping an hour when they awoke to a huge commotion. Teresa looked at her protector with a terrified expression. Alejandro got up and headed for the door.

"I'll have a look at what's going on out there. I'll be back in a second."

"I'm scared. Don't leave me here alone!"

"I'll take care of you, my dear!" he replied with unusual familiarity, which told Teresa that she was not the only one afraid.

Ten minutes later, Alejandro returned, holding some sort of pulp in his hands which stank terribly.

"There are a lot of soldiers down there. Now," he nodded at his hands, "I have to smear this on your face."

"What is it?" she asked in disgust.

"Unfortunately, my Lady, this is horseshit, but you must endure it. Don't ask any more questions, we have to act quickly."

Then Alejandro smeared her face, hair and clothes thickly with the fresh horse dung. Then, they quickly collected their things and left the room. They met no one in the upstairs hallway, but as they headed down the stairs, the sound of voices intensified.

"Everyone stay where they are until they've been questioned!" someone shouted.

When they got down, people stood in fear by their tables, the room was filled with armed soldiers. In the centre, stood the Commander. Alejandro suddenly grabbed Teresa's shirt and began pulling her directly towards the Commander.

"Damn this bloody servant!" he shouted. "I can't trust him to do anything!"

"What are you shouting about there?" the commander growled at him. "If you don't shut your mouth, I'll teach you how to be silent."

"My lord, look here," he shoved the stinking, shit covered girl before him. "I asked this halfwit to tie up the horses and he gets covered in shit. What more, he had the gall to come up to my room. Look at the state of him!"

The Commander took a step back in disgust.

"Take this pile of shit away from me! If it touches my clothes, I'll hang the pair of you!"

"Yes sir, Commander Sir. Excuse me, I'll take him to the well, and we'll only come back when he's clean as a whistle."

They quickly left the room, soldiers and guests moving quickly out of their way. As they exited, they ran to the stable, freed their horses and were soon riding through the dark woods.

"My Lady, forgive me, I could think of nothing else."

"It's alright. I did not think you were so crafty, sir."

"What will we do now?"

"If we ride till dawn, we'll reach the woodland hideout where you will be safe. I will leave you there, we cannot go on together because we will be caught. And even if we aren't, I cannot cross the whole of Madrid with you without causing a scene."

"And what will you do?"

"I will speak with Councillor Pedro Garcia and everything will be alright."

"It's not nice of you to consider me such a child! They won't even let you into the castle, and even if they do, you will never get an audience with the Councillor."

"Don't underestimate me, my Lady."

"I don't know who you are, Alejandro, but I am certain that you are not who you claim to be."

"Why, my Lady, do you remember me claiming to be somebody?"

Head Liquidator Sanchez stood before Garcia's desk. His legendary calm seemed to have left him. The Councillor was surprised by the uncertainty he saw in his soldier's eyes, but it also sparked his interest.

"Is something wrong, Head Liquidator?" he asked as he placed the papers down on his desk. *Things don't look too bright*, he thought, *I could do with some good news, but this certainly won't be it.*

"My Lord, Alejandro Leon sought me out here in the castle."

"This cannot be true," Garcia erupted and looked at Sanchez, feeling ashamed of his sudden outburst. The news was obviously true, or the Head Liquidator would not have said it.

"Why did you not capture him? All the liquidators combined could not defeat him?"

"The situation is more complicated, Sir," Marcos Sanchez's voice belied offence and impatience. The Councillor knew full well that he was able to make independent decisions, and if such a situation were easily solved he would not be standing there.

"He wants to speak with you."

"You know I think highly of you, Marcos," the Councillor said, impatiently, "but we both know that if we let Leon in here, then we can have as many soldiers on duty as we like, we are still dead men."

"This is true, Sir, but, with your permission, I don't think it's about that now. He said he has news of Teresa de Cantabria, more precisely, he claims to know where she is."

For a few moments, Garcia pondered this, he clasped his hands before him in reverie. For a while, he did not move, and then reaching a sudden decision, he spoke.

"I see, you made the right decision as always. Bring him in at once!"

"Do you not want protection, sir?"

"You know it's useless. If he wants to attack, no one can stop him, but if he wants to talk, I'll need no protection."

Sanchez left, and the Councillor sunk back into thought. He had not seen Sanchez in ten years, he hadn't even known he was alive. He'd left him suddenly and without warning, in the same manner that he now arrived.

There was no one more dangerous in the world, but he had to meet him now. Teresa's life was crucial to the future of the kingdom. In fact, the situation of the Spanish Kingdom was crucial to the fate of the Known World. So he had no choice but to speak to him.

The door creaked and the tall, swarthy figure of Alejandro Leon appeared. He approached the Councillor slowly. His movements were deceptively youthful. Neither of them spoke, they just stared at each other.

Leon sat opposite Garcia and looked at him with sharp, ice-cold eyes.

"It's been a long time, Alejandro," the Councillor said, breaking the silence, "you've aged a little, there's more grey in your hair than brown."

"The years have been no kinder to you, Pedro," the unwelcome guest replied in a measured tone.

They knew they would have to get down to business soon, but old wounds made their conversation difficult. They'd parted without farewell, Leon simply had not returned from a mission.

"Before we get to the point, please tell me why you disappeared without telling me the reason for your departure."

"If I'd told you, would you have let me go? I don't think so." Garcia knew that Teresa's fate was at stake here, but he could not resist prying open the past.

"When you killed your father, one of the most important people in the kingdom, I gave you refuge. Later, I protected you when they wanted to kill you for being a mutant. Yet, this is how you thank me?"

"Let us, at least, be honest between us here." Leon's voice belied no emotion. "You did all that to have control over my abilities. I killed many people to fulfil my debt to you."

"I offered you a position among the liquidators, a great career could have been yours but you did not want it."

"True, and still, I was the best killer the Kingdom ever saw. When I felt like the debt was paid, I left."

"And I did not send a search party after you, though you would have deserved it."

"And I did not kill you, though you would have deserved it."

The two men calmed their tempers, as if speaking these words had released them from their pressures. They'd never liked each other, and no one had ever liked them, this much they had in common, as well as their dark pasts.

"Why did you come after such a long time?"

"Let us not play games, Councillor. I would not be here if Sanchez had not told you about the reason for my visit."

"Alright, then tell me what you know about Teresa!"

"I found her in the street, quite far from the place where you'd been guarding her. Three men were trying to rape her and I intervened. And now I'm protecting her."

"What do you want for her?" the Councillor took a fat pouch from the drawer and threw it on the table. The dull clinking indicated that it was full of gold.

"Nothing. I want to bring her to you, but if we arrived together you would have thought that I kidnapped her. And I cannot know who here means her ill. And you can shove your gold up your arse!" Leon looked dismissively at the gold and then at Garcia.

"If you did not do it for gold, then why?"

"You wouldn't understand. She's just important to me."

"You didn't harm her, did you?"

Leon sprang to his feet. This sick determination was too much, even from the Councillor.

"Do you have such disgusting thoughts because you judge people as you judge yourself? No, I care for her, not like a woman. This is a feeling you cannot comprehend, because it is foreign to you," Leon sat back down and looked into Garcia's eyes, "do you even know what love is?"

"I've heard of such a thing, but I admit, the feeling is foreign to me, because, so to speak, it is foreign to reason. But you must admit that such a thought is logical when speaking of the most notorious killer of the kingdom. I could not imagine a stranger pair than the two of you."

The Councillor was about to ask Leon to bring Teresa to the castle when he had a better idea.

"Look, you keep hold of her for a while, speak with Head Liquidator Sanchez weekly, I will send a message with him when the castle is secure."

"I agree," Leon replied curtly and with a lithe movement, he stood and left the room.

Garcia stayed deep in thought for a long while. Life had cast him an ally, whose help he would never have expected.

Teresa waited with concern for Alejandro's return. The little house in the woods was to her taste, it didn't have many creature comforts, but the birds sang so loudly there that they made up for everything else. She just sat on the porch and wondered at them.

But her joy was not undisturbed, because she worried that her benefactor may have come to harm. Although she knew that there was no greater warrior than him, he could still not take on the whole castle in combat.

Late in the afternoon, he arrived with a full bag over his shoulder.

"I brought you lots of good things to eat and fresh spring water. Later, I will go hunting."

"Who cares about food?" she replied happily. She was very happy that he had returned. "Tell me what happened in the castle!"

"I met the Councillor," Alejandro said.

"Do I have to draw every word out of you with pliers, Sir?"

"The point is that you must stay here with me for a few days, but it maybe a few weeks."

"Well, that's wonderful, you could not have returned with better news."

"You don't mind, my Lady?"

"How can you ask such a thing? I can be with the person I love most. You will have to answer so many questions, you can't imagine."

"I have an inkling," he replied, with a smile.

Chapter Thirty-One

Ponga and Jules had been in the King's castle for a week. Everything had turned out as they'd arranged it, they were easily hired.

Because there was always a shortage of people who spoke the old languages. They did not meet the Councillor. Perrier had a lot to do in those days, so he had no time to deal with the details of the library. True, it would not have been a problem if they had met, because Fifi had done their makeup well, and they were unrecognisable. And they started each day in front of the mirror, Jules adjusted the makeup on their faces, they put on their wigs and kept their disguises working flawlessly. Head Librarian Lalonde did not recognise Jules, who would have liked to hug the old bookworm for helping him escape back in the day. Unfortunately, he could not, but he determined that if he survived this ordeal, he would thank Lalonde a hundredfold. Ponga's lack of languages was not discovered because Jules had told the Head librarian that they translated the books together. They had not been able to gain access to the restricted section yet, Jules was certain that their time would come, and if all else failed, they would go in by force, because the knight alone was worth as much as an army. The volume of 'The Brief History of the Dark Ages' occupied Jules more than anything. Then, suddenly, everything changed.

On the day of the King's death, Jules got word that his old mentor, Marquis Bastien de Caulmont was in the castle. He took the news straight to Ponga.

"Get ready, tonight we'll go to the city through the secret tunnel."

"I don't understand, you said that we would only leave the castle with the book," Ponga said, confusedly.

Jules had to admit that he owed an explanation, so he told Ponga the news. Since Ponga understood nothing, he was forced to reveal who the Marquis was, and spoke of the soon-to-be-King and revealed Henri and his own past. Ponga did not interrupt, he listened attentively through his friend's confession.

"I've long suspected that you are an important person but I still don't understand why we have to go out."

"You know the Councillor cannot be trusted, he tried to kill you too. The Marquis never trusted him, he just had no other choice but to ally with him. We need to tell Marquis Caulmont that we're here, he may have use for us."

"Alright, but then let us visit the others, if only for five minutes," Ponga replied, though he was thinking only of Fifi.

"We can't. It's too dangerous."

"We do nothing but dangerous things. You could do this little thing for me."

Jules realised his folly. Ponga followed him blindly and when he told him their plans were changing, he did not step back. He could not deny him a meeting with Fifi, it was simply his due.

"Alright, but just five minutes really. And now, let us go, our aids await us!"

They left. Ponga suspected that they would go to the stables from where the door led to the secret tunnels. They had used this tunnel for their escape. If they passed through the castle gates, the guards could be suspicious, they may even take them straight to the Councillor.

As they entered the passageway, they had to light torches. In the twilight, Ponga had an ominous feeling. These tunnels had a dark history that people today could not comprehend. What sort of people were the ancients? Why did they tunnel into the ground? What did they use these passages for? He was certain these questions would never be answered. The road they took was much shorter as they did not have to leave Paris and did not have to pass all the five city gates. A few minutes later, Jules led him up a flight of stairs to the surface. Men were waiting for them there with clothes, which they quickly changed into. Jules did not introduce Ponga to his friends, he simply exchanged a few words with them. Ponga could not hear what they were talking about, but it looked like Jules was passing out orders and the strangers listened, nodded and then left. After they'd changed their clothes, hiding their clothes under the stairs, they headed towards the others in the comedians' wagon. Ponga hugged Fifi so tightly she could barely breathe, but she would not have complained, not for all the jewels in the world, she wanted nothing more than his closeness. They did not speak a word to each other, they did not want to waste time chatting, or perhaps neither of them wanted to spoil the magical moment. Jules took care of that for them.

"Come on, five minutes are up!"

The couple did not want to leave each other's arms. Finally, Fifi pushed him away from her.

"Go, my love! Go, do what you have to do, then we can be together for the rest of our lives."

Ponga did not know what to say, he just nodded and stroked her face. Then he quickly turned on his heel and as he walked away, he felt that if he did not leave now, he would not able to do so later.

For a while, they walked through the narrow streets and Ponga realised he had no idea where they were going.

"How do you know where to find the Marquis?"

"Let's not talk on the streets, sounds are carried far at night! My men have found out, let that satisfy you for now." They got past into the central district of the city where elegant restaurants stood in rows. Soon, they arrived at an elegant building where two soldiers were waiting for them who immediately led them to the Marquis' chambers. Without knocking, they were shoved into a large hall. Marquis De Caulmont was waiting for his guests, staring into the fireplace, a pipe hanging from his mouth.

"Since I sent you away, we've barely met," the Marquis began and turned towards them as he spoke, "do you remember Hubert, how we used to stare into the fire together?"

De Caulmont approached his guests, embraced Jules and then shook Ponga's hand.

"Who have you brought with you? How reliable is he?"

"My Lord, this is Sir Ponga, who I saved from the clutches of the Councillor and took to the swamps. I'll vouch for him."

"Alright, answer me," the Marquis leaned so close to Didier that their faces almost touched, "are you loyal to me and your King-to-be?"

"Honestly, my Lord?" Ponga asked as Jules' eyes flashed in concern, but he did not dare speak.

"Remember, my son, I value honesty over everything, even if it hurts. Obsequious lying is as disgusting as is it is sly."

"I do not know you, Lord, and I know nothing of politics. For me, one King is just like the next," the Marquis' eyes shot sparks, but he let Ponga speak on' Jules tried to wave his companion off, but Ponga did not notice, or did not want to notice the warning. "But I know my companion, Jules, well, and I will be loyal to him till my death, and if he says he serves you, then so do I."

De Caulmont smiled and patted the knight on the shoulder.

"That's what I'm talking about. You don't beat around the bush, my son. By the way, I've heard of you. Is it true that you could finish any of us with ease and that my sword would mean you no challenge? Though I have to admit that the years have not been kind to my fencing skills."

"My Lord, I mean no disrespect, but I would easily best you if you were but twenty."

The Marquis laughed loudly, and then offered his guests a seat and wine. Jules told him about the reason for their visit that they were in the castle again, prepared to do anything to get the book.

"Leave that damned book. Though it is very important, it is not the most important thing now. Now we must help our future King with all our might."

"But, my Lord," Ponga interjected, "how could we help if we don't even know where to find him, nor do we even know who it is?"

"True, but you are the closest to the fire and if something happens, you will be the first to know. Watch the Councillor secretly, if the King surfaces, send me a message and protect him with your lives. Never trust Councillor Perrier, you know Hubert, he wants to capture you and he wants the knight dead. Currently, I can do nothing more than pretending to trust him. I've not mentioned it, but the Councillor gave me Marquis Bertrand's head, that is, he allowed me to defeat him in honourable combat."

"Then perhaps he's with us, after all?" Jules asked.

"We cannot know for certain, and I certainly don't believe him. I know of no one more evil and wily than him. Perrier always acts in his own interests, but only he knows what he truly wants."

"My Lords, excuse me, I know it is impolite for me to probe, but…" Ponga began uncertainly. Meanwhile, Jules pulled at his robes, but Ponga pretended not to notice the indiscreet warning.

"Enough of your damned politeness," the Marquis snorted, "it is true that I outrank you, but remember well that we fight on the same side. Ask me anything! Ask away!"

"When you saw him last, he was a child, and now he is man. What if the Councillor does not want to bring the true King to the throne? Whoever he appoints, you will be forced to believe him."

"You see, Hubert, it's worth listening to others. Anyone can have a good insight."

"And, my Lord," Jules asked, "what is your response?"

"Naturally, it has occurred to me, a long time ago, and I'm not worried about this matter."

"How will you recognise the King?" Ponga even forgot to say 'My Lord' in his excitement. Marquis De Caulmont smiled mischievously and answered.

"Unfortunately, I cannot tell you that, but I will soon show all my cards."

On the road leading to the castle, Ponga and Jules did not speak much. They both sank deep in thought and felt like they were merely pieces of a huge jigsaw puzzle, the entire image of which they had no clue of. In fact, this was the truth. And yet, they would have liked to know more about the game into which life had swept them, but no matter how hard they thought about it, they became none the wiser. Ponga followed his friend blindly through the dark Parisian streets. Then he became aware that they had come to the underground passage. They went down, lit torches and changed back into their librarian clothes. In the blinking light, Jules checked their face paint and their wigs, then they continued on their way. They reached the stables without issue and carefully climbed out. Taking great care, they put the door back where it had been. It would not have been good if the stable boys discovered the passageway. Quietly, they crept back along the corridor and entered their shared dormitories, barred the door and lit torches. The scene illuminated before them was shocking. Fabian, Henri and Fifi sat tied to chairs in the centre of the room, the liquidators standing behind them held knives to their throats and Councillor Perrier stood to one side, smiling.

"My dear Sirs," the Councillor began jovially, "unfortunately, I must ask you to sit down on those two empty chairs because we must bind you to them. If you should resist we will cut this charming woman's throat first."

"Don't listen to him, Didier," Fifi shouted, "he's going to kill us anyway. Don't think about me, save yourself!"

Ponga was unable to act, he assessed that his speed alone was not enough to save her. He had no other choice but to allow them to tie him up.

They were not gagged so they knew they were going to be interrogated. In their desperation, they imparted the choicest curses on their foes. The Councillor listened to the company delightedly, it seemed like the curses were only making him happier. When he'd sufficiently savoured the moment, he spoke.

"There is no better feeling than being so popular, but I must get to the point. I do admire your bravery, or at least your unbounded stupidity astounds me. If someone is so disrespectful towards their captor, they will quickly learn humility. Fire and iron make lambs of the bravest men, believe you me."

"But if Marquis de Caulmont finds out what you've done to us, you will not escape his wrath!" Jules said.

Perrier wagged his head, smiling, the assistant standing beside him looked sadly into space, as if his thoughts were drifting far away.

"My dear friends! I am not afraid of anyone, not even Marquis de Caulmont, but you misunderstand the situation. I am not your enemy but your ally."

The company looked at one another in confusion, their astonishment quickly changed to anger.

"How can you say that, Councillor?" Ponga spat besides himself.

"Look around! Is this how you treat your allies?" Ponga was very angry at himself, because if he'd not begged Jules to go see Fifi then she would not be here now, because they had led the liquidators to the others. The responsibility was his alone, and if he had not been so stupid then only Jules and he would be sitting there now.

"Looks can be deceiving, the saying goes," Perrier replied, "I am here to convince you that I am not your enemy."

"Then tell us why we are tied up?" Ponga asked.

"Because of you, dear knight, if it were not so then you would have killed us before I had a chance to explain. Therefore, I was forced to use the young lady to disarm you. As soon as I've explained the situation to you, you will be free to go."

They did not believe a word Perrier was saying, but they did not dare antagonise him further. As per usual, only Jules remained calm.

"We are all ears, Councillor Sir," he said in a distinctly mocking tone.

"Alright, then let us begin with Sirs Hubert de Godard and Edmond la Forge, or as they are known nowadays, simply Henri and Jules."

"We were placed in the library because you and the Marquis agreed on it, yet we had to escape from there," Henri burst out and Jules nodded.

"I don't like it when facts are twisted!" Perrier retorted. "Who gave you the task of copying 'The Brief History of the Middle Ages'? I did. You think I did not know you would make another copy? The truth is I wanted the contents of that book to be known by the Marquis. I knew he was interested in old history. Unfortunately, there were unexpected events and that damned Priest Gilbert blew your cover. I wasn't the one chasing you, it was your mistake that meant you had to escape."

"Didn't you chase us across half the country?" Jules asked.

"I don't chase anyone across the country, I catch the people I chase. You think I don't know about your secret hiding place in the swamp? In fact, I also know that the Marquis finances your supplies."

Suddenly, everyone was shocked, they would never have thought that the Councillor knew about the swamp. Fear and surprise paralysed their tongues. Even the lethargic Farall's eyes went round.

"You need not be afraid," Perrier went on, in a tone as blithe as if he were discussing the weather, "I've kept your secret till now, I will continue to do so. Naturally, I also knew that you, Sir Godart, or let's just say Jules, and Ponga had returned to the castle. In fact, I knew of the whole comedian troop. Your disguises have my highest praise, but I am not easily fooled."

Jules listened stoically, his jaw was locked so tightly that his teeth ground together.

"Furthermore," the Councillor went on feeling better and better, "if you like, dear Jules, I will list your men in Paris by name, and I also know of the entrance to the passageway in the stable that you love to use to get out of the castle. And just to completely convince you of my good intentions, I've brought you a little present."

The Councillor motioned to one of the liquidators who brought him a thick book. Perrier lifted it and held it before Jules.

"I guess you know what this is? This is 'The Brief History of the Middle Ages'. I had a copy made, because I could not wait for you to finish. When we're done here, you can take it to the Marquis. Have I convinced you yet?"

The bound group fidgeted in their chairs, the Councillor had indeed been convincing.

"Even if this story is true," Ponga spoke up, "you cannot deny that you wanted me dead."

"You would not have made it out of the castle if I did not want it, you could not have escaped to the swamp if I did not wish it, and finally, you could not have come back if I did not want it," Perrier replied dramatically.

"You expect me to believe that? You tried to kill me twice! Don't you remember? That's a fact. You cannot explain your way out of it."

"I don't want to make excuses, I'd rather provide some proof."

The Councillor turned to one of his men who nodded. Clearly they had agreed on something beforehand. The soldier went to the door and opened it and Perrier gave a sharp whistle. Soon, a small dog appeared in the doorway, a black triangle on its forehead.

The dog wagged its tail happily and ran around the room.

"You recognise it don't you, Sir Knight?"

Didier looked at the animal in disbelief, he couldn't understand it.

"How can this be? I saw it die with my own eyes, I gave it the food brought to me. It was certainly this animal, I recognise the triangle on its forehead."

"The dinner contained sedatives, not poison," the Councillor replied, "I wanted to move you aside gently, because the Archbishop accused you of being a mutant. I would have made good use of your special skills."

"And Sir Dimitar Borkov, who died because he was sitting next to me? You remember the poisoned arrow?"

"He is alive too, but has returned to his village. If you wish you can visit him, he too was merely sedated. Now I have only one question left, if we untie you, will you still wish to fight us?"

They looked at one another. They couldn't process the fact that all their secrets, their whole lives, were an open book to the Councillor.

"We reckon you've convinced us," Jules said, "you can release us now, Sir."

Perrier motioned to his soldier, who untied their knots and returned their confiscated weapons.

"May I ask what you wanted to use me for?" Ponga inquired.

"Not just wanted, dear knight, I will use you in the, not so distant, future."

"Then may I ask what, you want to use me for?"

"You may, but, unfortunately, I cannot give you an answer yet. You are my trump card, and you know the trump card has to be played at the right time in the card game, and that moment has not yet arrived. Please have a little patience."

On the way out, Ponga was deep in thought, both the Councillor and Marquis de Caulmont had mentioned cards, he truly hoped that their plans would not collapse as houses of cards usually do.

Not much later, Farall and Perrier were sitting in the Councillor's chambers. The aid sat on his usual uncomfortable chair and Perrier sat behind his desk.

"I see you are very troubled, Vincent. Pour yourself a cup, it will calm you. I am glad that these past events have jolted you little from your moodiness. Honestly, your constant silence was beginning to drive me crazy."

"I don't understand why you supported the knight when you had told me you wanted to have him killed. How come you don't want him dead, when the Councillors want all mutants dead? And why do you have to lie to me? I thought I was your confidant, but you toy with me just like everyone else on your imaginary chessboard."

"Will you allow me an answer or just continue to bombard me with questions? Let's take them one at a time, I am generally honest with you, and if I am not, there is a very important reason for it. I lied to you because even you cannot know about the tasks that await the knight. When his role becomes clear to you, you will understand why I had to keep it a secret from you. As I've mentioned it to you, Councillors are all different. Some take the rules seriously, and others are more relaxed. I am one of the latter, but I did not want to confuse you. I only speak of matters with you that I can justify, and in this case, I am still holding back a few surprises. I promise, you will see everything more clearly soon."

"Maybe I can even believe that Alain, but how many more mysterious cases you have hidden away."

Perrier smiled, he was so happy to be with his aid again, all other matters paled in comparison.

"You know, Vincent, if you knew all my secrets then you'd find me boring, and there is nothing more pitiful than a boring person."

Chapter Thirty-Two

Roy Davis stood on the deck, watching the sea. There was no storm, but a strong wind blew the Dreadnought on, its sails filled to bursting. The sailors ran about visibly without pattern, but the former Councillor's aid knew that everyone was doing their job and that no one was making even one unnecessary movement. The sleek battleship was just like Sir Lemmy Black himself: silent, quick and dangerous. The Strategist did not like monsters of the sea, they moved sluggishly in battle, he preferred the security of the smaller, but lightning fast hull of the Dreadnought. Roy's stomach was well prepared for sea journeys, not like Claire, who crouched in one of the cabins, getting acquainted with a bucket. Roy was almost always beside her and only rarely went on board to marvel at the terrifying beauty of the ocean. Roy had only been on deck for ten minutes and took big gulping breaths of the bracing salty air, but he already missed her. He spoke to her in his mind.

"How are you, my dear?"

"Well, as a matter of fact, I've felt a huge improvement these past few minutes," Claire's silent words revealed the same kind humour he loved so much about her.

"Soon I will come down to you, I'm just going to watch the sea a little longer. It is such a shame you cannot be here with me."

"Stay as long as you want, I will only get better when we reach land. And I'm as likely to see the ocean as I am the middle of my back."

"I love you!"

"Me too!"

They almost always ended their conversations this way. Perhaps, even unspoken, they felt like the words 'I love you' were so magical that they had to be said again and again to cement their love, or perhaps they just enjoyed saying it.

Roy thought with dread of their mission, of which they knew nothing in particular. The Strategist had said that he himself did not know exactly what the young couple would have to do, but he said he saw great potential in their special abilities. But this did not tell them much. Roy was not so much worried about himself as he was about Claire. The events did not give them reason for much hope, they were travelling on Sir Lemmy's notorious battleship, they did not know where, but they did know that the bowels of the ship held three hundred soldiers, armed to the teeth, and that Councillor Ed Wilder had been mutilated and was being guarded separately.

The Strategist entered the Councillor's cell. He wore black light-armour over his black clothes. Just as in his choice of ships, he preferred speed over security in his armour. He did not expect a sea battle on the way, yet he wore armour so that his soldiers would know he belonged among them. Besides, he took every opportunity he could to show that he was one of the soldiers even if he was first in rank among them. No wonder his men would cross through fire for him.

The old Councillor crouched in the corner, his good hand chained to the wall with nothing but a bucket beside him. The room was constantly guarded, so that he wouldn't harm himself in any way. There was always a soldier and a doctor with him who constantly checked his condition. His hand was healing nicely, the wounds had been professionally dressed, but his fever had only recently abated. Since he was not young, his body did not handle losing a few fingers too well.

"Councillor Wilder," Black began. He was almost whispering, and his monotonous tone revealed nothing to the Councillor, "I am glad you are well, under the circumstances."

He waved to the doctor and the guard to leave them.

"You are such a hypocrite, Strategist! If you truly cared about my condition, you would not have cut off my fingers," he said, staring in horror at the stubs where his fingers used to be. Despite being changed, often the bandage had bled through.

"My dear Ed, let us not confuse matters! You had to part from your fingers because of the ring, and your health is important because I have need of you in the coming days. Furthermore, if you did, perchance, lie to me, then you have to withstand much torture yet. You know what you went through will seem desirable compared to what's coming to you if I think you're not telling the truth. Councillor, I am not angry at you and yet I did this to you. Imagine what I will do if I'm angry."

Wilder could imagine anything from Black since he'd lost his fingers to him. True, he had often tortured men to death himself, but he only now truly understood their torments.

The fear of further pain spread through every corner of his mind.

"What do you want to know? I've told you everything!"

"I have to be certain, so let's go over it again. If any of your statements prove to be false in the future, you will suffer for days. But if you're useful to me, I will eventually let you go."

"I'm a broken old man, ask away!"

The Councillor did indeed seem broken, but his soul was hurt, most of all. He remembered his childhood, which he had spent in the same city they were on their way to destroy now, on his information.

"We've been sailing for ten days and are on unknown waters now, when do we land?" Black asked this question every day.

"I've told you I left Atlantis when I was thirty years old. Now I am sixty-seven, I've not been there since. I am not a navigator, you cannot know our methods of coordination, so I can only point you in the right direction. I think

248

we will have to land somewhere here, but be prepared that we will have to travel fifty miles, maybe more, after we land."

"Alright, then I will tell the captain to turn towards land. Now tell me about your country," the Strategist did not raise his voice, but the fact that Wilder knew he could be tortured at any time, made Black terrifying to him.

"In the Known World everyone thinks that Atlantis is in a faraway, cold place, beyond the countries of the yellow nomadic tribes. This is not so. It lies about ten days sailing to the South, in a valley between great rocky mountains. It is surrounded by little villages which help supply the city, because Atlantis is really a walled-in fortress."

"How many are you in the city?"

"Ten thousand, you have no chance, you cannot take it," the Councillor waved his good hand dismissively. If they failed, which they would, he would die with them. Black took no heed of the warning.

"How many soldiers?"

"About three thousand. There are another five hundred living there from outside who serve the city, the rest are all scientists."

"Are their soldiers experienced?"

"No, they only keep order in the nearby villages and protect Atlantis."

"What weapons do they have?" Black kept asking questions on purpose. In his experience, quick-fire questions were harder to lie to. At these times, people either told the truth or quickly got confused. He questioned the Councillor every day of their journey. He often asked the same question to test Wilder's honesty. He had a lot of experience in interrogations, so he was certain that Wilder was telling the truth.

"Like anyone else in the Known World, they do not want to be more conspicuous than necessary. This world has no connection with yours, but it is worth being careful. There are explosives in the castle which have never been used. Such materials are reserved for when a King does not want a Councillor, or does not take a Councillor's advice. Then we use explosives. And the people think it is the wrath of God."

"What exactly are those? What sort of destruction are they capable of? I've always suspected that you were behind the divine destruction."

"I've said it before, you wouldn't understand, but you don't need to be afraid, they only explode when a string is set on fire. Look, Strategist!" the old man looked pleasingly at Black. "You can still turn back. You only have three hundred men, and you have to attack, which is much more difficult than defending. How do you expect to win against such odds?"

"Don't worry about me! If there is a choice, I always side with attacking and I've no other choice now either."

"Every commander prefers to defend because it is much safer and comes with far fewer losses. Why do you think otherwise?"

"Those who attack have control, I can control the outcome of things," Sir Lemmy replied, then he turned on his heel and left. He'd already asked the Councillor all this before, but he wanted to hear the answers again, just in case he could squeeze some extra information from him. He determined that when they landed, he would interrogate Wilder thoroughly one more time about those explosives, they may prove the key to victory.

Roy and Claire felt the ship change its course. The wooden structure creaked, sailors shouted, and Claire's seasickness returned. Soon they noticed that the cool air was becoming warmer. Later, they began to sweat and came to the conclusion that they would reach dry land at any time. And so it was – an hour later, they heard splashing noises. The ship anchored down and boats were lowered. The young couple went up on deck and watched the preparations for landing.

The soldiers were twenty to a boat, each of which carried two pairs of oars. The three boats could carry sixty men in one go and the row to shore took no more than a few minutes. On the way back, only the rowers remained in the boats as they returned for more passengers. Roy guessed that in two or three hours, everyone would be ashore. From the boat they could see the desolate hills that dominated the shoreline. The plant life crept low up the mountainsides. It seemed as if the whole wilderness of dry land were growing straight up from the sea.

The air was hot and very dry – despite this, Claire was feeling better. The anchored boat was on calmer waters now, and the heat was not as bad as being on the open ocean. They sat in the last boat with Sir Lemmy and the Councillor who looked at them accusingly, but didn't say anything. They knew that Black had already told the Councillor who they were, and also that they were under his protection. The injured prisoner could not harm them, even if he had once been a powerful Councillor.

"Once we are all ashore, we will head inland," Black said to the Councillor. "At the first settlement, we'll find out how far we are from the city."

"This is madness, Strategist," Wilder began whining again, "you cannot believe the news of your troops will not proceed them to Atlantis?"

The young couple's eyes went round. So that was their destination, to conquer the Councillor's country. They didn't understand why they had come here, or why Sir Lemmy wanted to win this hopeless war, and they certainly did not know why the Commander needed them.

But they knew one thing for sure: they were unlikely to survive this adventure.

"Look, Councillor! If anyone should be worried it's you, not me. But I have little patience for your whining. A Commander has to accept the factors that he cannot change. Obviously, our news will proceed us, there's no skill in predicting that. Now, stop this tedious conversation, because these unfortunate souls," he said, pointing at Claire and Roy, "are scared to death. Our situation is not as hopeless as you see it, the task not so difficult, I simply have to destroy the Councillor's country."

"With three hundred men," Wilder added, wagging his head.

When everyone had landed, the officers distributed the supplies. They only brought what was absolutely necessary: weapons, tents and a day's food. It was past noon when they set out. Only the direct shoreline was flat. After a hundred paces, tall mountains barred their paths. They walked parallel to the ocean till they found a narrow valley, through which they headed inland. Black sent a search party ahead who would constantly send back news. Though the valley was far lower than the mountains surrounding them, it still proved to be quite steep. The soldiers set the pace, and despite bearing heavier packs, they moved faster than the others. Two hours later, the scouting team returned. Sir Lemmy allowed a brief rest, and sat down on a rock with the Councillor and the young couple.

The commander of the scouts waited to be allowed to report, he did not want to begin in front of the others till he received permission from the Strategist.

"You can speak in front of them," Black said.

"My Lord, the peasants working in the mountains know of our approach. From here, the first village is about an hour away. The path we're on, goes straight there."

"Alright, you go around the village and figure out the next route we will take."

The soldier saluted and nodded, and the Councillor began whining again.

"Why do you want to go the village? It's a waste of time, you're giving the city more time to prepare."

"Councillor, you worry as if you were actually on my side. What am I to make of this?"

"Whether you like it or not, I am in the centre of your army. If you lose, I will probably die too. So I am not worried for you, but for myself."

"My Lord, what is your plan?" Roy asked, his voice was not brimming with confidence either.

"I never discuss war plans with others, and anything I do say can change if the circumstances require it. But, once we're camped for the night, we can discuss a few things, and I will tell you what I want you to do," he looked at Roy and Claire.

For the next hour, they marched on in silence. The Councillor moved forward with gritted teeth, he was visibly struggling to keep pace, and there was always a few soldiers and a doctor near him.

He was slowed not only by his condition but also his age. The young couple awaited the evening with fear and anticipation, when they would finally discover what Sir Lemmy wanted from them. They were so deep in thought that they didn't even communicate telepathically. Sir Lemmy focused all his attention on the terrain, while scouts kept appearing, reporting on the situation ahead.

The officer at the head of the column suddenly raised his hand and everyone stopped. A soldier ran back to Black and reported that the village was in the valley ahead of them. The Strategist motioned to the officers to surround him.

"We are going in," Black began instructions, "kill a few people, but not many. I want the majority to escape, do not pursue them! Take a few prisoners, I want to interrogate them. Then burn the village down!"

"Yes, Commander Sir!" the officers replied as one and then left.

"I did not think you would take pleasure in killing and aimlessly taking lives," Wilder whined.

"Mark my words, Councillor, in case you did not know me after all these years, I never do anything aimlessly. And now stay here, a few of my men will watch over you. Don't ask me anything till nightfall, you will have time then."

Black didn't want to waste any more time talking, he quickly went to his men because he wanted to direct the attack on the village personally.

The peasants showed little resistance and the soldiers quickly did their work. When they set the houses on fire, there were only a few corpses in the streets, the others had escaped.

They had five prisoners, of whom one was led to Black.

"How far is Narun from here?" the Strategist asked – the Councillor had told him that Atlantis was called Narun here. For safety reasons, the Councillors had thought it prudent to only use the name Atlantis in the Known World.

"Not far, my Lord," the young peasant replied, though he used the common tongue, Back could barely understand him, "a day's journey from here. If ye follow dis road, there be a fork in a ha' day. There ye goes left and den you gets there."

"Alright. You're coming with us, and if I hear no complaints about you, I will spare your lives."

"Thank you, your Lordship," the older man said, though Black could barely understand him, "we will do our very best, we promise."

By nightfall, they'd burned three villages to the ground, they did not kill many people but they chased everyone away. At dusk, Sir Lemmy found a suitable place to spend the night. The soldiers followed the officers' order to make camp for the night. They set up the tents a small distance form one another with the Commander's tent in the centre, which was much larger tent. In the evening, Black called Roy, Claire and Councillor to him. Beside the Strategist stood Commander Caroll and Liquidator George Silver, who followed Black everywhere like a shadow.

"I've called you here because it has become necessary to initiate you into my plan. Since all of you have great tasks to complete, it is important for you to know what I want from you."

In the glimmering light of the torches, Black seemed terrifying and mysterious at once. His black clothes and hair moulded with the darkness, accentuating his white, pale face.

His reserved manner stood in contrast with his dangerously glinting, searching eyes.

"You said you would answer out questions tonight," Wilder said. His greasy hair fell in dishevelled waves over his grey Councillor's robes that no longer protected him.

"So it is Councillor, I'm listening."

"Why did you burn the villages?"

"You remember when I said that I don't do anything aimlessly?"

The Councillor nodded, everyone in the tent stared curiously at Black.

"If I burn the peasants' houses and put terror into their hearts with a few murders, they will flee to a place where they will be protected. There is only one such place around here, Atlantis."

The young couple had not spoken till then, but Roy now collected his courage and spoke.

"Why do you want it to be so, my Lord?" Roy asked.

"My Love, don't antagonise Sir Lemmy!" Claire warned him telepathically.

"Tomorrow, you will go ahead to the city fortress of Atlantis with five select men. You will wear the clothes of one of the prisoners and when the wave of villagers reaches the city, you will mingle among them and enter. Be careful, these people do not speak the Common Tongue as we do, so you will have to pretend to be a mute. We will stay in contact through your telepathy with Claire."

Roy looked suddenly at the Councillor, he did not seem surprised. The Strategist noticed the glance.

"As I've already mentioned, Wilder knows about your abilities, but he will not move against you, he is in no situation to harm anyone, anyway," Black felt that he had to calm the youngsters who still seemed afraid of the Councillor. "When you came to me, I decided to use your method of communication to my advantage. Roy, you will be my eyes in the city, and if need be, my hands. Councillor Wilder will be beside me at all times, so that if I have any questions, I can ask him," he turned to the Councillor, "which I hope you can answer in your own interest. Your advice will help Roy complete his tasks. Tomorrow, the Atlantians will send scouts, who we will chase away with a heavy attack, I do not want them to gain precise information on our numbers. If they think our power to be greater they won't risk attack, but lock themselves in their fortress."

"What if they send a large scouting party?" Wilder asked.

"They won't, I wouldn't. At such times, quick information is the key and a little scouting party will return much faster and are less conspicuous."

"So how are you going to spot the scouts?" the Councillor fretted.

"We will wait for them," Black smiled complacently.

"And then?" the old man was asking questions as if he had forgotten that he was a prisoner. The events of the past days had changed the wise Councillor into a shadow of his former self.

"For now, it is enough if you know this much, we can talk more later."

With that, the Strategist brought the meeting to a close. The young couple, the Councillor and his guards left. When they were gone, Silver spoke.

"May I make a remark, Sir?"

The liquidator was fidgeting nervously and was beginning to regret having spoken at all. Commander Caroll beside him looked at him disapprovingly, he certainly would only speak to the Strategist when spoken to. But Silver was far less disciplined.

"Of course!" Black replied, watching his soldier with interest. He like the man's informality. Liquidators were all dried up, the long years of training vanquished all emotions from them. Silver was different, he had not received a lesson in humility.

"I've heard many stories about you—wild and crazy things, but..." Silver suddenly went silent. He did not know how to finish the sentence.

"But?"

"But, you'll excuse me, I could never have imagined anything this crazy. Three hundred men against a fortress?"

"Is something not to your liking, Liquidator?"

Black furrowed his brow, but his twinkling eyes revealed him.

"Quite the opposite, Sir, it's so crazy, that's what makes it great!"

"That is very reassuring. I have to admit, I organised this whole campaign for your entertainment."

They all began to laugh, their voices carried far in the night air.

Roy and Claire stood at the edge of the camp, staring at the starry sky. The coming days frightened them, and it was reassuring to hold each other's hands. A few weeks ago, everything had seemed so simple, and now, here they stood in a strange world and would soon have to part from each other. They didn't even know for certain if they would meet again, but they did not dare speak of that.

"Roy, in a just a few days we'll be done with all of this, believe me!"

"I think so too, my love, we only have to make it through this little while."

"Then don't you go picking up some common whore in that city!"

He wondered at her, how her sense of humour was not lost even in times like these.

"How could I dare to do such a thing? I'm more afraid of your wrath than all the soldiers in the world."

"You'd better!" Claire replied and kissed him. There, in that moment, time ceased to exist for them.

Chapter Thirty-Three

Councillor Perrier glanced at the clock gathering dust on his office wall. It would be eleven soon, time to go to the Coronation day. His aid stared disinterestedly into space, curled up on his little chair.

The Councillor did not like Vincent's behaviour. The truth was that, despite regaining his memories, he was a changed man. While before he had been curious, open and even happy sometimes, nowadays, he looked like a man who just wanted his life to end.

The old Vincent would have been full of questions, after all, it was coronation day.

"And you did not even ask why I chose the jousting arena for the ceremony instead of one of the great halls of the castle," Perrier tried to gain his aid's attention.

"Why did you choose it?" Farall asked, but his faded voice was filled with disinterest.

"I see you are not interested, but I will tell you anyway. I wanted a place where we could fit not only the upper nobility, but even a huge crowd. I want a spectacle, a day fathers will tell their sons about when they grow old, a day no one can forget. I want anyone who does not come, to regret it for the rest of their lives."

"But, Alain, this is not a jousting tournament. It's not entertainment for the masses, it is a political ceremony."

"Nonsense," Perrier waved his hand, "they are one and the same. Anyone who thinks differently, knows nothing of politics. Today, we not only give the people a King, but create a myth. The legendary, mysteriously disappeared King returns under no less mysterious circumstances."

"Now, will you tell me where you're guarding the new King?" Farall asked this only out of a sense of duty, his thought were firmly fixed on Amelie. The fact that he had regained his memories did not mean that he had forgotten about the days he'd spent with her. In fact, they remained the most important to him. He was angry at Perrier for separating them, but mostly because while he appeared to be teaching him, he was just using him as a puppet like he did everyone else. He was crazed because he'd thought he was the only person close to the Councillor's heart and he was forced to concede that this man had no heart.

"I ask only for a little more patience from you," Perrier answered enthusiastically, though he could sense from his aid's voice that he did not care about any of it, but he pretended like everything was as it used to be between them. "For the security of King Fernand de Bellehache, I cannot tell you anything. Now let us go, you will see him soon."

Damn that duplicitous, hypocrite of a Councillor! Marquis Bastien de Caulmont raged besides himself. He paced impatiently up and down the largest room of the tavern, chewing rather than smoking the pipe that hung from his mouth. No one dared speak in the room. Ponga, the triangle specked dog in his lap, Fifi on his arm, Jules, Henri and Fabian stood before the fireplace watching the raging nobleman. They'd told the Marquis about the circumstances of their capture and release the day before.

The noblemen listened to the 'story' of the Councillor's innocence with disbelief.

"I still don't know where the King is, if he is alive at all," Caulmont grumbled on.

"My Lord," Jules tried to calm him, "just a few minutes and we can go to the Coronation ceremony, where everything will become clear. You see, it's turned out that the Councillor is not our enemy."

"That is just my problem. If Perrier seems like the good guy, something is wrong. Perhaps, he is using yesterday's events to distract us."

"May I speak, Sir?" Ponga began, and Fifi poked him in the ribs with such force that Ponga almost dropped the dog and Jules and Henri waved to him to indicate that it was not the best time to disturb the Marquis.

"Let's hear it!" Caulmont thundered.

"You're not easily pleased, Sir." Ponga received another jab in the ribs from the girl of his dreams. The Marquis did not answer, he just raised a bushy eyebrow.

"Not long ago, the Councillor gave you the head of your greatest enemy on a plate. Yesterday, we found out that he was not trying to kill any of us. In fact, he made a present of the book you've been wanting to get."

"And?"

"We're about to go to the Coronation ceremony. Perhaps you could give him a few more minutes before demolishing him."

"Perhaps you are right," the Marquis put his pipe down and headed for the door, "it's just strange seeing Perrier as the good guy, it's worse than a smiling wolf. And I know him too well to fall for it! Well, what are you waiting for? How long are you going to sit there? Let's go and see the Councillor's true face!"

The jousting arena was packed. The manmade hill was so full of people that the grass was not visible. The noblemen were seated on the road in front of the hill. Traditionally, only they would be present at a Coronation ceremony, but the Councillor had insisted that the people get to see the event. Opposite the road and the huge hill, was a wooden pedestal, far larger than a traditional stage. At its centre stood the empty throne, waiting to receive a King.

The crowd rumbled, rumours and speculations flew about wildly. The majority thought that the son of the recently deceased King would take the throne, but that the regent appointed to him would hold the true power. Some thought this would be Marquis Bertrand. Some of the high nobility had been informed by Marquis de Caulmont of Bertrand's death, they were certain that Caulmont would be appointed regent. As it was customary, there were always a few loud moths purporting to be in the inner circles. They circulated the wildest rumours and there were always people who believed them. The members of the swamp party received seats in the first row as confidants of the Marquis. The high nobility glanced disparagingly towards them.

"I hope it will be a good show, there's certainly a commotion," Fabian said bitterly.

"Who cares?" Ponga growled back. "All I care about is that we get to leave as soon as possible."

He could barely wait to continue his recently begun life with Fifi. He didn't care if they placed a donkey on the throne as King.

As a matter of fact, that was usually the case, he thought, but, of course, he kept his opinion to himself because the Marquis would have bit his head off for such a remark.

Directly beside them sat the people close to Councillor Perrier: Head Liquidator Luc Moreau and his aid, Vincent Farall.

The majority of the nobility were represented by family members because the army was posted on the shores of Normandy. According to the most recent news, the Strategist had sailed the Dreadnought from London, but had not headed for the shores of France. This act was just as inscrutable as his whole warmongering behaviour. Councillor Perrier and Marquis Bastien de Caulmont were last to arrive. Their escort of liquidators stayed below while the two men climbed the stage. The Councillor looked around contentedly, everything was as he had planned, a huge mass of people waited expectantly for the coronation. When they stopped, the murmuring of the crowd increased.

Perrier did not speak, the tension caused a sudden silence and only then did he speak.

"Ladies and gentlemen, people of France. We've called you here today with my friend, Marquis Bastien de Caulmont, to nominate the new King," he pointed at the throne beside him. The Councillor was an excellent orator. The people lapped up his every word.

"You must think that we are going to coronate the son of the dearly departed King, Lefebre. This will not be the case. Please allow me to begin with a very old tale," then he recounted, in detail, the murder of King Gaston de Bellehache, the evil plots of Marquis Bertrand and his recent death. The people listened as if to a fairy tale.

The Councillor exposed every detail of the plot, but did not mention the King's son, he was saving his story for last.

"You must know that King Bellehache had a son, Fernand, who was just two years old at the time of the assassination."

"He also died in the attack, as did all the members of his family," someone shouted.

"You are right, or so everyone believes," Perrier replied, playing the greatest role of his life. He was truly in his element, "but the truth is that Fernand de Bellehache is alive."

There was a huge uproar. The people spoke in disbelief of the news. The Councillor watched the wave his announcement made contentedly. The very nervous Marquis de Caulmont beside him whispered in his ear.

"Where is the King, you bastard?"

"You're going to have to make it through the next few moments, my friend," the Councillor whispered back.

"What happened? How come? We want to know the truth!" the audience shouted.

Perrier did not speak, he waited for their curiosity to reach an almost unbearable climax in a nervous silence. Then, he spoke again.

"My friend, Marquis de Caulmont, was there when the royal family was attacked. In fact, he was not merely there, but he did, in fact, save the young Prince's life."

The Marquis blushed at the words in his honour. "It was nothing, nothing," he said quietly.

The Councillor went on, "I made an alliance with the Marquis to save little Fernand. Back then, we could not announce that he was alive because Marquis Bertrand and his men would have tried to kill him. We had no choice but to hide him and wait for the right moment, which has now come. The Prince was under the Marquis' supervision for a while, and I've taken care of him since. When he came to us, we knew that one of us would not see the Prince for a long time. Though the Marquis and I trust each other," Caulmont muttered something under his breath, "we needed some assurance so as we could recognise the Prince after so many years. We decided to tattoo a brief poem on our three bodies so that we could identify the King who we've not seen in so long."

There was another uproar and everyone was shouting.

"Who ever heard of such a thing? Tattooing an innocent child?"

Then nobleman from the first row shouted out, "Would it not have sufficed to only tattoo the child?"

The Councillor smiled and held a little dramatic pause.

"It would have sufficed, but we wanted to share in the King's fate. If we had to cause him pain, then we would suffer with him."

People nodded their approval, Perrier knew how to capture an audience.

"One line was placed on the Marquis' back, one on mine and another on the Prince's head."

Not for the first time the Councillor had astounded his audience.

"On his head, why on his head?" they asked in unison.

"Because," Perrier replied, "the hair would grow over and cover it. And the little child soon forgot the unpleasant memory. In this way, later on, he would not know who he truly was. This was the only way to preserve his safety, even he could not know of his origins."

"Stop dragging it out! That's enough!" the Marquis whispered in the Councillor's ear.

"The time has come for everyone to know who will be the Ruler of France!" Perrier shouted. "You take off your shirt first, my friend, as you bear the first line," the Councillor said, turning to the Marquis.

"Tell me where the King is, already!" Caulmont said loudly, unable to contain himself.

"Let's stick to the plan, my friend. Please, take off your shirt!" Perrier asked again.

The Marquis did so grudgingly, he struggled to get his shirt off. His hairy, barrel chest was a strange sight among the well-dressed masses. Then he turned, slowly revealing the text written on his back:

Those who think him dead are wrong.

The Councillor read the first line of the poem aloud. The guests sitting in the front all sprang up from their seats and started for the stage to see the Marquis' tattoo for themselves. In the same moment, the crowd behind them wanted to surge forwards too, but Perrier had expected this and posted several row of soldiers between the commoners and the nobility, who tried to keep the crowd at bay.

"Stop!" the Councillor gave a huge shout. "If you don't stay where you are, then we will continue with just the nobility present. We can't have everyone running over here because it would endanger the King."

Suddenly, everyone stopped pushing and shoving. They were not worried about the King, but about missing the show.

"I promise," Perrier went on, "that everyone will get to know everything, but only if you stay where you are. So, now everyone knows what is written on the Marquis' back."

The Marquis stood with his back to the crowd, and twisted his head around to speak to the Councillor.

"Now the moment of truth has come! Stop dragging it out!"

"Alright, my friend, but I ask you to stay with your back to the audience and I will continue," Perrier answered.

"Here's the second line which was written on the Prince's scalp! Vincent, please, come up here and join us!"

Everyone was confused, a tornado of voices swept across the hill, the nobility sprang to their feet again. The Marquis shouted over all of them.

"Enough of this drama, I want to see the King. Who cares about your aid?"

Perrier crossed his arms in front of him but did not say a word.

"What do you say? What is your answer?" the people shouted, but the Councillor would not go on. After a while he raised his arm, indicating that he wished to speak. Silence descended over the crowd.

"If you'll keep quiet, I can tell you the end of the story, if you can't, then I might as well leave now."

"You're not going anywhere," Caulmont growled, "you're finishing this!"

"Provided you stop interrupting me!" came the Councillor's response. The Marquis conceded that he would have to wait for Perrier to finish, but he determined that if the King was not brought forth, he would kill the Councillor right there in front of everyone.

During this scene, Farall sat frozen in his chair. The Councillor had managed to shock him out of apathy. In that moment there, he was scared to death. What did Perrier want from him? What would he have to do, to say on stage? Where was the King who was far more important than him?

"What are you waiting for, Vincent?" the Councillor asked, then motioned to two liquidators to escort Farall on stage since he was petrified with shock. They approached him and gently nudged him towards the stage, up beside the Councillor. Farall stared in terror at the huge crowd. All eyes were on him and he would have rather been anywhere else in the world. That is, he remembered suddenly, there are places far worse than this. The death-scented torture chamber is worse, he determined. He did not know why he was thinking of this, but in any case, he drew strength from that fact that there were worse places to be.

"Bring the chair and begin!" Perrier gave the order. They quickly brought in a chair, onto which Farall sat and they quickly began shaving off his thick black hair. Meanwhile, the Councillor approached him and whispered in his ear.

"Don't be afraid! I'd never leave you stranded, trust me!" Vincent was silent and yet, somehow, it calmed him.

When the barber was finished, Perrier began to speak again.

"Stand up! Show your head to the noblemen," as he said this, he gently pulled Vincent forward and read the text tattooed on his head.

The Bald king

"He is the King! He is the King! The aid is our King!" people shouted. The Marquis quickly pulled up Farall's shirt and looked at his back. The Councillor spoke quietly to Caulmont.

"If you're looking for the birthmark beside his spine, it's there. Believe me it's him."

Then, he turned towards the crowd and took his own shirt off. There was not a spare ounce of fat to be found on his wiry, muscular body. He turned his back and read the text on his own body out loud.

becomes self-aware.

The crowd began chanting the poem, and they shouted it louder and louder till the entire hill seemed to shake.

*"Those who think him dead,
beware:
The Bald King becomes
self-aware."*

Marquis de Caulmont stood up and then dropped to one knee.

"Long live the King!" he shouted.

The crowd followed suit, bowing to their knees before Vincent Farall, now King Fernand de Bellehache.

Vincent could not comprehend what was happening to him. One moment he had been the Councillor's aid, the next he was the King of France. His first thought was that his soul was not suitable to the task. The responsibility was too great, he did not like to be in public, and a King did little else.

He would have liked to refuse it, but it was impossible under the circumstances.

"Let's hear the King!" the crowd shouted. Perrier moved in beside him and said.

"Your highness! I know this is very hard for you now, and that you need time to process all this, but you still should speak a few words to your people."

Farall stepped forward, he had no idea what he was supposed to say. They probably expected great words from him, but he would not be able to live up to their expectations. Before he realised what he was doing, he began to speak.

"I am just like all of you. You did not know what was going to happen here, neither did I. You've been led by the nose, so have I. You too are afraid of what the future will bring, but believe me, together we will be strong and we will oppose our fate, because your fates and mine are the same."

The crowd went wild and everyone sang the young King's praises. Meanwhile, Perrier and the Marquis escorted Farall off the pedestal and headed for the palace.

"This isn't so simple," the new King burst out, "you tricked me, you lied to me my whole life, when we reach the castle I want to discuss this with you."

"Yes, your Highness," the Councillor and the Marquis said as one.

After a few steps, Perrier spoke again.

"If I may remark, for a new ruler, you made a very good speech."

"What I don't get," the King sulked on, "is why we needed such a great commotion? Lots of people, the stage, the tattoos, not to mention the scalping," he said, stroking his bare head.

"Your Highness, we did not only crown a King today," the Councillor replied, "but a legend. We've lifted you into the realm of myths, from the very first day of your reign."

"I'd have preferred to have a quiet ceremony," Fernand said in a tired voice.

Perrier just smiled and did not answer, what could he answer, the King was missing the point. As for the excellently planned, perfectly executed events of the day, the ancient people would simply have said: 'show business'.

Chapter Thirty-Four

There was a great commotion in the Spanish castle, everyone was waiting for the royal heir to be born. The stable boys and soldiers made bets on whether it would be a boy or a girl.

Those in the know explained how the birth would rearrange the political situation. The servants buzzed about, because they had to prepare the new-born's room, which could not be too far from the Queen's chambers, but not too near either. The child's crying could not be allowed to disturb Esmeralda's sleep. Archbishop Oscar Martinez had chosen four wet maids, who were prepared to receive the child. They were already living in the castle with their own children. The servants waited elegantly dressed, and there were flag and flowers everywhere, just as it was customary on King Carlos' birthday. The doctors saw it time to report to the King that the Queen would have to go to the birthing room on that day. The ruler was so excited that he could not bear to stay in the castle, but on the recommendation of Councillor Pedro Garcia, he went to the nearby woods for a little hunt. He left instructions to be informed as soon as the royal heir was born.

Esmeralda lay contentedly in her bed. Her contractions were becoming more regular and she did not have long to suffer until the birth. She had taken every precaution for her own safety these past months.

She had not given the Councillor any opportunity to get near her. She was constantly at the King's side, and a few minutes later, she would go to the birthing room where he could not hurt her in front of the doctors. She had won, and she wanted to enjoy this feeling to the fullest, so she sent for Garcia. The Councillor could only come into her room by passing through the many guards in front of her door. That bastard would not hurt her anymore. Her only worry was that she hoped the pain from her contractions would not ruin the joys of the coming conversation. Slowly, she stood up and carefully waddled over to the comfortable chair next to the bed. She sat down gingerly and waited for her victory to be confirmed.

Soon Garcia entered, bowed slightly and then approached the Queen.

"I am glad, my Queen, that you are so well despite your condition."

The Councillor's voice was sweet, as if that brownnose Archbishop Martinez were speaking. It seems that the arrogant, dangerous Councillor had conceded his defeat and was forced to bow to her now – the recognition filled Esmeralda with glee. *But I still do not want him to get away with it*, she determined, *he has to feel that he is a failed man!*

"Your useless flattery comes too late to improve our relationship, Sir. You should have recognised my power earlier."

"You are right, my Queen, but perhaps it is not too late to atone for my sins. I admit I have no other choice, you have won. And for me, there is no choice left but to bow my head before you."

The Queen had never seen her arch-enemy behave this way, and for a moment, she considered sparing him his life. If he stayed this submissive then she might yet forgive him. Then a much stronger, more enjoyable, urge overcame her, a great pleasure she could not resist: revenge.

For now, she would pretend to desist, but after the birth, she would have the Councillor taken to a torture chamber and she would watch his suffering till his last breath. She would forbid the jailers to touch his tongue so that she could hear his pleading as many times as possible.

"Let's make a truce," she said magnanimously. "But now leave me, I have to prepare to bring this child into the world.

"Yes, my Lady," the Councillor replied as he backed out of the room, making sure not to even accidentally turn his back on the Queen

Esmeralda felt more contented than she had ever done before.

"So, have you decided?" Teresa asked Alejandro.

"What, my Lady?" he had no idea what the question was regarding.

"Oh, come now, don't pretend like you don't know."

"You ask me so many questions, suddenly I don't know what I'm supposed to answer now."

"I ask you every day, but today, you must answer! Do you like birds? And I won't take 'I think so' as an answer. Be careful what you say, because I adore them."

"I so like them, and I like them because they make you happy." Teresa smiled at the answer, visibly filling her with warmth. They sat on the balcony of the woodland hut, as they had often done in the past days. Neither of them spoke of the future, they did not mention the dreaded moment when Teresa would be called back to the castle. Alejandro stole a glance at Teresa and he remembered that he had no idea what he was going to do when Teresa returned to the castle.

He would not be able to continue his life as before. His future seemed desolate and hopeless. His aimless wondering had not bothered him, or he had not allowed it to bother him till now, but his attachment to this girl would burn his heart from now on. Alejandro saw his Lady's unbounded joy. Only children could live so intensely in the present, not caring about the future, not worried about anything, just enjoying the joy of the moment.

"My Lord, you like to show yourself off as simpleminded, but you are not at all. It is just how you wish to escape from giving serious answers. You don't like people to know your true emotions."

Alejandro was surprised at how well she knew him. She noticed things about him that no one else did. Perhaps, it was because she was the first person to take interest in his thoughts. She was not indifferent towards him, but the word was.

"So, what is it, Alejandro Sir? Have I managed to touch on the truth again?"

He could not reply. It was often the case when conversing with Teresa that her questions demanded honesty when he did not want to face the truth himself.

"You may be right, my Lady. You know it is a lot simpler to make people believe that you are stupid, than to be honest."

He gently stroked her head and then looked at his hands. The hands which he believed were made for killing. Soon their time together would end and then he might find his way back to his old life. He could not live in just the present and he was afraid of parting with her. It played constantly on his mind that any of their conversations might be their last.

"Alejandro Sir, are you not afraid of death?" Teresa asked.

True to her custom, she changed the subject so fast that he could not follow. Then after a brief pause, the truth spilled out of him.

"No, my Lady, I am only afraid of life."

Esmeralda entered the birthing room. The Royal doctors had prepared everything, the decorative bed was lined with buckets, forceps and tweezers. The Queen was momentarily frightened by all the metal objects which closely resembled those found in a torture chamber. *I cannot be weak now*, she warned herself, *this must happen! Soon, all the power will be in my hands, at the price of suffering through this birth. So be it, I will pay the price*, she determined, and shuffled over to the bed. The doctors could not stop flattering her.

"My Lady, carefully! Don't be afraid, my Lady, we will take care of you. Your Royal Highness, try to relax!"

"Enough!" Esmeralda said. "Stop this silly simpering! I am not a child and I have no need for it."

The Queen's rage had the desired effect, the doctors went silent and focused on the task at hand. One of them, the oldest one, would have to speak because they couldn't just undress the Queen without her permission.

"Excuse me, my Lady, but you must take your clothes off," the doctor stood before the bed with his eyes on the ground.

"What? You think I don't know that women don't give birth in clothes? What are you standing around there for? Help me!"

They all sprang to the bed and began peeling the fancy clothes off her. When they were finished, they could not take their eyes off her body which was attractive even with her huge belly.

In a few moments they came to their senses and stretched a blanket out under her breasts. The snow-white material was fixed to ropes hanging from the ceiling so that Esmeralda could not see what was happening between her legs. This was customary among nobles, protecting the birthing mother from the grizzly sight. But they could not relieve them of the pain, the mother had to bear all of that, even the most powerful ones.

Meanwhile, the contractions became so frequent they were almost continuous. The Queen tried to maintain her composure, but she could not stop from groaning.

"Excuse me, my Lady," the oldest doctor said, "but we will have to gag your mouth. This will stop you from biting your tongue. Then I have to bind your hands too, this will keep you safe."

"Do what you have to!" Esmeralda replied roughly.

The old man nodded silently, then taking a smooth stick, he placed it in the Queen's mouth and then tied the ropes at either end of the stick to the headrest. When he was done, he produced two thick ropes, looped them around her wrists and tied them tightly to the sides of the bed.

Esmeralda watched the doctor. She thought it strange that she had not seen him in court before, though doctors had frequently examined her in the last few months. Suddenly, she had an ominous feeling, tied up as she was at their mercy, and somehow the old man's twinkling eyes were suspicious to her. *All that suspicion must have made me crazy*, she tried to calm herself.

"You can go now!" said a voice on the other side of the sheet. At first, the Queen could not comprehend who it was. She didn't understand it

Why someone was disturbing the doctors, and how dare anyone come in when she was laid on the bed with her legs spread.

"Two men by the door, you stay!" came further orders. And Esmeralda recognised the voice of Councillor Pedro Garcia. In her fright, she peed herself and the warmth soaked the bed. She tried to shout, but gag in her mouth allowed only a faint moan to escape her. She began to toss herself about, but she felt strong hands grasp her untied legs.

"My dear Queen!" the Councillor said, appearing from behind the screen.

"If you don't stop this futile resistance then I will be forced to plunge my dagger into your belly."

Esmeralda froze in terror, she could certainly imagine the Councillor actually making good on his threat.

"That's much better," Garcia said. The Queen felt the sadistic glee radiating from him.

"As long as you cooperate with me, you can save your child's life, provided it is a girl. Unfortunately, I will have to kill a boy. It will be very exciting, I can barely wait, and believe me, you won't be bored yourself. I would like to ask for your help, please hurry up, if you hold it back I will have to take it out myself and that would be very painful. If you've understood me, please nod."

Esmeralda's eyes filled with tears. She was surprised by the new feeling spreading through her brain. Fear was replaced by a mother's anxiety for her child. She never would have thought she could feel this way. Her own life was no longer important, only the child's was. She nodded and prayed that it would be a girl. Not long ago, she would have given anything for a boy, but that was then, and this was a different situation entirely. Professional hands gripped her, the wet bed linens were pulled from under her and fresh ones were put in their place. Soon the birth began, she was cooperative, though she knew that as soon as she gave life, her own would be taken from her.

She was not afraid, she had never felt so brave in her life. Would she have loved her child this much if this had not happened? *Yes*, she answered herself –

because she felt that it was truly a special thing to become a mother. Nothing else interested her, only the life of the child.

It did not take long. After a few minutes of suffering, the new-born cried out. Esmeralda's heart was filled with pride. The joy only lasted a few moments, then she came to her senses and looked in terror at Garcia appearing from behind the sheet.

"So that part is done then. We can make another deal," the Councillor said with the perverse glee of a child receiving a long-coveted toy. "If you do not resist much, I will tell you the gender of your child before you are killed and I'll even let you have a little look at it. You know, you just need to nod."

The Queen knew that the Councillor was toying with her. He was enjoying his victory and took great pleasure in the ruthless game. But she could not lose, she could have the greatest moment of any woman's life, as Garcia was going to kill her anyway. She sighed and prepared her soul for the great meeting, then she nodded.

"Then we are agreed," the Councillor said, wanting to make her as desperate as possible. If he had suspected how much good he was doing with Esmeralda, he would not have raised the child, but Garcia was just a man, who had no idea what a mother could feel."

"As you can see, it is a girl," he held up the infant, quite close to her face, "so, I can spare her life. Don't worry, she won't want for anything. In fact, come to think of it, I could do her no greater favour than killing you, since what kind of life would she have had with a mother like you?"

Esmeralda didn't even hear the Councillor's mocking voice. She looked at her beautiful child and felt like these few moments were well worth dying for.

Then, Garcia quickly swept the infant away and motioned to his men. One of them pushed a pillow onto her face. Esmeralda did not resist. She was happy to die with the image of her child burned onto her retinas.

The gate guards of the Spanish Royal Castle watched with fearful respect as a tall, hooded man escorted Teresa into the castle. The news of their arrival had preceded them. Head Liquidator Marcos Sanchez indicated that Alejandro Leon would be escorting Teresa. Sanchez had ordered that no one bar their way into the castle, they would be greeted in the courtyard. There were some who knew of the famous assassin personally from a long time ago, but those that had not personally met him still knew his name. The floating unbuttoned cloak revealed the sword and dagger hanging about the waist of the rough man. Only noblemen and on-duty liquidator were permitted to carry weapons in the castle, Leon was not one of them, yet, no one dared mention it to him.

The crowd parted to let them pass, and so they proceeded to the central courtyard where fifty liquidators awaited them with Marcos Sanchez at their head. As they stopped, the Head Liquidator greeted them.

"My Lady! I am glad to see you well."

"Greetings, Sir Sanchez! Allow me to introduce Sir Alejandro."

The two men sized each other up with hostility and then Sanchez broke the silence.

"Alejandro Leon and I have known each other for a long time. I've come before you, my lady, to lead you to the Councillor."

"I will take her there," Alejandro replied in grating voice. He did not seem nervous, but there was something frightening in him.

"I know you, Leon, but you cannot seriously think that this many men could not stop you?" Sanchez was not the kind to be intimidated.

"Try it!" Leon replied, avoiding addressing Sanchez by rank, which was an insult in itself.

They were almost at each other's throat when Teresa intervened.

"Aren't you ashamed of yourselves? You want to fight in my presence? I forbid it!"

The Head Liquidator embarrassedly waved off his men who had reached for their weapons. The tense situation was diffused by the arrival of Councillor Pedro Garcia.

"Soldiers, weapons down! Didn't you hear what the Princess ordered? Welcome to the castle!" he turned to Teresa and nodded at Leon.

"Come to my chambers, we can talk there with refreshments. Thank you, gentlemen," he turned to Sanchez, "you may go now."

They left. The men did not speak on the way, or would not have if Teresa had not asked them questions constantly.

"You know, Councillor, so much has happened to me recently."

"You will have time to tell me all about it, my Lady."

"And did you know that Alejandro is real hero?"

"Yes, I've heard about his wonderful deeds."

They went on like this to the chambers, Teresa questioning one man and then the other. When they arrived, the Councillor offered them seats, but Leon preferred to stand. Garcia sat behind his desk and was very pleased with himself.

"My Lady, unfortunately, I have to break some bad news to you. Queen Esmeralda passed away giving birth. Your Royal father is very broken up about it, but your visit will surely give him strength."

"Poor thing," Teresa replied, "it is true she treated me unkindly but her death is still sad to me."

"And to me, but, at least, the child is alive."

"Is it a boy or a girl?" Teresa asked. Alejandro interrupted him.

"I swear on my life that it's a girl." The Councillor's head snapped up and he looked angrily at his former assassin.

"How do you know?" Teresa asked him.

"Just a gut feeling, my Lady. My gut feelings are usually right, aren't they, Councillor?" Leon did not say Sir, which even the King would have added when speaking to the Councillor. But Garcia ignored the insult.

"Thank you, Sir Leon," he emphasised the word 'Sir', "for bringing Teresa here. You may go now."

Alejandro glanced at Teresa one last time, then turned around and without saying goodbye, he headed towards the door. He was afraid he would shed a tear, and he could not bear the shame for the Councillor to witness that.

"Stop!" Teresa shouted.

The two men were taken aback. Leon turned around and Garcia looked inquisitively at her.

"Councillor Sir! I've obeyed you my whole life. Right?"

"Yes, my Lady."

"I've taken all your advice as Holy Scripture. Right?"

"Yes, my Lady," Garcia was very curious to find out what Teresa was getting at.

"I never asked anything of you. Right?"

"Yes, my Lady."

"And I won't ask you now. I command you, for the first time in my life."

The Councillor was surprised, he had never thought she could be so determined. Alejandro was glad to be close to Teresa, at least until she finished talking.

"Your wish is my command, my Lady," Garcia did not argue with her that could wait till she asked for something he did not want to complete.

"I command that Alejandro Leon be my bodyguard! He can protect me best."

Alejandro looked lovingly at Teresa. Suddenly, he understood that Teresa had not been worried about their parting, because she had come up with this plan long ago.

The Councillor did not rush to answer, he though through the possibilities seriously.

"Alright, my Lady. If you will continue to obey me, then I will appoint Alejandro Leon as the commander of your guard. He can choose his own men, but he will have to join the liquidators to do this."

Alejandro looked at Teresa, the Councillor seemed to see a smile flicker across his face, which astonished him. He'd never seen Leon smile before. She watched nervously as Leon went quite close to Garcia's desk and spoke.

"I understand, Sir, and I accept the offer."

"Alright, Commander Sir," Garcia replied, using the correct rank, "then we will discuss the details once Teresa has left."

When Teresa left the chambers, she laughed at Alejandro in a way that he would have made a deal with the devil to hear again, which, as a matter of fact, he had.

Garcia waited for Teresa to leave the room and only then did he speak.

"So you will stay beside the girl, but I will request your help from time to time. Not as often as before."

Leon felt like he was back in the prison he'd escaped from many years ago, but this time the bars were made of gold.

"Alright, but don't forget, Councillor, currently Teresa's safety is in your interest, but if in the future, you wish the opposite, you will have to face me."

"No one can live forever, commander, not even I."

On the way out, Leon thought of how a man cannot avoid his fate, no matter how fast he runs. He would serve the Councillor once more, but he could be together with the person who gave his life meaning.

Chapter Thirty-Five

Roy Davis waited nervously before the gates of the fortress city of Atlantis. Thousands of people crowded the huge area. They'd come from all directions. The news of burned villages had caused people to flee to Narun. Only here could they hope for sanctuary. The atmosphere of panic turned the crowd into a buzzing hive. The guards kept strict order, allowing only twenty at a time to pass through the gates. They wanted to check everyone so that no enemy would infiltrate among them. Roy was dressed as a peasant and waited for the opportunity to be allowed inside. Through Claire, he kept Black informed of what was going on. Beside him were Silver and Commander Caroll, but they could only escort him as far as the gates. The two soldiers had wanted to infiltrate the fort with Roy, but Black had forbidden it, because the local dialect differed significantly from theirs. Roy would pretend to be a mute, and the sight of three mutes would probably raise suspicion.

Claire spoke inside his mind.

"My dear, Sir Lemmy says that you should not go in yet, the checkpoint is too strict. He thinks they won't be able to keep letting in only twenty people at a time, the crowd is always growing. When they let a lot of people in at once, go with them."

"I got it."

"Oh, and Black says that if Silver and Commander Caroll dare to enter with you, he will tie ropes about their waists and drag them home behind the Dreadnought."

"I'll pass it on. I love you!"

"Me too."

Roy conveyed the Strategist's message verbatim, and the two soldiers looked at him as if he had come up with the plan.

In the next two hours, the situation became worse. The guards shouted from behind the walls for everyone to stay calm, but the people's patience had run out. At first, little scuffles broke out, then the whole square turned into a seething mass of punching bodies. They could not get organised into lines, and the fights broke out and got worse. The peasants were afraid that the enemy would appear when they were still outside waiting to be admitted.

The Atlantians saw that if they did not come up with something now, the people would kill each other. Sir Lemmy had been right, someone appeared over the gate and shouted down.

"People, calm yourselves! The enemy is still hours away and we will speed up the admittance process. If you behave calmly you can all come in, if not, you can stay outside."

The brief speech had its desired effect, calm settled over the area once more. Hope and the threat sobered the peasants up. Silver and Caroll began gently making way for Davis through the crowd. A few minutes later they stood before the huge gates. The guards lifted the metal bars halfway and began letting people in. Roy did not notice when his two companions disappeared from beside him. Suddenly, he was alone in the thronging crowd. They swept him along till he stood before the guards who were no longer asking questions. They just stood there, trying not to get trampled.

Inside, young men were sorting out the new arrivals.

"The injured and I'll go right, the rest go left," one of them shouted.

Inside the walls, they reached a huge square. Roy was directed left with the healthy people. They were lead across the square and then followed a short street which also lead to a huge square. They were expected there and after a few questions, the refugees could move on. A soldier approached Davis.

"Where did you come from, boy?"

Roy groaned and pointed, first at his mouth, then over the wall.

"Well, you don't make it easy do you?" the soldier grumbled. "Are you coming from a Tura?"

Roy nodded vehemently.

"Alright, you'll get food over there," the soldier pointed at a corner filled with pots, "do you understand what I'm saying anyway?"

Roy nodded and pretended to be a bit crazy, he thought they would leave him alone, and so it was. The others were interrogated at length because the soldiers wanted to know everything about the approaching enemy. The soldiers wanted to know their numbers, their weapons, but the terrified peasants gave contradictory answers. All they knew for certain was that the enemy was completely ruthless and killed anyone in their path. The introduction of the refugees lasted till nightfall and by then there were a vast number of them. The Atlantians did all they could to accommodate them but such a huge crowd arriving so unexpectedly could not be prepared for. The food was gone, and they used corners draped in tarps as latrines, which also proved to be insufficient, forcing many to relieve themselves in the public squares.

Young children cried, women moaned and men cursed. By late that night, the noise died down, fatigue overcame their fear and desperation. Roy sat in a corner, relatively comfortably, because at least he could lean against the wall as he reported back to Black. Through Claire, he told Black the number of soldiers in the square, the height of the walls and their thickness, and the estimated the number of refugees. Sir Lemmy wanted to know everything, especially about the prevailing mood inside, from which he could deduce his enemy's morale.

"You're taking care of yourself right, my love?" Claire asked.

"Did Black ask that too?" Roy joked.

"You'll pay for that when you get back!"

"I can't wait for you to give me a scolding!"

"Sir Lemmy says that you should wait for everyone to go to sleep and then he'll give you further instructions."

"Alright, I love you!"

"Me too!"

It was well past midnight when the majority of the refugees had gone to sleep. Roy determined that he would wait a few more minutes to be safe. He looked around. The silhouettes of soldiers and torches lined the tops of the high walls. There were a lot of them up there, and even more on the square where Roy was. The injured could not be too far, because the sounds of pain carried through the night air. The temperature dropped fast. People slept cuddled up to one another, some of the larger families formed veritable piles. Earlier, a young, well-endowed peasant girl had approached Roy and asked to cuddle up to him, because she'd lost her family and felt so alone.

Roy did not have to play the fool for long to chase her away. Later, he saw her resting in the arms of a large peasant boy. Roy figured that the fort was silent now, and it was time for action.

"There won't be a better time than now," he said to Claire, "but it's still impossible to move around unnoticed."

"Alright, Black says to take a torch and go to the latrines, there you should light the canvas in as many places as you can. When it's alight, wait for people to panic and then Sir Lemmy will tell you where to go."

Roy knew that Councillor Wilder had told Black the city's layout, and he certainly had a good plan. Though he could not imagine what he could do alone.

Slowly, he stood up and headed towards the latrines, the stench of which filled the square. As he approached them, the stench became increasingly unbearable. He pulled the curtain behind him and took a torch from the holder on the wall nearby and lit the canvas in several places then he went back to his place. Soon, all the tarps were burning, spewing caustic smoke. The light breeze helped to quickly spread the fire. People, waking from their sleep, flew into a panic. They began running from the flames. If they'd thought about it for a second, they would have stayed as the fire could not spread anywhere. The soldiers could not control the sudden commotion, they too were overcome with fear. They shouted for everyone to stay put even as they too were running away.

"Everyone is running away, even the soldiers," Roy reported.

"Good," came the response, "then follow the wall out of the square, but not towards the main gate, the other way."

He began to run and as he did, so he figured out why the Strategist wanted him to stick to the wall. The panicked peasants trampled and shoved one another to get away from the flames, while close by the wall, he managed to make it out of the square without event.

"I'm out!"

"Alright, look around! You're in a little square, you see three streets. Take the middle one, the narrowest one all the way, tell me when you're there."

"What if I'm stopped?"

"Just grunt and look scared. They won't bother with you for long!"

He ran as fast as he could. He did not think that if he was caught they would let him on, but he had no choice but to run. He got to the end of the lane quickly and got further instructions. A quarter hour passed by the time he reached a large building which was guarded by a few soldiers. On the way, he saw a lot of people running by, but no one paid him any heed in the commotion. The Strategist directed him behind the giant, stone building, there was no one there.

"I'm here," Roy said to Claire, "there's no one back here."

"What do you see?"

"Above me, about three men up, is a small vent window."

"Climb up! Go inside!"

Roy started up, the gaps between the stones made the climb easy. He managed to push the little window open without difficulty.

Then, he squeezed himself through somehow. Inside there was barely any light, but when his eyes got accustomed to the dimness, he saw that the whole room was full of chests. He didn't even have to jump, he could walk down the chests to the floor as if they were stairs. Inside were two torch holders in which the torches were still flickering weakly.

"The whole room is full of chests," he said.

"Open one!"

Roy pried open one of the lids and dug his hand into the dust which filled the chest.

"There's just some sort of dust."

"Good, now pay close attention! There has to be some rope around there somewhere, find some!"

"I got it."

"Take the rope and push one end of it deeply into the dust in the chest. Then lead the rope all the way to the entrance door and use the torch to light the end. When it's done, run. Leave the building and run back the way you came. Good luck, my love!"

Davis finished quickly. When the rope began to burn, he turned to leave. He climbed up the chests, out the window and down onto the road, from where he ran as fast as he could. Soon, he heard a thunderous bang, louder than any thunder he'd ever heard. The ground shook beneath his feet, buildings swayed and collapsed. He ran even harder now though he thought he'd been running at full pelt before, but the terrifying noises doubled his strength. Meanwhile, Claire spoke to him.

"What's going on, my dear?"

"There was a huge bang! I'm running back now."

"You did that with the powder." Roy could not believe it had been him. How could some lousy sand do that?

"When you're back, make yourself scarce, Black will begin the attack. We will be together again soon. I love you!"

"Me too!" Roy replied as usual.

The explosion had destroyed the armoury and the barracks beside it where the majority of the infantry had been resting. Many buildings were damaged, but what was most important to the Strategist was that a part of the city wall had collapsed. That is where they penetrated Atlantis. The city was in an uproar, no one knew what was going on exactly and people ran in all directions. Atlantis was like a huge human anthill. Black's soldiers surprised the confused enemy who didn't even comprehend that they were under attack. The attackers split into small groups, and cleared the city house by house. It was easy to identify the Atlantian soldiers from the scientists as they wore their own uniforms. The shock of the explosion, followed by close combat, paralysed the defenders. A well-planned butchery ensued. Sir Lemmy had given orders to spare the peasants but to kill the locals because if they got their wits about them they could easily rebel. Commander Caroll's unit took the streets and squares while Silver and Sir Lemmy took the houses. Many fled to the open main gates, especially the peasants, but locals fled the city in cast numbers too. Black had predicted this so he had ordered that they pursue no one, they did not have enough men for that. The Atlantian soldiers were not used to true danger, and their training was insufficient, so Sir Lemmy took the city with his three hundred men in just two hours, and more than half of them survived.

They did not take prisoners, their goal was just to demolish the city.

The Strategist wanted to take five scientists with him. Any more prisoners than that would have hindered his retreat, and he wanted to return to England as soon as possible. He did not want the French conflict to turn into actual war. The whole tension with the French kingdom was only necessary to distract the attention of the Councillors so that he could easily overrun Atlantis.

President John Neville was overcome by strange calm, the torturous anxiety of the past few months evaporated. When he heard the explosion he knew that the Strategist had arrived, and he also knew that the time of Atlantis was over, as was his own. He watched his ring, which he would soon use. The President allowed the sad feeling of certainty course through his veins. He smiled, perhaps it was better to know the end of something than to be ground down by hope. He only wanted one more thing – to meet that unpredictable, peculiar foe, Sir Lemmy Black, the dreaded Strategist. He was very curious about him. He wanted to see the man because of whom he was the president to lead Atlantis into ruin.

The door opened softly and Neville prepared himself to use the ring, but the hope remained in him that he may speak with Black before his death. A slim, noble-faced, handsome man dressed in black, entered the room. His movements were more like those of a dancer than a soldier. He headed for Neville.

"Don't come any closer or I'll use my ring immediately!" the President warned him.

"May I just sit down in the chair opposite you?"

The greying man pointed at the chair and the black clothed man sat. His straight posture did not change when seated.

"President Neville? if I am not mistaken?"

"Yes, and you are Sir Lemmy Black, the Strategist."

Black nodded.

"President, Sir, you should know that I do not wish to kill you. If you join my side, you can choose your life. Together, we could achieve much."

"You know, it cannot be so. I am still alive because I wanted to see the man who beat me. How did you do it?"

"Let's make a deal," Sir Lemmy replied, without a trace of emotion on his face, "I will tell you how I got here and you tell me the story of Atlantis."

The President agreed and Black began. He told him about everything, from the capture of Councillor Wilder to the help of Roy and Claire. He'd learned the structure and population of Atlantis from old Ed. Then he spoke of the explosives, which had been significant in the attack. Neville did not interrupt him, he listened attentively to the person who had singlehandedly defied the Councillors. The President only asked when Black had finished.

"So, the fleet on the French shores was just a distraction?"

Black nodded and allowed himself a faint smile.

"Naturally. I wanted to be here with the Dreadnought before my news made it. If you had prepared for the attack and knew the numbers of my army, I would have had no chance."

Since the attention of the Known World and the Councillors were on my fleet, I could silently head for Atlantis.

Neville furrowed his brow and stroked his beard. It annoyed him that the Strategist had mislead him with such a simple trick. As per an old saying, he had not seen the woods for the trees. *It doesn't matter anymore*, the President thought. Then he asked Black the question which he most desired the answer to.

"Why did you turn against us?"

"I did not see the point of what the Councillors are doing. You ruled us. You told us how big our ships could be, which god to worship, who to war with, who not to fight. Why would I obey?"

"I see. What did you know about us before you captured Councillor Ed Wilder? You could not have known how strong our army was. Not to mention that everyone in the Known World thinks that we live in some cold inland area."

"You are wrong. I've suspected that you could not be far for a long time, because you could not react quickly to unexpected situations from afar. But you were prepared, and that suggested that you were close by, and if you were close by then you could not have hid a large country from our sights. Now it's your turn! Tell me the story of Atlantis!"

Neville sighed and looked at the man sitting before him. He got the feeling that Black had destroyed Atlantis simply because he could not bear not being able to explain something. Sir Lemmy had only enslaved them to get answers to his questions, and now he would get his main prize, and he deserved it. Then, the President began the story that no one in the Known World had heard before.

"I don't know how much you know of the ancient people?"

"I've read many copied books, but I always had reservations about their contents as the originals had, long ago, fallen apart, and anyone could have rewritten the copies."

"So it is. We wanted to hide many things from the past from you, and we had good reason to. But let's take it one at a time. If you don't understand something, feel free to ask. So, what do you know of the ancient age?"

"A lot of people lived on earth," Black began, "or so they called their world. They did not only live in the Known World but on a much larger area. They lived in huge cities, and used many strange structures, of which we have no conception as to their workings or purpose. They represented a higher culture, and yet, for some reason, they disappeared. Then the majority of people died out and the rest sank back into chaos. There was nothing left but destructive hoards. Then the Councillors appeared, who built the world we know today, and kept it under their supervision."

"You knowledge is correct, thought fragmented, but I have to know what you know and what I must tell you."

Neville could see a childlike desire glimmer in the eyes of the seasoned warlord.

"Back then, some two thousand years ago, an incredible number of people lived in incredible comfort. True, there were also a lot of poor people which lead to constant tensions, but the majority of people lived better than our Kings do now. Their wasteful ways led to the dissipation of the Earth's reserves and their environment began to deteriorate. The countries of the world convened the greatest scientists they had to find a solution to this problem.

The greatest minds from all the sciences, representing the majority of the knowledge on Earth. The countries did not want the scientists to take the limelight, so they organised the several weeks long summit in a deserted icy corner of Russia. Because of the extreme cold, they built an underground city to house the five thousand scientists. There were another five thousand people there, mostly soldiers, to guard them, as well as serve them clean after them and so on. At the end of the summit's first meeting, the history of humanity changed forever, and almost ended. Back then, there were many tools with which people could speak with one another from any distance, if you don't mind, I won't go into their mechanics, you wouldn't understand them anyway. So, the scientists were informed that the majority of earth's population had died, and in just a few hours civilization had been wiped out. They had used some sort of chemical or biological weapon, an invisible killing tool that killed humans but left buildings intact."

"How is that possible?" Black did not want to interrupt but he felt like he had to.

"Imagine it like smoke, it spreads through air but does not harm buildings. The difference is that these substances were invisible, by the time they noticed the trouble, it was too late. No one knows which country started it, but we are certain that whoever it was also demolished in the counterattack. We still do not know how the survivors remained alive. Perhaps they were not in the streets like the scientists, or their bodies coped with it somehow, we will never know.

The survivors soon attacked each other, and the population of Earth continued to dwindle. Meanwhile, the scientist-city considered their options.

They knew that the information they held, all the knowledge on Earth, would be demolished if they did not save it in a way that it would survive. You can't even imagine how much information one of those machines they called computers could store, and they had to write it all down as the computers would sooner or later break, and the machines sending them energy would also break in due course. Their luck was that because of the cold, the complex was self-sustaining, so they didn't need anything from the outside. They worked for two generations for a part of the knowledge to be saved. They knew that even they would sink back in time, as the production of their machines would have taken several million people, further machines, factories and professionals. Meanwhile, they sent out small scouting parties but they only received little news because of the barbarous conditions that ruled the world. They knew that there were a few survivors, but there was nothing they could do for them till they'd copied their remaining knowledge form the computers. Then, they left their icy home and settled in an out-of-the-way location which they called Atlantis after a long forgotten world. They came to the determination that they would not allow humanity to simply wipe itself out. They would help them, but also control them.

The scientists studied human history and came to the conclusion that they would recreate one of the longest periods of human history and make it constant—they called this the Middle Ages. More precisely, the so-called Palaeolithic period lasted much longer, but we won't get into that, no, because it is not relevant to the story. So they chose this period because that time had the least progress, and they wanted consistency that could be controlled and maintained.

The middle ages seemed most appropriate for this because during this period, humanity's use of the Earth's resources did not lead to the destruction of the Earth. In short, it seemed like an eternally sustainable status quo.

Of the few books that reached you, they carefully took out the references to the middle ages, because they did not want you to recognise your own world in this long-gone era. They developed the Councillor's order, and you know the rest.

Our goal, to this very day, was to stop you from progressing, because it was the only way we could protect humanity from committing another fatal mistake."

"And everything went smoothly until now?" the Strategist asked in disbelief.

"Of course not, there were many problems along the way, such as the constantly occurring mutations. Since we retarded technological development, humanity chose biological evolution instead. It seems that even we cannot overwrite the laws of nature."

"Then why did you not leave the mutants alone?"

"You have seen what an advantage they have in battle. If we did not intervene, small skirmishes would have turned into huge wars, and slowly but surely, we would have reached a point where we do not want to find ourselves again, the destruction of humanity. Sometimes we may have seemed cruel, but our goals were noble. Don't you think? Look, if you agree with us then you could help us rebuild Atlantis. We could rule the Known World together. With your help, we could correct the mistakes made till now and we could create a perfect world."

Sir Lemmy seriously considered what he had heard, he had to assess it all. He could choose the Known World as it had been, or he could accept the President's alternative truth.

"If you meant well, you blundered greatly. You had no right to take our futures, and what is even worse is that you cannot oppose the laws of nature."

"What are you thinking?"

"Change is a part of life, no one can go against it."

"So, we should have left you to wallow in your misery."

"No, but you still took our futures from us. You could have helped shape it, instead of stealing it."

"Perhaps you are right, Strategist," Neville smiled, and then he suddenly clenched his right hand. The poisoned ring ended him swiftly.

Black stood up and approached the dead president, he pried his hand open, took the ring from his finger and put it in his pocket. From the doorway, he turned back and spoke to the corpse.

"For what it's worth, my victory brings me no pleasure," he said out loud. *It seems that King Mortimer is right, I'm developing a habit of talking to the dead,* he thought, *though they make excellent conversationalists, they never argue back.*

Chapter Thirty-Six

Vincent Farall, that is, King Fernand de Bellehache sat on his favourite chair, the simple, hard, uncomfortable trash that stood beside the Councillor's desk.

The Councillor could not contain himself.

"Your Highness, may I suggest…" Perrier began.

"No!" Farall interrupted angrily. "I am the King and I will sit where I please! Or is that not so?"

"Yes, your Highness!" The Marquis and the Councillor replied in unison.

Emotions were swirling wildly in the new King. He was disappointed because his adopted father, Perrier, had tricked him, he was afraid of his duties as King, and he was sad because he missed Amelie Chanel.

Only a few minutes had passed since he'd been elected King, but he felt like years had passed. He insisted on discussing the situation with his two mentors who had lied to him his whole life. More precisely, he wanted an explanation for their inexplicable actions.

He looked around. The room which, until now, had meant safety to him, now seemed foreign, and the people nearest him seemed like enemies.

"The whole thing is one big lie," Fernand began," you know well that I am not the son of Gaston de Bellehache. My parents had sent me to the priests long ago because they were unable to raise me."

The two men stood before the King, they did not dare sit in the comfortable chairs while the King fidgeted on his uncomfortable perch.

"The truth, my Lord," the Marquis replied, "is that the people you knew as your parents were my people. You were two years old when I saved you from the Marquis Bertrand's people, and I knew that you could not stay with me, because it was the first place they would look for you. I was forced to hide you, so I handed you over to family loyal to me. When they picked up your trail again, I ordered them to give you to the monastery."

"But they found you there too," Perrier took over, "it was not pirates who stormed the monastery. I mean it was them, but on the Marquis Bertrand's orders. Unfortunately, I arrived too late to save you, but you hid yourself well. That is when I decided to hide you in a place where no one would look for you, since who would think that you lived in the King's Court. Your enemies searched the whole Kingdom for you, but not in their wildest dreams did they think that you were right there under their noses. I did not even tell Marquis Caulmont where you were."

The Marquis hummed nervously and then could not restrain himself.

"And then you raised the King to be your man!"

"Stop it! I'm not either of yours! Until now, I was your puppet, from now on, things will be different," Fernand announced determinedly, though in reality, he had no idea what he was supposed to do. But he knew one thing for sure, ruling did not suit him.

"Your highness!" The Marquis said with concern, "when your family was killed, we wanted to save you. We weren't acting on our own interests but in yours. Perhaps we made a mistake, but our intentions were good."

However angry Fernand was at them, he had to admit that they were right. In reality, he only had fate to blame, but all the lies still hurt him.

"Alright, we cannot change the past anyway. You two will be my advisers, but I make the final decisions. I will not be anyone's pawn on the chessboard. If I think you are putting your own interests first, I will have you replaced."

"Yes, your Highness!" they replied in chorus.

"And if I am the King then I can do as I please. Is it not so?"

"Yes, your Highness," the Councillor replied immediately. "Though, if I may observe, we are here to warn you of possible mistakes."

Fernand stood up and approached the window. Outside, everything was so peaceful, if he went down for a walk now, people would bow before him, he could not blend in with the crowd. *Nothing will be the same again*, he thought desperately.

"You did not ask me if I wanted to be King," he turned to the men standing motionless behind him, "but I swear, I will give back the crown if you do not follow this request, or actually, my order! Have Amelie Chanel and her family brought here immediately, I want her to be my wife!"

"I understand, but..." Perrier began.

"No buts! This is my condition, if you do not like it then you can go find yourselves another King!"

"Yes, your Highness," the Councillor replied reluctantly, "but I must mention that we are missing a huge political opportunity with this. Rulers do not marry based on emotion, but they can keep lovers."

"Councillor!"

Perrier was shocked by the hard, authoritative voice coming from the boy who had once been so close to him.

"I did not ask you, and if you hurt so much as a hair on her head, I will put you in the torture chambers you love so much!"

Perrier thought he knew people, especially the person he'd spent the majority of his time with, but the King's sudden harshness threw him off balance. He was not frightened, not only because of the Councillor's ring on his finger but also because he had not suspected such determination lurked in his once apprentice. He replied briefly and to the point.

"The deal is made, your Highness. If you'll allow me, I'll retire now."

Without waiting for a response he turned on his heel and left the room. Fernand could barely resist calling after him. He felt he had been too rough with the man who had been so important to him, but if he was not determined enough, it could easily cost Amelie her life. After the Councillor's departure, Fernand quickly dispatched the Marquis as well. He remained alone in the Councillor's chambers and he was well aware that the loneliest night of his life was ahead of him. He would have no company but for his confused thoughts.

Sir Ponga was inconsolable, even Fifi sitting beside him could not cheer him up. The day before, just after the Coronation, Perrier had told him he would be appointed head of the King's guard.

Not long ago, back when he had won the tournament, this would have been the best thing to ever happen to him. It seemed to him like that was a long time ago, so long ago that he could barely remember it, as if the proud winner of the tournament had been a different person entirely. Now, all he wanted was to return to the swamp with Fifi, he did not want a life in the King's Court. He sat there in his own chambers and felt as if all the riches in the world could not compensate him for his lost life.

Fifi stroked his head and tried to pour some strength into him.

"It's all not so terrible, my dear. I am here with you, only, of course, if you want me to. Not so long ago, you would have been very happy to be honoured in this way. You've become a powerful Lord, everyone will follow your orders."

Ponga looked at her, took her hand and smiled sadly.

"I know you are sad too and yet, there is more strength in you than me. You console me though it should be the other way around. The truth is that I will have to spend most of my time beside the King and I can only be with you a little while. In the swamp we could have spent all our time together, but that damned Councillor has ruined everything."

"Don't you care that I'm sticking with you? Or perhaps you'd prefer a dame from the court?"

"How can you say that, Fifi? If you were not with me, I would go crazy, or in fact, the situation would not bother me at all. What am I saying? You know what I mean!"

"The man who loves me should be strong, not whimpering like a little girl!"

Ponga was touched by the kind words but he could feel that she would be happier in the swamp too, but she was also right in saying that he could not afford to let himself go in this way. His mind raced feverishly. He had to duck out from under this somehow. He'd been Commander only one day, perhaps he could speak with the King and reverse the appointment. Yes, he began imagining it. He would not tell Fifi, it would not do for her to get hopeful or worry about him. King Fernand seemed like a good guy, if he told him about his emotions honestly, perhaps he would understand and let him go and then that damned Perrier could do nothing to him.

"You are right, my dear," he touched his forehead to Fifi's, "I will collect myself, but I have to go check the guard now."

"At this hour, it's passed eleven?"

"It'll do me good to clear my head."

Ponga knew that the King had been up all of the previous night. With a little luck, he could talk to him privately. He was certainly surrounded by people during the day, and then he could not raise his personal matter. He went along the corridor, the guards stood to attention as he passed them. Not long ago, he would have felt so proud, but now it did not touch him at all. Reaching the King's hallway, he sensed something strange. He could not define what it was, but something was different than the night before. When he got closer, he realised what the matter was. There were four guards in front of the King's door, though there should have been only two, the other two guards should have been in the hallway but they stood by the door. When he got closer, the guards turned towards him.

"Why are there four of you here?" He asked them as he heard noises through the door. Before they could answer, he knew there was serious trouble going on.

He did not hesitate but charge the two guard closest to him. The attack was so swift that his opponents had no chance of defending themselves. He smack one in the throat with the heel of his right palm, and killed the other with the dagger from the man's belt. The two remaining soldiers pulled their swords, but they had no time to strike. By then, Ponga was holding a weapon in each hand and neutralised them at once. The whole fight only took a few seconds and Ponga quickly tore open the King's door. Inside, a guard was about to strike Fernand, and the table upturned between them did not sufficiently protect the King. Ponga moved closer and recognised his former opponent, the son of the late Marquis Bertrand: Auguste Bertrand.

"If you take another step, the King is dead," the assassin threatened, pointing his sword straight at the King.

"You've experienced my speed once before, why do you want to feel it again?" Ponga asked, just to win some time, the distance between them was still too large to strike. The King solved the situation. He kicked the upturned table, forcing Auguste to look down which gave Ponga ample time to leap between them like a flash of lightning. The blade hit Ponga beneath his left shoulder and came out his sword. In the heat of the fight, he did not feel pain, he stabbed the assassin in the heart and then fell to his knees. Fernand helped the knight sit in a chair and shouted at the people who had run in at the sound of commotion.

"Fetch a doctor immediately!"

"I'm fine, your Highness," Ponga said, trying to stay conscious. He was terrified that he would black out and could not tell the King the reason for his visit, "I only dared intrude on you at this hour because I wanted to ask you something important," he could not go on because the world went black before his eyes.

A woman screamed from the crowd at the door.

"He's not going to die," the King said to the woman, "he just fainted. Are you with him?"

"Yes, your Highness," Fifi replied in shock.

"Do you know what the Commander wanted to request from me?"

"I do, your Highness."

In the hour after the attack, the commotion in the King's chambers was like a tavern at rush hour. Councillor Perrier took over control. He questioned the King, had Ponga taken away, making sure Fifi could stay with him and reprimanded the head of the guards, then he discussed the next steps with the Marquis Caulmont. Fernand just sat there and let Perrier do his job.

When the Councillor was done and had sent everyone away, he too made to leave.

"Stay here a little, I want to speak with you," the King said. They sat down but neither of them spoke. Fernand knew that he would have to break the silence but he could not find the right words. They both knew that sooner or later they would have to discuss their situation.

"I am not a different person," Fernand forced the words out through gritted teeth.

"What do you mean, your Highness?"

"Don't make it more difficult for me! Just because you made me a King, I have not become a different person. I just can't get over the fact that while you were the most important person in the world to me I was just a tool in your hands."

The Councillor did not reply immediately, he too, was lost for words, which never happened to him.

"I took you to the monastery, because I had to, but I did not make a puppet out of you. Think about it! If you had been just a tool then I would not have raised you like a Councillor. I did something that is forbidden to me, I passed on our secret knowledge. I did this because I did not want you to think what you are now saying. I treated you like my son even if I could not be completely honest with you all the time. I knew that one day, I would lose my son and receive a King in his stead."

Fernand had never seen the Councillor so distraught. The usual prideful, cynical act was gone. Perrier stood and headed for the door because he felt like he had said everything he had to. The King called after him.

"I want to ask you something."

Perrier looked back inquisitively.

"When we're alone, could you call me by my name, Alain?"

"Of course, Vincent," the Councillor replied. Then he headed for the door. His hand was on the handle when the King added.

"And don't you dare have my chair removed from your chambers!"

"I wouldn't do such a thing, Vincent," Perrier replied and then closed the door.

Chapter Thirty-Seven

Councillor Aleksandr Petrov trembled as he headed towards the secret meeting. It was night and the glimmering torches barely illuminated the castle hallways. The guards saluted him when he passed by them and he could see in their eyes that they were afraid of him.

This would have given him pleasure, but on that evening he was not able to enjoy the power his position afforded him.

The storm caused by the murder of Boris Kurilov was beginning to settle down when Sergei Giakin, Prince Ivan Genisei's man had approached him. He had passed on the Prince's invitation to the late-night meeting. After the dinner that had cost so many lives, Petrov knew that Ivan knew no limits. Despite his young age, he was a raging monster who was capable of controlling his emotions if the situation demanded it, but as soon as he could, he brutally dispatched his enemies. The location of their meeting did not reassure him. What sort of sick person would arrange a meeting at night in the woods beside the castle?

Before he left the castle, he took a torch with him. He'd been passing through the pines for about fifteen minutes when he noticed a campfire. He approached the flames and soon reached them. There were ten men standing around the fire as no one felt like sitting down.

"I appreciate your punctuality, Councillor," Genisei said crudely, simply calling him Councillor. Petrov noticed the presence of Commander Vladimir Niachejev, who had escaped with his help. The Councillor had thought that Niachejev was not in Moscow, but had escaped to the inner lands to the yellow people. He was almost as scared of the Commander as he was of the Prince and the thought occurred to him that it might have been a mistake to come.

On the other hand, he could not hide, the situation would not simply solve itself. Since the assassination, he had been pondering whether it had been a good idea to form an alliance with the Prince. True, if he had not, he would no longer be alive.

"We are gathered here today, to form an alliance, and discuss the future," Ivan went on. "Everyone here is loyal to me and any of you would give your life for me. Only you remain to show your true colours, Councillor Petrov. You have to assure me that you are by my side. Tonight, you must make a decision. If you do not wish to serve me and you choose Atlantis, though by the sound of it, there's not much left of your country, then you may leave."

Petrov was certain that he would only leave the campfire alive if he swore fealty. Atlantis was finished anyway, and who knew how long his Councillor's power would last.

"My Prince, I have been by your side since I've arrived. Who has done more for you than I?"

"Don't you understand or do you not want to understand the point, Councillor?" the Prince's tone turned sharp and threatening in a moment. "What you've done till now, you could have done for tactical reasons, simply because it served your interests. I want so much more than that! Those who serve me, pledge me their lives!"

"Prince Ivan, I am here, is that not enough? You can kill me now if you wish, my life is in your hands. How could I further prove my loyalty?" Petrov had never been so scared in his life. He did not know what the Prince was getting at but he felt that the others did not trust him, especially Niachejev.

"Give me your ring!" Ivan said, holding out his hand.

"But my Prince, if they see my hand in Court they will suspect something is wrong, it is the symbol of my position. We must maintain appearances, I can only be useful…"

"Give it here! I'm not used to having to ask for something twice."

The Councillor took it off and felt as though he were handing his power to Ivan. The Prince took the ring with an evil smile, opened the vial containing the poison and emptied it on the ground. Then he handed the ring back.

"Here, now you can keep up appearances, like you said. Commander Niachejev, cut off his little finger!"

Petrov didn't even have time to protest. Two men held him down and the Commander chopped off his finger with a well-practiced move. The Councillor fell to the ground moaning. The Prince approached him and whispered.

"Those who best serve me, are afraid of me."

Well, Petrov was afraid. Until then, he had not known that this was the strongest feeling on Earth.

Alejandro Leon was walking with Teresa de Cantabria in the Spanish Royal gardens. This green area surrounded by high walls was Teresa's favourite place. She came here almost every day with the stern-faced Leon.

They sat down on a stone bench, opposite which was her favourite fountain. Teresa liked it so much because the water was spat out by stone sculptures of birds.

Alejandro could barely follow Teresa's barrage of words, which would have been fine if he had not been expected to answer.

"So Alejandro, what's it to be?"

"Excuse me, my Lady?"

"You're not paying attention again! You think I'm asking the questions from myself, or from you? You always zone out and stop paying attention to me."

"Sorry, my Lady. What was the question?"

"Which bird do you like the best? You remember, a few days ago you told me that you like birds. If that was true, and I hope you did not lie to me, then tell me, which one is your favourite?"

Leon checked from the corner of his eye to make sure that the men guarding Teresa were far enough away, and only then did he answer.

"My Lady, I have a secret answer to your question, but I don't want to offend you so I'd rather not answer."

"Oh! Alejandro Sir, I insist that you tell me. Excuse the expression, but you're a gargoyle, and if you do want to tell me something secret then it had to be done right."

Teresa quickly stood up opposite the seated liquidator and ceremoniously asked him again.

"Which bird do you like the best?"

"You, my dove!"

Teresa wagged her head and planted a kiss on his hairy face.

"You really wormed your way out of that one, but you've never said anything as kind to me before."

Then, leaving Alejandro there, she headed towards the rosebushes. Alejandro reached into his pocket and produced a sealed envelope. Recently he'd received many such letters from Councillor Garcia. They always had a name on then, the name of a person belonging to the circles of the recently deceased Queen Esmeralda. The Councillor was doing a full clean-up in the yard, and had taken complete control over the Kingdom. Leon opened the letter, smiled and thought how he would enjoy doing this job. He stood up and pocketed the paper on which the name of Archbishop Oscar Martinez was scrawled.

Sir Lemmy liked the atmosphere of the London Castle by night. The silence was undisturbed. He went along the battlements, the guards all saluted him and he asked them a few questions about the night's watch.

The tower clock struck midnight, Black left his men and headed for the King's chambers. He did not want to be late to the late-night meeting. Only at this hour could he discuss private and confidential matters alone with the King.

When he entered, Mortimer greeted him smiling.

"Sit down, my friend, help yourself!" the King said, before Black could greet him.

"Good evening, your Highness! Thank you," he replied, sitting down and pouring himself a cup. Mortimer had known Black for a long time and he saw immediately that he was preoccupied.

"What's troubling you, you just scored a huge victory? Out with it!" Mortimer said, getting to the point.

"We won, my Lord, this much is true, but the meat of the matter is yet to come."

"We cut off the enemy's head, the rest should be easy," Mortimer said confidently as if they had already won the war.

"That's not how I see it. It is true that Atlantis is defeated, but the Councillors are still in power in the other kingdoms. We cannot underestimate them. They are sure to unite against us, and we will have to face the armies of many countries."

"You've said before that it would be so. Why are you surprised now?"

"You are right, it was not hard to predict, but that is not the biggest issue."

The King looked at Black, nonplussed.

"When the president killed himself in Atlantis, he did not seem defeated."

"Don't wind me up, if someone kills themselves in front of their enemy, do you think they are the winner?"

"There was peace in his eyes, not resignation. Also, I think the city was too big for the population that was there. And my biggest problem is that Atlantis was a lot further away than I thought. It would be impossible to control the Known World from there."

"What are you getting at?"

"I don't know, but something is not right," as they spoke, Black produced his long-stemmed pipe, but did not light it, he just chewed the end.

"You're imagining things, my friend. Light your pipe, maybe the smoke will vanquish your daemons."

"Have my daemons ever proven to be imaginary, my Lord?"

"Admit it, Strategist, that this time you are wrong!"

"I would love to, but the situation is I am never wrong."

Roy and Claire were retelling the story of the siege of Atlantis for the umpteenth time on Commander Mallory's request. The old soldier listened to them like a child listens to his favourite fairy tale. When they finished, Mallory kept repeating.

"I'm proud of you!"

They were in the little house by the Castle preparing for lunch, a special lunch. The Commander wanted to prepare the food himself for, as he was fond of calling them recently, the heroes.

"I know it is woman's job to cook, but I wanted to surprise you with something, and I cannot buy you a big present, so you will have to make do with this."

"Daddy," Claire said, "do you think gold is the most important thing in life? Don't let me hear you say that again!"

They laughed and Mallory began serving the food. Claire could not allow this, she took the fragrant dish of duck legs from him and served the men herself.

For a while, they ate in silence. If they did speak, they complimented the food. When they were done, a pitcher of wine appeared and their tongues loosened.

"After all this, I cannot wait what Sir Lemmy has planned for you in the next battle."

The young couple looked at one another, they had heard this said by the Commander more than once. The Strategist had called Roy to him that morning to tell him how he imagined their future.

"I don't want to ruin our pleasant day, my dear," Roy said telepathically to Claire, "but we have to tell him!"

"You are right, my love, we cannot lie to him. And the truth would come out anyway."

From their silence Mallory knew they were speaking to each other, specifically, to leave him out of the conversation. He did not contain his annoyance.

"You think I don't know what you're up to right now? You're talking in that silly speak so that I'm left out of important matters!"

"That's not it, daddy," Claire said as she stood up and approached Mallory. She hugged him and looked him in the eye, "we just don't want to ruin this beautiful day."

"Is something wrong? Is Sir Lemmy displeased with you?"

"Mallory always spoke of the Strategist as if he were god, his word was the most important to him in the world.

"Not at all," Roy took over, "he summoned me this morning and told me his plans for us."

"Then why haven't I heard about this yet?" Mallory's voice was offended and accusing at once.

"We did not want to cause you grief because we know that you would like us to go to war again," Roy took a deep breath and then spat it out, "but Sir Lemmy wants something else."

"I see," Mallory said, though he did not understand it at all.

"He has a much more important mission for us," Claire took over.

"I would not have been happy to see you go to war, but what could be more important than fighting by Sir Lemmy's side?"

"Daddy, if we fight it's only two people. We have been ordered to collect and train those like us. Then we will have many such people fighting for our Kingdom."

"Great," the Commander said in relief, "then you will quickly get married and I will move from here."

"The thing is, we also haven't told you yet that Roy has been made Captain, so he outranks you now. If he says you will live with us then so it will be."

They laughed, Mallory enjoyed Claire's humour just as much as Roy did.

"So what is your order, Captain Sir?" the Commander asked the boy.

Roy looked lovingly at Claire and tried to force himself to be as serious as possible.

"The thing is, Commander Mallory, that no matter my rank, there is someone who is above me in this family. We are both forced to follow her orders. So you are going to live with us whether you like it or not."

Didier Ponga recovered his senses. He was in a strange room, not as if there were many rooms he could call home. A woman standing with her back to him was rummaging through something he could not see what. He wanted to sit up to see the slim but curvaceous stranger. As he moved, a pain shot through his shoulder and he groaned softly. The woman turned at the sound.

"You should not be ferreting about yet, my Lord."

"Fifi! What are you doing here? I don't even know where we are. What happened to the King?" Ponga suddenly remembered the image before he'd passed out.

"If you keep asking questions I won't be able to answer anything," she laughed. That laugh contained everything. Relief that Ponga was alive and love, which made it all the more beautiful for him.

"So you saved the King, but you were injured. I've been taking care of you since."

"What happened to the assassin?"

"You killed him, as you usually do those who stand against you."

The memories of the past washed over him. He remembered the brief but happy time in the swamp, the mission, the Coronation and his appointment to commander of the guards. He was saddened because he knew now why he had gone to visit the King at midnight, and how he had lost consciousness before he could make his request.

"Does it make you so sad to have killed the assassin? You don't seem yourself," Fifi chided him as she stroked his hair.

"It's not that, I just want to be in the swamp again with you."

It would be so nice to help out on Happy Island again.

"And?" she acted as if they had not spoken about it on that night.

"The thing is I went to the King because I wanted to ask him to…"

"I know."

"That can't be unless I told you in my dreams."

"In fact, I spoke to the King myself."

Ponga was so surprised he sat up and then sank back in pain.

"If you jump around like that, I won't tell you anything," Fifi frowned at him. "So I took care of everything."

"What do you mean?"

"You are no longer in the King's service. He's excused you. In fact, he even promised to help the swamp dwellers. Just like the Marquis Caulmont. When you're strong enough, we can go. Fabian will come with us, but Jules and Henri will stay here in the Marquis' service."

"Then let's go at once."

"When you're better! Besides, I did not mention that I have a condition."

"Consider it done!" he blurted.

"Good, then we'll go see your parents on the way home. Maybe, they would like to live in the swamp, and if not, you still need to clear up your relations with them."

Ponga wanted to protest but he knew her too well, when she looked at him in this way there was no arguing with her.

"Alright," he gave in, "but you're going to have to go first."

Councillor Alain Perrier was pleased. He usually did not like this feeling because it made one inclined to inattention. But on that morning, he felt like he deserved to lean back a bit, not only in the literal sense but also spiritually. He was drinking his second goblet of wine, and had turned his favourite chair towards the window, watching as the rays of sunlight illuminated the flecks of dust dancing in the air. It was pleasantly cool inside, the summer heat could not yet penetrate the thick castle walls. The voices of people passing below and the shouts of playing children wafted through the open window and they did not bother the Councillor one bit. In fact, the happy buzzing calmed him. Everything had gone to plan, and his years of preparation had paid off.

Vincent was on the throne, de Caulmont was an excellent ally, and Bertrand, his archenemy, was dead. True, the Strategist had seriously rearranged the powers of the Known World, causing him much grief along with the other kingdoms. But no matter, such is life, when one matter is solved, many step up to take its place. He most regretted that he had to allow Ponga to leave on the King's request. He would have been a one-man army, eternally by Vincent's side. The Knight's presence would have guaranteed the safety of his long plans. On the other hand, the King had to feel that the Councillor's will was not always absolute, and so, he preferred to concede on this case for rather than a far more important one. The appearance of flexibility had to be maintained, after all a perfect puppet is one who does not know he is on a string. The King was, in fact, the masterpiece of his life's work, a tool that could be used to perfectly rule the Kingdom.

He poured himself a third glass of wine, it did not go to his head, he was too accustomed to it to feel it, but the alcohol washed pleasantly over his body. He observed once more that all his hard work had paid off. A long story was coming to a close, he could finally speak those magical words that were the favourite of all storytellers, which adorned the last page of all novels and tasted so good after a long hard road, it felt so good to say:

THE END

Councillor Perrier had not made many mistakes in his life and never had he made one so great.

Epilogue

The presidency sat at the rectangular table. Only one chair stood empty which was the president's seat. The members fidgeted nervously. No one knew what to expect. Their new leader had not shared his thoughts on the future with anyone. Their tongues were ready to lash out in disapproval as such lateness was insulting, the President was insulting them, but none of them dared to speak. The silence was broken by the youngest, barely thirty-five-year-old member of the President's council, Adan Perez. He stood slowly, his large coat failing to cover his scrawny body. He ran his hand through his pitch-black hair and spoke.

"My Lords, this tardiness undermines the presidency's respectability," he looked around but no one wanted to answer him. He wiped his sweating brow, his brown skin leaked not only because of the head, but also out of rage.

"We must do something! I suggest we leave the hall!"

"There is no call for this, my Lords!" a voice called out from behind him. The men gathered there looked as one at the voice and Perez turned. The new President, Pedro Garcia, accompanied by Head Liquidator Marcos Sanchez, stepped into the room. When they reached the chair, Garcia sat down and Sanchez stood behind him, his stern expression, the weapon on his side and the fact that he stood opposite the seated men, was threatening to them.

"Excuse our lateness, but I had to take care of an urgent matter," his light, nonchalant style, and feeble excuse did not calm the others, though they all acted as if nothing had happened.

"As is well known, the Strategist has destroyed Atlantis. Our only luck was that our late President Neville and I had previously agreed to move Atlantis to the intermediary base, of which I am the leader. This was necessary as I'm sure you well know, because it was increasingly difficult to rule from so far away. A long time ago, the base was created for this reason, because a lot of cases demand immediate intervention. The move was not nearly completed and the majority of our men were still in Atlantis when Sir Lemmy attacked. It was a heavy blow, but we will recover. In fact, we will show the Known World where the true power lies. I officially announce that here, where we sit now, is the New Atlantis, the location of which must remain a secret. If anyone discovers where our base is, we are done for."

"President sir!" Perez raised his hand. "May I speak?"

Garcia hated being interrupted, but he steeled himself and motioned to the young council member to speak.

"Before we get into the details, I will mention that Council is secret, and only we can take part in it, yet the Head Liquidator is still in the room."

A few members nodded approvingly, and Garcia drummed his fingers impatiently on the table.

"My Dear Perez! We are living in a new age, everything will change. Consider this a state of war. Commander Sanchez is part of our little circle, because our security is the salvation of the future. You know what the Strategist did to our city. This cannot happen to the new Atlantis."

The answer did not satisfy the council member, but no one wanted to speak out.

"If there are no more questions, I will continue," the sharp remark cut the silence like a knife.

"From now on, we have a new strategy. Until now, we have strived to maintain consistency in the Known World from the shadows. That is over, the genie is out of the bottle and balance is an illusion."

"What are we to make of this, president Sir?" Of Course, it was Adam Perez who'd spoken.

"We are unable to control the ever-breeding mutants throughout the Kingdoms. Their abilities speed up an area's development, and the Strategist is collecting them. The blow we suffered is forcing us to change. Our current numbers and resources are insufficient to continue our activities. We will forego consistency and enslave the Known World. We will control by force."

"We cannot do that! We intervened long ago to help humanity," Perez interjected angrily.

"We must adapt to the new times, otherwise humanity will wipe itself out once more. If we cannot herd them, we will take them on a short leash," Garcia replied.

"Impossible." The young council member protested, "if we did not have enough men till now, how could this new plan work?"

"We must show strength, which is much easier than trying to lead them on the right path, and we must control the power of the Councillors. Recently, some Councillors have been behaving like Kings, those that will not get in line will be replaced."

Pedro Garcia looked around at the Council Members and saw the fear in their eyes. *Good*, he thought, *you should be scared!*

"And I will not tolerate disobedience even within Council circles. You know the saying: 'If all you have is a hammer, everything looks like a nail'. Follow that proverb."

At the meeting's end, the members left their heads bowed like shamed dogs. Garcia took Sanchez' arm.

"You stay a little longer!"

When the others had left, the President, the Spanish King's Councillor, turned to his man.

"Next week, we must find someone to replace Adan Perez, who tragically died in an accident. Give Alejandro Leon the job, I want it to go smoothly."

The Head Liquidator nodded silently then left.

Pedro Garcia looked out the window. On the distant horizon, the snowy peaks of the Pyrenees Mountains scraped the sky.

Colophon